I0722979

THE WINE-DARK DAUGHTER

DAMIEN J. COLUCCIO

The Wine-Dark Daughter
Copyright © 2024 by Damien J. Coluccio

All rights reserved. No part of this book may be reproduced or used in any manner, including stored in a retrieval system, or transmitted in any form or by any means, electronic, mechanical, photocopying, recording, or otherwise, without the prior written consent of the copyright owner. The only exception is for the use of brief quotations or excerpts in a book review.

Without limiting the author's and publisher's exclusive rights, any unauthorised use of this publication to train generative artificial intelligence (AI) technologies is expressly forbidden.

This novel is a work of fiction. Any names, characters, places or incidents are a work of the author's imagination. Any resemblances to actual persons, either living or dead, or locations, or events is purely coincidental and not intended by the author.

Damien Joseph Coluccio is the owner and publisher of this work.
[978-1-7635940-0-5]
Year of first publication: 2024

Published with the assistance of Authors Own Publishing Services Pty Limited
Edited by Danikka Taylor
Cover design by Casey Grills
Map by Angeline Trevena

For more information visit:
https://www.damienjcoluccioauthor.com/
https://authorsownpublishing.com/

To all of us who long to sail the wine-dark sea.

ESQUILINO
VIMINALIS
CELE
EMP
PALANTINUS
CAELIUS
ADURIC SEA
QUIRINALE
CAPITOLINUS
AVENTINUS
ARIL
URRUC
MIDD
N
TO OPUNI

TO ARYDOR
COLD SEA
THE LEAGUE OF KINGDOMS
DRAMAKI
TAS
TETHALIA
THEVAI
TRILOS
DELPHON
ATHANAI
APASA
KORIITHOS
PHORONIA
PALLAN
ICARII SEA
SOLMATHUS
ANAMA
KONOSO

Content Warning

This story has been written with a mature audience in mind and contains strong themes and occasional descriptions of violence. Readers should exercise discretion and prioritise their well-being.

BOOK ONE:
SACRILEGE

PROLOGUE

Smoke from the dying incense swirled around the dark columns, the temple filled with shadows as the moon rose a fine sliver in the sky.

Embers cast a smattering of light across her path from the firepits and bronze braziers, but she knew the temple better than the valleys of her own body. She could be both blind and deaf, yet never falter in her step – for this was the home of her goddess.

No one else walked the marbled floor of the naos at this time of night.

Clothed in a loose robe of pale green, her feet bare, her arms and neck shed of the adornments of her title. She left her hair unbound down her back, rich and deep, like wine pressed fresh beneath the feet of girls from the field; blessed hair that none except one other boasted in the League.

Her daughter.

They two alone were crowned by the goddess with her own hair, dark as the sea's wild heart at sunset.

She approached the statue at the end of the naos, her goddess carved so vividly that in the moving shadows one could almost believe it was flesh and not stone that was seated on the throne.

She slid to the cool floor and leaned her head against the base of the statue. 'Please, come back,' she whispered, her words heavy with emotion. 'Come home, my goddess.'

She was the twelfth since the city lost its divinity.

The twelfth high priestess to rule the temple since their goddess left them.

She could feel the tears gather in her eyes but even here, alone in the dark, she could not let them fall. She was the strength of her people, the undying devotion, the enduring flame. She could not express what rotted away in her heart.

Their goddess had abandoned them.

It had been five hundred years since she had last called Apasa, the place of her birth, home.

When she had been chosen to replace her aunt as the next high priestess, she had remained kneeling in the naos for two days, alone and without interruption. It was for her and the goddess to commune.

But she heard only silence. No matter the prayer or plea she gave, she heard nothing in response. On the second night, fallen into a trance-like sleep, she had glimpsed the goddess, flashing and fleet, turning down a corridor; but no matter how fast she ran after her, she never found her again.

And so she told her first lie as high priestess.

And, for fifteen years, she had led her people and city in devout worship, never hinting that doubt writhed inside her for every unanswered question to the heavens, the smoke from their sacrifices rising into the ether – never to be consumed.

Theirs was not the only city without a goddess. Only two gods from the Holy Twelve still lived within the League, for the rest had moved across to the Empire, bestowing their love and gifts upon them.

But she would never give up hope.

She would bring her goddess back to the city, back to her true home.

For why else would she have been blessed with a daughter that rode the waves with the heart of a true heroine? Both fierce and bright, honour for her home carved deep into her bones?

If this journey was triumphant, if her daughter found her mark and brought home the prize, then the goddess would have no choice but to return.

She must ...

'Hear me, my goddess,' she pleaded, her words burning with fervour. 'Hear my prayer, unending, for my love for you will never cease. I have been loyal and devoted all my life, as has my aunt, my grandmother, and greatmothers tenfold before her. My blood flows still in my daughter, who seeks your glory with sail and sword, instead of robe and altar. Your home cries out for you – a hearth without a fire.' Her fists balled up in her robes, shaking. 'Do you not love me? What could I have done to be treated so by you, Goddess of Love?'

The darkness seemed to grow deeper, the scent of rose and apple growing until she felt her chest constrict. She looked up at the statue and, for one moment, its face was illuminated by the last breath of life in the embers below. For a single heartbeat, the statue was looking down at her instead of out across the hall. Her breath seized as she gazed into its sea-green eyes, its rubied lips tight, its face stern as it stared down at her.

She was dust, an ant, a crumb. She was nothing before pure divinity.

Falling on her face, hands clutched to her heart, silent cries wracked her body as the temple swelled with the might of the goddess. Rose and apple effused the very stones, choking her with their fragrance, the scent twining into her lungs and growing thorns. The air thickened and came alive, waves crashing upon her, beating her into the stones as though she weighed nothing.

And then it was over. She forced her eyes to rise upwards, but the statue had resumed its position.

She rose shakily to her feet, bowing deeply before kissing her fingertips and circling her heart. The sign of devotion marred by the purse of her lips.

Though she loved her goddess, she was angry at her. Centuries of ceaseless worship seem to mean nothing. But she would bring the goddess back, one way or another.

High Priestess Timothea would one day kneel before her goddess in love and Turan, Goddess of Love and Desire, would embrace her.

This she vowed to herself.

CHAPTER ONE

Sparkling salt spray swept over the bow of the trireme, its twin sails grasping at what little wind ruffled the air as its triple bank of oars cut into the sea.

Desma stood in the centre of the ship, one hand on the main mast to steady her while the rowers grunted in timed exertion below, their efforts encouraging the ship faster and faster. Home was almost in sight and hearth beckoned, bolstering the flagging strength of the rowers.

Her hair flowed behind, freed of its usual braided constraints. Desma's mother, famed for beauty and grace throughout the League of Kingdoms, had hair like summer berries and fresh-spilled blood. But her daughter – her daughter was said to have been gifted her hair by the goddess, Turan, herself. Hair as rich as northern wine, shimmering with all the colours of the fertile, red fields of Tuscanai.

Desma could not keep the smile from her lips as another playful spray from the sea left brine on her lips. Her hand brushed over the pouch tied directly to her waist under her dress. Since its discovery, it had never left her person – nor had she loosened it to peer at its contents. The next time it was opened would be in the presence of the high priestess.

She was eager to be home once again, to present her triumph at the temple. To see her father sitting at his potter's wheel, content to let the world come to him. To relax under the fig and pomegranate trees, drinking syrup and sumac water, listening to the lyres being plucked in the small courtyard theatres – to bathe *every day*.

A laugh caused her to turn, smiling at the antics of her friend.

Dressed in a sage-green peplos with a belt of woven horsehair, Cela had adorned her brow with a crown of seaweed and was teasing two of the men into kissing her. Hair like sun-kissed wheat fell in tresses down skin the colour of honey-mixed milk and her laugh was as golden as the rest of her.

'Come, now,' Cela said, shaking her hair back to expose a creamy shoulder. 'Do I not look exactly like one of the sea nymphs? A daughter of wave and tide, waiting endlessly for a burly mortal to grant me but a moment's excitement from the dreariness of everlasting life?'

One of the sailors grunted something Desma couldn't quite catch.

Cela gaped at him for a moment before erupting in laughter yet again. 'Oh, you dirty dog!' She turned to Desma. 'Did you hear that? He said he hopes he would last longer than a moment.' She turned back and pinched his rather muscular arm. 'Well, I hope so too,' she said with a sly look.

Desma groaned. She and Cela had been companions since birth with both their mothers being priestesses in Turan's temple – Desma the elder only by a month. 'Cela, leave them alone, for Uni's sake,' she called out, invoking the Goddess of Dignity and Composure.

Cela removed her seaweed crown and placed it with great solemnity upon his head. 'My lord,' she said with a bow that caused her sleeves to slide further down her shoulders before spinning away to join Desma by the mast. 'Do you think Mynta will be in the city?' she asked as she perched atop a water barrel.

'I cannot say.' Desma shrugged. 'Depends how things are going with Trilos.'

'I hope she is,' Cela said wistfully. 'Three months with nothing but shirtless, sweaty, dusty men becomes tiresome.'

Desma snorted. 'You say that as though you would not have climbed them like olive trees had I not intervened.'

Cela opened her mouth to retort.

'City sighted!' The lookout crowed.

They both sprinted to the bow and clung on to the ropes as the city came into view.

The Kingdom of Apasa, ruled by the Hero-King Sophocles, was a city of cream and rich browns, built from the stones of the coastal cliffs and from marble quarried further inland. One of the richest city-states in the League, it was also the youngest, only founded two thousand years ago.

The buildings flowed like a tumbling river down from the cliffs into the ocean, some even becoming submerged at high tide, their faces etched by the constant caress of the sea. Terraces and pillars, olive trees and temples, weaving roads and bright statues gradually came into focus as Desma and her crew steadily approached, the last leagues of their journey shrinking before them as the city loomed larger.

The harbour's three great stone piers, each a mile long, jutted out far into the ocean like a welcoming hand. The larger ships berthed at the ends that settled into the open ocean, while the smaller ships were tied off in the shallower waters closer to shore. The quays were ringed by a single, crescent-shaped building comprised of warehouses, offices, and taverns for the trade coming and going from the city. To the north was the great sea amphitheatre where the stage was a single large block of stone in the water, tall enough to remain dry no matter the height of the tide. The seats of the theatre began on the beach – where the attendees were most likely to leave with wet legs – and rose eighteen levels high.

The city faced into the setting sun and as it dropped below the horizon, the sky ablaze with reds, and deep blues, and tinted blush, the city became ... incandescent.

As the trireme sailed closer to the harbour, Desma heard singing from the triple ranks of rowers beneath her feet. It was an old song, as old as the first stone laid, the first foot on the beach, the first offering burnt on the cliffs. Short and sweet and ancient. It was a song sung to the rhythm of the final pulls upon the oars, sung with hope and relief and love.

Desma and Cela joined in upon the second cycle of the song. Cela was silver bells and harps. Desma was thrumming strings and echoing halls. The song was a rope flung out to the city and Apasa caught it with both hands, gladly pulling them into her safe shores, always the welcoming mother and protector.

It was still another hour before they could disembark. Desma left firm orders with the captain to allow no one on or off the ship until the temple guards arrived. The hold was filled with treasures both dreadful and beautiful from the broken city of Urruc – a place few dared to brave, let alone plunder.

'Straight to the temple?' Cela asked as they crossed the pier, the ship having berthed halfway along the northernmost one.

'I thought we could see Father first,' Desma replied, glancing at the sky. 'He should still be in the shop.'

They passed through the crescent warehouses quickly and were soon in the city proper, where the scents, sights, and sounds hit Desma like a bolt of lightning to the chest. It was a pain that was welcomed and cherished.

Apasa was a paean to their patron goddess, famed for small pink roses that burst from every garden and park, as well as the heady rosemary bushes that suffused the stones with its fragrance. Roses and rosemary – the flowers of Turan, Goddess of Love. Legend was that when Turan rose from the oceans on a wave of foam and coral, born from the slain fragments of her parent's body, her first step was upon the beaches of Apasa.

Statues of her, lovingly carved and painted, stood in every square. Doves and swans, considered sacred and protected by the goddess, featured in frescoes and mosaics. The many sons of the goddess, known collectively as her Lovers, could be seen standing guard in doorways and shop fronts.

The sun had finally disappeared beneath the horizon and the stars were just beginning to gleam in the thickening twilight. It wasn't long before they reached a small stone street, the buildings leaning forward until they were almost touching. Some shops had small signs proclaiming their wares, but others used the more traditional cloth hangings: yellow for food, green for clothes, red for wine, black for metal. And orange for pottery.

Palamaon's work was not famed or sought by nobles and kings. They were good everyday wares that mothers bought to store their oil or taverns for wine; farmers bought them as gifts for their wives or for dowries for their daughters; men bought the small clay medallions for their sweethearts and children.

He was a good and fair man. Desma could understand why her mother had asked him to marry her all those years ago. He was a grounding presence for someone who spent so much of her time communing with the heavens, surrounded by the wealth of kingdoms.

She pushed open the wooden door and stepped into the dimness of the shop, the only light coming from the back.

Carefully, they passed between shelves of pots, platters, cups, and vases. Some were the simple brown or terracotta of the natural clay. Others, blazoned in black and orange, depicted motifs of everyday life and scenes from heroic adventures.

They found him in the back, hunched over his wheel, a lump of clay spinning slowly as his hands roved with purpose, creating a vase with a wide lip, before squashing it back down. He then repeated the process, shaping a bowl, then a cup, then another bowl; each time simply stopping his hands until the clay clashed against his fingers and the spinning shape dissolved once more into a mere lump of clay. Crafting and destroying. It was her father's end of day process to clear his mind of the day's work and worries and to remind him of the simple joy of pottery.

'Father!' Cela cried into the calm stillness, throwing herself on his back and making him fall onto the wet clay with a squelch.

'Hello, Father.' Desma smiled fondly as she pried Cela off Palamaon.

'Girls!' Palamaon's face crinkled with joy as he shrugged out of his tunic and grabbed a clean one off a nearby hook. Once it was settled on his shoulders and his hands wiped clean, he embraced them both. 'You've returned so early. Thank Turan for your safety.' He stepped away to cast his eyes over them both. 'You are unharmed?'

Desma nodded. 'We are safe, Father. Turan had her hand over us throughout our journey.'

He gripped her shoulders and stood back to study her, his knowing gaze seeing more than just the physical marks of the journey. Her skin, though always bronzed, was darker now after three months of searching through the ruins of Urruc, under the sun in the deserts on the southern coast of the Middle Sea. Her hair, always the pride of her parents and of Apasa, seen as a symbol of the blessing of their goddess, now bore touches of glittering starlight where the sun, the salt, and the sea left their mark. Her eyes were gold-tinged brown, large and slightly tilted upward – common among the eastern coastal city-states – and when her father's gaze landed on them, she knew he saw more there than she wished him to.

He took her cheeks in his rough hands, still cool from the washcloth, his eyes searching hers with care. 'I see marks within you, daughter,' he said quietly. 'Your flesh may be whole, but how is your heart?'

She leaned forward to place a kiss on his cheek. 'Nothing that home cannot mend.' She wondered if the words sounded as hollow as they felt.

He kept his hands on her for a moment longer before letting go, the crease in his brow not quite smoothing away.

'We brought you something,' she said quickly, handing him a small bundle wrapped in sailcloth.

He slowly uncovered it and drew out a small clay bowl, little bigger than his palm. It was worn and crumbling on the edges, much of the colour washed away by time and sand, though it was clear to see that it was once the same hue as wine. Stamped around the rim were black geometric patterns with the outline of a white snake in the middle. He traced his finger over the serpent. 'This is very, very old.'

'We found it in one of the oldest parts of Urruc,' Desma confirmed.

'Remarkable.' His voice grew wistful. 'Imagine, a simple potter like me sat at his worktable and crafted this small piece. And, centuries after his bones and the bones of his people have crumbled to dust, his art is still here, miles away across the sea, in another city, in another potter's hand. He is remembered.'

'Or she,' Desma smiled.

'Or she,' he agreed, looking up at her face. 'Thank you.'

'Come with us to the temple,' she said, grabbing his hand. 'We can both surprise Mother.'

CHAPTER TWO

The moon was bright above them as they climbed the cliff road through the city to the tableland that overlooked Apasa, broken by a few dales and trees, turning the sky the glorious purple of evenfall.

They told their father tales of their adventure in Urruc, laughing as his face turned from shocked to terrified to dismayed as they described the giant flies, scorpions the size of cats, and winds that sounded like wailing cries.

Though some things they kept to themselves, to only tell the high priestess.

In turn, Palamaon kept clear of the shadows that tainted their voices, only saying over and again how glad he was of their safe return.

Cela drew strength from his smooth hand in hers, worn from decades of wielding clay and water. He had given her lessons, though they both soon learned she did not have the patience for pottery, unable to get the vase walls thin or tall, her creations turning into stout mugs or thick plates that she gave to the kitchens at the temple.

It was not known who had laid with her mother during one of Turan's amorous festivals, a nameless worshipper who may have left Apasa shortly after, or whom she passed every day in the street. But she did not care for that man. Desma's father was all she could ask for and more.

And she could have asked for no greater sister, to gift her own father without jealousy or possessiveness. She had truly been blessed by Turan for the love of her chosen family.

'And I hope you did not cause too much trouble among the crew, Celadine,' he said to her now, lowering his brows in mock-scolding.

She blinked her eyes innocently. 'Who, me? Uni herself would be proud of how I conducted myself.'

His eyes widened in fear and he let go of her hand, backing away as he looked worriedly at the sky. 'Oh, thank the gods,' he sighed after a moment, gripping his chest in relief. 'I thought for sure Uni would strike you down for such ridiculousness.'

Cela cried out indignantly as she swatted his shoulder, sticking her tongue at Desma, who laughed loudly, wiping tears from her eyes. 'It is not my fault that men are driven to idiocy at the very sight of my beauty.'

Her father rolled his eyes while Desma snorted.

'Jealous, the both of you.'

'Both my daughters are beautiful,' he said, taking up their hands once again. 'I thank Turan every morning that I have such children who are brave and noble.'

Cela leaned over to whisper loudly in his ear. 'We won't tell Desma that I am your favourite.'

'Oh, shut it!'

Many a pilgrim had fallen to their knees in tears at their first sight of the temple. And though she was practically raised within its walls, Desma could not deny the pang she felt each time she saw it.

One king had wanted to build a road of marble and silver that linked the city to the temple, but the high priestess had decreed it was not the will of Turan. The goddess wanted her worshippers and supplicants to walk through the dust until they rounded the final rock outcrop and viewed her temple in all its divine beauty.

Constructed of white and grey marble that shone gold under the sun and silver under the moon, the temple was open on all four sides, with twelve steps leading from the dust to the pristine stone, where the first of the columns stood in eternal vigil. The hundred-more columns were themselves gilded with the purest silver and gold. Crowning the top of the columns was a frieze depicting the birth and life of Turan: her emergence from the sea, her creation of the mirror, her marriage to Sethlans, her grief at the death of Atunis.

Spurred on by the thought of seeing her mother, Desma picked up her pace. Cela and her father were clearly in agreement as they hurried with her up the stairs and into the vestibule, where they were greeted by more columns of marble, wreathed in garlands of myrtle and apple flowers fashioned from gold. It was boasted by the people of Apasa that only the Under-God Aita, in his Halls Beneath from where all metals and gems poured forth, had a house richer.

They waved at the temple guards, many of whom they had grown up with, and headed into the naos, the centre of the temple. As the guards pushed open the applewood doors the scent of rosewater and myrrh swept outwards, beckoning seductively with shy whispers and open promises.

Tension slipped from Desma's shoulders as the scents of home embraced her.

Taking up a full third of the temple, the naos was home on earth for the goddess.

Myrtle trees lined a path blanketed with a carpet of cerulean. That alone was worth the treasury of the Hero-King himself. But it was the statue of Turan that caught the eye and held it in silken bonds.

Set upon a dais before a burning altar, the statue was the work of the Smith God, Sethlans, himself. The throne was carved from the same marble as the temple. But Turan was sculpted from lunar-stone that was a gift from Tiur. The effect was she glowed forever with the ethereal light of the moon, draped in robes crafted from rose quartz made to look like the softest wool instead of sparkling stone.

Her eyes were the colour of sea foam, green and untamable; lips painted with crushed rubies, her smile both alluring and motherly; her hair was the same colour as Desma's, sculpted so that it seemed to be suspended by a constant breeze. A crown of doves carved from pearls bound her brow, wings of sea glass and gold peered shyly over her bare shoulders. Built at the height of twelve men, Turan was unmistakable: a goddess. Untouchable by man, Queen of Love in all its forms, she demanded the worship they gave her willingly.

After supplicating themselves before her, they each threw a handful of rose petals and incense into the fire pits in thanks for a successful journey before heading out the back of the temple.

Situated behind the building was a small, walled community that lived in service of the temple itself. Priestesses, guards, acolytes, weavers, farmers for the apple trees, gardeners for the rosemary bushes and roses, and the courtesans all lived there in a tight-knit community.

They waved at old friends they passed and quickly discovered Desma's mother in the agora, sitting by the fountain featuring three of the winged Lovers. She was discoursing with several other women as they peeled vegetables into giant pots for the communal evening meal, her cream peplos girded with a soft-green belt. As Desma watched, one of the women said something and her mother tilted her head back and laughed, her wise smile crinkling her eyes.

The sight of her mother sitting with her friends in the firelight, her cowl falling slightly back to reveal her deep-hued hair, sent tears flashing down Desma's face.

'Mother!' she cried out across the agora, dropping all sense of grace as she broke into a run.

Timothea's head whirled in her direction, her mouth dropping in surprise. She hurriedly discarded the knife and peels in her lap, casting vegetables about without a care as she leapt over her friends and flew to meet her daughter in her arms.

Together they fell to their knees in the dust, the temple residents circling them as they shared in their joy and love. Palamaon joined them on the ground, arms wrapped about them both, a circle closed to the world, bound together once more.

It was several long minutes before they could reign their emotions in enough to speak. Her mother smoothed back Desma's hair and held her face in her palms. 'Welcome home, daughter,' she said, placing a kiss on her brow. 'Welcome home.'

Cela's mother had also been peeling vegetables and spent long moments embracing her daughter. Afterwards, both mothers pushed and prodded them towards the bathhouse, although neither of them needed much encouragement.

It was over an hour later when Cela's mother came to fish them out of the tubs, claiming she could cook stew in less time than it took for them to get clean. Night had completely fallen, yet the cloudless sky was bright with stars.

She gave them both soft robes dyed the barest blush, anointing their hair with cassia oil and rosemary wreaths. Soft slippers with flexible leather soles took the place of their toughened travel sandals, and they emerged from the bathhouse cleansed and refreshed.

They moved through the village, heading towards the temple, when Desma saw her father talking to the grizzled captain of the temple guard, Theokritos. They moved to head towards him, the captain nodding curtly once at them before moving on, back straight as a spear.

'We got a nod from him,' Cela noted. 'He must be in a pleasant mood.'

'He is glad to see you both returned safely,' Palamaon said. 'Some men are born hard, others are driven to be hard. It is wise to know which a man is before taking their character.'

'We are going to see the high priestess,' Desma said. 'Were you invited as well?'

He shook his head. 'This is the business of gods, not potters. I will see my wife later tonight. For now, I will sup with old friends and learn the happenings since my last visit. Goddess be with you both, daughters.'

Cela glanced at her friend as they entered the small rooms Desma's mother kept at the rear of the temple.

In the time they had taken to bathe, Timothea had transformed from grateful mother in the market to powerful high priestess.

Her simple peplos was replaced with robes of pure silk, dapple-green and rose-red, a thin diadem of gold set with a single white diamond gracing her brow.

As they entered she waved for them to take a seat on the stools across from her desk. The small smile tugging at her lips was the only crack in her official mien.

'Praise be to Serene Turan for your safe return,' she intoned as she kissed her fingertips and circled her heart, an ancient gesture for the goddess.

'Praise be,' they whispered back, mimicking the gesture.

'I trust your expedition was successful?' she asked.

'Yes, High Priestess Timothea,' Cela said. 'It was marvellous!'

'Any troubles?'

Cela looked to Desma to answer.

Desma gave a small sigh as her voice hardened. 'Nothing we could not handle.'

Timothea studied her daughter. 'Were there others in search?'

Desma shook her head. 'Not from the Empire.'

The high priestess' eyes were piercing, the same gold-tinged brown as her daughter. 'We will speak further on this later, daughter mine.'

Desma gave a curt nod.

'But, regarding the reason you were sent, the rumours of the tomb of the Sand-King ...' There was a glint in Timothea's eyes. For centuries, kings and heroes from both the League and the Empire to the west had died – or worse – in the pursuit of the riches of the Sand-King. Urruc was the first city, founded before the gods had yet emerged in the myriad of ways divinities were birthed. It was older than deserts and seas, its language the first tongue to be spoken, its weapons the first to kill, its tools the first to create.

The people of Urruc were the first to mine the earth and learn what was mud and what was gold, to place value in the stones that gleamed and glowed and glinted. The first to understand art and the ability to capture beauty forever in their works. The gods themselves were known to shower blessings on devotees who presented items from Urruc. And those were far and few in between. The city and its lands were cursed so that no god or goddess could step foot upon the land. Otherwise, there would have been a celestial war fought over who had dominion in Urruc.

It had been Desma who found the tablet, buried under a shrine on a small island off the coast of Artas, its location hinted at in a tattered scroll. Desma who spent three years working with the scholars of the Library of Kelus in Apasa. Timothea had nearly stripped her backside bare when she spent eight hundred silver drachmae to bring over the elderly librarian from the oracular temple in Delphon. He was nearing his eightieth year and had demanded a hundred drachmae for every decade of his life. But Desma felt it was worth it, and it was.

He was the only person in the League who could read the language of Urruc with any competency. And it was from the tablet that they learned where the tomb was located within the city. All the measurements were in lengths and dimensions that made no sense to Cela or Desma. The people of Urruc used the sun in all their measurements, and some things could only be measured at certain times of the year. Hence why it took three years for them to figure out what some of the dimensions were. And so, Cela learned that eighteen shadows of a temple brick on the third day of the month of cold winds was the same as twenty-seven hands. It was an arithmetic nightmare she hoped to never again have to experience.

But when they removed the rubble from the tomb's entrance and saw what lay beneath ... it was worth *everything*.

'Nothing in all the scrolls and books or on temple walls came close to describing what was there, Mother,' Desma breathed. 'It was untouched. After all these millennia.'

'So, you mean to say ...'

'Our ship docked at the quay contains all the wonders of the dead city of Urruc, a treasure worthy of all the Holy Twelve.'

'And it will all be dedicated to the beauty of Turan.' The high priestess' eyes were bright with reverence and pride and something Cela could not quite name. 'Our temple rivals even that of the Sky-Father's grand temple in Quirinale, both in wealth and beauty. And now ... now we will be the undisputed star descendant. The gods will rage in the heavens at their sister's fortune. Perhaps it will even be enough to entice our goddess home.'

Desma could hear the catch in her mother's voice at her last words. She reached out and grabbed her hand. 'I think we can make it even more irresistible.'

Timothea's eyes were filled with confusion and hope. 'What do you mean?'

'Because we found something else in the ruins.'

The high priestess' grip drew tight. 'Show me.'

Desma withdrew her hand to take out a small pouch from the folds of her robe before placing it on the desk and loosening the drawstring. With a slight tremble in her hands, she drew out what lay inside.

Timothea's breath seized in her throat. 'No. It cannot be – is that ...'

Desma placed a simple woven belt between them reverently. At first glance, it appeared the same as any belt used by the women in Apasa to gird their peplos. But something about it drew the eye, then the breath, then the heart. What at first glance looked like fresh wheat before it bronzed in maturity were bands of flowing sea foam. And what appeared to be sprinkles of dew catching the light were scatterings of miniature stars collected from the heavens. Cela knew that to touch it was akin to feeling what a first breath, the oldest wave, the lustre of pearl, what mirrored sunlight felt like. It was beyond man, woman, or personhood. Beyond dust and ash and smoke. Beyond field and hill and grove.

It was divinity.

'The Belt of Turan,' Desma whispered at last.

Cela remembered the story. When Turan first stepped from the sea, carried to land by waves and coral, and placed her feet upon the blessed sands where Apasa now stands, goddesses appeared and crafted clothes from the magic of her creation, clothing her in herself. This Belt was circled about her waist by the hands of nature themselves.

The Belt she then gave to the first mortal she took as a lover. The first mortal to dare break a goddess' heart. The first curse cast down from heaven to earth. The first love spoiled and tainted.

'Returned at last to her home, to forever be the final flower of the Grand Temple.' Desma looked up at her mother, whose face had gone slack in the relic's presence, and gave a half-smile. 'Are you pleased, Mother?'

CHAPTER THREE

A celebration unlike anything in the temple's history was to be thrown. No expense was to be spared. The temple treasury was thrown open and gold spilled out like a river. The high priestess almost emptied the temple of its guards to safely fetch the contents of Desma's ship. Every wagon and cart from the temple community was taken with blankets and cloths to cover the loads. Her mother had even requested the Hero-King send his own soldiers to vacate the piers and crescent harbour building. None were permitted to see the contents beyond the people of the temple.

The high priestess cloistered herself away with several other priestesses to commune with Turan to determine when the celebration was to take place. Two days later, they had emerged exhausted and exhilarated. One priestess refused to speak, taking an unending vow of silence after hearing words from the goddess herself. She would not sully the memory with her own voice.

Timothea had stood in front of Turan's statue and declared that the goddess had entered the room and whispered to them. Turan was pleased beyond measure at the offering and decreed the celebration would be in three weeks, on the night of the new moon. The temple would be closed to the city for the duration, the road sealed and patrolled by the temple guards.

Desma had dinner with her mother that night. Since making the announcement, Timothea had fallen quiet, scarcely responding during the meal. Eventually, Desma stopped her mother's hand as she reached for more bread.

'Mother, what is it?' she asked.

Timothea frowned at her daughter's hand before her gaze slowly moved upward. Her eyes were bright and distant. Desma watched as they slowly dulled and her mother blinked, almost in surprise at seeing her. 'Daughter? I'm sorry. Today has been ... wonderful. And strange, if I dare say.'

'Did the goddess truly speak to you?' Desma asked.

A beatific smile wreathed Timothea's lips. 'Yes. My grandmother used to speak with her almost monthly when she was high priestess. But since her death, it was as though the last tie to Apasa was severed and Turan has been fading like smoke in a fierce summer's breeze. No matter what I or my aunt before me have done ... nothing has brought her back. Nothing seems good enough ...' She caught her words sharply, her breath coming swift.

Desma understood. Some scholars had started calling it the Exodus. The goddess had started spending more and more time in her temple in Aventinus, in the empire across the Aduric Sea. No matter the wealth, renown, and glory Apasa brought to Turan's name, it was never enough to have her move her court back to her birthland.

It was bittersweet for the priestesses. They were acknowledged as the most wondrous and beautiful of the holy houses, but they were godless. What was a priestess without a goddess?

'What was her voice like?' Desma asked, never having been blessed by Turan's presence.

'How do you describe a voice?' her mother asked. 'You compare it with other beautiful things. Silver bells. Songbirds. Pure crystals. Azure springs and brooks. Golden lyres. Her voice is what these things seek to imitate. But words are all I have to compare it to ...' She took a steadying breath. 'Her voice was all the things we think of when we think of love. The slide of a thigh on silk sheets. The sound of flour falling on a kitchen bench as a mother makes bread for her children. The rustle of hay as two lovers couple in secret in a barn. The heavy breathing of two men sparring as they have been since they were childhood friends. It was soft and indomitable. It was bright and dangerous. It was love in all its gentle and cutting forms. When you hear her speak, you know that the Goddess of Love is speaking.'

Desma felt like a child sitting around a fire, listening to a storyteller speak of the wondrous deeds of heroes past. Despite being raised in the temple, divinity was as untouchable as it was always present. 'And you told her of the Belt?'

'Yes,' Timothea breathed. 'When I told her of the treasures of Urruc, I could sense her joy and desire to possess them. But when I mentioned the Belt …'

Desma waited. The silence stretched. 'What?'

Her mother's hands trembled in her own and Desma squeezed encouragingly.

'Her voice … turned ravenous.' Her mother's eyes took on that glossy, far away look again. 'Ravenous,' Timothea whispered. 'A midnight snarl. Ocean deep. Heart blood. Want. Need …' She trailed off.

It made sense, Desma thought. The Belt was as much part of Turan as her hair or skin. It was with her at her birth. It was given to her first mortal lover and had been lost ever since. Desma could only imagine how she would feel if she was in the goddess' place.

She waited for her mother to keep speaking. But Timothea simply seemed to withdraw further from the present the longer Desma sat watching her, the shine in her eyes taking on a star-like quality that scared Desma more than any creature she had encountered on her journey to Urruc.

'Mother,' Desma said cautiously.

Timothea stood abruptly. 'I am tired. There is much to prepare for the ceremony. I'm going to retire. Please clear the table, daughter mine.' She kissed the top of Desma's head as she passed and disappeared into her room.

Desma was left sitting in the kitchen, concern twisting in her gut. She listened for the sounds of her mother turning in, but heard nothing.

She rose slowly from the table and crept to the door. Placing her ear against the wood, she heard her mother's voice. She was chanting. But it was not with the usual grace and calm, a meditation before sleep.

It was fast, breathless and fervent.

She was pleading.

Desma reached for the latch, but paused.

This was not between mother and daughter. It was between priestess and goddess.

She left the door and cleared the kitchen before going to bed herself. Throughout it all and well into the night she could hear her mother's voice, too soft to discern words but loud enough to feel what her mother was feeling.

Want. Need. Fear. Love.

Mynta gazed out on the city below from her window high in one of the bright towers, banners bearing her family sigil streaming proudly in the breeze above her.

Trilos was ancient and proud. The land east was rich and fertile, trees and farmland vanishing past the horizon provided food for the city and for the many of the Kingdoms. Further to the north were low-lying hills from which the mighty river Skamidros flowed, first looping away before doubling back to the city to pour out into the ocean. West of the city was hard-packed, rocky ground that eventually softened into fine sand that melted into water so blue it stung the eyes.

The land was once ruled by Aplu, who allowed his famed singing cattle to graze the once sweeping plains of sweet, sun-drenched grass. When the land became bare, he gifted it to Sethlans, who discovered veins of gold and copper in the hills and set up his Forge, founding the city to ensure he had helpers and supplies for his work.

The city was famed for its strong walls and tall, square towers. Its gates had never been breached, and her armies bore weapons direct from Sethlans' flames.

But it was the giant automatons who guarded the gates and stood sentinel throughout the city that caused Trilos' enemies to pause and think twice before attacking.

The automatons varied in size from twice the height of a man to being able peer over the walls. Cast from bronze and stone, they were fashioned into fearsome warriors wearing ancient helms and armour. The secret to their workings were known only by the Clevers, who maintained them, and the King, who commanded them.

Once a year, in a great ceremony, the automatons were awakened and rotated around the city. The clashing of their gears and inner workings, the rumble and shake of their steps, the shadows they cast as they passed by, always struck a note of fear in Mynta's heart while the rest of the people cheered wildly. All she could imagine was what it would be like to face one on the battlefield. It was only by Sethlans' order that they be used solely to safekeep Trilos and her lands that past kings did not use them to conquer the other kingdoms.

Some centuries ago, a king, more arrogant than his predecessors, tried to move them south against Apasa, but when the automatons reached the edge of their territory they froze. It was said that the king was in such a rage he picked up a war hammer and struck one in the chest, causing the automaton to fall to the ground, where it began to bubble and hiss, before slowly turning into a pool of molten metal. Then, in front of the king and his army, the metal reforged itself into chains and struck at the king, binding his hands and feet.

For the rest of his days, the man was then shackled; so he had to hobble when he walked, and needed to be fed as he could not lift his hands to his mouth. It was only on his deathbed that the Forge God forgave him and freed him from the chains, allowing him to embrace his family for his last breath.

Mynta always wondered if the punishment was proportionate to the crime? She did not know by what standards a god judged his people. She would not know what she would do if she was divine. She knew that was a blasphemous thought but, sometimes, when the sky was still and the moon danced slowly across the clear sky, she wondered what kind of goddess she would be: what she would rule, what she would want from her city and devotees.

She remembered mentioning it once to her mother when she was a child. Her mother had dropped her wine in shock and had priests of Sethlans and Uni gather in their home to bless and cleanse her. That was when she began to withdraw, to build walls, and only portray what she knew her parents preferred. That was her first lesson in only showing people what they wanted to see.

Sometimes it was hard to remember there were two people inside her. The image she showed to society would be on display for so long, she often forgot there was a second person, waiting for the moments she could be free – usually when she was in Apasa.

'Come, my dear,' her old nursemaid said, holding up a dress of wheat and apple-red. 'Let us get you to breakfast. Your father requested your presence, remember?'

She rose from her seat and allowed her ladies to dress and groom her. The dress was bound around her body and her hair was swept up high. She studied herself with interest in the polished bronze mirror as jewellery was strung across her neck.

She was no longer the slim, idealised beauty from her younger days. Her mother had done everything in her power to make her as beautiful as possible. Her father had great plans for her, she used to say.

Mynta had always enjoyed food, but never questioned when her portions were controlled. She learned quickly not to reach for another fig, or loaf, or slice of meat. She had long since lost count of the slaps her hands had received over the years.

She had always been pale and lithe, but as the years went by it became a hollowness.

She was tired all the time. Weak. Unable to do the simplest tasks without losing what little strength she woke up with in the morning. Her parents subjected her to a host of remedies. Poultices applied to the stomach, herbs burned under her nose to give her muscles strength, soaking in baths of milk and wine to refresh her skin and fire her blood.

As a last recourse, her nursemaid had brought a priest of the Healing God, Esplace, who declared she was not ill from evil humours who sought her destruction. She was sick from being denied the bounty of Horta's blessings. Food.

She was starving to death.

The priest had said that she must be allowed to eat what she wished, to be denied nothing. His god would ensure gluttony would not enter her mind and her body would know what she needed to be what the gods had planned.

And so, to their great reluctance, her parents allowed her to fill her own plate.

At first, she was hesitant. Only eating what she knew would make them happy. But her nursemaid begged her, late at night, tears streaming down her face as she offered bread and honey, fruit and cheese, rich wine and cream. Eventually, Mynta had found she could not deny the old woman's pleas any longer and began to slowly eat a few pieces to appease her.

One year on, and she felt as though she had been born anew. She woke refreshed each dawn, strength and vigour flowing through her body, eyes bright and undarkened by exhaustion. Her hair, rich as ink and with an unruly tendency to curl, was silky without need for oils, and her skin was smooth, without blemish. Most importantly, she no longer felt hollow.

But, she thought as she turned to examine her side profile in the mirror, she was no longer the slim and slender maiden she had been; not like the rest of her peers. Her body was now curved and full, rolls where before there were ribs. She was not willowy or lissom, and she did not want to be. She had never felt stronger, more capable, more herself.

She knew her parents were disappointed. She saw it in their eyes each time they looked at her. Her father had said that they would need to pay a larger dowry to compensate for her appearance.

Words that landed like daggers in her heart.

But she would not go back to those years of exhaustion and weakness. To wither away. She refused.

'Come, Amynta,' her nursemaid said, shaking her from her reverie. 'Do not keep your parents waiting.'

Mynta turned from the mirror and braced herself.

All of Trilos had heard that Apasa had retrieved a great host of treasures from Urruc. Mynta shivered at the name, for all children were brought up on the dark tales of the cursed city.

And yet her friends had braved the sands of the dead city and gods knew what other dangers, not only finding the treasure but also bringing it safely back to Apasa along with each other. She was filled with pride that the two women dearest to her heart would be forever heralded in history for their discovery.

She remembered when she had first met them four years ago in Apasa. Being the only child and daughter of Trilos' emissary to the city, she was always expected to carry herself with dignity – never knowing if the next son she was introduced to would be her future husband. Her parents used to parade her like a great jewel, flashing her at parties and dinners, always tempting and promising. That night, most of Apasa had turned out for a debut play and, after being presented to all the eligible bachelors, she was set aside with a cup of watered-down wine and told to remain quiet.

Which she obeyed – right up until Desma and Cela kidnapped her.

The next morning, two hundred city guards, and later three hundred rubies from the city vaults to appease Mynta's enraged father, a firm friendship had been established between the three women.

But she knew breakfast this morning was not going to be a celebratory one. Her father had sent a messenger by fast ship to the Grand Temple of Turan, conveying his attendance at the celebration that was now only a week away. A reply had arrived last night politely, yet resolutely, barring anyone not of the temple from attending. It did include a note that the Hero-King would be hosting his own celebrations in the city which the emissary was welcome to attend. Her father had raged the night before, and Mynta doubted his disposition had much improved upon sleep.

It was a grave slight. To deny an emissary attendance from such a momentous occasion his delegated kingdom was holding was unheard of. But Apasa had risen mightily. All kingdoms in the League boasted small troves of Urruc artefacts, a few swords or spears, a handful of cups or jugs, jewellery in some rare instances.

Though it had not been formally declared, rumours told of wagons lining the road from the harbour to temple when Desma and Cela returned home. *Wagons!* Mynta could not even begin calculating the wealth, though she was sure some lords in Trilos were trying.

She had heard her father talking to other councilmen that Delphon was outraged no share of the treasure was being sent to them, despite their scholar helping Desma to translate the tablet that led to the tomb. The Delphonii could be terrifying to deal with, for their patron god was Aplu, the Golden Seer, and oft they knew of things yet to come about.

She could only pray to the gods that Desma and her mother did not fall from the heights they now walked. History was littered with tales of the fates of mortals who rose too close to the gods.

CHAPTER FOUR

The days passed quickly.

The city was thrumming with rumours and gossip about the upcoming celebration. Nobles, and merchants, and heroes sent servants bearing requests for invitations.

Each was sent back with the same answer: a rose tied with a myrtle sprig. Temple community only.

Bribes came after. Gold and silks, rare oils and incense, bouquets of roses and rosemary. The high priestess sent a reply to each of them, thanking them for their charitable offerings to the goddess. Again, the message was clear: bribes will get you nothing but the temple's thanks for the gifts.

In bringing the contents of the tomb back safely, Desma's task was completed. She left the priestesses and acolytes to organise the details of the ceremony. The temple guard captain, Theokritos, was grizzlier than ever. He had the temple guards running constant drills and launching surprise ambushes on off-duty men, and already had plans to expand the guard's number. Desma had already passed along the offer to her crew, in case any wanted to retire from a life at sea to become a temple guard. A few were mulling it over, but there was no rush.

Until the temple sanctioned another expedition, Desma and Cela were bound to Apasa. Not that either of them really minded waiting in the paradise that was their home. They spent the first two weeks after returning enjoying the pleasures the city had to offer. And they took hold of those pleasures with all the fervour of two twenty-year-old women reaching the zenith of their youth.

They first set out to determine if Mynta was visiting the city with her family, but had no luck at the emissary's home. Nor did the servants know when the family would be visiting next.

Resigned to remaining a duo, Desma and Cela took the drachmae the temple paid them for completing their task, including a generous addition as a token of the temple's thanks. They could have both bought a villa atop the cliffs overlooking the sea and retired happily into indulgence.

Instead they took their crew out drinking at taverns, their gold ensuring wine flowed faster than the swiftest river current. Days passed with the heady fragrance of the finest Thevan wine never leaving their lips. Desma had the vague recollection of paying a band to follow them wherever they went so that they would always have music. Strings and reeds pranced and leapt about them noon and night, firing their blood, raising their voices until she was sure she had no sound left, but still she kept singing.

Feasts of honey-soaked pork, fennel, and thyme sausages, fig-stuffed ocean fish, spiced lamb wrapped in vine leaves, roasted grapes and apples, artichokes and olives – all the foods of home.

Desma would dance until her legs were covered in dust from the street and bruised from the taverns' wooden floors. She danced until her hair was thick with sweat and glistened as darkly as the wine she drank. When her peplos got dirty, she would simply step into a shop and buy another. Some being simple and spun at home by a wife looking to make a few more drachmae, others sewn with sapphires and pearls. She dispensed gold for poor and rich alike with an extravagance she could not explain.

She felt like Phersipnai, wife of the Under-God Aita, She of Two Lands. Half the year she danced among the wildflowers with her mother Horta, Goddess of Crops and Harvests. And the other half she ruled the dark world beyond life with her husband, keeper of all the treasures of the deep earth. When she stepped from the dark to the light, she would bring with her chests of riches to share with the living world, uncaring of status or history. All were given gifts.

And so Desma and Cela acted.

Somewhere in the back of her mind, a small part watched herself with amusement as she danced, and sang, and drank, and spent. She noticed the nobles lift their lips in disgust as she stumbled from tavern, to shop, to theatre. She saw some shopkeepers brace themselves to deal with yet another spoiled, rich youth – and others wait with bated breath and helpless hope, wishing she would walk into their shop and stave off the debt collectors for a little while more. She saw priestesses from the temple give pitying glances at the wild waste of youthfulness, saw city watchmen roll their eyes at the disturbance they created.

Desma felt like she was all the different women the people saw her. She was drunk, and selfless, and delinquent, and brash, and entitled, and more.

She was a child of the temple and a potter's daughter, she was adventurer and sailor, she was fearless and brazen, foolish and clever. She was a finder of lost treasure, hero to city and goddess.

She was a looter and a thief. And sometimes so much worse.

But here she was home, a daughter of Apasa.

Here she could wrap her people around her like a cloak, a shield, a sanctuary.

Here she could almost imagine she was not something else.

Someone she did not sometimes hate.

Desma opened her eyes and let out a low hiss, shutting them again tightly.

Light blazed through the window with almost malicious indifference.

She cracked her lids slightly and breathed through the sharp pain that lanced her head. Minutes spread like cool honey until she was finally willing to push herself up into a sitting position.

It took a moment for her to realise she was in her bedroom at her father's shop. It was plain, with only a bed, table, chair, and few shelves on the wall. The shelves held a vase her father had made her, painted with olive trees and rabbits, and various trinkets she collected when she was young. The beginnings of her career.

She found a jug of water on the table and nearly tripped in her haste to reach it. She gulped half of it down with barely a swallow before she heaved it all back up into a bowl conveniently placed next to the jug.

Once her stomach settled, she finished the rest of the jug slowly. Feeling a little better, she quickly pulled a comb through her hair that was in desperate need of a wash. Her dress had some wine stains, but would suffice for the moment.

She left her room and crept downstairs, not trusting herself to take the stairs at any great speed.

She found her father folding up a bedroll from the shop floor, a blanket and pillow already stored in a crate next to him.

'Father?' she managed to whisper hoarsely, already feeling thirsty again.

He turned, a frown marring his usual placid features that almost had her worried until she saw the suppressed twinkle in his eyes. 'Cela is in my bed. With a ... friend.'

She looked at him puzzled before understanding dawned. 'Oh. My. Uni.'

'I thought I might have had to sleep outside with the noise they were making,' he said as he finished packing his bedding away.

'I am so sorry. I don't even ... I don't know what to say.'

'Think no further of it, daughter mine,' he said. 'Celadine is a daughter of one of Turan's priestesses. She was raised from infanthood to celebrate all forms of love. The love of two strangers sharing a night can be one of the most passionate and memorable.'

Desma felt like throwing up again. 'For the love of the gods, please stop talking.'

Her father chuckled. 'Breakfast?'

She dropped into a chair by his worktable, temporarily cleared of clay and tools. 'Please. And tea.'

He placed bread, goat cheese, and figs in front of her with a steaming cup of tea so strong it puckered her lips. 'Oh, gods ... honey!' she spluttered.

With a not-so-innocent grin, he pushed a small pot towards her. 'Nothing like a well-brewed cup of tea to clear the head.'

'Demon,' she coughed as she tried to clear the acrid taste from her mouth. She didn't bother with a spoon. She poured the honey straight from the bowl until her cup was at the brim. With a careful sip, she let out an audible sigh. 'Much better.'

Her next sip nearly resulted in the scalding contents spilling over her as the door to her father's shop slammed open hard enough to set his wares clattering.

'Palamaon,' a woman shouted as she stomped inside, 'are you awake yet?'

'For all the gods' sakes, Korinna, you're louder than Laran himself on the battlefield,' Palamaon shouted back, naming the infamously ill-tempered God of War. 'How would I still be asleep after that entrance?'

Korinna appeared from behind the shelves bearing a tray of food. She was around the same age as Desma's parents and had brown hair streaked with iron-grey that was always pulled back in a loose ponytail, a face lined from a lifetime of joy, shoulders slightly too broad to be seen as demure, and a voice to match the roughest general.

A farmer's daughter who married relatively later in life compared to her four older sisters, she had waited for the right man – a wine merchant – who took her from the fields to live in Apasa. She spent her days caring for the other shopkeepers in the street, always bearing a tray of food or a new sampling of wine lifted from her husband's stores, and she always paid special care to Desma's father. With Timothea spending nine days out of ten in the temple and her father refusing to give up his shop, it was often a relationship held across a distance. Not that it ever seemed to dim their love for each other.

Korinna gave Palamaon a glare. 'The day I find you sleeping past dawn is the day Tinia decides to blind the Sun-God,' she said, before smiling sweetly at Desma. 'Good morning, dear. You're looking a little peaky. Here, eat some yoghurt, it's sweetened with my own berry syrup. Don't forget the cinnamon. Is Cela here? Cela!'

There was a heavy thud from upstairs. The three of them listened to the sounds of clumsy stumbling and the clattering of furniture, followed by the crack of something fragile hitting the wooden floors accompanied by a barrage of cursing. A few moments later a head surrounded by a cloud of magnificently golden bed-hair peered around the corner of the stairs.

'Whoever is shouting better have something to appease me,' Cela snarled. Unfazed, Korinna lifted one of the cups from her tray. 'Mead, dear?'

'Aunt Korinna!' Cela exclaimed, all enmity erased as she leapt from the stairs to grab the cup and hug Korinna one-armed. 'Have I ever mentioned that you look just like Mother Horta bearing the harvest of the seasons? So full of dignity, love, grace, unparalleled beauty ...'

'Be quiet,' Korinna laughed as she shooed Cela into a chair. 'I hope you got your homesickness out of your systems. Two weeks gambolling around the city with that thug crew of yours must be a record.'

'Three months of sleeping in sand, living off camel meat and brackish water, not a bathhouse in sight – it was enough to drive a woman mad,' Desma said. 'We were just trying to catch up on three months of the simple joys of life.'

'And being a terror unleashed on the city,' her father said disapprovingly. 'I think you have had enough frivolity, daughters. I would ask peace from you and your crew.'

They both nodded, faces shamed, though he softened his words after with a smile.

'You are too harsh, Palamaon,' Korinna scolded. 'Poor little lambs. I could tell you stories from my youth that would get many a young man's spear raised high.'

'Korinna!' Palamaon exclaimed, covering his ears.

Desma and Cela laughed as Korinna began a ribald tale of her and an oil maker's nephew, causing the potter to make haste and disappear back to his wheel.

CHAPTER FIVE

The sky was turning from peach to blue, dawn forming a glimmering path along the horizon, the air filled with the scent of rosemary and brine. The city was slowly gaining colour as the sun rose higher, rich grey to earthy bronze. The sea was a sheet of glass, azure blue giving way to rich sapphire which, in turn, changed to ethereal green.

It was a perfect day to enjoy the ocean.

They left the trireme at the pier. It was too much hassle getting the two-hundred strong crew together for a simple pleasure cruise.

Instead, they took Cela's small craft she kept for just such an outing. Single sail, a bright sea-green with just four rowers, a small hold, and enough cushions to furnish every bed in Apasa, it was perfect for just such a day. Desma decided to invite her command crew with them as a slightly more leisurely gathering than their two-week tavern crawl.

There was the captain, Khufu, who came from Opuni in the Great Lands to the south of the Middle Sea. He was a large man, with rich, umber skin like mountain earth in summer shade, hair always cut short, his accent nearly eroded after a lifetime among the League. He wore loose trousers and a sleeveless tunic of red and cream, a gold torc his only adornment. He had been their captain for the last four years and ran the crew with a calm surety that Desma had come to trust.

Then there was the helmsman, Bion, who hailed from the island kingdom of Konoso. Bion was built like a bull and was nearing six-foot-five, his body covered in wiry black hair, with a face both pleasing and blunt. He was fiercely protective and ferociously disciplined, expecting nothing more or less from the crew than he did not give himself.

The quartermaster was as thin as a whip, and perhaps the deadliest of the crew. Cosmas got the position after Desma caught him sneaking on the ship and poisoning the evening meal during a trip to Pallan. She had not initially seen herself offering him a job at the end of their conversation, given she had been holding a knife to his throat at the time, but sometimes the gods enjoyed throwing an adder into the nest. And, so far, every meal since then has been delicious – even if he did have an over-generous hand with the cinnamon at times.

Delphinus was the piper who kept the three banks of rowers in time as they sailed. His mouth was always full of song and his pockets empty of coins. He was a handsome youth, only a year or two older than Cela and Desma. His eyes were as green as the far sea with hair like dulled copper, but his voice was his winning feature, rivalling any court bard in skill and variety.

The last of Desma's command crew were women.

The daughter of Apasa's leading shipwright, Arete had both known and forgotten more about boats than most people would ever learn. With a mind clever enough to give Menrva, Goddess of Wisdom, a run for her drachma – always designing and planning, tinkering and building – she was as much their battle commander as well as their shipwright. Desma couldn't count the number of scrapes they had made it through thanks to Arete's strategies. She was able to outthink and outfight most of the crew, her solemn eyes never wavering, much like her belief in herself. More than once Desma had found herself quietly envying such confidence.

Her overseer and the youngest member of the crew at eighteen, Kassandra, was from Trilos. Though her age did not diminish her fearsome reputation in the harbour. Not a single rower dared question one of her orders.

Overall, six command crew, another ten sailors, twenty men trained solely for spear and arrow, and one-hundred-and-seventy rowers made up the crew of the trireme. To a man, hand-picked by Desma and Cela when the high priestess gave Desma the ship as a gift for her sixteenth birthday. Naturally, Cela had opted to join her rather than enter the temple as an initiate and they had spent a year being trained by the best sailors and warriors Apasa had to offer alongside their newly formed crew. They were held apart from the temple guard, a special group focused on hunting down the ancient treasures of Turan and her Lovers, bringing riches and history to her Grand Temple, her divine birthplace.

There was a time that Desma's mother had nurtured hopes of her daughter becoming an initiate of the temple, but it soon became clear when Desma was caught climbing Turan's statue in an attempt to try on her dove crown that devotion was perhaps not the path for her. The first time, admittedly, Timothea said she had believed it to be a sign of Desma's path in the temple to succeed her as high priestess. The fourth time she tried to get the crown, however, Palamaon was able to convince her that Desma just wanted it because it was shiny.

As much as Desma loved the temple, being raised among the incense and offerings and glories, she knew the priestess path was not for her – and gods knew she did not have the patience for her father's craft. And so the high priestess took a chance, forging a path for her daughter that had not existed before. And, after this trip, bringing home the treasures of Urruc, finding the Belt of Turan itself, Desma knew this was what she and Cela were meant to be doing.

They let the ship settle right where the deep blue turned to glass-green, leaving it to drift on the waves, the rowers keeping it in check.

Delphinus played casually on his lyre, the music lazily floating around them as they lounged on the cushions, passing trays of meats and cheeses and bottles of honey-wine.

Kassandra laid draped over Bion's chest, idly popping grapes into her mouth and pegging them at others when they were not looking.

'Have we been told where we might be going next?' Arete asked, who was also leaning up against Bion, feet propped on the railing.

'I hear that in the middle of the Sea of Red Spears there are items blessed by a rageful and jealous god,' Cosmas said quietly, sipping a cup of spiced tea. 'Weapons powerful enough to summon plagues and part oceans.'

Arete rolled her eyes at him. 'Yes, and I heard there is a magical book of obsidian buried in a sand dune and made of gold that can raise the dead. And on an island far, far to the north, across a channel of frozen grey water, there is a magical sword trapped in a rock. If you can pull it free, you will be crowned king of the island. Do you desire a crown for your head, Cosmas?'

'Someone's a bit snarky today,' Delphinus said as he fiddled with his strings.

Cosmas simply sipped his tea, eyes never leaving Arete's face.

Desma interceded before a bloodbath could begin. 'It might be a while before we are issued a new assignment. The temple has a lot to occupy them. Besides, is anyone really that anxious to leave Apasa already?'

'Not all of us call Turan's city home,' Cosmas said blandly.

It was true. Alongside Desma and Cela, only Arete was from Apasa. Delphinus came from a small town on the border between the League and the Empire. And Cosmas never mentioned where he was born or where he grew up. Desma let him keep his secrets in exchange for his skills.

'Maybe after the ceremony we could sail up to Trilos?' Cela suggested, sitting up on the bow, looking for all the world like a sea nymph emergent in her dress of sun-kissed green. 'We could see Mynta.'

'We could visit the Copper Markets and Gears Plaza, maybe swing by the Thinkery,' Kassandra said excitedly. 'Who knows what the Clevers have thought of since we were there last! It's been ... what ... eight months?'

'Closer to ten, I think,' Arete said.

'I have no objections, but only if we can see The Forge,' Bion grumbled, thumbing his knife. The Forge was where Sethlans himself used to craft weapons of awe and dread when he resided within the League of Kingdoms. He was the first god to leave for the Empire. Now, The Forge was run by acolytes with arms thicker than Desma's body. The only place to rival the weapons and tools from Trilos was The Workshop across the Aduric Sea in Quirinale, the City of Gods.

'It's settled, then,' Desma said, flicking her red hair from her eyes. 'Granted the temple does not send us elsewhere, we sail for Trilos two days after the ceremony.'

Kassandra twisted around on Bion's arm to face Khufu. 'Isn't Trilos where that woman tried to castrate you?' she asked innocently.

A glare darkened the captain's face as the rest of the crew failed to hide their sniggers. 'It was a small misunderstanding.'

'That's probably why she didn't succeed,' Delphinus said, pretending to grasp something elusive. 'Too small to get a good grip.'

Desma spewed honey-wine.

Khufu threw an apple that hit the piper hard enough to split the fruit. 'Says the man who we had to rescue hanging naked from a rooftop after the man's wife found you in bed together.'

'How *did* she manage to get you both suspended from that rope?' Kassandra asked.

Delphinus blushed. 'I didn't realise how quickly women gather when one is slighted. I barely had time to *find* my clothes let alone put them on before she had all the wives in the street pinning me to the floor.'

Once the group's laughter faded, Arete turned to Desma. 'Explain again why we are not invited to the temple's celebration?'

Bion and Khufu groaned in practised unison.

'It doesn't matter how many times you ask, Arete,' Kassandra said. 'The high priestess said no. Not even King Sophocles was invited – and I heard he sent two of his most beautiful horses from his personal stables, one laden with gold and the other with scented oils. And she sent him a thank you note and a reminder of where his soldiers were to be stationed!'

Desma did not find her mother's action surprising. The Hero-King held his peoples' loyalty and love, Timothea held their hearts and devotion. Sophocles could imprison and kill his citizens – an angry goddess could do much worse.

Arete's hazel eyes did not waver from Desma.

She sighed. 'I told you – I asked my mother a dozen times for you all to come. I argued that you helped us find the treasure and get it back safely to Apasa. She said no every time.' She decided to forgo the details of their exact conversation where the High Priestess had threatened to cut out the tongues of her crew if she asked one more time. Considering the strange mood she had been in since communing with Turan, Desma did not wish to press her mother any further. 'The goddess' orders were clear. Only those who live in the temple can attend.'

Arete's eyes flashed but she did not say another word.

Desma went to speak, but Cela nudged her with her foot and shook her head. She was right. There was nothing she could say that would change the situation.

Delphinus started singing softly, a song of a shepherdess who refused to lay with Arekles, godling son of Turms, the Trickster God of Silver Tongues, and the crew settled in to listen pleasurably.

The tale told of the woman not being impressed by the youth's looks and fighting back when he tried to take her. Turms chose to punish them both, the woman for striking his son, and the youth for using muscle instead of words to win her. Though the tune was pleasant, the story itself was sad, ending with the shepherdess turned into a tree for the crime of defending herself from a brute.

'And so,' Delphinus finished softly, fingers barely brushing the lyre's strings, 'the woman passed from the history of man into the songs of legends, her name forever locked within her boughs and known only to the Corded Goddess, who doles out the lives of mortals with frugality and intent.'

The music dissipated into the balmy air, the crew each within their own minds as they gazed across the glittering sea.

Desma wondered if the shepherdess' family ever found out what happened to her before they died, or if they heard the song one day and never knew it told the end of their daughter.

'Empyreans.' Cosmas' voice broke like thunder on a clear day.

Every head whipped around to the west to view the large, gleaming quinquereme sailing towards Apasa, its five banks of oars causing the ship to plough relentlessly onwards. Its single, giant sail was emblazoned with the Empire's sigil – a bronze, double-headed axe vertical behind a snarling, gold she-wolf. But beneath them was a sign Desma never thought to see within the waters of Apasa: a blush swan bearing a crown of roses. It was the symbol of Turan's temple within the empire, as the myrtle and dove were her symbols within the League.

'Oh, sweet Esia, please descend upon us,' Kassandra whispered, calling upon the Peaceful Goddess.

'Back to the harbour,' Desma said urgently, casting cushions aside in her haste to get to her feet. 'Get this ship moving – NOW!'

'To stations, you pathetic heaps of cow dung,' Bion roared as he surged to his feet like a black bear, flinging Kassandra and Arete off him. The rowers scrambled back to their seats and grabbed their oars. 'Delphinus, triple time. Play!'

The copper-headed youth set a furious tune on the pipes drawn from his tunic. The ship lurched forward as the rowers sent the ship flying. Though they had a fair lead, their small ship had four rowers compared to the three hundred on board the quinquereme, and Desma could almost hear the snap of the oar-masters' whips. Empyrean ships often used slaves for their rowers – and they rarely cared if most survived the voyage.

'Golden Turan, born of sea and air, show us your grace,' Cela was chanting from the stern. 'Lend us your speed. Send us a breeze. Ask the waves to help and not hinder. Take these gifts as unworthy devotions to your power, Serene One.' She began to cast silver drachmae into the white wake of the ship.

Arete joined her. 'Nethuns,' she called to the hoary God of the Deeps. 'Get us back to the city before those bastards and we will give you a statue from Urruc.'

Before Desma could do any more than gape at the shipwright, a groan sounded from far below the ship. Water frothed around the hull until they were surrounded by a roiling pool of ocean. With another groan the ship lurched forward, its speed increasing until Desma could barely keep her eyes open in the spray that drenched them, the wind howling in her ears, her hands clenching the rail so hard splinters pierced her skin.

All at once, whatever force was propelling them fell away and the ship came to a gentle stop next to the furthest point of the middle pier.

Desma and Cela did not even wait for the ship to be tied off before jumping the side onto the stone pier. They took off towards the city, leaping crates and barrels, dodging sailors and ropes. Desma glanced back to see the quinquereme coming about faced by eight Apasan triremes. It would take them time before they gained permission to dock. Apasa was the furthest kingdom from the Empire and little love was lost between them.

When they reached the end of the pier and the harbour crescent, Desma looked back again and gasped in dismay. A small vessel was already rowing swiftly toward the city, flying the standard of holy diplomacy. By law, twelve priests with two guards and a servant apiece were allowed to enter the city without obstruction.

'Desma, here,' Cela called. She had found two mounted city guards. 'Please,' her friend panted. 'We need to get to the temple. Empyreans.' She pointed behind her.

The guards looked at the harbour, saw Desma's flaming red hair, and promptly jumped off their horses.

'Turan give you wings,' one of them prayed.

Mounted, they took off in clatter of hooves on stone. There were several paths up the cliffs from the city. Some were for walking, others for donkeys, and some for wagons. The one they took was for riders and, though it was longer and less steep than the path for donkeys, it was faster for being less crowded, and within ten minutes they were at the top.

It was then they gave their horses free rein. Used to gently plodding around the crowded city, the horses let out shrieks of freedom and proved their worth. Desma's stomach rolled at yet another lurch of speed. First the ship and now the horse. If she made it to the temple without losing her stomach, it would be a miracle.

It was no coincidence that an assembly from the Empyrean temple would arrive in a city they have not stepped foot in for over two hundred years only six days away from the unveiling of Urruc's treasures.

Why they were here – and what they hoped to achieve – she could only guess. All Desma knew was that she needed to give her mother as much notice as possible. She knew the Empyreans would have sent no messenger or word of their coming, a classic tactic to throw the temple off-balance.

They obviously did not know her mother well.

She almost felt sorry for whoever was in charge.

TALE OF THE SHEPHERDESS AND AREKLES

The day was fine and clear, the oak trees casting deep shade on the edge of the field where the woman was enjoying the warmth of the sun. Her sheep grazed around her, little clouds floating on a sky of undulating green.

From the trees emerged a youth, strolling across the field towards her with all the arrogance of a lordling – for he was Arekles, son of the cleverest god, Silvered Turms.

The woman was not impressed with the youth's burnished limbs or rich locks of hair, nor his dazzling smile and quick words. He came upon her and proclaimed his godling blood, letting his chiton fall about his waist so his body was clear before her eyes, carved and cut with muscles.

But she had no need for men and their foolishness, nor their weakness for untamed pride.

Undeterred by her rejections, Arekles quickly grew tired of her frigidness and tried to grab her. He reasoned that if he subdued her with force, then she would simply fall in love and be his to claim. But she was quick, and such thinking earned him a shattered jaw and a broken arm when she laid into him with her cypress staff.

Leaving the arrogant Arekles broken and bleeding in the shimmering sweet grass of her mountain home, the woman spat on him and walked away to tend her sheep, sending a prayer of thanks to Artimi, Goddess of Women Who Defend Themselves.

From his seat high in the clouds above his patron-city, Tethalia, Turms heard the cries of his son and flew down to the earth with his winged helm, blazing streaks of colour in his wake. Upon observing the pitiful sight of his offspring, Turms chastised his son for allowing anyone to get the better of him and for resorting to force over the power of words. He was the son of Turms after all, not of the brute Laran.

With a spell, he healed Arekles' wounds, though leaving the veins in his face and arm to glow blue and silver. Then, with another spell, Turms caused his son's muscles to fade and his strength to flow into the earth, where it was then drawn up by a nearby strawberry tree, which forever gave those who ate its fruit increased strength and speed. Arekles would now need to win his lovers – be they man or woman – with words and cunning as befitted a son of the Trickster.

With that, Turms turned his attention to the shepherdess. As foolhardy as his son had been, the god could not let someone shame a member of his family. But Turms, who was the Herald of all the Holy Twelve, could see the aura of his half-sister, Artimi, surrounding the woman. For the moment, the girl had the favour of the Huntress, and Turms did not dare enter into a fight with his sister – not over this son, anyway. He had other plans in the making. For while his brother Aplu used his powers of prophecy to see what lay ahead, Turms relied upon his intelligence.

A grin full of guile spreading slowly across his face, he plucked a few blades of grass from the field and blew them gently with his divine breath towards the retreating woman. With the flash and shudder of godly magic being wrought, the shepherdess screamed as her staff fused to her hand.

Inch by inch, the wood crept along her skin, her hair feathering into leaves that perfumed the air. Soon, the woman was gone and in her place was an indomitable cypress tree, sacred to Artimi and her coven, forever untouched by man's unwanted hands.

Pleased with the compromise, for both parties had been punished, Artimi allowed the matter to pass from her mind as she continued to prowl the hills of Dramaki to the south. Even if she had been inclined to, she could not save the shepherdess, for no goddess could undo the power of another god.

Turms flew back to Tethalia and resumed his games with Aplu.

And Arekles left to marry a woman who would bear him several sons, and it seemed perhaps he had repaired his ways ... until his wife discovered he had betrayed her with her sister.

As for the shepherdess, she remains in her field, though her sheep were long taken by wolves, her branches plundered by men for firewood.

But, still, she stands and gives shade, waiting for the day she is felled by axe, or age, or lightning, for that was the destiny of all trees, be they silent or filled with spirit.

CHAPTER SIX

The doors of the naos opened with a groan to admit the Empyrean assembly and twelve priests entered, their guards and servants kept waiting at the bottom of the temple stairs outside.

It was the first time Desma had ever seen their priests. Part of her teachings as a child was to learn about the empire across the Aduric Sea, focusing on Turan's temple and her devotees.

The priests were dressed in rich robes of white and red, heavily adorned with jewellery that flashed and glittered in the torchlight. The priest leading the group had a stole of deep blue, matching the carpet upon which he walked; it was the colour of the insanely rich, the royal, the divine. He was younger than most of his cohort, perhaps no older than forty.

His eyes, the colour of uncracked walnuts, gleamed with learning. He had a neatly trimmed beard that covered his jawline and chin; it almost looked like his brown hair had a strap about his face. His lips were set in a vainglorious smile that made Desma's hand twitch, itching to slap it off him. She took a breath to steady herself and glanced up at her mother.

Timothea was every inch the powerful high priestess of an ancient goddess.

When Desma and Cela had crashed into her chambers, words spilling out faster than their thoughts could keep up, she had listened without speaking until they were done. Then, in a matter of moments, the temple had exploded into activity as she left her rooms, calling out orders as she shed her clothes to the floor without shame. Attendants flew to her armed with brushes, scented oils, dazzling gems, and robes of softest wool and silk. Guards poured from their homes behind the temple, fresh roses and apples were brought into the naos, mirrors were polished, incense lit, floors swept, and instruments tuned. All within the space of a half hour before a runner boy came shouting that he could see the Empyreans.

Timothea now stood on the dais before Turan's statue, a solid copper brazier burning at her feet, sending plumes of sweet smoke wreathing about her hem. Behind her, the goddess rose in majesty, watching the proceedings with a sultry gaze.

Clothed in a peplos of sunset pink, brooches sculpted from gold into roses pinned her dress in place, with a belt of pure white horsehair round her waist, and sandals painted a startling red inlaid with gold studs peering from underneath. Her deep red hair was bound intricately atop her head and set with goose feathers and pearls. Scented orange blossom oil glistened on her skin, necklaces of silver and topaz around her throat, with matching bracelets at her wrists.

The high priestess was adorned with all the beauty and wealth of Serene Turan.

Flanking her on either side down the dais stairs and beyond were the priestesses of Apasa, beautiful and graceful, all staring with silent disgust at the priests who dared tread on their territory.

The lead priest stopped a few paces from the dais and waited.

The only noise was the crackle of flames and the rustling of myrtle leaves. Desma's mother stared straight ahead, over the tops of the Empyreans' heads, as patient and silent as the moon.

Eventually, the priest gave a small, quiet laugh and inclined his head. 'High Priestess Timothea, it is a pleasure to finally meet a woman of such a formidable nature as to be heard of even so far away as Aventinus. I bring greetings and wishes of good health from the Holy Mother of Turan's Grand Church.'

Slowly, Timothea lowered her face to meet the priest's eyes, the movement of a few inches seeming to take an eternity.

'I acknowledge the words of your priestess,' she said coldly. 'Welcome to the first Grand Temple of Turan, Bishop.'

'Ahh, you know my rank,' he said with some surprise.

'But still not your name,' she answered. 'I'm sure in the Empire you may be known, but here, where Turan was born ... you are but a stranger.'

'Then I shall remedy the situation immediately. I am Bishop Camillus from the Celestial Empire, born in the village of Remnun, raised in the service of Golden Turan, and now emissary for our Holy Mother Valeriana.' He turned to the other priests. 'These are, in rank of seniority, Fathers—'

'I care not for them or their names,' Timothea interrupted. 'I doubt you will allow any of them to speak on your behalf, so there is no need for me to hear their names and then forget them.'

Camillus gave a grin that sent shivers down Desma's spine. 'Formidable woman, indeed.'

Her mother raised a brow. 'I am only formidable when I find a worthy opponent. Maybe one day you will witness it.'

Camillus went to reply when one of the priests, an older man of about sixty, touched his arm. The bishop snapped his head around and Desma thought he was going to strike the old man. To his credit, the priest did not flinch but simply withdrew his hand.

Camillus turned back to Timothea with a more amiable smile. 'We come bearing gifts for your temple, though they are unfortunately still onboard our ship. I will arrange for their delivery as soon as possible. In the meantime, our Holy Mother herself gifted this particular item from her own possessions, as a token of friendship across the seas.'

From his robes he withdrew an exquisitely crafted glass rose. The stem was a vibrant emerald with softer, sage-coloured leaves. Thorns that were both dainty and sharp glinted along its length. The flower itself was a deep red in the centre, that lightened to blush on the outer petals that were then rimmed in gold dust. Glasswork was difficult, and most of the products produced by the League were simplistic bowls and jars. In comparison, this was a kingly gift.

Camillus approached the dais and ascended the steps until he was just below Timothea. 'High Priestess,' he offered.

Timothea did not make a move to take the proffered gift, but met the bishop's eyes, her gaze cold as old iron. It was then Desma noticed that there was no safe place for her mother to take the rose – Camillus held the flower balanced on his fingertips, under the smooth leaves and petals. The only remaining place for her mother to grab was the stem covered in glass thorns.

Without breaking her eyes away from Camillus, Timothea reached forward and took the rose. The priest waited, but she gave no sign of any pain. With another of those grins that made Desma's palms itch to hit something, he turned and walked back down the dais.

Once he reached the bottom, Timothea held the rose above her head. All could see the streaks of blood running down her palm and forearm. Several of the priestesses hissed.

'We thank the Empyrean temple for its humble gift,' she intoned. 'And offer it to Turan in the hopes its beauty will be pleasing to her eye.' With that, she cast it into the brazier at her feet, the smashing glass ringing throughout the silent hall.

Camillus' smile froze on his face but, again, the older priest touched his arm in warning. The bishop bowed towards the statue of the goddess. 'For the love of Turan,' he prayed.

Timothea clasped her hands in front of her, making no attempt to hide the blood that was soaking into her peplos and dripping on the marble floor. 'Formalities completed,' she said bluntly. 'What do you want, *Bishop*?' The foreign word was spat like an insult.

'News has reached Aventinus of the glorious treasure that has recently arrived in Apasa,' Camillus said. 'Treasures and riches of far lost Urruc and its Sand-King.'

'Strange,' the high priestess replied. 'I sent no word to the Empire. Nor an invitation to you or your Mother. And, yet, here you stand.'

'News of such a discovery spreads far and wide – faster than even the wings of gods,' Camillus said smoothly. 'Only ill news travels faster.' His eyes flashed with something that set moths of unease in Desma's stomach. 'The Holy Mother did not wish to risk causing offence if we were to arrive late to your – no doubt glorious – celebration due to any possible past ... misunderstandings.'

'Are you sure you are not better suited to be a priest of Turms, Bishop?' Timothea asked. 'Your words are more precious than silver, and as sticky as honey.'

'Diplomacy is the weapon of the wise, High Priestess.'

'And false sweetness the last tool of the desperate,' she countered.

'Enough!'

Both Camillus and Timothea turned in surprise to face one of the priests who had pushed his way forward. He was older than the bishop, and used to a life of good-eating with no fear of when his next meal would be. His nose was red with large and broken purple veins. His mouth was twisted in a scowl as he shook a fist at the high priestess.

'We are emissaries from the Grand Church of Aventinus, sent here by the blessed Holy Mother after she communed with our goddess. And you stand up there spitting weak poison with no cause. We have come bearing gifts and pleasant words. Our hands are open and our words honest. How dare you stand up there like some rich Thevan whore and insult our Bishop? You stand in front of the Goddess of Love with nothing but hate in your speech and your eyes. Contempt is not the province of this temple!'

The priest was almost shaking with anger as he tried to approach the dais. Camillus stepped in front of him, pulling his head close to his mouth, lips moving furiously. Desma was too far to hear what the bishop was saying, but it was obviously unpleasant as the older priest went white as parchment. When Camillus released him, the priest bowed once to Timothea and walked rigidly from the temple. No one spoke until he vanished behind the naos doors.

Camillus turned back to Timothea, but the high priestess cut him off before he could speak. 'As presumptuous your companion's words were, I feel there is a ring of truth about them,' she said. 'If you have truly come here in friendship, then perhaps an accord can be met.'

The bishop went to speak but she raised a hand again. 'I am going to ask a question, and I bind you in this place of worship to speak only truth. Turan sits before you and hears – lie at the risk of her displeasure. What is it you want?'

The bishop straightened his cerulean stole. He once again reached into his robes and this time he pulled forth a scroll, tied with gold ribbon and set with wax as red as blood. 'The Holy Mother wrote this in her own hand, sealed and bound, with orders to only place it in the hands of her sister in Apasa.' He again climbed the dais and proffered the scroll to Timothea in a similar pose to before, palms flat, waiting for her to take it.

Desma could see the question flash in her mother's eyes as she accepted the document about whether to read it in private or open it now. Whatever the reason, she broke the seal and untied the ribbon, letting it flutter to her feet.

A furrow appeared on her brow as her eyes scanned the paper. Though greatly educated, Desma guessed the letter was written in Empyrean script, which was infuriatingly similar yet distinct from their own written language. Her mother had scribes aplenty to read and write any missives in the Empire's language. And Desma doubted the holy mother would have made it easy to read.

After a few moments, Timothea held out the scroll to one of the scribes, who darted forward to take it, her eyes flashing across the words.

'Your language has never been essential for me to adeptly learn,' she said to Camillus. 'I know that you are aware of its contents. Tell me what she wants.'

'Why, is it not obvious?' Camillus asked innocently. 'Our Holy Mother Valeriana has requested the treasures of Urruc to be released into our custody, where we will ensure its safe passage back to Aventinus.'

CHAPTER SEVEN

Desma admired her mother's composure.

She made no movement or sound at the Empyrean's statement.

Desma, on the other hand, was physically restraining herself from stabbing him in the chest. A sentiment shared among the priestesses, if the whispers flying faster than knives between them were anything to go by.

Timothea though was frozen. The scribe beside her said something softly to her – no doubt confirming the wishes of the Aventinus witch. When the high priestess did not acknowledge her, the scribe stepped away, the letter crushed in her grip.

'Well, Domiini Timothea,' Camillus said, Desma identifying the Empyrean word as 'lady' or 'mistress'. She couldn't keep the snarl from her face. He was relegating Turan's high priestess to a mere household matron, rather than the match for his own priestess. 'Shall we retire to your chamber to discuss the logistics? We are happy to wait until after whatever ceremony you have prepared—'

'Get out.'

The words echoed like a sword dropped on stone.

Camillus blinked slowly. 'What?'

'Get. Out.' They were cold and final. Desma could only imagine it was what the voices of the Gods Beneath sounded. Like doom.

'I know that the Domiini would not be so brazen as t—' Camillus was cut off once more.

'I will order my guards to cut out your tongue and burn it in this brazier if you address me as such again,' Timothea said. '*I* am the High Priestess of the Grand Temple of Turan.'

'In a city where the goddess no longer lives,' Camillus said smugly. 'She has not resided here for five hundred years. Her city within the empire is boasted as the most beautiful, the most graceful, the wealthiest of all the Holy Twelve. *We* have brought her more honour and devotion and tribute than this outpost of a city could ever hope of achieving. *We* are her home now. *We* are her true children and she loves *us*. Not you. Not anymore.'

Desma had never wanted someone to hurt as badly as she wanted to hurt this bastard.

Timothea took a step towards the bishop. 'Remember upon what ground you stand,' she said coolly. 'It was here that Turan stepped from the blood and the sea. It was here that Love was born. A few hundred years are but a blink of the eye in the time of gods. Enjoy the company of Turan while she holidays in your little empire. Urruc's treasures will reside in Apasa, from now until the end of the world. We have not forgotten our goddess. But history will one day forget you.'

It was at that moment the fire in the sacred brazier roared to new heights beside her, flames gold and blush, the scent of rosemary and apple smothering them all. The statue of Turan began to glow with a matching light until Desma thought, for just a moment, that the stone was going to turn to flesh.

But nothing further happened.

The light dimmed. The fire died back down. The scent faded.

Her mother looked tired and pale, her arms still streaked with blood.

After one last, defiant glare, she turned her back on the bishop.

Without needing an order, the temple guards closed in, hands on spears, forming an impenetrable wall that steadily pushed the Empyreans out of their goddess' home.

Desma did not take her eyes off the priests until the naos doors sealed them out; then she hurried to her mother's side.

'Your hand ...' she began to say.

'Theokritos,' her mother called to the captain, who materialised from behind a column. 'Double the men you have on duty at any given time. Call upon all reserves. Keep the temple community here – no trips to the city. All wagons are to be inspected by your men one mile from the temple and again once it arrives. Am I clear?'

'Yes, High Priestess,' the captain grunted before disappearing into a crowd of guards.

'Leontia,' she called to Cela's mother. 'Take Melitta and Sophia with you. Pay a visit to King Sophocles and request he attend me as soon as his pleasure allows. Take a chest of golden swords as a personal gift and as thanks for his haste in arriving. Desma, Cela – come.'

Once the three of them were closeted away in Timothea's rooms, the high priestess turned to them. 'Your resting period is over,' she said, placing her bloody hands on her desk. 'I do not want a single one of those priests to be unwatched for a moment. You and your crew are to keep track of every Empyrean. The ceremony is in five days, and I have much to attend to. Anything that is suspicious, or unexplainable, or gives you an ill feeling in your gut – you are to report it to me immediately. Am I clear, daughters?'

Both Desma and Cela bowed. 'Yes, High Priestess.'

'Desma, daughter mine,' Timothea said gently, 'if all goes well, it means I may not see you until the day of the ceremony. It would be best if you remain in the city proper. For this, and to keep your father company. I miss him.' Her eyes fell to a small vase on her desk, one of Palamaon's creations.

'All will be well, Mother,' Desma said. 'Turan's blessings are upon us. The witch in Aventinus has no power over our temple. We answer to no one but our goddess.'

At her words, her mother's head jerked up from the table, her eyes wide and startled.

Desma was taken aback. 'Mother?'

'That will be everything, Desma,' she said. 'Blessings on you and your task. You too, Cela.'

'Thank you, High Priestess.' Cela bowed with a tug at Desma's sleeve. 'Let us go.'

As Desma was closing the door, she saw her mother slide slowly back into her chair, red-stained hands holding her head. For a moment, she was tempted to rush back in and offer whatever comfort she could. But this was not the trials of her mother, but the challenges of her high priestess.

She closed the door.

Desma sipped on a cup of wine while she stared out her window.

She was in her room above her father's shop, her father had gone to a tavern to drink mead with friends. Desma and Cela had left the temple immediately after receiving Timothea's orders, riding back to Apasa on the borrowed horses that they returned to the city barracks. From there, they walked to the docks where they found their crew waiting still. They reboarded Cela's ship and Desma explained her mother's commands.

Kassandra went to find out where the priests were staying in the city. Khufu and Bion left to check out where the servants and guards would be living while off-duty. Delphinus was given the task of watching the Empyrean ship in the harbour. Cosmas quietly said he would check in with some friends and disappeared. Desma let him go without a word. She did not need to know the details.

All reports would funnel back to the shop, where Desma and Cela would set up their headquarters. Cela was currently across the street at Korinna's home, learning how to make honeyed walnut bread, giving Desma some privacy.

For Desma was waiting for Arete.

The only order she gave the shipwright was to meet her at sundown.

They had some things to discuss.

It was the last thing she wanted to do right now, with not only the ceremony nearing but now the sudden arrival of the Empyreans and their blatant disrespect in laying claim to the treasure of Urruc that *she* had discovered.

Desma still did not understand what the bishop hoped he would achieve by demanding the treasures. He must know there was no eventuality where the temple would acquiescence to their request. Nor would the Hero-King himself allow it. News of the artefacts would bring much trade to the city.

The Empire and the League had strained relations at the best of times. The Empire itself was only officially founded less than a thousand years ago, when the tribes in Tuscanai banded together under the leadership of the Hill King Velch. Within a hundred years they conquered the entire peninsula and were soon spreading outwards. At the time, the League did not exist and often the city-states were at war with each other. But after the sudden and unprovoked sacking of Artas, the cities rallied together and attacked the entire west coast of the Empire. It was only after the Empyrean sea-city of Viminalis was blockaded for over a year that a treaty was reached, the first to be signed and the first to be broken when the Empire tried to assassinate the three archons of Athanai.

Apasa and Trilos, being the furthest from the Empire, were fortunately spared from the attacks and scars left on the other city-states. But it was them the other kingdoms called on for ships and money. Though the last skirmish had been over twenty years ago, Apasa had lost five warships and had since forbidden any Empyrean trade entering the city.

Desma would do as her mother commanded. Though Sophocles was King of Apasa, her mother wielded equal, if not more power and authority. But it was a relationship of mutual respect and friendship. Other city-states often erupted into civil wars between temple and throne. Perhaps because Apasa was the home of the Goddess of Love, king and priestess were often able to strike affable accords. She would leave the issue of the Empyreans to the wisdom of her mother and king.

There was a sharp knock on her door.

'Come in,' she answered.

The small shipwright opened the door and slipped inside, closing it firmly behind her. She approached Desma, who was sitting on the only chair at the small table, and waited, hands clasped loosely in front, her solemn eyes never leaving Desma's face.

'Arete,' she said, taking another sip of her wine.

'Desma.'

'You know why we are having this talk.'

'My promise of tribute to Nethuns.' Her words were flat and to the point.

Desma's hand clenched on her cup. 'Explain to me where exactly you got a statue from Urruc.'

She shrugged. 'A small crate of artefacts may have been misplaced during Cela's cataloguing. And no, she did not know about it.'

Desma had already questioned her friend about it. Cela admitted that she thought there should have been one more small box but assumed it was an error of miscounting. A search had revealed nothing. But for the shipwright, who knew every nook and cubbyhole of a ship, it was an easy enough task to hide it.

'Why?'

Arete blinked. 'Why would I not?'

Desma slammed her cup down on the table, wine splashing her hand even as the rush of blood stained her cheeks. 'Do not dare be flippant to me. Not at this moment. All of Urruc's treasures were to be presented to the temple, to my mother – to bloody Turan herself! And you *stole it from the goddess.*'

Arete did not bat an eye at her outburst. She never did. In the middle of a storm threatening to tear the ship apart, or under a hail of arrows and blood, Arete always kept her head.

'I stole nothing. The treasures of Urruc were not the property of Turan until they were presented. That is the law. Until they are presented to king, or temple, or master, or guild, that which is found belongs to the one who discovered it.'

'Then, by your own admission, the treasure was mine.'

'Not at all, Desma,' Arete said. 'I found the box. We had cleared out the antechamber to the tomb and I found the box behind a fallen rock, hidden on a shelf. It was my discovery, and so the treasure was mine to do with as I please.'

Desma could not believe what she was hearing. 'Do you not realise what your slyness has done? What it could do? You hide behind words like a sophist from Athanai, slipping and sliding to avoid the bright truth. All of what we found in Urruc was to be given to the Grand Temple. You stole it. And why? You were paid extravagantly for your services. You received gifts from both my mother and me. What was the need to take what was never yours?'

'Urruc belongs to no one anymore,' the shipwright said simply. 'And thus it belongs to any who claim it. I took one small box, one that was never missed and was the reason you managed to give your mother time to prepare for the Empyreans.'

Desma took a steadying breath. Realising she would not be able to win this argument against Arete, she attempted to change tactics. 'You will give the box to me and anything else you found in Urruc. You will find another suitable offering to Nethuns. I don't care if you have to empty your money purse into the ocean. That is your problem. And—'

'I have already dedicated the figurine to the ocean.'

Desma leaned back in her chair and closed her eyes, hands pressed to the edge of the table. A priceless artefact was at the bottom of the harbour. Goddess, help her. 'Give me the box. I will try to find some way to explain it to my mother ...'

'I cannot.'

Frustration almost made Desma reach across and strangle her friend. 'Why?' she asked through clenched teeth.

'I don't have it anymore.'

The tenuous hold she had on her patience snapped and Desma smashed her wine cup from the table, splattering wine across the room. 'What do you mean?'

Arete stared stonily at her. 'I shared the contents of the box among the crew. I assume by now the pieces have been sold across the city.'

Speech failed her. If Desma was armed, she would have been mightily tempted to draw her blade. Eventually, she managed to unclench her jaw. 'You idiot.'

Arete did not move.

'Do you not know what will happen when word reaches my mother that treasures from Urruc are suddenly springing up around the city? She will have you all tied to a tree and burned. She will whip me to within an inch of my life and then I will be consigned to the temple community until the end of my days. And that is if she is *merciful* to us.'

'We are not so stupid,' Arete snapped back. 'The items were sold to traders from other cities, all of whom have long since left – their discretion as to where they procured the items guaranteed. There are always rumours of Urruc treasures appearing across the League. Your mother will pay no heed to them – especially when all tongues will be wagging about what now lies in her temple.'

'And what of the figurine? Why was that not sold?'

'Because I wanted to keep it.' Arete shrugged. 'I was meant to sell it to a goldsmith from Konoso, but I found I could not part with it. Who knows? Maybe the fates knew I would have need of it beyond coin.'

Desma found she suddenly couldn't stand the sight of the shipwright any further. 'Leave me.'

Arete spun on her heel and headed for the door. As her hand reached for the handle, Desma added, 'Let the crew know: if any of you have kept the smallest token or talisman from Urruc – keep it hidden. If I ever see one, I will have you thrown into the ocean with rocks tied around your necks.' The shipwright opened the door. 'And Arete ... I have not yet decided what to do with you. Until I do, you are suspended from my service.'

Desma watched her friend's spine stiffen. She waited for one final word from her, but Arete left silently without turning back, closing the door with a too-gentle hand.

Desma was staring unseeing at the wine stain on the wall when Cela slipped into the room, a loaf of bread in her hands.

'I take it things did not go well,' she said despondently.

'Not as such.'

Cela came over and perched on the edge of the table, her wheat-gold hair gently brushing Desma's face as she leaned down to her. 'Don't make any quick decisions,' she advised. 'Cruel and harsh are the judgements of the fast.'

'She stole from us, Celadine,' Desma said quietly. 'She stole from Apasa, my mother, the temple, from Turan. She *lied*, and she got the whole crew in on her lie!'

'Did we not take something?' Cela asked quietly, softly.

Desma looked up so quickly she almost slammed her head into Cela's chin.

'It is true, Desma. We took the bowl we gave your father.'

The words stuttered in her throat as what Cela was saying sank in. 'But th – that is different.'

'How?' Cela pressed. 'You – using your own words – stole a treasure from Urruc. Yes, you did not sell it, but you gave it away. It did not go to the temple, it did not go to the glory of Turan, you never told your mother – and I doubt your father would have mentioned it to his wife. He knew what us giving it to him meant.'

'That is different,' Desma said, though the uncertainty was clear in her voice.

'Is it? Be honest with yourself. The only difference is you think because you are the leader, you can make exceptions for yourself. But look at it from the crew's perspective. You set the example. You took something for yourself, so Arete took something for herself and the crew. It should not have come as a surprise.'

Desma groaned, resting her head in her hands as her arrogance became clear. 'Gods, why do you have to make things worse with your common sense?' Desma scolded. It was true. She took the bowl for her father. And, looking back at it now, she accepted it was because she wanted to do it and she was in charge. No one was there to question or overrule her decision. But if her mother ever found out, she would demand the bowl be returned – and that is exactly why Desma did not tell the high priestess. Arete did the same, except it was to Desma. And there was nothing to be done about it now.

In the four years they had been sailing together, Arete had been a steadfast member of her crew. Never a word out of place, except when Desma opened her ideas to debate and then Arete's insights had ever been helpful. Always loyal, always dependable, always willing. One mistake should not be the ending of four years of unfailing friendship.

'Find her,' she said to Cela. 'Tell her that I expect a donation of a hundred silver drachmae to be made to the Grand Temple, one week suspension from the crew, and after the ceremony I expect her on the ship when we sail for Trilos. All forgiven.'

'All forgotten,' Cela laughed, leaping from the table.

CHAPTER EIGHT

It was the day before the ceremony and the city was packed with people from the countryside and other city-states. Though no one from the city was allowed entry to the temple itself, the city was more than happy to host its own celebration. Every statue and mural of Turan had been freshly repainted. Roses, in wreaths, in garlands, and bouquets of all shapes and sizes festooned every nook, step, window, and bridge in the city.

Rosemary and applewood burned in giant bronze braziers in squares, the fragrant scent perfuming everyone's clothes and homes. Parades were scheduled, music never-ending, plays depicting the wondrous tales of the goddess were set to perform in every theatre. The great sea amphitheatre was to perform the story of Turan averting a war with the dead with the help of her friend Phersipnai.

It was rumoured the Hero-King Sophocles had his royal forges craft twelve times twelve golden roses that he would award to artists and actresses and musicians who caught his attention.

But it was not a night off for everyone. The meeting Timothea had requested with the king was not to discuss pleasantries. The army was out in force, with troops being recalled from outlying villages. Warriors were seen on every street in the city, with patrols sweeping the road to the temple and beyond.

Desma's crew had kept watch over the Empyreans. Every move was reported back to Desma and Cela, who in turn sent updates to Timothea. As far as they could tell, the priests spent their time either in their rooms or taking strolls around the city, seemingly to admire the smaller temples and watch the preparations.

Beyond their small ship occasionally going back to their quinquereme to fetch supplies or pass along messages, there were no further movements. Their soldiers remained on board, enjoying the free time.

Which is why Desma was surprised when Delphinus burst into her room in the late morning, breath ragged and dripping sweat.

'What's happened?' she demanded, already slipping on her sandals.

'Your mother has summoned the bishop,' he managed to gasp out.

Stunned, Desma almost stopped moving. 'Why?' she asked as she headed for the door.

'No reason was given,' he said, following behind down the stairs.

'Cela,' she called out. Her friend appeared from between the shelves, confusion on her face. 'Are the horses out the back?' They had purchased two horses to keep behind the shop in a neighbour's small stable, in case of a moment of need such as this.

'Yes, they just came back from being reshod. Where are you going?'

'*We* are going to the temple. My mother has summoned the bishop. Hurry.' Desma was already out the door.

Within minutes, they were thundering once more along the road up the cliffs. When they reached the top, they looked down and saw the Empyreans had reached the bottom. There was only the bishop and three other priests, all mounted. They would not be far behind them.

With a shout, the girls put heels to their horses and set off at a gallop.

They arrived at the temple and asked the first priestess they saw where they could find Desma's mother. She was in her small room at the rear of the temple. She raised her hand when they entered, finishing dictating a letter to a scribe. Once the scribe had sanded the ink and left, the high priestess turned to the girls.

'Daughters,' she acknowledged them with a nod of her head. Her hair was brushed back and ruby earrings glittered from beneath her locks.

'High Priestess,' they chimed, making the sign of Turan.

'What brings you here, daughters mine?' she asked, her words clipped.

Desma stepped forward. 'We heard you had summoned the bishop, so we hurried here as fast as we could.'

Her mother raised a carefully sculpted brow. 'Why?'

Desma glanced back at Cela, the worry she felt reflected in her friend's eyes. 'We thought we should be here.'

'I did not realise you needed to be included in all the goings of my temple.'

Every sense of dread Desma had learned to trust on their journey to Urruc was now singing in her blood. Her mother was acting strangely. There were times when clear distinction was needed between priestess and mother. But today, the person before Desma just seemed cold and angry, neither Desma's mother nor the priestess. And Desma wasn't sure how to act.

'I don't ... I just thought ...' she stuttered.

'Never mind. You are here and, by the stamp of boots, it sounds like the priests have arrived.' She waved her hand dismissively. 'Stand behind me and do not make a sound.'

Desma and Cela moved to flank the high priestess, quickly smoothing their dresses and combing the wind out of their hair with their fingers. They stopped fidgeting, hands clasped gracefully beneath their breasts in the fashion of the priestesses when the door opened.

Theokritos entered with a face like a sullen thundercloud. He banged his spear on the marble floor, the iron-shod butt ringing shrilly. He gestured impatiently to the men behind him.

Camillus came first, his intelligent brown eyes darting between the three of them, his smile maddeningly sly and charming, his hand absently brushing an invisible crumb from his cerulean stole – a clear reminder of his rank.

Three unnamed priests came behind him, each with a triumphant look upon their faces.

'Domiini Timothea,' Camillus said. 'How happy we were to receive your invitation.'

Her mother nodded her head to him. 'I am happy you answered my summons, messenger of Valeriana,' she said calmly. 'I would have hated to have you dragged before me.'

The bishop's eyes flashed angrily at her refusal to use his name or title. 'I am sure the Holy Mother would be glad to see us treat each other with respect and friendship. After all, she sees Apasa as another daughter of Turan, no matter how far from her home you may be. I am sure that she would be open to welcoming another bishopric into the fold.'

Timothea ignored the remark. 'I have summoned you here to formally invite you and six other priests to the celebration at the temple tomorrow.'

Desma could not keep the shock from her face.

Camillus glanced her way with a grin and she felt suddenly dirty under his gaze.

The bishop turned back to her mother and gave a shallow bow. 'I am most overjoyed at the news, Domiini. Sweet Turan came to me in my evening prayer and told me the happy news, but to hear the words from your lips brings me a delight that is almost transcendent. I will invite Fathers Gnaeus, Alban, Festus, Balbus, Egnatius, and Decimus to attend. I will be sure to introduce them all to you personally on the night.'

Timothea inclined her head. 'The celebrations are to start at dawn, with the ceremony beginning at twilight. We will see you tomorrow.'

The bishop made no move to leave the room. Theokritos went to usher him out when the high priestess stopped him. 'Is there something else, messenger?'

'I was just wondering about the other matter?' he asked innocently.

It was the first time her calm facade cracked. 'I will make the announcement during the ceremony.'

'Ah, well then, we will leave you to your preparations. Love be with you, Domiini.' He gave a shallow nod and turned to leave.

Desma's mother made no move until the door was closed. She gave a weary sigh and asked Cela if she could fetch her some lemon syrup water.

'At once, High Priestess,' Cela said, throwing a worried glance at Desma before leaving.

Once they were alone, her mother reached out for Desma who clasped her hand tightly, kneeling beside her.

'Why would you invite them?' she asked.

'Because Turan came to me last night.'

Desma slid to the floor, still holding her mother's hands. 'Tell me. Please.'

Her mother looked down on her with a gentle smile. 'Oh, my darling. I hope that there will never come a day when you hear her voice. It is a heavy burden and a great trial. Sometimes, it is better to escape the attention of the gods than to be blessed by them. For blessings can become curses as swift as a spring day can turn to storm.' Timothea lifted a lock of Desma's hair, rubbing the scarlet strands between forefinger and thumb. 'She came to me long after night had deepened, when nothing is awake, when even lovers have fallen asleep, spent from their exertions. Her voice was like the waves on the cliffs, unending and enduring. Nightshade and rose thorns. Breath when it turns from fear to passion ... and back to fear. It was beauty. It was terrible.' She paused, her voice fading to nothing as she dropped Desma's hair. Her mother's eyes were far away and misty. Desma did not speak, instead capturing her mother's hands in a bone-cracking grip, attempting to bring her back with touch alone.

'She commanded me,' Timothea said eventually, 'and I had to obey. Seven priests were to be invited. And everyone loyal to the temple is to attend. Everyone.'

Desma frowned. 'I do not understand. Who has been excluded?'

'As Turan said, "All from the crown to the sole are to attend. High priestess to scullery boy, courtesan and cleaner. Every warrior and guard. All are to take part and to imbibe – to leave one out is to forbid the love and joy you seek to honour." So, I have ordered Theokritos to bring all the temple guard at dawn to celebrate with us.'

'But ... Mother,' Desma gasped. 'We cannot be unprotected.'

'Do not fear, daughter mine,' Timothea soothed. 'Sophocles has promised that the road will be lined with soldiers and the temple surrounded by rings of iron. Nothing can go wrong. And, as you have reported, the Empyreans seem content upon their ship. We have the eyes of the goddess upon us – all will be well.'

Despite her mother's words, Desma could not quash the unease that was blooming in her gut. 'And what of this other matter the bishop mentioned?'

Timothea's face went cold, the person Desma didn't quite recognise returning.

'That is a matter between the goddess, myself, and the bishop. It is nothing for you to be concerned about. Is that clear, daughter?'

Desma kissed her mother's hands. 'Yes, Mother.' She paused for a moment, debating her next question. 'Does Camillus know of the Belt?'

At that moment, Cela returned with a cup of lemon water. She paused when she saw them, Desma on the floor, the clasp of their hands. 'Sorry, I can go ...' she stuttered.

Timothea withdrew her hands from Desma's and gratefully accepted the cup. 'Thank you, dear one. I have much to do before tomorrow – I should get back to it.'

Desma climbed to her feet and joined Cela in leaving.

'Desma,' her mother called after her.

She paused.

'Could I ask for you to spend the night with me? Perhaps we can have supper together with your father?'

Desma smiled. 'Shall I get some of the peppery goat cheese from Iason? I heard his new batch is ready.'

'That sounds lovely,' her mother said. 'Until tonight.'

Desma closed the door. Her last glimpse of her mother was her staring into her drink with a solemn expression, looking like a prophetess scrying the future in the water. But what was she trying to see?

CHAPTER NINE

Desma spent the rest of the day collecting food for dinner. It had been weeks since she and her mother had spent a meal together, and she wanted to make an effort. She got some of the cheese from Iason, aged thyme-infused olive oil, a floral red wine that was a particular favourite of hers, and a special treat of oranges in saffron-honey.

She also stopped to see her father. He had been invited to the temple for the celebration but had declined. He rarely took part in the temple's holy days. Even though he was married to the high priestess of a goddess that exulted in freedom of bodies, desires, and inhibitions only rivalled by the God of Wine, he was a quiet, introverted man. He would rather visit the temple afterwards to help his wife nurse her hangover and debrief the events of the night than take part in them himself.

Desma pushed open the door, basket of food heavy in her arms. 'Father,' she called passed the shelves. 'You in?'

No answer.

She headed into the back of the shop and found the fire stoked in the kiln, so he could not have gone far. She set about tidying up the dishes from his lunch – most likely brought to him by Korinna – and wrapping the leftover cheese and fruit.

She turned as the shop door opened to find her father walking in, holding two halves of a vase and shaking his head.

'Father.'

Palamaon started and nearly dropped the clay pieces. 'Aplu and Sethlans preserve me and my craft,' he scolded. 'Put a bell around your neck, girl.'

'It would clash with my dress,' she laughed as she flung her arms around his midriff, carefully avoiding the vase. 'Where did this travesty come from?'

'It is Korinna's. A gift from her mother-in-law. Or, as she delightfully calls her, a long-lost sister of the gorgons. She broke it by accident and she needs it fixed by next week. I can put it back together but not without there being a seam on the inside. If her mother-in-law looks inside, she will see it was broken.'

'Why in the kingdom would she look *inside* the vase?'

'Because she is a monstrous woman with harpy blood flowing through her veins'—he smiled—'or so it was explained to me.'

'I'm sure you will make it as perfect as possible,' she said, watching her father place the pieces next to his turntable. 'Mother has asked if you are free to have dinner with us tonight?'

His eyes lit up. 'That would be lovely. We have barely supped together, the three of us, since you returned.'

'I wish you were coming to the celebration tomorrow,' she said wistfully.

He kissed her on the top of her head as he walked past. 'I know, Desma. But it is easier for your mother to not have me there when she must be the high priestess. And though I would never ask her to be anything else ... sometimes it is hard for me to see her as such, too.'

'Why?'

He paused as he pondered his words. 'Mortals cannot touch the divine without being changed, this is what I have observed. Your mother is not the same woman as when I married her. We all change through life, this is the nature of being mortal, for we do not have enough time to be the same person for long. But sometimes I worry for your mother and the burdens upon her.'

'Do you ever get jealous?'

He thought for a moment. 'I used to. Not at first. When we married, I often spent a lot of my time at the temple. I was younger and did not mind the travel back and forth. It was only after my business began to grow that I started to spend more time in the city. But then I was too busy to notice the absence too much. It was after you were born when I felt the first pangs of jealousy.' He smiled at Desma affectionately and she returned it warmly.

'Your mother kept you at the temple, nursing and raising you within its walls. Of course, I was always welcomed but it was rare when Timothea would make the journey to see me here. That was the hardest time for us. But it was because I was filled with this new and burgeoning love – one that eclipsed all else in my life. My love for your mother is absolute, and your birth took nothing from her, but it was as though I suddenly had to find more room in my heart for a love that was its equal. Unfortunately, that sometimes came out as jealous and selfish arguments.' He scoffed at his own foolishness. 'But by the grace of Turan, we figured it out. Our love is enduring. I know that the first thought in her mind when she wakes is of us. And the last thought she has before sleep. Just as I have the same first and last thoughts. In that moment, at dawn and twilight, we are connected. That is the blessing of Turan.'

'That is beautiful,' she said.

'You will find it yourself one day, daughter,' he said with a knowing smile. 'Turan will bless you as she blessed us, I am sure.'

Desma nodded with a tight smile.

Her father gave her a concerned look that he quickly wiped away.

Desma, unlike Cela, was not as open to meeting people. She had had a few dalliances, mostly when she was greatly intoxicated and at the urging of her friend. But marriage at this time in her life was about as likely as her sprouting wings.

'So,' he said, changing the subject, as he took a seat at his turntable. 'How goes the bishop-watching?'

She grabbed the rope he offered gratefully. 'Same as before. They do nothing but sit in their rooms and walk around the city in pairs. I still cannot believe that Mother has invited them to the celebrations.'

Palamaon nodded as he slowly began to wet a block of clay. 'It was inevitable. If only to avoid sparking a holy war between Aventinus and Apasa. What can they do to us? Let them witness the splendour and awe of our temple. The reason why that bishop is so sharp is because the Empyreans know they can never have the history and prestige we have. This will always be Turan's homeland, her birthplace. We are her true people. Let them sling their barbs and whispers. At the end of the day, they will go home to a temple not even half the age of ours – and without the treasures of Urruc.'

But they have our goddess, Desma thought silently to herself. Her father's face told her he was thinking the same.

It was not long after sundown when Desma arrived at her mother's house, the air warm and fragrant, the soft evening scents of apple, and rose, and myrtle as comforting as a hug.

She wore a fresh lilac peplos that accented the richness of her hair, a belt of pale lemon and green, and a bronze necklace with a matching pair of earrings.

She pushed the door open and greeted her parents in the kitchen. Her father was wiping down the table and her mother was drawing out a dish of lamb from the clay oven, somehow managing to look both homely and resplendent. Her dress was the same mottled purple as the basket of figs on the table, wrapped with a belt of soft vermillion, and adorned with gold and topaz jewellery. Her hair was coiled messily atop her head, but was allowed to spill down her back in rivers of red, and she looked more at peace then Desma had seen her for the last few weeks. Her brown eyes, though still ringed with signs of too-little sleep, were warm and content. Here, she could shed the temple mantle and simply be a quieter part of herself.

'Is dinner ready?' Desma asked as she unloaded her basket onto the table.

'Just as you walked in,' Palamaon said, moving dishes over from the kitchen. 'Grab the jar of olives from the cupboard. Oh, and a bowl!'

Soon, the table was filled with a delicious spread. Mint-crusted lamb, soft bread spiced with cassia, eggs boiled with rosemary, the peppery goat cheese, lashings of lemon juice, and honey-soaked oranges, all accompanied by wine that tasted like wildflowers.

They spoke of nothings and everyday things, the world growing smaller to encompass just the three of them.

At some point in the evening, Desma found herself sitting on a pillow in front of her mother having her hair brushed. Her father propped his feet in front of the small fire pit, nursing a final cup of wine, his eyes drooping.

Desma couldn't remember the last time her mother had brushed her hair. It would have been nearing five years. She had missed the steady rhythmic movement, the slight *hush* of the brush, the gentle caress of her hands. They fell into a comfortable silence, with only the flicker of the candles and occasional spark from the dying fire.

Desma was overcome with a sudden wave of nostalgia and she opened her mouth to ask her mother something, but caught herself. She was not a child. There were some things that were left behind when one grew older. But ... still, she wanted to ask.

'Just spit it out, daughter mine,' Timothea said, her words jerking Palamaon awake.

'What?' Desma started. 'What do you mean?'

'You want to ask me something.'

'How do you know that?'

Her mother laughed. 'Because every time you're about to ask, your breath hitches as you summon the courage. Then you let out a sigh when you change your mind. It's annoying.'

Desma chuckled. 'It's childish.'

'Then who better to ask than your own mother?'

She had a point.

'Can you sing to me?' Desma finally blurted in a rush, biting her lip once it was out, waiting for her answer.

The brush stilled for a moment. 'Sing?' Timothea's voice was soft, faraway.

'I just thought ... it would be nice. Like when I was little. But I understand if you do not—'

'It's been a while since I sang just for the pleasure of it,' Timothea mused. 'It's always hymns, or devotions in front of crowds. I cannot even remember when I last hummed to myself.' There was a pause. 'What should I sing, I wonder?' she asked, her voice trailing away, the question for herself.

Desma waited silently, wanting the choice to be her mother's. Her father was also silent, a small smile on his face as he gazed at them both.

After a few moments, she felt her mother softly swaying behind her. She hummed a few bars before starting to sing.

It was the story of a blacksmith's wife near Dramaki, Rhoxane, whose husband had gone to war. One day, she saw the beautiful and proud Myrto in the river and passion grew like a weed in her heart, consuming her. She spent many sleepless nights crafting beautiful gifts that she left in secret at Myrto's door, until the final one – which she delivered herself. Upon seeing who was pursuing her, Myrto gently turned Rhoxane away, kindness softening her words though they still stung Rhoxane to her core.

The blacksmith's wife went home and prayed to Turan and her Lovers, prayed that she would be able to touch Myrto, smell her hair, hold her body, to be each others.

And so Turan sent one of her sons forth and, in doing so, destroyed the lives of both Myrto and Rhoxane, for the gods give gifts and curses alike – and it is not always clear which had been delivered.

Timothea's voice trailed away as the ballad ended.

It took Desma several moments to draw herself back to the present. Her mother's singing voice was fair, though it often went wandering to find the right note. But it was the voice of her childhood, and staying up late, and lunches on the beach. She would trade listening to the great choirs of Aplu for a song from her mother.

But the story her mother chose troubled her.

'Why did Turan punish Myrto? She did nothing wrong. She did not abstain from love like a coven-member of Artimi. She just did not want to be with Rhoxane, and told her to wait for her husband as is proper.'

Timothea was quiet for so long, Desma thought she wasn't going to answer. 'You have to remember, daughter mine, gods are not mortals. They never were. They are a separate race to us, granted such power and magic and long life that it is impossible for us to understand them. Think about the woodland tribes to the north of the Kingdoms. We know almost nothing of them, and yet they are closer to us than the gods.'

Desma thought for a moment. 'Sometimes, I get worried I will say the wrong thing or do something to the wrong person and the next thing I know I am going to find Horta or Fufluns turning me into a snake. How is someone meant to avoid that?'

'Be as unremarkable as possible,' her mother said seriously. 'Do not be noticed. Hide by being plain and boring. The gods ignore the mundane. Do not be beautiful or hideous. Do not be rich or powerful. Do not be loud, or proud, or unique. Be unnoticed. Be like dirt.'

'I guess Father is the only safe one in our family,' Desma joked, looking over at him to see his eyes resting unwaveringly on his wife.

Her mother cracked a faint smile. 'Perhaps.'

There was one more question Desma wanted to ask. 'What was the other matter Camillus mentioned today?

Timothea stiffened before abruptly standing. 'It is a concern for myself, daughter. Come, we have a big day tomorrow. I need to pray before sleep. Are you okay to clean up?'

Desma nodded and began to clear the dishes. Her mother stopped her briefly to kiss Desma's brow before taking her husband's hands and retreating to their room.

When Desma finished cleaning, she had one last cup of wine before blowing out all but one candle. She went to go to her room but decided that, if her parents were asleep, she might slip into their bed. She knew she was being childish, but she wanted to spend time with them both tonight, the three of them together.

She carefully opened the door to her parent's room and froze.

Her mother was standing before her tall bronze mirror, still in her clothes from dinner but, draped around her hips, was the Belt of Turan. Its sparkling sea-foam green was unmistakable in its divinity. The Belt was meant to be deep in the vaults of the temple, guarded by twenty-four of Theokritos' most loyal men, and supervised by four senior priestesses at all times. Yet here was her mother, committing an act of blasphemy by wearing what only a goddess should wear.

Her father was sitting on a chair a little behind her, his hands clasped in his hair, tears wet on his cheeks. He was leaning so far forward, as though every inch of him wanted to grab Timothea, hold her, bring her back. But he did not move, held back before the high priestess, for he would not interfere with divinity.

Desma's choked gasp caused her mother to turn away from her reflection. Her eyes, normally warm as the brown cliffs, were cold like hoarfrost on the earth. But as she turned, Desma saw that her dress was torn open and her midriff covered in claw marks with blood seeping down her stomach, the Belt distressingly clean.

'Mother—'

'Leave me, Desma.' Her voice cracked with ice.

'But ...'

'I am your High Priestess,' she snapped, her words a whip that struck a blow. 'Leave me, by the goddess' command.'

Desma looked to her father, but he did not turn from his wife. His mouth moved silently, as though trying to call Timothea back from wherever she now walked. Desma was a shade to him.

She could do nothing but close the door, where she then remained standing, unable to move, the sight of her mother seared into her mind.

Soon, her mother began to keen. It was long, and primal, and shrill. It took Desma several moments to discern what she was saying.

'*Serene Turan, hear me.*

Serene Turan, forgive me.

Serene Turan, don't leave me.'

Over and again.

There was a clatter of wood and, though she could not see, Desma knew her father must have discarded the chair. Was he holding her? Stopping her nails from carving further grooves in her skin? Or was he on his knees, pleading for his wife to come back from the heavens, to be with him in their bed, human and mortal?

Her heart beating worse than any time she had to fight with a blade to save her life, Desma ran to her room, tears searing down her face. But her mother's voice travelled clearly. For hours she lay with her pillow atop her head, waiting for a silence that she feared may never come again ...

Until, eventually, with only a couple of hours before dawn, Desma fell into an exhausted sleep, plagued with images of red spears and wolves and roses dripping with blood.

Tale of Myrto and Rhoxane

Myrto was a beautiful woman from an island off the coast near Dramaki, with sun-lightened brown hair and bright, green eyes that helped to soften her oft-sharp words. She was a woman who refused the role of mother and wife, choosing instead to enjoy her life for herself. Though past the age of forty, she had lost none of her vivacity, her body smooth and ample from indulging in the rich food and wine of her island; she was the subject of longing for many men, both youth and widower ... and of a few women.

One such woman was the wife of the island blacksmith, Rhoxane. The same age as Myrto, though with a few more wrinkles and the first signs of grey, she had borne one son and a still-born daughter. Her hands were marked with hard work, her face lined with the worry of motherhood, her clothes always smelling of charcoal. Her husband had left three years prior to fight in the battle with Pallan to the south. Others had returned, but there was no sign of her husband – or news of his death. By Dramaki law, she had to wait ten years before she could assume he was not returning and seek a new life.

But one day, when she was washing her sheets with some of the village women down at the river, she noticed Myrto join them. She had seen Myrto many times before. But something was different. Rhoxane could not say if it was the way her hair turned to bronze under the dappled shade of the trees, or how her cream-and-green peplos hugged her body, the dark splotches from the water soaking it in tantalising places, or the way she threw back her head to laugh at the ribald stories the newer brides were telling of their wedding beds and the enthusiasm of young men.

Whatever it was, Love struck Rhoxane with all the strength of a hurricane stripping the coast, with all the force of an arrow striking the breast. With the same power a whispered word at the right moment could bring about release, the blacksmith's wife knew she had to possess Myrto.

That night, she toiled away at her husband's forge, and in the early dawn she crept to Myrto's house, leaving her gift on the doorstep. Later in the day, she saw Myrto in the agora, a necklace of silver and bronze flashing like divine fire upon her chest. Rhoxane heard her telling the other women of the surprise present and their guesses on who might have left it.

The next two nights, Rhoxane again gave up her sleep gladly, hammer ringing and bellows pounding. Until again, in the grey light of a new day, she left her gift on Myrto's step. When it neared midmorning, she heard a clamour among the village women and followed them to Myrto's house, where it took three women to lift the great shield she had crafted. Shining like the sun, ringed with bronze and tin, beaten upon its surface were images of Myrto: carrying pomegranates in the marketplace, picking flowers in the meadow, standing with her feet in the sea, lying in repose with a sheet draped scarcely upon her. The women again chattered excitedly about who the suitor could be.

One woman turned to Rhoxane and called out, 'My dear, yours is the only blacksmith on the island. Surely this was crafted at your husband's forge?'

'Indeed,' another woman, Rhoxane's neighbour said. 'I heard the banging and clatter of the forge last night. Has your husband returned? Do you know who commissioned this shield?'

Rhoxane shook her head. 'Alas, my beloved husband has not yet returned from Pallan, Laran grant him strength and speed. And what you heard last night merely was my own poor attempts to mend a broken pot of mine. Surely this shield, with such mastery of the art and beauty, came from the Clevers in Trilos?'

The women turned from her in agreement. Only those divinely inspired by the Smith God could have made such a shield.

Rhoxane went away with a smile, her next gift already planned in her mind. That night she forwent the forge and instead began to sculpt the block of clay she bought from the potter that day. Once it was ready, she spent the next two days firing it using the forge's heat in place of a kiln. Not for a second did she leave its side, her eyes never flickering from the flames, her thoughts consumed by

Myrto, until – at last! – it was ready. By then it had been five days since she had felt the gentle hand of sleep caress her brow. But love fueled her.

This time there was no secrecy. She approached Myrto's door just as dawn spread her pale wings across the sky. Heart thundering, head filled with clouds, eyes red and wide, she knocked on the door both timidly and with purpose.

Myrto opened the door, robe wrapped tight around her, hair wild from sleep, the silver-bronze necklace peeping from beneath the fabric. She blinked in surprise at the sight of Rhoxane before flicking down to what she held.

It was an exquisite clay bowl, wide and shallow with a curved lip. Emblazoned on the outside were scenes of the two of them: holding hands beneath a laurel tree, kissing in the river, bare-chested on a couch, making love on a mound of pillows and roses.

Myrto's face turned scarlet as she realised the gifts, the secret admirer, were all the blacksmith's wife.

'My Myrto,' Rhoxane said in a gush, dropping to her knees, bowl held out between them. 'I bring you this bowl as a sign that you will always have wine, and milk, and bread, and berries. I brought you a shield to show that I will always be there to protect your body, your heart, and your life. I brought you the necklace because beauty deserves beauty.

'You are my flower, my wind, my sun, my water, my fire, my blood, my passion, my desire. You are me, and my, and mine. I love you, Serene Turan and Mighty Tinia as my witnesses. Please, say I can be yours. Let our lives be one and entwined. What say you?'

Then Myrto spoke the words that blackened her heart and filled her with unfathomable despair.

'Dear, brave Rhoxane,' she said as gently as her shock would allow. 'I cannot begin to express how wonderful your words make me feel, for how can one's heart not delight at such praise and description. But, alas, I must say no to your proposal.'

Rhoxane's hands shook as they bore the weight of the great clay bowl. 'But why?'

'To spare you, I wish there was but one reason to quickly explain and end this conversation. But there is a myriad, as – deep in your own mind – you must

also know.' Myrto took her hands from her robe to unclasp the necklace from her throat. As she did, the material pulled away, revealing her naked curves.

A passionate fever erupted in Rhoxane.

Myrto, seeing the ravenous look take over the woman's face, quickly covered her body and dropped the necklace into the bowl. 'You are a married woman. What you propose is illegal before the law and before Uni, Goddess of Matrimony, the most spiteful of gods when her laws are broken. I will not be ravaged by a goddess because of your lust, as that is what this is. It is not love. It is not enduring. It is the grips of an affection that will slacken away. I will not build my own destruction on something so fleeting.

'Please, Rhoxane, take back your gifts and go to your home. Sleep in your marriage bed, and pray to Laran, and Turms, and Menrva to bring your husband home safely.' With that, Myrto rolled the shield from where it stood inside, leaning it once more against the doorstep, before gently closing the door with a final pitying look.

Rhoxane remained, still on her knees, hands gripping the bowl tightly as she gazed at the shield, unable to understand how such love could not be returned.

All at once, with a great cry, Rhoxane flung the bowl, shield, and necklace from her. The bowl smashed on the ground, the shield dented as it struck the wall, and the necklace came apart into a hundred sparkling pieces. But Rhoxane didn't see any of it.

She fled to her home.

But it was not to do as Myrto suggested.

Instead, she prayed to different gods.

She prayed to the Lovers, Turan's children.

She prayed to Aminth, Avenger of Unrequited Love.

She prayed to Turnu, the Impetuous Love.

She prayed to Erus, the most ancient and Cruelest of Love.

And she prayed to the Goddess of Love herself.

She prayed for revenge on Myrto and her cold heart. She demanded pain and disease on her for accepting her gifts when she thought it was from a strapping young man, and then rejecting them once learning they were from her. She wished for Myrto to change her mind, to realise her mistake, for her heart to warm and soften.

She prayed that, even if it was for just one night, she could feel her body, touch her face, kiss her, be with her.

Eventually, sleep claimed Rhoxane, even as her thoughts and words still rushed with rage and desire.

Far away in her temple in Apasa, Turan and her children heard the pain and fervour in Rhoxane's words. The strength of her emotions caused her prayers to be heard over the thousands that poured in every day.

And Turan listened with intrigue.

Dramaki was the domain of her sister, Artimi, whom she hated most of all the Twelve.

Though she was only one of the Trinity of Virgin Goddesses, she was the most baleful towards love in all its forms. Sex and bodily pleasure were as disgusting to her as manure and poison. Perhaps it was time for a little scandal.

She turned to her son, Aminth, who fluttered beside her in barely constrained excitement, his thousand-coloured butterfly wings ablaze and his long hair flaring at the breeze caused by their beats. She raised a hand and plucked a wine-dark strand of hair from her head. As it came away, the hair stiffened and hardened, sharpening. In a moment, it was a crimson spear that glinted angrily.

She passed it to her son. 'You know what to do.'

And so, Love set her Lover upon the world.

Aminth flew from Apasa and entered Rhoxane's island home in a fierce whirlwind.

The blacksmith's wife came awake with a cry at finding a god in her house.

'Do you love Myrto?' the Lover asked, his voice hard as silken metal.

Rhoxane threw herself prostrate before him. 'Yes.'

'Do you wish more than anything to lie with her body, touch her skin?' he asked.

'Yes.'

'Will you do anything to make her yours?'

'Yes.'

'Then take this spear,' he said, holding out the red weapon. 'As dawn approaches, creep into her house. Wait until the moment she awakes before plunging the spear into her heart. Do this, and you will be together forever.'

Rhoxane took the spear, the touch of divinity burning her hands. 'Thank you. And thanks be to Turan and all her powerful glory.'

Aminth gave her a smile that was both encouraging and chilling. 'Love should always be returned.' With a flash and beat of his brilliant butterfly wings, he was gone.

Rhoxane almost thought it was a dream, but the burning spear in her hands told her otherwise. Peering outside, she realised night had fallen while she slept. Not wasting a moment, she left her home, slipping into Myrto's house through a window, the spear clutched firmly in her grip.

There she stood, unmoving for hours, watching the woman of her dreams sleep peacefully. Myrto's hair was turned silver by the moon, the shadows hiding and revealing her body just as much as her sheet did, sliding from her curves as she moved in her sleep.

Finally, Thesan, Goddess of the Dawn, left her sky palace to farewell the night.

A shard of sunlight as pure as gold struck Myrto's eyes.

Slowly, she left the cobwebs of her dreams behind.

She opened her eyes to the sight of Rhoxane standing poised above her, a spear as red as lamb's blood held over her body.

Myrto screamed just as the spear plunged into her chest.

Rhoxane waited, hands clenched on the spear, for the magic of Turan to begin. But instead she watched as Myrto writhed on the end of the spear, the deep-dark of heart's blood soaking the bed, her eyes wild with pain and pleading. She watched in horror as her love coughed up more blood, her breath rasping and faint, until at last all movement ceased.

She realised that the goddess never meant to give her what she wanted, what she prayed. She threw herself over Myrto's lifeless body, blood cooling and thick. Her tears mingled with the blood as she touched the woman she loved for the first time, face buried in her hair as she clasped her against her body.

The voice of Aminth whispered in her ear. 'Remove the spear from her chest. Kiss her heart.'

Rhoxane started at the Lover's words. But, once again, her hope was revived. With a wrench, she pulled the spear from Myrto's chest and, through the gaping hole, she could see her still heart. With reverence, she bent down and pressed her lips directly to the ravaged muscle.

With a great flash, Rhoxane went blind and deaf.

When her senses eventually returned, Rhoxane realised she was lying down. She lifted herself up and saw her own body on the floor, bloody spear next to her. She looked down at her blood-covered body – Myrto's blood-covered body – and screamed. She was in Myrto's body, but Myrto was not in hers. She was dead.

'Why?' she cried out to the heavens.

Again, Aminth's voice came to her ear. 'You prayed to be together forever. To be able to touch her body. Is this not what you envisioned? You have her body – forever. That is what attracted you to her, is it not? Turan has answered your prayers, mortal.'

She cried out again, begging another god to help her, to step in and reverse the atrocity. But none did, for no deity could unweave what another god has wrought.

Unable to stand what she had done, Rhoxane-Myrto leapt from the bed and ran to the cliffs that jutted out to the sea. She flung herself over the side, hoping that the jagged rocks beneath would make the end quick.

But Turan had promised they would be together forever. If she died, Rhoxane would be separated from Myrto's body. So, the goddess sent a sea breeze to catch her and lift her back up to the cliff, where Turan then turned her to stone; an undying effigy to the consequences of love unreturned ...

CHAPTER TEN

It was a celebration like no other.

The temple, already renowned for its grandeur, was bedecked like a divine bride on her wedding day. The hundred-more columns were wrapped in miles of golden cloth, and entire apple and pomegranate trees were moved in giant pots to line the road leading to the temple. The steps were covered in layers of rosemary and myrtle, each footfall sending out bursts of fragrance.

The revelry had begun at sunrise, with the ceremony set to take place at twilight. Dawn and dusk were sacred to Turan as the times when lovers met and separated, when two became as one then dissolved, when bodies entwined and came apart once more.

Each member of the temple was gifted a pendant of golden coral, symbolising the birth of Turan as she rose from the waves and blood of her creator. Scattered about the hills and dells surrounding the temple, people lay gathered in repose, drinking wine and feasting on the breads and honeys of the Kingdoms on the finest pillows of silk and lambswool blankets. Entire roasted swans were served redressed in their plumage, baked fish in a sea of lemon water, mountains of fruits surrounded by spring flowers.

In the middle of each gathering, glowing braziers fed by a steady stream of cinnamon, cassia, fennel, and clove breathed a gentle haze of smoke into the laden air. The mingling of scents was almost overwhelming, heady to the mind, smoothing over the edges of thoughts and brushing away inhibitions. Music, soft and playful, was teased from lyres with expert fingers, from pipes that set the blood simmering, and covered cymbals that rang with a low hum. The youths and maidens of the community sang songs of lovers' quarrels and returned love, their hymns sweeping and tangling among the revellers.

Desma and Cela spent the day with friends they had known since birth and were careful to only sip at well-watered wine, politely refusing to partake in the dream powders that came from the east. They had a part to play in the ceremony and needed to be as clearheaded as they could manage in such an atmosphere. But that did not mean they could not partake in other pleasures.

Desma spent much of the afternoon dancing from one band to another, despite her lack of sleep the night before. Cela disappeared twice, each time with a different, well-muscled man. She returned with a beatific grin and knowing wink. Unlike the more composed festivals of Uni or Menrva, Turan was the Goddess of Sex. Nothing was shamed in her house – beauty and pleasure in all its forms were celebrated. For to deny what was sacred to a goddess was to blaspheme.

Twice Desma caught sight of the Empyreans. They all wore their red and white robes, the bishop with his blue stole, a large swan with a rose-crown embroidered in crocus-purple on each of their chests. Camillus carried a strange staff of gold; it was taller than him and curved at the top, so it resembled a shepherd's crook. Yet his staff ended in a rose bloom and was studded with thorns. To Desma it looked vicious.

The priests appeared to enjoy themselves, although the people they sat with looked uncomfortable. One Empyrean reached out a hand to caress one of the courtesan's breasts but she pushed his hand away, which seemed to annoy him. With speed, his hand shot out and grabbed her breast roughly. The woman cried out, smacking his hand off and shouting at him. Outraged, the priest slapped her face.

Within moments, Theokritos was there with six off-duty guards, who firmly separated the priests from the others. Two priestesses arrived to smooth over any ruffled feathers, explaining the customs of their temple while the guards swept the courtesan and her friends away.

Desma wondered with dread what their festivals were like in the Empire.

Not long before the appointed hour, Desma and Cela went inside the temple. The naos had been sealed except for the priestesses, who were readying it for the ceremony.

'Gods above and below,' Cela gasped as they entered the temple proper. Desma understood the feeling.

Everything was draped in gold and blue. Suspended from the ceiling on silken ropes were doves and geese and sparrows wrought from solid gold and silver. Large mirrors stood between the columns, reflecting the fire that refracted off the precious metals. The temple was ablaze with coloured light softened by shadows. Incense swirled through in a haze with all the fragrances of Apasa and the sea, yet still the air was crisp and clear. A great curtain was erected along the dais, hiding Turan's statue and no doubt the treasures from Urruc, ready for the grand reveal.

Priestesses in robes of white, topaz, and pale-pink hurried about in final preparations, each anointed with oil of rose and crowned with myrtle and apple.

Cela grabbed Desma's hands excitedly. 'Let us get ready,' she said, pulling her towards a small room where Cela's mother, Leontia, waited to help them.

They removed their dresses and were quickly wiped down with cloths and warm water. Leontia then anointed their skin with the same oil of rose before sprinkling apple and clove oil into their hair. With practised hands, she braided their hair and wove them around their brows until they resembled diadems. Thornless spray roses, petite clusters of apricot and blush, were threaded into the braids and sprigs of myrtle leaves and rosemary filled the gaps.

Cela's dress was the colour of summer sand and flowed down her body like water. Desma's was the same rich colour as her hair, with small golden doves scattered on the fabric in sparkling flocks. Leontia then pulled out a small chest and opened it with a smile.

Desma gave a small shriek.

Cela nearly fainted.

The chest was filled with some of the most precious jewellery only worn by the high priestess on the holiest days.

'Mother said we could wear these?' Desma asked, reaching out a hand but too afraid to touch the contents.

Leontia nodded. 'As thanks for all you have done for the temple.'

'This one's mine!' Cela's hand darted out to grab a stunning necklace of sapphire and sea glass.

'Cela,' her mother admonished. 'Serenity and grace, remember?'

'What do you expect when you open a chest filled with treasure in front of a pirate?' she said as she studied her reflection in the mirror.

'We are not pirates,' Desma scolded.

Her friend gave a disbelieving grunt in reply.

Desma chose a gold bracelet with green gems, several rings, and a necklace of rubies so dark they appeared black, set in a bramble of rose thorns.

She caught Cela gaping at her from the corner of her eye. 'What?'

'You look more beautiful than even Turan.'

'Tinia protect us,' Leonitia said. 'Don't blaspheme, daughter.'

'Oh, but Desma looking like that is not blasphemous?'

'Her beauty – as is yours – is a gift from Turan and deserves to be celebrated. But do not compare yourselves to the divine. You should know enough stories to understand the risk of such pride.'

'Turan could make you fall in love with a great-grandfather who likes to eat onions for breakfast,' Desma said with as solemn a face as she could maintain.

'I am not marrying Theokritos,' Cela said, aghast.

Desma couldn't keep back her laughter.

'You two are monstrous,' Leontia chided. 'Get out of here and try to keep yourselves presentable for the next five minutes.'

'We will have to join the wrestling matches later then,' Desma joked to Cela as they left the room.

'Gods save me,' they heard Leontia sigh.

One of the senior priestesses, Melitta, appeared behind them. 'Girls, this way. Quickly.'

They followed her to the dais and were positioned on the steps to the left if one was facing the statue, Desma one step higher than her friend, the curtain right behind their backs.

'Do not move,' Melitta warned before disappearing just as abruptly in a flurry of robes.

'Damn,' Cela swore under her breath.

'What?'

'I have to make water.'

Desma snorted. 'Cross your knees.'

'That doesn't look very dignified.'

'Better than wetting the temple floor.'

'Just be glad you're upriver.'

'That's disgusting!'

Before Cela could retort, the doors to the naos were thrown open and people began to enter with hushed excitement. There was no order or rank, people pushed to be at the front, jostling their neighbours good-naturedly. All except the Empyreans. The Apasans moved aside like water before a ship's prow until they had an uninterrupted view directly at the bottom of the dais.

Desma had to fight to keep the distaste from her face.

Camillus gave her a smile that made her skin crawl.

'Ignore him,' Cela whispered, pretending not to notice the murmured compliments from men and women about her. She was beautiful. Not just on the surface, but in her spirit as well. Her confidence and ofttimes brazenness made her shine. She was truly blessed by Turan.

After a few minutes, the temple was filled to bursting with still more people straining to see and hear from outside the doors. The sun had since disappeared beneath the horizon, streaks of rosy pinks and blush oranges melted into a deep purple glittering with stars.

Minutes stretched with nothing happening.

The priestesses had taken up their positions lining the walls of the temple, hands folded in front of them, hoods drawn deep.

People began to shift and the bishop whispered to his brethren, a frown marring his face.

Desma felt sweat bead her brow. It was getting warm with the press of bodies and the many fires burning. Had something happened? Where was her mother?

At that moment, the priestesses raised their hoods and began to sing.

Young women who were acolytes to the temple threw damp bundles of herbs and spices into the fires, sending billows of scented smoke high into the shadows of the ceiling above.

Musicians hidden behind columns began to accompany the singers. The song was a hymn to Turan's beauty, her grace, her sensuousness, her power over man and beast and bird and fish; love in all its endless forms.

As the hymn reached its crescendo, Timothea pushed through a gap in the curtains, the fabric rippling with the movement, as the High Priestess of the Grand Temple of Turan in Apasa took her place on the dais.

Timothea was beautiful and dreadful.

Cela felt her breath flutter in her throat at the sight of her high priestess.

Her peplos was heart-blood red, girdled at the waist with a belt of pure gold, and embroidered with doves in white thread and golden myrtle leaves. Bracelets of rose quartz and topaz covered her arms, her throat was encased in a torc studded with precious gems, and a necklace of tarnished copper set with more rubies hung beneath.

Her hair was a river of liquid flame and soft wine, waves falling endlessly down her back, delicate braids framing her face. And upon her head was a crown of orichalcum, the most valued metal in the Kingdoms and Empire, a golden metal lit with celestial fire within. It was worn by gods and goddesses and those most revered on earth. Only the highest priests of Sethlans were gifted with the knowledge of its creation. And to Apasa they sent gifts of orichalcum to honour the marriage of the Smith God to their goddess.

Cela's heart swelled at the vision of Timothea. She truly was the most blessed of Turan's followers, the representative of Love in the world, a mortal goddess.

Timothea raised her arms and silence fell across the temple.

'My children, disciples of Turan, Goddess of Love and Desire and Unity. Welcome. Welcome to what will be known as the one of the most celebrated days in all of Apasa's history.' Her voice rang out like diamond on stone, strong and unbreakable.

'I know that you all are aware of why we have gathered here,' she continued. 'But it is good to be reminded and to understand, from the beginning, why this day is so great.'

She took a deep breath.

'Far back in the past, before our goddess rose from the sea borne aloft by a wave of coral, before her brothers and sisters were born, before the Kingdoms were founded, before any of our histories had yet begun ... there was Urruc.'

All citizens in the League and across the sea knew the story. This was the time before gods. There was no Tinia with his lightning and his judgements. There was no Uni, with her dignity and spite. There was no Nethuns with his monstrous children and fickle temper. No Horta who calmed the earth and brought forth food. No cunning and devilish Menrva. No light and song from Aplu. No spells and wildness from Artimi. No bloodshed and rage from Laran. No craft or creation with Sethlans. Colours less bright as there was no Turms. No sense of home and family and hearthfire as Ethausva was not yet born.

This was a time of Beings. Creatures Without Name. Unbound power and unconstrained chaos. Dreadnoughts who were giants and titans compared to the gods. Theirs was creation from the insanity of an unknown cosmos. These Beings made the first peoples, men and women with unchecked abilities and talents. A race of divine heroes. No laws were placed upon them. No limits or boundaries. No divine eyes to keep them in their place.

Free, they built the first city. From the shifting sands and howling winds, under the blistering sun and by the untamed seas ... they built Urruc.

A city that has lasted for over ten thousand years. A city that still brought wonder and reverence and desire to the tongues and minds of those living.

Ruled by Dune-Kings and Wind-Queens who worshipped a Being who was the Light in the Night, a city never before seen and ever after sought, rose from the dust and clay. Towers, pillars, domes, pyramids, bridges, aqueducts, palaces, temples, walls unending. Art and poetry and song that was said to have even made the terrible creatures as they battled for supremacy pause to listen in wonderment. Weapons that did not break. Shields that would not give way. Clothes that never dulled. Metal that did not rust. Jewellery that never lost its shine. It was a city that would be the first and be the last. Everlasting.

But then the gods were born. From the Beings known as Fundament and Firmament, creatures before sex and gender. Before love. From them came the Eleven, who would raise their thrones and craft their crowns from their own flesh and power. Alone among them did they ascend to rule. All others born to serve. These were different to the other creatures born from the Beings. They defined themselves. On the mountain known as Eharhul to the south of Urruc they gathered and worked their magic. There they lived and coupled and grew. From them came the other gods we know and worship. But the Beings became jealous. They were slaves to their nature, chaotic and volatile, changing ever. They saw the gods settle and divide creation between them and they hated them. And so the war began. A universal war of powers great and small and incomprehensible.

The gods were young and not yet fully stepped into their power. They battled and bled ichor and died. For only at the hands and teeth and claws of the Beings could the divine be darkened.

But the people of Urruc saw what the gods offered: order and knowledge and surety. A chance to live in a cosmos that did not threaten to implode at a moment's notice. And so they turned their minds and hands to crafting weapons and strategies against the Beings. They came to the gods' aid.

Death, the only Being to side with the gods and thus be given a name and purpose, wept at his task. For so many souls came to his lands that he could no longer greet them himself but had to create the Charuns to carry them across the rivers of cosmic blood.

Such death and destruction the world has never witnessed again.

In the end, the Beings were vanquished. Some died. Some fled to the far corners of the cosmos. Others were imprisoned. And some begged the gods for forgiveness and were given roles to play in the new divine order. But one Being refused to bow. It was the Firmament who was Sky and Storm and Wind and Space. Alone, It was unmatched in power. But alone It was, for all others had fallen. It stood before the Eleven and their armies and the wicked designs of

Urruc. It knew it had no hope of victory. Still, the Firmament fought, and the world was at the brink of utter devastation when finally the gods triumphed. With a blade forged from his blood and lightning, Tinia smote the Being that was the Heavens.

'And in pieces and bleeding ichor that was red and black and deep blue, still the Being held its consciousness,' Timothea said, her voice a trance that held the naos captured. 'It said unto the gods, "Today you have killed what should never die. And from me I will give life to one last creation. They will have power beyond anything you have witnessed. They will be soft and sharp and sweet and striking. They will be the end of so many things, pain beyond imagining. Through them I will have my revenge. Fear them, for they will be your destruction."'

With one last strike of his sword, Tinia ended the Firmament. The gods threw its pieces into the wide ocean and went home to their mountain Eharhul to rest and revel in total dominion of the world.

It was here Timothea paused in her telling. The fires began to dim and the priestesses pulled sheer cloths over the mirrors to dull their light.

The assemblage was caught in the story. No one dared break the silence and even the Empyreans were as spell-struck as the others. This was the story of their history as well. The history of their goddess. And she very much doubted their Holy Mother could be half as captivating as her high priestess was in this moment.

Cela looked at her friend, her sister, one step above. Desma's face was beatific, her eyes wide and glimmering with pride at her mother. Pride also filled Cela's chest as she gazed at Desma and Timothea, a mother and daughter favoured by Love and now forever heroes of her home.

She remembered when she first saw Turan's Belt, drawn from the Sand-King's tomb, glittering in Desma's hands. Her sister's face had been bathed with the Belt's holy light, reverence and awe clear in her eyes. Cela, for a moment, had held the blasphemous thought of how like a goddess her friend appeared.

The high priestess continued.

'Wine-dark sea and wine-dark blood. Salt and divinity. Hatred and passion. Pain and revenge. Pleasure and desire. The ocean, a Being bound by Nethuns and Tinia, roared at the slaying of its brethren. Rage and chaos. Change and volatility. All these things thrown into a spell that wrought the greatest magic of any age.

From this mixture rose a creature that was both Being and Goddess, ancient and new, a bridge to everything that was and all that would be.

Turan.'

CHAPTER ELEVEN

Muffled cries came from the crowd, several people falling to their knees, tears flowing freely. Desma almost wanted to join them. She regretted any impure thoughts she ever had against the goddess. Sometimes she forgot exactly what and how Turan was born. She was not just the Goddess of Love but a daughter of death and blood. She was part of all things, all dominions, all powers and feelings.

Timothea spoke again. 'The gods, fearing this creature who rose from the seas and upon the beaches of Apasa declared her domain of Love, offered her a throne among them. And so the Eleven became Twelve, thus satiating the urges of the Firmament that reside deep within our goddess.'

But it was not the end of the cosmic wars. For Fundament, spouse to Firmament, who was also parent to the gods, could not bear the loss of their companion. For now that Turan was born, so was Love. And when Love dies, there is Loss.

Outraged and filled with an emotion that never before existed, the Fundament lashed out one more time and destroyed Urruc. The earth roiled like the sea waves. Mountains fell like sand dunes. Rivers were flung afar. In remembrance of their love and the power of Firmament, the Fundament pulled the earth from the skies – giant rocks of flame that smashed entire temples and palaces into dust. It took the strength of the Holy Twelve to contain their rage to Urruc and bind them into an eternal sleep over which Horta and Aita keep watch.

When the world settled, Urruc was destroyed, its peoples gone, heroes of the First Age dead, and the land was cursed. No god could stand upon its ground or sail its seas or fly its air. It was lost to the divine.

'And since then,' Timothea said, 'anything retrieved from the treacherous sands and rocks of Urruc have been prized by both man and immortal alike. A sword is worth a city. A necklace the wealth of a temple treasury. Wars have been fought, assassinations committed, treaties bargained, blessings bestowed, honours given. All these for trifles. But today … today I devote to the everlasting glory and serenity of Turan, the fabled treasures of the Sand-King!'

At her announcement, the priestesses removed the mirror covers and threw oil on the fires to send their flames leaping. The great curtain that hid Turan's statue and the back of the temple fell away.

Desma was not prepared for the thunderous cheering that arose. People clapped and stamped their feet, men wept and women jumped. And Desma could not keep the proud smile from her face.

The items she and Cela and the rest of their crew had retrieved were on display all around the base of the statue and spilling down the dais. The treasure had been cleaned and polished until it gleamed brightly. Swords, helms, spears, shields, bowls, jewellery, vases, amphoras, statues, carvings, censers, tools, cups, brooches, even a chariot.

It was impossible to describe the artistic flair of Urruc and drawings done by others did them no justice. The designs and symbols were as different to the League and the Empire as gold was to topaz. The sun and the moon featured heavily, with snakes and camels and oases. Even the simplest design caught the gaze. Urruc script was a mixture of strangely familiar symbols and sharp angles that covered everything, telling stories that few could now read.

There were hundreds of artefacts. If every kingdom in the League and all the cities of the Empire emptied their treasuries, it would only afford half of what was on display.

It was wealth beyond counting. And it all belonged to Apasa, the Grand Temple, and to Turan.

This alone ensured Desma and Cela's place in the annals of their city. Her mother had mentioned King Sophocles was planning a new square in dedication to the achievement. Turan would stand in the middle, with Cela, Desma, and Timothea in three of the corners. The last corner would have a carving of the ship that brought the treasure home safe. Though a little bashful at the idea of modelling for a statue, Desma could not deny a large part of her was excited. Cela made no attempts at being humble and had already made requests for her hair to be of solid gold.

Desma looked up at Turan's statue and she felt that the goddess' usually alluring smile was wider and filled with glee, though she dismissed it as fancy brought on by too much wine and the clouds of perfumed smoke distorting everything.

Her mother brought her hands together in a sharp clap that cut through the cheers and shouts. Silence fell once more.

'I also wish to address one more thing. Rumours have reached me of what is to become of these treasures,' she said, indicating the artefacts behind her. 'A lot of speculation and worries. And the presence of priests from the Empire has only added fuel to those fires.' She acknowledged the Empyreans with a nod and the bishop gave a slight bow, his sneering grin returning on his face.

'I wish to put to bed these fears. The treasures were recovered by none other than my own daughter, Desma, and another temple daughter, Cela. They and their crew sailed across the Middle Sea to the sands of Urruc, which, if memory serves, lies not three days south of Aventinus. Is that correct, Camillus?'

'Yes,' the bishop said warily.

'They spent three months living on cursed land, endangering their lives with sandstorms and other nightmares. They found what hundreds have failed to do. With Turan's blessings.' She kissed her fingertips and circled her heart.

The temple mimicked her gesture.

'They then transported the items, from right under the nose of the Empire, passed the pirates of Konoso, home safe to Apasa. This is a clear sign. The treasures of Urruc will remain here, in the Grand Temple of Apasa, forever dedicated and safeguarded to Serene Turan, Goddess of Love!'

While the temple erupted into cheers once again, Desma stared down at Camillus, who made no effort to disguise his anger. Was this the matter he had tried to discuss with her mother the other day? But did that mean Turan had commanded her mother to release the treasures to the bishop? If that was true, then what her mother did ... it was divine treason. It was blasphemy. She looked up at the statue and this time it was not her imagination playing tricks. The goddess' face was cast in half-shadow, but it was furious. Gone was the smile and in its place was a barely constrained snarl. Dread, cold and cutting, ripped through her. What was her mother thinking?

Camillus took a step up onto the dais, his hand white where it clenched his staff.

A sharp ring sounded.

Camillus' face turned as white as his hand.

Between his feet was an Urruc dagger, as sharp as the day it was forged, its bronze handle in the shape of a cobra with the sun in its fangs. The blade had sunk up to the hilt into the stone.

'A gift.' Timothea's voice was ice. 'From Apasa to Aventinus.'

And a clear message.

The bishop looked as though he was going to rush the dais to strike her. But one of the young priests grabbed his arm and pulled him away while another wrenched the dagger from the marble step.

In silence, the Empyreans left the temple. When sight of them had vanished into the crowd outside, Timothea gathered their attention.

'Let the celebrations continue. Love be with you all!'

Music struck up and people surged forward to grab their high priestess' hand, or kiss her hem, or ask for her blessing.

It was several minutes before she was able to extricate herself from her adoring disciples and made her way over to Desma and Cela.

'My girls,' she said with a wide smile, gathering them into her arms. 'You look so beautiful.'

'Thank you, High Priestess,' Cela said as she squeezed her back.

'Mother,' Desma said once they drew apart. 'I don't understand. Why ...?'

'Not today, daughter mine,' Timothea stroked her daughter's hair. 'Dance, drink, make love. Live today. Let us worry about the future tomorrow.'

'But what about'—she lowered her voice—'what about the Belt?'

Timothea shook her head sharply. 'Not as long as those Empyrean snakes are in our city. It will stay hidden until they depart. And we will have another celebration – this one for all Apasa. We can never have too many parties.'

'That is the truth,' Cela said with a tight smile, trying to defuse the tension.

'Please, Desma, enjoy yourself. Let me enjoy myself. Let us dance. Show me what is new down in the theatres of the city.' She pulled them both towards the floor of the temple where already people were swaying and leaping. 'Dance with me, daughters!'

Laughing, Desma and Cela spun their high priestess around and began to dance. Music and incense, strong wine and stronger laughter, all began to blur into the night.

But no matter how hard she tried, Desma could not shake the feeling of being watched. And she refused to look at the statue again for fear of what she would see staring back.

Desma found herself naked, running through a plain of bloomless rose thorns.

The brambles ripped at her skin, tearing already wounded flesh open again and again, but her feet would not stop. Something was coming. Something ancient and awful and filled with unspeakable rage.

She cried out when her ankle caught on a large stem and brought her crashing into a large patch of thorns. The sharp spikes pierced her deeply until it felt every organ was slashed. She looked up, crying again when her neck was wrenched as her hair got caught. The sky was black and blush, as though sunrise and deepest night had collided. She felt her coming.

Pain and pleasure slammed into her, tears and gasps falling out of her. Her mind splintered and stretched, waiting for a shattering, a release, that never came.

She was so small. She was nothing. She was a flicker. Smoke in the wind. Raindrop in a desert.

She was coming.

'Desma, wake up!' A scream tore through her dream, followed by a slap. She sat up, startled, hair falling into her eyes.

'What?' She brushed the strands from her eyes to see Cela in a singed dress, a bloody smear on her cheek, and a sword in her hand.

Adrenaline flooded her body, flushing out the wine and tiredness. She leapt to her feet naked, grabbing the closest garment and throwing it over her head. It was then she realised she could hear screams and clashing of weapons. She had gone to bed in the late hours of the night, in her room at her mother's house behind the temple.

'What is happening?' she asked Cela as she snapped on her sandals. Her friend handed her another sword, also covered in blood. Desma grabbed two knives as well. She bound her hair in a strip of cloth.

'It's those bastard Empyreans,' Cela spat. 'A whole army of them.'

They ran out of the house and headed for the temple. Women and men were appearing from other houses, running to gather the wounded people streaming from the temple. Guards ran past, some only half-clothed in armour, calling on Turan and Laran to fight by their side.

'I was in the temple, asleep on one of the couches, when the shouting started. We have no idea where they came from. The naos was suddenly filled with warriors. They were slaughtering everyone.' Cela's voice caught, sobs barely held in check.

'Get everyone away,' Desma said. 'Head for the city. Find the city soldiers on the road and send them here.'

'No,' Cela snarled. 'I'm coming with you.'

'Cela—'

'My mother is in there, too.'

Desma couldn't argue with that. She nodded and they both climbed the steps and entered a scene from their nightmares.

The temple, just hours earlier, had been full of beauty and riches and joy. Now, the steps of the dais were awash with blood, the braziers collapsed, spilling coals and fire, bodies strewn across the floor. The carnage made them both gag.

Warriors in armour bearing the swan and crown fought against Apasan men wearing the myrtle and dove. Farmers and craftsmen from the temple community also fought with discarded weapons and tools snatched from their homes. But they were dulled with wine and sleep. The Empyreans were fresh and prepared.

Cela pointed at three priestesses backed against a column, two waving large candleholders at a group of Empyreans bearing down with sword and spear.

Desma did not hesitate. They both descended like the Demon-Goddess Vanth, the Fury of Beneath, slashing and cutting in silence until the four warriors were dead. The priestesses, pale and speechless, nodded their thanks and ran for the outside.

Desma and Cela moved on.

They appeared from the shadows and smoke like wraiths, death following every blow, vanishing in moments to find their next prey. But soon they became engaged with warriors who recovered quicker. They traded blows, Desma and Cela moving in unison as they had trained since they were sixteen. But Desma cursed herself inwardly for forsaking her training for the last five weeks. She had not picked up a blade since they departed Urruc and her arms were starting to shake. She wished she had her crew by her side. But they fought on.

Desma caught one warrior's sword on her own blade, but another lashed out with his spear and grazed her thigh. She let out a gasp and stumbled away. The warriors pushed forward but Cela spun like a dancer away from her opponent and cut the backs of their legs. As they collapsed to their knees Desma skewered one through the eye and plunged a knife up through the chin of the other. By the time she had recovered, Cela had finished dispatching the other warrior.

'Thanks,' Desma said breathlessly.

'Always,' Cela said with a vicious grin.

The battle raged thick. She could not tell which side was winning, as the dead all blurred into one amid the smoke and screams. Eventually, they found themselves at the rear of the temple where her mother's chambers were located.

Inside they found two priestesses, their robes torn, wielding a knife and broom to hold back the Empyrean who taunted them.

He never saw Desma kill him from behind, his head falling from his shoulders. The younger priestess ran from the room before they could say a word. Cela turned to give chase but Desma stopped her. The other woman was wounded in her leg and needed support to walk.

They hauled her to her feet. She was barely able to keep upright, but she clung to them stubbornly. They left the room and saw a group of women running down the hall, chased by ten warriors. The priestess at the rear glanced back for a moment.

'Mother,' Cela cried, letting go of the woman's arm and dashing down the corridor.

'Cela, no!' Desma cried after her but she was gone.

'Leave me,' the priestess said. 'Help her.'

For a heartbeat, Desma considered letting the woman fall and abandoning her to the swords and darkness. But Cela was armed and able. This woman needed help. With a grim expression, she held onto the woman in a firm grip and kept moving. They made it back to the naos where the fighting was still going strong. She caught sight of Theokritos wielding a great war hammer, smashing Empyrean soldiers apart, roaring orders, bolstering his men and gathering them together. He truly looked like a son of Laran, God of War.

A large Empyrean, the blush swan on his armour darkened with blood, appeared in front of them. He swung his sword and Desma barely parried with her own, her arm shuddering under the force. The warrior lifted his foot and kicked her in the stomach, sending both women flying back. Desma rolled to the side to avoid the downward swing of his sword but the priestess was not so fast. When Desma got to her feet she saw the woman had nearly been severed in half. Rage bloomed inside her and she threw herself screaming at the warrior, battering his sword aside until both weapons fell to the ground. Not stopping, she barrelled into his chest, sinking a knife into one side of his neck and her teeth in the other, bringing him to the floor with a crash.

She raised her head, blood dripping down her chin, eyes feral and hair come unbound. Several warriors who were approaching blanched at the sight and fled. She looked up at the Turan's statue, glowing faintly in the light of the fires spreading throughout the temple. The goddess was smiling with delight, but it was cold and cruel. The rose quartz glowed crimson and black, melding together until it was the colour of Desma's hair. The goddess was enjoying the destruction of her temple and people.

Desma rose to her feet but a shield came flying out of the darkness to strike her in the head. She fell back onto the marble floor, ears ringing, the slaughter around her becoming dull and distant. As the darkness began to steal her away, she could not take her eyes from Turan, resplendent in the death surrounding her throne.

CHAPTER TWELVE

Desma woke to the snap of a whip and a shriek.

Her eyes slowly opened in protest to the predawn light of a day not yet birthed. Her head throbbed painfully and it took a moment for everything to stop swaying and fall into place.

She was in an open cart inside a hastily constructed wooden cage. Her wrists were bound together to the top bars so she was crouched painfully, not quite kneeling but unable to stand due to the low height. There were a dozen other women with her, not all priestesses, but everyone showed signs of rough handling. Twisting to see where they were, Desma peered over her shoulder, through the red tangles of her hair.

The cart was ambling slowly along a road with the sea to their left, so they were heading north. But to where? Trilos? Empyrean warriors formed lines both in front and behind them with other wagons dotted throughout. All the other wagons she could see were covered, so Desma prayed they were the only ones captured. She assumed the rest were carting the Urruc treasures and no doubt as much of the riches of their temple as they could steal.

But how did they get to the temple in the first place? King Sophocles promised his warriors would protect them. There was no way they could have arrived at the temple without alerting anyone. It made no sense.

'Cela.' She swung around to look into everyone's faces, but neither Cela nor her mother were there and she breathed a sigh of relief. 'How are you faring?' she whispered to the other women.

They ranged in age from sixteen to late thirties. She knew them all from everyday living at the temple but was not close to any of them. Then she saw Melitta and Sophia. If Cela's mother, Leontia, was Timothea's right hand, then Melitta was her left, and Sophia was Melitta's niece. Both appeared unconscious.

'Melitta,' Desma called.

'Shut it,' a nearby warrior shouted, coming close to slam his spear shaft against the cage.

The noise caused Melitta to stir. She blinked her eyes and focused on Desma. 'Oh gods,' she groaned. 'Sweet, sweet, Turan, why?'

'Melitta,' Desma said again, careful to keep her voice low. 'Are you hurt?'

'Just bruised,' she said, shifting uncomfortably. 'Do you know where we're going?'

'I'm not sure. We can't be going to Trilos. Their ship must be anchored somewhere along the coast.'

'It mustn't be too far,' Melitta noted. 'The only horses they have are pulling the carts – and they need to be back on the ship before the King catches up with them.'

That was true, Desma thought. She should have seen that herself. That meant they had even less time than she had hoped to escape.

Sophia woke suddenly, took one look around, and started screaming.

'Sophia,' Melitta said, trying to press her body against her. 'It's alright, my niece. Be calm.'

'Shut her up, or I'll do it,' the same warrior growled, lifting the butt of his spear to thrust between the bars.

'Sophia, be quiet or you will get us killed,' Desma snapped, giving the priestess a sharp kick in the thigh.

Sophia grunted at the blow but fell quiet, eyes swimming with tears, her hollow gaze now locked on Desma. The guard stepped away.

'We will get out of here, I promise you all,' Desma said. 'But we need to stay calm and think fast. I don't know what exactly is going to happen but we all need to take ownership of our fates. We can survive. Is that clear?'

'Turan decides our fate,' Sophia said.

'Do you really think that Turan wants us to be captured, to spend weeks on a ship being raped by these men, to be sold into slavery in the Empire?

Or worse?' Desma asked, eyes flashing. 'While we are breathing we must keep fighting.'

Sophia stayed silent but her lips still moved in prayer.

'What are you thinking, Desma?' Melitta asked.

'I don't know.' She tugged at the binding at her wrists but the leather strap was tight and had no give. 'Does anyone have anything metal or sharp?'

They all shook their heads, except Sophia, who now had her eyes closed.

'A hairpin? Paring knife? Brooch? Anything.'

'I have a needle,' a soft voice whispered.

Desma twisted around to an earth-toned priestess with curly black hair. Her face was half-covered in a giant bruise and she was missing several teeth. Someone had bashed her face in.

Desma searched for her name. 'Zoe.'

Zoe smiled tightly and waggled her fingers, showing a thin bone needle.

Desma fought to keep her voice calm. 'Do you think you could pass it to me?'

Zoe shook her head. It was true. Desma was in the middle of the cart and Zoe was at one end, with several women in between them. She didn't have enough leverage to try and toss it. If it fell there was no way for anyone to pick it up.

'Can you try to start undoing your knot?' Desma asked. 'But don't untie it all the way. Just be close and wait for my signal. Okay?' She glanced at the guards, who were keeping a wide circle from the wagon.

Zoe nodded and set to work, carefully sliding the needle into the knot at her wrist and beginning to pry away.

'It is the will of Turan,' Sophia whispered, her eyes now glazed and faraway.

'Or it is a test,' Melitta said firmly. 'We must fight to restore the honour of our temple.'

'If we do manage to get out of the cage, what then?' one of the priestesses asked.

Desma was not sure.

She could not see all the Empyreans, but she counted at least fifty immediately surrounding the cart. They were on a flat stretch of sea-cliff with no hills to head towards, nor were there any paths leading down the cliffs to the sea. If they came upon a beach cut off by heads, they would be just as trapped as in the cage. Worse, they had no weapons and she was the only one with any fighting experience. She sent a prayer to Menrva, Turms, and Aplu. It was clear she would need all the intelligence and trickery she could muster to fight for their freedom.

A flash of red in the brown and olive landscape caught her eye and she narrowed her focus on the spot ... there! Again, she saw, for the briefest moment, a red cloth waved from behind a large rock.

A hurried glance at their captors showed that none of the warriors seemed to have noticed.

Desma looked back to see a familiar head poking up from behind the rock. 'Arete,' she breathed, her heart swelling.

The shipwright raised her hand, making a fist with her thumb out sideways. It was their signal to say all the command crew were there except Cela. Arete flashed her hand open once before closing it quickly. Five additional men from their crew were with them. Desma did not know how they found them so quickly, or at all, but she had never been so happy to know they were near. The plan fell out in front of her like a well-spun tale. She and Arete had spent so much time over the years devising stratagems that she knew her friend had the same plan in mind.

Desma waggled her fingers to show she got the message and then made a double fist before holding up four fingers, then opening her palms like a flower.

Acknowledged. Four minutes. Distraction needed.

Arete nodded before disappearing into the landscape.

She could not see where the others were hiding, but she knew they were out there. They had to move fast. Eleven crew, Desma, and a dozen unarmed women, against at least fifty warriors within spitting distance of the wagon – with more men within a moment's run. She'd had worse odds. At least that was the lie Desma told herself.

'Zoe, how's it going?' she asked.

'Got it,' the priestess said. 'One jerk and the rope will give way.'

'Okay, listen up everyone,' Desma said. 'My crew are out there ready to help rescue us, but we all need to work together and work fast.' They had three minutes. 'Zoe, untie yourself. You four, cover her from view while she works to untie you. When I shout, you five hurry to untie the others.' They did as instructed. Two minutes. 'Listen, this is going to be the hardest thing you have ever had to do. Some of us are not going to make it. Some of us will be caught again. Some will be killed. You must not care. Run. Fight. Escape. Leave the dead to Aita. Even if you see your sister cut down with a sword and fall screaming. You. Do. Not. Stop. Running. No time for tears. No time for arguments. Pray that your feet be given wings.' One minute. 'Zoe, are you done?'

'Yes, Desma.'

'Pass me the needle.' Zoe's arm shot out from the women shielding her, the needle pricking Desma's fingers but she grabbed it. 'When the diversion starts, stay where you are. Wait for me to open the cage. Then run. If you don't meet with my crew, then keep running inland until noon before you turn back south and head for Apasa. Does everyone understand?'

They all murmured in assent – except Sophia, who was still staring out to the sea. Less than a minute.

Desma felt the ropes loosen around her wrists. They were as ready as they could be. Just a few more seconds ...

There were shouts from further in front and behind them as arrows began to pepper the warriors, each shot striking its target in the throat or eye. That would be Arete and Kassandra. The caravan had reached a section of terrain that had a few small hills and on top of one appeared a fearsome figure. If Desma did not know he was there to rescue them, she would be terrified.

Khufu stared down at the Empyreans with disdain, almost as though he was deciding if they were worth dirtying himself with their blood. Dressed in the battle garments of his home, Opuni, he was bare-chested with a skirt of scaled bronze, arms ringed with bands of tin and copper, his usual gold torc accompanied by a collar of fanned spikes strapped onto his shoulders and standing higher than his head. On his brow was an ivory horn from one of the fierce beasts from the Great Lands. He bore a great curved sword designed to reach around enemy shields and an ornate axe fashioned so the blade was the wing of a fire bird.

The men around them murmured, shifting uneasily, but the women kept their eyes on Desma, waiting.

Khufu thrust his sword high in the air and began to scream in his birth-tongue. The guards flinched. Harsh and rhythmic, the words suited his powerful, deep voice, the battle cry both mesmerising and terrifying.

From behind him, hidden from view, someone began throwing sacks high into the air. When they landed, the bags burst open and dozens of snakes spilled out. Some of the men were struck directly and they fell in a screaming heap as the frantic snakes began to bite and hiss. Ranks dissolved as the serpent bags were followed by more arrows.

'Now!' Desma shouted, wrenching her hands free and throwing herself at the door to the cage. As she jammed the needle into the lock it snapped. Swearing, she began to kick viciously at the wood. It was thin and hastily constructed but it held despite her best efforts.

'Hey!' one of the guards yelled, shoving his spear between the bars.

With a twist, Desma dodged the blade and grabbed the shaft, slamming the butt into the guard's face before pulling it through to jam between the two bars the lock was holding. She heaved and grunted, but the lock held firm. Melitta and Zoe joined her and, finally, under their combined weight, the wood splintered and gave way.

The door sprang open and Desma threw the spear through the opening, taking one of the guards in the chest. She leapt through and grabbed his sword, clashing with another guard. The women poured out behind her, grabbing fallen weapons and forming a tight knot behind the cart, with nowhere to run as the guards closed in.

'To the Beneath with you all,' someone yelled.

Out of nowhere, Bion and Delphinus came crashing into the guards. Bion wielded an axe and shield, using brute strength to smash men apart, roaring like a bear as he went, a great thundercloud that never gave way. Delphinus spun around him, two blades dancing like golden fire, singing songs of great heroes who never fell, eyes flashing on the edge of sanity.

The Empyreans fell back, leaving the women an opening.

'Run,' Desma shouted, leading the way. Her sword flashed and flew, slashing and biting men, not stopping to finish them off but simply trying to get them out of the way. Soon, they broke free of their captors' lines.

Men came sprinting after them, but Kassandra appeared from behind a rock and fell on them like an avenging harpy, face streaked with blood, her sword tinted red by the sacred fires at The Forge in Trilos. The five other crew members ran at her side, yelling their war cries as spears clashed.

'Keep going,' Desma said, slowing to check how her crew were faring, and the women continued on, headed for the small hills.

Arrows from Arete continued to rain down. Several brave soldiers had engaged Khufu, who continued to roar challenges even as he cut them down like wheat before a sickle. These were her warriors: brave, daring, and completely mad. Eleven against fifty with more Empyreans running towards them. One would not find a more potent mix of insanity and confidence in all the League. Desma's chest flared with pride.

'Bion,' she called behind her. 'Grab Delphinus and let's go.'

The helmsman scooped the almost-crazed piper into one arm and caught up to Desma and the slowest of the women easily, axe flashing left and right, and they all ran at a dead sprint with thirty warriors giving chase. Bion put down the piper and picked up two of the more injured women, carrying them with ease, and they slowly put distance between their pursuers. Kassandra was covering the rear with her men, fighting off the faster Empyreans who got too close.

Desma dropped back to help Melitta, who was struggling to support Sophia. 'Go ahead,' Desma said breathlessly. 'Come on, Sophia, we're nearly there.'

'It is her will,' Sophia gasped, stumbling on the rocks in her bare feet. 'It's your mother's fault.'

Desma tried to ignore the priestess, but there was a note of doom in Sophia's voice that made her skin prickle.

'She wanted the treasure for herself. She was meant to give it to the bishop. I know. I heard her talking to herself. She was rambling. She chose to disobey our goddess. No, not hers. My goddess. She broke her promise. She betrayed Turan. *She betrayed my goddess.*' Sophia fell heavily, her hands iron claws on Desma's dress, dragging her down with her.

'What are you doing?' Desma said, barely avoiding impaling herself on her sword, struggling to get out of the other woman's grip.

'You are her daughter. Poisoned sapling from the tree. You will die just as she did!'

Desma froze. 'What did you see?'

'I saw her fall into fire and stone and darkness.' Sophia laughed as she clung to Desma's arms, her fingernails sinking in and drawing blood. 'Turan cursed her and now she curses you.'

'Get off!' Desma screamed, kicking out at the woman. The Empyreans were only a few seconds away.

Sophia's eyes were wild. She grabbed Desma's hair, ripping at it with force as the thunder of their assailants' approach drew nearer. 'Accept Turan's punishment!'

CHAPTER THIRTEEN

Desma jammed the palm of her hand into the priestess' throat. Sophia's eyes bulged and she let go as she struggled to breath. Desma rolled away and leapt to her feet just as Kassandra appeared next to her.

Three warriors reached them, yelling war cries as their swords clashed. Faced with two opponents, Desma ducked a swing and struck out viciously, spilling one's bowels onto the dirt. While she was still kneeling, the other warrior stepped over her and brought his sword down in a crushing blow. Kassandra twisted away from her opponent to block the strike, allowing Desma to stab him through the chest and his sword dropped to the ground from limp fingers.

But before Kassandra could bring her sword around, the last remaining Empyrean struck her hip in a wild blow. She cried out, stumbling away, her hand clasped over the spilling blood. Desma stepped into the warrior's guard and elbowed his face before grabbing his head and ramming the hilt of her sword into his throat, crushing his windpipe.

'Cut his balls off for me,' Kassandra grunted, grabbing Desma's shoulder for support.

'Let's go,' Desma said, glancing back at the remaining soldiers. Arete was still shooting arrows and, with half their group now dead, the rest of the Empyreans began to retreat to the caravan. Khufu was gone from his hill.

'What about Sophia?'

Desma did not even bother looking back. 'Leave her.'

They rounded one of the small hills to find the crew waiting, warily watching, with ten horses. All the captives were already mounted. Besides Sophia, two other women did not make it.

'Where's Khufu?' Desma asked, realising her captain was missing.

'Do not fear for me,' his voice said from behind her.

She turned and flung her arms around him, not caring that he was drenched in blood, dust, and sweat. 'Thank you,' she whispered fiercely.

'We will always come for you,' he said, stroking her hair gently. 'But it is not I who you should be thanking for the rescue. For that, you need to turn to your shipwright.'

She let go of him and turned to Arete, who was holding the reins to one of the horses, pointedly talking to the woman in the saddle.

Delphinus coughed politely. 'Perhaps we can continue this somewhere far, far away?'

Desma nodded. 'Right. How are we going to get back to Apasa?'

'We have ten horses, and there are twenty-one of us,' Khufu said. 'Each of you will ride with one of the women and I will keep to my feet.'

Desma did another swift count. 'Where is Cosmas?'

'He headed back to the city after throwing the snakes,' Delphinus said. 'None of us were particularly keen on carrying them here, and he seemed comfortable enough procuring them. He should hopefully have some of the king's men meet us on the way.'

Desma nodded and mounted up with Melitta, who clung to her back, the older priestess' face growing tight as Desma told her of her niece's actions.

They set off at a gallop, the horses eager to be away from the scent of iron and blood. Arete explained as they rode that Cosmas had awoken them in the night with news of the attack. How he found out, he had not cared to share with them. By the time they had arrived on stolen horses, the Empyreans were already gone. They had found one of the cooks, who told them she had seen Desma captured. Desma's heart dropped when Arete said they had not yet found Cela.

It was a little over an hour before a large smudge appeared on the horizon that grew with their approach, revealing itself to be a giant cloud of smoke.

The temple, Desma realised in horror.

By the time they reached the road connecting the city and the temple, the horses had slowed to a trot. She ordered the rest of the group towards the city, turning her own mount toward the temple. Melitta slid off behind her and joined another priestess, Bion happy to continue on foot.

Arete spurred her horse over, one of the women wrapped tightly around her with eyes squeezed shut. Desma gestured her away. She doubted any danger awaited at the temple. But she had to see.

Her mother.

Cela.

As she approached the temple, her tired horse struggling to produce the speed she demanded, the wind began to shift, blowing the smoke towards the sea. Soon she was almost blinded in a choking, black soot. She wrapped a strip of her dress around her face, squinting to keep the temple in sight. The closer she got, the stronger the wind seemed to blow, whipping past her head, as though begging her to turn back.

Steadfastly, she eventually made it to the temple steps and the wind died away.

She could hardly breathe at the vice grip that seized her chest.

The white marble columns were marred with black and grey. Fire-scorched and with several pulled down, shattered on the stairs. The dust and ash mixed with blood left patches of thick ooze that reeked of death. Bodies lay where they fell or were kicked aside. Warriors in nightclothes, farmers with rakes, women fleeing. The Empyreans did not care. All they saw were Apasans.

Desma climbed the stairs and entered the vestibule. The alcoves that rose from floor to ceiling and once held great treasures were now empty. Their treasures stolen. Instead, there were the severed heads of people Desma had grown up with. Her old teacher, Agathe. The leatherworker, Antipatros. Cela's summer lover, Georgius. The herbalist, Ligeia. A guard whose name, to her shame, she couldn't remember.

The desecration almost made her vomit, the bile burning the back of her tongue. But she made herself look at them all. None were her mother or Cela, so she clung to the hope that they were both in the city, safe, as carefully as she would a candle flame in a gale.

She stepped onto one of the naos doors, ripped down so their golden hinges could be hacked off, and entered the temple centre.

Where a mere day before it was a vision of heavenly beauty and divine fragrance, now it was a hellish scene that burned her throat and eyes.

The myrtle trees had all been cut down. Wine and food were thrown about, their jugs and bowls gone. The cerulean carpet was stained with blood and gore, large sections cut away, stolen by the intruders, and the bronze mirrors were cracked, braziers overturned, the rich cloths ripped down.

Parts of the temple were illuminated by the morning sun, as sections of the roof had caved in from the heat of the fires that had raged in different areas. Ash and dust swirled in silver and gold, a mocking echo of the treasures that had been looted.

Desma began the sickening task of searching the dead, rolling bodies over, wiping away the muck that obscured faces. There was Lykos, the friendly cook who always snuck her honeyed figs as a child. Zotikos, the smith's apprentice, had his stomach ripped open. She found Charmion, the oldest priestess at the temple, nearing ninety in age. And Glaphyra, the courtesan who had struck the Empyrean priest. It was clear that she had suffered.

Tears made tracks in the grime on Desma's face but still she kept moving, a prayer to the gods of the underworld falling from her lips. Aita, Phersipnai, Mania, Soranus, Orcus – anyone who would listen. She prayed that they gathered the dead of Apasa in peace and let them enter unhindered into the Crocus Vales.

She eventually made her way to the dais, where Turan's statue was obscenely clean. The goddess would not abide any dirt to fall upon her holy self. The lunar-stone glowed faintly, matched by the soft roselight from the quartz. Her sea-green eyes and wings set off her wine-dark hair. Her dove and pearl crown flashed brightly, a reminder of her divine authority. The dais was empty of the artefacts from Urruc – the true prize the Empire was after.

Desma spat on the statue.

The world dimmed. The stones trembled. The walls shuddered.

The goddess was angry.

Desma waited for lightning or fire or blessed wind to strike her down. But nothing.

Instead, a stone slab a few feet away shifted and a shaft of light broke through the soot to strike something rich and dark – the colour of blood.

Her mother's hair.

Desma stumbled over the rocks and scattered debris. She reached the stone slab and there was her mother, the high priestess. Her legs were crushed under a section of roof that had given way. Her dress was bloodied and scorched. And her hair, what had attracted Desma's attention, had been shorn off and left by her head.

'No, Mother,' she cried, afraid to touch her. She was pale under all the grime, her face the fresh violet of new bruises, her lip cut open. Desma reached out and gently brushed her cheek.

Her mother's eyes fluttered.

She was alive.

Desma could find a priest of Esplace, God of Wounds and Disease. Their strange sect could take the pain and illness of others unto themselves as they were the only ones their god would deign to bless with his healing magic. There was always at least one in the city. She could be there and back in just over an hour. She folded up a scrap of clean cloth and gently lifted her mother's head so she could slide it beneath. When she went to pull away, Timothea's arm shot up and she grabbed Desma's shoulder in a tight grip.

'Daughter,' she rasped. 'Water, please.'

Desma looked around but there wasn't an intact jar or amphora left in the naos. She dashed outside to the well, which was fortunately clear of pollution, and ran back inside with a bucket and cup. She carefully lifted her mother's head and let a small trickle of cool water dribble through her parched lips.

'Thank you,' Timothea said with a clearer voice. She coughed and grimaced, breathing sharply through her nose. 'Dear gods ... shit.'

'Let me fetch one of Esplace's priests,' Desma said desperately. 'They can save you. They can fix your legs.'

'No, dear one,' Timothea said with a tired voice. 'I do not have long and I would rather spend my last moments with you then alone. Please.'

Desma could not keep the sobs away. She curled up around her shoulders, her mother's head resting into her breast.

'What did we do wrong?' she asked, her question disappearing into the empty temple.

'It is not anyone's fault except mine,' her mother said. 'I disobeyed Turan. And this was her revenge. She told me to give all of Urruc's treasures to the bishop. And I said no.'

'But why?' Desma struggled to keep the anger out of her voice. 'Why not give it away and she would have left us in peace?'

'Because ... I love her.'

Her words rang out.

'How can you?' Desma asked, picturing all the dead she had seen.

'Because she is my goddess. And my mother's. And my grandmother's. And yours. She is my life, my worth, my purpose.' Coughs wracked her body again. Desma held on to her mother until the wave of pain passed. Timothea continued. 'I thought that if I kept the treasure, she would come back. She left just as all the other gods did – to play with their new shiny empire across the sea. But we are her home, her family. We always will be.'

Desma swallowed the bile that rose in her throat.

'But, in my desperation and eagerness, I forgot who I was dealing with.' Her mother's voice grew dark. 'We forget how terrible the gods can be. They are just like us. Good and bad. Evil and wonder.' She broke off with a low cry, her face grey and damp with sweat. Desma could only hold her, wanting to take her pain into herself, but it was without hope.

Timothea gathered herself. 'She is all things. Do not forget! She is Lover and Love, Sweet Whispers and Great Pleasure. But *all* love is within her domain.' Her hands scrabbled on Desma's arms, her broken nails drawing lines of red down her skin. 'She is Temptress. Mistress. Abuser. Her power is invoked when wife makes love to husband and she is there when man forces himself on maiden. She is every moan and scream. She is cruelty and pleasure, taking and giving, willing and unwilling.'

Her chest heaved in her frantic fervour. 'We forget at our own peril. Nothing is more vicious than Love that is jealous or thwarted or betrayed. Nothing can be more vengeful or spiteful or hateful.' Her eyes widened and her voice filled with awe as she stared upwards. 'It moved. It was dreadful. She raised her hand far up towards the ceiling, her face devastating in her rage. With a gesture, she sealed my fate, handed down my sentence. The roof shattered and I was struck down.'

Her mother's voice lapsed and they laid on the cold stone together, her breath becoming short and sharp. Desma did not know what to say, what words of comfort to give. A daughter was not meant to care for her mother in this way.

Desma was tempted to spit on the statue again. To find a hammer and smash it to pieces. To grind the marble into dust and cast it out into the sea. To destroy it as the temple was destroyed. Anger flooded her, electrifying her skin because it had nowhere to go, no outlet. It was all futile. What could she do against a goddess?

'What do I do?' she asked, laying her cheek on her mother's shorn head.

'Live and be forgotten,' was her answer, a whispered echo of Timothea's advice the night before the celebration. 'Do not seek revenge. There are enough stories of the folly of men and women who dream of casting the gods down. All have failed and been destroyed. Go to your father. Disband the crew. Marry a simple man. Go find a village and be a contented wife. Or else seek the haven of the Virgin Goddesses. Only they can shield you from Love's wrath. But promise me, daughter mine'—she reached for Desma's hand, clutching it with too-cold fingers as she pressed them vehemently to her lips—'promise you will do nothing to anger Turan.'

Coughing seized her again, her body curling up, blood leaking from beneath the stone crushing her legs but, still, she persisted breathlessly. 'Stay away from the Empire. Pray you will pass from her mind. She has what she wants. Do not give her a reason to turn her eyes towards you. Promise me!'

'I promise,' Desma said helplessly. She had no strength left to do anything else, the daughter of a dying high priestess in a temple burned. She would leave retribution to the Hero-King.

She stayed there, holding her mother's body long after her spirit went to the Under-God's Halls Beneath, not daring to open her eyes to see the lifeless corpse her indomitable mother had become. But eventually she did. She looked down at her grey, dirtied, blood-soaked body, with her hair shorn and her dress burned, her legs buried under stone.

Timothea, High Priestess of the Grand Temple of Turan in Apasa, was dead.

Desma threw back her head and wailed. Her cries and shrieks ripped from her throat and shattered on the broken marble, folding and echoing back until the air was filled with her despair. She reached up and tore handfuls of hair from her head, blood and flesh still clinging to the roots, casting the strands down to join her mother's hair. She ripped her dress open, beating on her chest until she felt her own heart would stop. Her nails seared down her skin, fresh rubied drops splattering her hands and her mother's face. Tears and snot flowed down her face, her sight blinded by the salt, barely able to breathe but she found the air because she would not stop screaming. Again and again, her wails left her body, draining her soul. Her grief felt like a smothering wave that was suffocating her, driving her towards insanity at the impossibility that her mother was gone.

She had no memory of leaving her mother. No memory of her way back to Apasa. There was nothing but dulled greyness and piercing agony.

She knew nothing until sleep's dark cloak claimed her.

CHAPTER FOURTEEN

Bishop Camillus stood on the deck of the quinquereme, an absent smile on his face as he watched the last of the cargo ferried onboard from the shore.

Once the festivities of the temple ceremony had died down, he and his brethren had left to a small encampment a mile away. There they waited until Turan's Empyrean Swan and Rose Guard arrived. A small phalanx of warriors escorted them back to another quinquereme that was waiting a few hours north in a small inlet. The ship in Apasa's harbour left during the night to meet them, and once they set sail they would meet up with a third quinquereme in the sea halfway between Pallan and Konoso. He was charged with bringing back the greatest treasure the world has ever seen, and so he demanded no less than the twelve hundred men the three ships carried to protect him and the fruits of his labour.

The thought of the screams and clash of arms he heard from the temple as he rode away still elicited a pleasurable thrill in him. It was disappointing he could not have watched it himself, but he preferred not to be placed at risk. Perhaps after returning to Aventinus, the Holy Mother would permit him to spend some time in Capitolinus to attend the Impareum and watch the bloodblades battle to the death.

He was astonished that these so-called devotees of his goddess would forget an integral part of her divinity: she was the lover of War. Ancient tales told of her prowess on the battlefield, her fierce protectiveness when her favourite heroes were facing mortal peril. The only difference between love and war was how one directed their bloodlust. Turan had sent a fine mist that covered the eyes of Sophocles' men, allowing the Empyrean guard to cut them down as they approached the temple.

He breathed the salt air deeply, his shoulders losing some of their tension now that all he was tasked to retrieve was in his possession.

His second, Father Spurius, approached with an open scroll, his eyes glancing back and forth as he skillfully dodged sailors and cargo.

'Bishop, the last Urruc artefacts are about to be loaded,' he said, his young brow furrowed at the contents on the scroll, his scruffy auburn hair ruffling in the wind.

'Excellent,' he said. 'Have you located the relic?'

'Not as yet, Bishop,' Spurius admitted. 'It is concerning. Before loading onto the ship, I and the other fathers checked each bowl, box, vase, amphora, figurine. We did not find it.'

Camillus' face darkened. 'It must be here. Once we are underway, I want everything searched again. And again, if need be. It must be here!'

'The High Priestess did not display it during the ceremony,' the younger priest noted. 'I thought that was strange. Could she have guessed at what would have happened? Could she have hidden it?'

'I ordered her chambers searched,' Camillus said. 'Every room in the temple, from alcoves, to baths, to pantries. Surely, Turan would have sent a sign if we had missed it.'

Spurius pursed his lips. 'Who knows what tricks the Apasans are capable of committing? But, by Turan's grace, we will have it. I will bring it to you myself the second it is found.'

'Do so,' Camillus said, dismissing the priest.

Serene Goddess, please let Your blessings fall upon us and all Your dreams fulfilled, he prayed silently, a heavy stone of dread settling in his chest.

The city was grieving.

Desma walked near the head of the procession, wrapped in dark robes, her face smeared with coal and her hair dripping with seawater, leaving a trail of tears behind her. Surrounding her were the women of the temple. Priestesses, wives, courtesans, and daughters. The female family of her mother.

When news reached the Hero-King of the attack on the temple he had sent a thousand men. The warriors he had set to guard the road and hills surrounding had all been killed, their throats slit or hearts stabbed. It was said he fell to his knees and wept when he heard of Timothea's death.

Almost all the temple guard, three hundred strong, had been killed in the fight. Dozens of priestesses were slain or missing, and while most of the community had escaped, they were not entirely unscathed. The Empyreans set fire to their houses when they left, reducing most of them to charred rubble.

A few treasures and riches were recovered, those pieces unseen in the chaos or dropped in the mad rush. A drop from the ocean of wealth the temple had hoarded.

It was three days since the attack. Three times had the sun risen over the land where her mother no longer walked.

Desma was not alone in her grief. So much death had been wrought by the Empyreans, so many loved ones taken away. Grief was at high tide, showing no sign of receding.

The procession was thousands strong. The city had gathered by the great sea amphitheatre, where dozens of wagons waited, cradling their precious cargo. Hundreds of bodies, wrapped in linen and covered in garlands of myrtle and crowned with celery flowers, lay stacked like bundles of wood.

At the head of the convoy was an ornate cart with heavy marble wheels and gold carvings, pulled by a team of four horses. Desma could scarcely look at it. Wrapped in a blush cloth with thin bands of orichalcum, the body of her mother looked like an unformed puppet, waiting for life to be carved and drawn into its features. But life had long since left her vessel. Desma could only pray she was greeted with easy passage to the Crocus Vales to spend her days in bliss and peace.

The wagons led the way up the widest path to the top of the cliffs.

King Sophocles walked behind the high priestess' wagon, his family and noblest lords clustered around him.

Then came Desma and the cloud of darkly-wrapped women who sang dirges, beat their chests, pulled at their hair, screaming their pain and distress to the heavens so the gods could know the loss.

But Desma did nothing. She had not even been able to ready herself that morning. Arete and Kassandra had come to her father's shop and, with soothing words and gentle touches, dressed her for her mother's funeral.

Cela walked beside her, songs of grief pouring from her mouth, eyes glimmering with tears that shed freely. Even surrounded by such darkness and sadness, her friend shone.

Cela had managed to rescue her own mother, escaping with others to hide among the dales until the sun rose, when she led them to the city, unable to leave the frightened and wounded to search for Desma.

Leontia had not been able to attend the procession. She had suffered a savage cut to her leg and so remained in the healing house, still wounded and sick with fever. Desma worried for how she would fare. The gods had not been kind of late.

King Sophocles had sent word to the kings of Trilos and Konoso, as well as the archons of Athanai and the queen of Pallan, of the attack and offering a reward for the capture of any Empyrean quinquereme. Desma noted that none of their emissaries were present for the funeral, for she had looked out for Mynta and her father. Apasans walked alone.

The king had also announced plans to fund the rebuilding of the temple until it surpassed its previous beauty, with walls many feet high to protect the jewel of Apasa from all danger. He called upon Turan to bless them and shelter the city in her hands while they tended their wounds.

But not all his citizens shared his faith.

For the last three days, the city had been in upheaval. Some citizens flocked to statues and shrines to Turan, crying for her mercy, begging forgiveness for whatever crimes they had committed that displeased her.

Others gathered at the goddess' shrines as well but in anger and rage. They vandalised her statues, carving obscene acts and words into her stone flesh. Some tore down the marble altogether, shattering her countenance.

Large groups called for war on the Empire, citing old alliances and promises between the League cities, vowing the destruction of Aventinus and the return of their treasures. The old men watched the youths shouting their bravery with weary dismay, knowing well the true ravages of battle. Some families were fleeing the city altogether, fearing this was the start of the fall of Apasa.

The League's history was rife with stories of great cities that fell when their patron-deity was displeased. The most famous was the tale of the city of Ravna, to the north of Dramaki in the heart of the mainland. They worshipped the twin brother of Tinia, Summanus of the Dark Lightning. The Lord of Night Storms was a volatile god, so erratic in behaviour that even his siblings tread lightly in their dealings with him.

One hot summer night, he saw the youngest daughter of the queen asleep, naked, on her bed and felt such overwhelming passion that he turned into a great bird of prey and descended into her room. In his rush to have her, Summanus only half changed back to his man-form, resulting in a great beast of hands and feathers and lips and talons. At her screams, the queen mother rushed into the room, spear in hand, and seeing a monster on her daughter she struck a great blow.

In pain, bleeding ichor from a weapon made by Sethlans himself, Summanus turned himself into a storm of unspeakable power and let loose his fury, seeking release in destruction. When Thesan left her sky palace to farewell the night, the sun rose on a swath of blackened earth. Not a single building was left standing, a single citizen allowed to escape, a single clay pot left to survive. Ravna was obliterated in the Night of Violent Passion.

This was the story being told around Apasa in homes, taverns, agoras, and shops. This was the first taste of Turan's displeasure. And she was wife to Creation and lover to War ... nothing was impossible.

The procession reached the top of the cliff and headed south towards the tombs of the city. Few people were buried within Apasa itself, for there was little land between cliff and beach.

Low drums accompanied the funereal singing, a lone pipe weaving its sorrowful melody, gently cutting with its sweetness. Desma turned to look for her father and glimpsed him behind the women, Melitta on one side and Korinna on the other. Her heart crumbled.

Her father – her sweet, gentle, homely father – was a void.

When she finally made her way to the shop, after being found at the temple by the king's men and escorted back to the city, covered in dirt and ash and blood, he had opened the door anxiously. One look was all he needed to know the worst had happened.

Her father was not a strong man. Timothea had been the strength they drew from, the unbreakable rock from which they both took shelter and comfort. Without her, Palamaon was a ship without a sail or a guiding star.

When he saw her on the shop's step, he fell to his knees, face slack, eyes wide and glazed. Neighbours had to rush to help Desma carry him to his bed. Humourists were fetched to see if they could balance the elements of health, but grief was without medicine. Korinna ended up shooing them from the shop after two days and she sat by his side, feeding him clear soup and lemon water.

Korinna had enough heart and warmth for a dozen people. She cleaned Desma and gave her fresh clothes, brushed and scented her hair to get rid of the foul stench of smoke that would not leave. Even after three days, Desma could still catch a whiff of the temple fire underneath the scents of mint and almond blossom.

Even after her father came out of his initial shock, he was a greying of his former self. He stopped making pottery, stopped talking to his friends, and could barely stand looking at his own daughter.

She had not wanted to attend the funeral. As they drew closer to the tombs, dread wailed inside her. Already, she could spy the great pyres hastily constructed, smell the freshly cut pine and cypress, the oil drenching the green wood so it would burn hot.

When they arrived, the priestesses of Aita started to ferry the bodies of the deceased to the pyres and the king began to speak, his voice rolling out over the silent crowd. But Desma heard nothing. She could only watch as the high priestess of Aita and high priest of Phersipnai lifted her mother's body and carried her to her own pyre. They laid her body reverently on the wood, placing a vial of rose oil on her chest as a gift to the Charun who would carry her across the blood rivers.

Desma's heart cracked when the torches were lit.

The king was reaching the summit of his speech, arms thrown wide as his voice, great with passion and sorrow, touched the hearts of his people, rousing their love for city and goddess.

But the fire consumed Desma's sight.

Her mother was going to burn, releasing her last hold on this life, to her and her father.

Her mother was going to leave her.

The flame touched the pyre and it roared to life, like a demon from the Halls Beneath, rippling through the wood, devouring.

Her chest broke apart as a sob wrenched itself from her lips. She fell to her knees, breath stilled in her lungs, bones frozen, as the linen caught alight.

The scent of rose and apple oil rolled from the pyres, smothering the assemblage.

'Timothea ... NO!'

Heads turned to see her father pushing his way through the women, his face a shattered wreck, despair twisting his features. Melitta and Korinna had given chase but he was filled with an unknown strength, shoving priestess and courtesan alike out of his way as he sought to reach his wife's pyre.

'Father,' Desma called, but her voice was weak. She struggled to rise to her feet, Cela gripping her arm.

Two of the king's guards stepped into his path, but he gave no heed, slamming into their armoured bodies. But he was no match for their strength. They halted his approach and held him firm, their own grief clear on their faces.

He fought against them in vain, his wave of strength draining away as suddenly as it had surged forth, leaving him limp like seaweed abandoned on the beach. 'Please,' he begged, his words hung alone in the air, for all watched in silence as the husband of their high priestess broke before their eyes. 'Please, let me go to her.' His words were knives to Desma. 'Timothea ...' He slumped in the guards' arms.

Fires raged and smoke filled the sky.

Grief and sorrow suffocating the heavens.

Desma was silent as she watched her mother's body burn.

The rest of the funeral passed. Aita and Phersipnai's devoted called upon their king and queen, asking for safe and calm passage into the realms Beneath and for honour to those killed in service of their goddess. Libations of wine, oil, and wheat were poured over the smouldering embers. The ashes were carefully collected and poured into an urn ten steps wide. The king had ordered it brought forth from his vaults, crafted over a hundred years ago. It was a war urn, used for when the number of those slain was too great for individual burial. It was a great honour, for all consigned into it were pronounced brave warriors, defenders of Apasa.

When what was left of her mother had been swept away, Desma made her way to her father, who knelt on the dusty ground, his fingers buried in the earth. It took several minutes before she and Cela managed to coax him to his feet.

'I need to take him home,' she said to Cela. 'Go and be with the others.'

Her friend opened her mouth to argue.

'Please, Cela,' she whispered, her words as thin as the strings of fate.

Cela nodded, kissing her father on his cheek and embracing Desma before heading back to join the temple women.

Desma made the slow journey back to the city, her father not speaking or seeing, barely able to put one foot in front of another. Eventually they made it home and she took him upstairs to his room. She helped him remove his chiton and washed his limbs, almost forcing him to sip a cup of mead, before letting him roll onto his bed. As she left the room, she saw him reach across and pull the other pillow to his chest. Her mother's pillow.

She went to her own room and poured a large cup of wine, drinking it in one before pouring another.

Time was meant to be a healer, but he was measly in its doling out. How long would this pain last? When would they start to piece their broken parts back together? Or was that ignorant of her to imagine?

She sat alone while the sun sank, until she was in shadows and gloom.

Her eyes were heavy and she was almost falling asleep, two jars of wine emptied next to her, when her bedroom door slammed open.

She jerked wildly upright, eyes blinking rapidly, as Cela and Arete made their way over, both with stern looks on their faces.

'Desma, you need to come with us,' Arete said. 'Now.'

CHAPTER FIFTEEN

Cela had not wanted to go to Desma, today of all days, but Arete had been insistent.

'When Cosmas says we need to come *now*, you don't argue with him,' was all the shipwright said as they hustled through the streets to her father's shop.

The funeral rites had just ended when Arete had found Cela standing with the other women from the temple, now homeless and living in halls and friend's houses in the city. Cela felt like a wrung towel, shedding more tears than ever in her life. Her heart all but broke when Desma had cried. And to see her father, shouting for his wife, held back from the flames ...

She did not judge Desma for seeking the comfort of wine, for Cela was still fortunate to have her mother, though the healers said she was not yet out of danger.

'What is going on?' Desma asked as she tried to stand up unsteadily.

'Just come,' Cela said. She grabbed Desma's arm and, with Arete's help, escorted her out of the shop.

They walked swiftly through the city, heading towards the crescent harbour, avoiding groups of both the faithful and the faithless, dodging patrols and sticking to quieter streets. They both refused to say anything about their purpose or destination. The cool sea breeze held a hint of smoke and roses from the pyres.

Eventually, they made their way to a small, disused warehouse. Arete pushed open the door that was swollen by the brine air and ushered Desma inside. The space was almost black, but in one corner there was a dim light. They rounded some emptied crates and found Cosmas sitting on a stool, eating a stem of grapes.

'Cosmas,' Desma said, clearly surprised. Cela wondered when she had last seen the quartermaster, for she had not seen him herself for over a week. 'What are you doing here?'

'Having a talk with my friend,' he said, jerking his fruit towards a bleeding man tied to one of the columns holding up the ceiling.

'What …?'

'He's one of the bishop's men,' Arete said flatly.

Cela watched as Desma's already wine-flushed face flooded with a black rage and she stalked over to the man, her deep red hair falling about her face. He was around thirty, probably not that much taller than Desma, with mousy brown hair, muddy-green eyes, and a slim beard that hadn't been trimmed in a few days. Barefoot, both his hands were bandaged and he was wearing a cream, sleeveless chiton that was stained red from numerous cuts across his body.

'Where did you find him?' Desma asked.

'Yesterday, in your bedroom,' Cosmas said, his muted blue eyes watching Desma with interest. Cela noted he had flecks of dried blood on his clothes and in his sun-whitened hair. 'I caught him and brought him here to discuss the trespassing. He has not been the most forthcoming.'

'What have you managed to get out of him?' Desma's face was inches from the Empyrean. The man's brow was beaded with sweat and blood dribbled down his chin from where his teeth clamped into his lips. He met her gaze like an animal frozen before the hunter.

'He was left behind by the others to watch how the city reacted to the attack,' Cosmas explained. 'But he interestingly received new orders two days later. Quite urgent orders.'

'What were they?' Desma asked, just as the man stiffened violently.

Cosmas appeared by her side and pulled her away as the man vomited red and grey bile down his front. His face was twisted in agony, but every time he tried to draw breath to scream his body wracked in spasms and caused more vomit to gush forth.

'Gods above, what is that?' Cela said, jumping well back from the scene. 'It stinks.'

'It seems my grapes do not agree with him,' the quartermaster said with a cruel smile.

Cela raised a brow.

'It is an interesting powder. It causes one such pain people have been known to throw themselves to their deaths rather than deal with it. Death by nausea. I rarely get to use it, because it causes irreparable damage to the organs. Oh, nothing so immediate but bad enough to cause months of lingering sensations that cripple one terribly.'

'You sound so remorseful,' Arete said with a swift grin.

'Truly broken-hearted,' he said, shaking his head.

'Why was he in my bedroom?' Desma asked.

'To get to you,' Cela said. 'Apparently, something was missed in the attack and they think you have it.'

'What?' Desma was puzzled. The man had finally stopped convulsing and sagged against the ropes, face slack but eyes still watching her.

'The Belt,' Cela said.

Desma froze.

The Belt of Turan. A holy relic of pure divinity. It wasn't presented at the ceremony because Timothea had wanted to wait until the bishop and his priests were gone from the city. Desma had told Cela that Turan had commanded the high priestess to give it to the Empire along with Urruc's treasures. But she had refused, and she was killed for it.

'I don't have it,' Desma said. The Empyrean picked up at her words. 'And it can't be at the temple. It was searched by the king's men and the temple survivors. No stone was left unturned.'

'Then where could it be?' Arete asked. 'Who could your mother have entrusted it to?'

Desma shook her head.

'Father?' Cela suggested.

'He already searched your father's shop,' said Cosmas.

'What about one of the priestesses? Your mother, Cela?' asked Arete.

'I don't think so,' she said. 'Unless it was before the ceremony. But then Timothea would had to have known the attack was going to happen. And she would have warned us ... wouldn't she?'

'I don't think she knew for certain,' Desma said, 'but she suspected something. She provoked the goddess – retaliation in some form was to be expected. But she did not think that Turan would have sanctioned the destruction of the temple.'

'But what was the purpose of all this?' Cosmas said. 'It seems a senseless risk.'

'She wanted her goddess back,' Desma said quietly.

The gods had resided within the cities of the Holy Twelve since the destruction of Urruc thousands of years ago. But over the last ten centuries, they had slowly begun moving across the Aduric Sea to the Empire. A collection of hill tribes that within the span of a few generations were a fledgling empire, their greed and prowess and wealth soon capturing the attention of the gods. The kingdoms had never bothered with their neighbours to the west, but focused their attention among themselves and the east, and had unknowingly allowed an empire to rise that rivalled them.

First was Sethlans to leave, tempted by the great fire mountains around Capitolinus. Followed by Nethuns, who fell in love with a city built on water. Once Tinia and Uni decided to move their court from Konoso and Phoroniaa to a city men said was like a star had descended onto the earth, the others joined in a flood. The only gods who still claimed the League as home were Turms in Tethalia and Aplu in Delphon. And now Turan had no home in the League, destroyed by her own hand.

As to the whereabouts of the Belt ... if the Empyreans did not have it, then Timothea either gave it into another's safekeeping, or it was buried in the temple rubble. Maybe once a new high priestess was raised, whoever had the Belt would come forward. Or if it was still within the temple it would be found during its reconstruction.

Cela's eyes lingered on Desma, who was staring at the Empyrean. They had never lied to each other before ...

'What was he meant to do if he could not find the Belt?' Desma asked, breaking off Cela's thought before it could fully form.

'He had orders to capture you, torture you, and – finally – to kill you,' Arete stated coldly.

The man was no longer vomiting but was shaking from the exertion, his skin pallid and his eyes bloodshot. But still, he would not stop looking at her.

'Are there others?'

'Ah, this is the one question he will not answer, despite my careful administrations,' Cosmas said. 'Which I think we can take as the affirmative. It would be strange to leave just one man deep in enemy territory. I believe there is a ship somewhere with a small crew.'

'He will not talk?' Desma asked, stepping closer to the Empyrean.

'Not yet,' the quartermaster admitted. 'But perhaps soon.'

'You've had him for over a day,' said Desma. 'If he hasn't spoken by now, I don't think he will.' She leaned closer to his face, their noses almost touching. 'Am I right?'

The man spasmed again, his breath coming harsh and fast. 'I ... am ... alone.'

'Liar,' she snarled, and jammed a dagger she pulled from her belt into his gut. Blood fell over her hand as the man shuddered, eyes glazing over as the last waves of pain accompanied him down to the Beneath.

Cela stepped away quickly, shocked by the sudden violence. Desma pulled out her dagger, her dress and arms splattered with his blood. Her eyes were stone.

'Now, why did you do that?' Cosmas said with dismay.

'He wasn't going to say anything,' Arete said. 'He would have kept repeating he was alone, or told you anything. He knew he was going to die. Maybe you're losing your touch, my friend?'

Cosmas bared his teeth at her.

'Scary,' she said with a smirk.

Desma grabbed a towel from a nearby table, wiping her hands clean. 'We need to find that boat,' she said, tossing the soiled towel onto the floor. The killing of the Empyrean did not seem to affect her. 'Cosmas, please clean this up. Arete, tell Delphinus to start making the rounds in the taverns to see what he can hear. And have Bion check the markets. Cela, let's talk to Khufu and see if we can set up a little surprise visit for the Empyreans.'

'Should we not report this to the king?' Cela asked. 'Perhaps we need time to heal rather than fight.'

The look Desma levelled at her was chilling, yet it echoed the hollowness she felt inside, like a hearth fire doused in winter.

'It was your home too, Cela.'

And she realised Desma was right. The call, the need to strike out, the uselessness and impotence. And here was a chance to let vengeance free. But would it make either of them feel whole again?

It was another two days before Delphinus sent word that he found the boat. It was a small, twenty-man ship, built for speed and hidden off a small beach south of the city that was not easily accessible by land.

Desma was in her room at her father's shop – which she realised was her only home now that her mother's house was burned at the temple – getting ready as the sun drifted below the horizon. A black, tightly woven chiton, a strip of dark cloth binding her hair away from her face. A sword was strapped to her hip, with a dagger and another knife sheathed on her thigh. Cela was going to meet her soon and they would catch up with their crew outside the city.

She was doing one last check of her blades when her father opened the door.

'Desma ...' He paused when he saw her.

'Now is not a good time,' she said. Her father knew well what she did for the temple. What she used to do. He never spoke to her of any concern or trepidation on her chosen path, but she remembered the fights he used to have with her mother. They were the only arguments she ever heard them have – and they were over her.

She never understood how her parents wove their lives together so well. Timothea was known throughout kingdoms and walked with royalty and divinity. Palamaon made pots for housewives and farmers. Yet their love was unbreakable; flexible like silk yet never tarnished. She did not know what her father dreamed for her; he had never spoken to her about it. Probably a husband and children, making bread in the morning and gossiping with her friends in the agora. But she could never have given him that life. To be a wife and mother was a different strength, with its own battles and wounds and triumphs. She only hoped that no matter what she did, she did it well enough to make him proud.

'Daughter,' he said, his voice like a leaf landing on water, gentle yet shattering. 'Must you do this? Can you not rest? Let others do what needs be done.'

Desma shook her head, her hair – her mother's hair – breaking free of its constraints. 'I must do this. This is temple business.'

'There is no temple,' he said, grabbing her hands, his large and familiar palms both rough and soft from working with clay. 'There is no high priestess to give you orders. There is no goddess to serve.' He pulled their hands to his chest. 'Please, Desma. Stay home with me. Eat dinner. Sleep. Be here.'

'Father,' she said, resting her forehead on his. 'I cannot. You know who I am. I need to do something.'

His face, slowly being creased by life, weathered by simple joys and worries, was haggard. His eyes were blackened from little sleep and his hair knotted from lack of care. 'Do not follow your mother into this fight,' he whispered. 'Leave it alone. Live your life. For me ... please.'

Her heart was stretching in two. She wanted to do as he said, to give him happiness and peace. But she knew she could never be what he wanted her to be. If only he knew truly what his daughter was capable of, then he would not fight so hard to keep her.

'I will see you later tonight.' She kissed his cheek and drew her hands away. She stepped around him and went through the door.

'Be safe,' she heard him say after her.

Be safe.

It took a little under an hour for them to make their way to the beach. The ship was anchored just beyond the almost closed natural harbour created by a broken circle of rocks. The Empyreans kept the ship dark and used a small boat to ferry back and forth. The beach was in a depression of rock, which kept them sheltered from the wind and hid the light of their fires.

Desma and her crew slowly crept across the rocks, thankful for the waxing moon that lit the surface, conveniently riddled with cracks and crevices. All of them were wearing dark clothes and were armed to the teeth. Little discussion was needed on their way from the city, they were well practised in this art now.

They spaced themselves out and once they reached the edge of the depression Desma peered over to take stock. She counted four fires and seventeen men. That meant two were left on the ship. They were all relaxing with wine and the remnants of their evening meal around them – one even played terribly on a pipe, to the great hilarity of his companions.

Desma nodded to Cela and Arete. Cela moved to the left with Bion and Kassandra, while Arete went right with Cosmas and Delphinus. Khufu followed Desma.

It was a six-foot drop from the lip of the rock onto the soft sand. The eight of them fell with the slightest swish, masked by the sound of the waves. The light of the fires did not extend across the whole beach, so they were hidden in the dark grey of the moonlit night. Like wraiths, they crept across the beach, weapons drawn, faces set in grim determination. All Desma saw was the sigil of the blush swan and rose-crown embroidered on one of the men's tunics.

It consumed her vision.

When they were feet from the encampment, one of the Empyreans glanced over his shoulder briefly and blinked stupidly at the sight of her crew emerging armed from the gloom. Before he could shout, Kassandra's thin blade ended his voice. The spray of blood sizzled as it hit the campfire and the Empyreans all leapt to their feet, shouts ringing as loud as the swords being drawn.

The sixteen men left standing met Desma and her crew with a clash. She ducked under a sword, rolling in the gritty sand, before kicking out sharply to snap one Empyrean's ankle. As he fell, she stabbed her sword into his chest.

She looked up and watched as Bion threw Cela through the air, her friend spinning gracefully as she took out two men on her own, her sword a shimmer of silver flame. Arete was fending off two men twice her size. Desma ran over and blocked a blow set to separate the shipwright from her left arm.

The Empyrean turned his attention to Desma then, relying on his considerable strength as he smashed blow after blow at her, his sword leaving notches in her own blade as her arms began to shake holding up under his assault. She leapt away to give herself a second's respite, but the warrior spun, his sword tip in the sand, flicking it up into her eyes.

She shielded with her arm and stumbled away, glimpsing his advance through her tears and flailing wildly in front of her. He dashed her sword easily to the side and slammed his shoulder into her body, knocking her to the ground. Dazed, eyes streaming, Desma tried to gather her thoughts as the man slashed his sword downward.

A wild shriek soared through the firelight and shadows to resolve into Delphinus leaping onto the man's back and bearing him down. Desma rolled out of the way of the two men, getting to her feet to see the piper sawing at the back of the Empyrean's neck.

'Delphinus, enough,' she ordered.

The piper turned to her and she stepped back, unnerved. His green eyes were wide and deep, glinting with madness, his copper hair aflame. 'Delphinus,' she said gently but with iron. 'Enough.'

The piper looked down at the almost-decapitated man and blinked rapidly, drawing himself back from wherever he went when the battle-lust took over. He dropped his sword as he dismounted, scooping up sand to rub the blood off. 'I'm back,' he said as he scoured his hands. 'I'm back.'

Desma gave him a reassuring nod and turned back to the battle. All the Empyreans were dead, some without a chance to even find a weapon to defend themselves. She quickly scanned her crew and, besides a few shallow cuts and bruises, everyone was unharmed. 'Wait, where's Cosmas?' she asked.

Kassandra pointed her sword towards the sea.

Desma stepped forward so the fire was behind her and squinted. The two Empyreans left to guard the ship were distant outlines in the dark. They knew something was wrong and were on deck, looking at the shore. It was then Desma noticed something disturbing the water, only noticeable under the moonlight. The disturbance turned into Cosmas as he reached the hull and swiftly climbed onto the deck. The men must have heard him and turned, drawing their swords, both collapsing before they could take a step. Cosmas was deadly with knives.

'How did he swim that far so fast?' Cela asked, appearing beside her with a smear of blood across one eye, giving her a fearsome look.

'How does Cosmas do anything?' Desma replied. 'Mysteriously.'

'What do we do now?' Khufu asked from the other side the fire. 'Leave them to become dust?'

'No,' Cela said sharply. 'Gather the bodies and row them to the ship. Let's send them back to their home.'

The others looked at them uncertainly, but Desma nodded her assent and they began moving.

It took four trips to row the bodies back to the ship. Once they were all piled on the deck, Desma and Cela produced two sacks and covered them in myrtle branches and dove feathers, symbols of the Apasa temple. They unfurled the sails and set it pointing west, letting the wind and tide take it away from their homeland.

They gathered back on the beach, watching in silence as the ship bobbed and dipped in the silvery water, eventually disappearing behind the waves.

'What are the odds it will actually make it back?' Kassandra asked.

'None,' Arete answered. 'But it will no doubt be found by another ship or drift into one of the islands. Word will travel of a shipload of dead Empyreans covered in tribute to Turan. Aventinus will know what it means.'

Kassandra still seemed troubled. 'Do you think it was wrong to act without seeking word from the king?'.

'I don't think it is contrary to his current position,' Cosmas said.

'I heard he already sent emissaries to The Forge in Trilos to request weapons,' Bion said. 'Do you think we will really go to war with Aventinus?'

'Not alone,' Khufu said firmly. 'We are not strong enough and too far away. We would need allies, supplies, and ships from others in the League – whether or not they will help us is another story. They may see this as an issue contained only to this city-state. Only Aplu knows what the future holds.'

'What do you think, Desma?' Bion asked.

Desma did not answer. She kept watch, even though the ship was lost to view. The tight lid she kept on her feelings, that had been in place since she mourned her mother in the ruins of their temple, was beginning to come loose. Anger, hot and wild and useless, boiled beneath, wanting release. But she knew it was no good. Even the deaths of these Empyreans did nothing to smoulder the fire.

Her mother was right. There was nothing for her to do but fade away. Gods knew she had enough money to live comfortably for the rest of her life. Lavishly even. She still had her ship. She could sail around the Middle Sea, visit Mynta. Perhaps even find love in a husband and have the children her father craved. Or a wife. She had honestly never given it much thought. But maybe the last four years was all the adventure the gods were willing to give.

'It's enough,' she said quietly. 'Let's go home.'

CHAPTER SIXTEEN

The days passed with little interest or colour.

Desma often found herself wandering the city. It was still beautiful, even though its heart had been ripped out. The fountains still splashed, the flowers bloomed and attracted bees that bumbled through the air without care for the affairs of the wingless. The statues of heroes and gods still stood strong and inspiring, giving hope to the citizens. The sun set over the brown and cream buildings, painting the cliffs pink and apricot and yellow. The sea invigorated with its clean salt and brought in ships to trade.

Spray roses bloomed in every nook and crack in the stone and pavement, rosemary scenting the air with its heady fragrance. Orange and fig trees dipped their branches for any to grab a quick snack. Musicians continued to ply their trade, performing in the small courtyards and terrace steps, trying their best to soothe the troubled hearts of Apasa.

The city had been dealt a great blow but she was strong. Their Hero-King made sure he was present, walking through the city, dispensing gold and silver, laughing at the jokes of housewives and admiring the skills of youths. Apasa's official response to the atrocity committed by the Empyreans was yet to be announced, but there was a constant stream of messengers flying to and from the city to the other kingdoms. Khufu was probably right: the other city-states would not want to get involved in a dishonour only one of the League suffered. Perhaps starting a war would not be in the best interest of the city. They had already lost their goddess. Why waste the lives of their citizens for treasure that was never theirs and a deity who did not want them?

Desma had volunteered her two-hundred strong crew to assist with clearing the temple and helping to rebuild the community buildings. Many of them expressed the desire to join the recruitment of new guards Theokritos was holding. The temple captain was more taciturn than ever. He rarely spoke except to give orders and Cela said she sometimes found him late at night, standing on the steps of the temple weeping silently.

Cela herself was busy helping her mother, who had assumed the interim leadership of the temple, running temple business from her sickbed in the king's own palace, her leg still not healing properly. They were all worried that there would be little choice but to remove it soon.

At the end of another day walking aimlessly around Apasa, avoiding speaking to people where she could, Desma made her way home slowly. Their house was silent now. Her father rarely spoke, and Desma did not know what to say to him. He had stopped making pottery, his orders going unfulfilled, and his clients, even the most loyal, had taken their business elsewhere. Not that he needed the money. He owned the building and had drachmae aplenty from the temple allowance as husband to the high priestess. But he had no more purpose. Korinna kept saying to give him time and they had no shortage of that.

For the first time in her life, Desma felt rudderless. Her mother had always known what to do, the next step in their lives they had to take, guiding, leading, even ordering. She was the keystone of their family and, now that she was gone, their house was crumbling.

She turned into her street and bumped into Korinna. 'Sorry, Aunt,' she said, grabbing the older woman's shoulders to keep her upright.

'Oh, Desma, I'm glad it's you,' she said, holding her basket. 'I've just come from your house but no one answered the door, so I assumed you were both out.'

Desma blinked. Strange, her father had not left the house since the funeral. 'I'm just heading home now. Did you have a message for him?'

'Oh no, no,' her aunt said, flustered. 'I just wanted to drop some food off. Here you go.' She passed the basket over.

Desma gave her thanks and promised to visit Korinna's house soon – maybe even dragging her father along – and continued up the street. The coloured cloths announcing the wares being sold fluttered wistfully in the breeze. She stopped outside the two-story stone building with the wide orange cloth for pottery flapping. She unlocked the door and went inside, putting the basket on the table.

'Father,' she called out. 'Are you here?' Maybe he was asleep. She checked the back of the shop and the downstairs storeroom just in case he had started working again. Empty.

She climbed the stairs and knocked gently on his bedroom door. No answer.

She started to move away but paused. An uncomfortable feeling was beginning to settle in the pit of her stomach. She knew that if she did nothing she would sit in her room worrying, so she decided to quickly check. She nudged the door open, cursing the squealing hinges, and peered into the room.

It was dim, as the curtains were drawn, but the fabric was thin so it was bright enough to easily make out the furniture, clothes, her father lying on the bed.

The blood.

The shock of seeing the pooling red brought the memory of her mother lying crushed under burnt stone, her hair cut from her head, red on red on red.

The door cracked as she slammed it open, running to her father's side, hands searching for the wounds. His chest was slick with blood. That was when she saw the knife, the thin blade he used to delicately carve patterns into his pottery before they were fired in the kiln. It was lying by his open hand on the floor, its bronze shining beneath the crimson.

'Father! What happened?' she cried, grabbing the blanket and pushing it against the wound. 'What did you do?' She turned to call for help, hoping someone on the street would hear.

'No,' her father said weakly, his eyes fluttering open. 'Don't, Desma.'

'Why?' Tears poured hot and fast down her cheeks. 'Why would you do this?'

He reached up and stroked a finger across her cheek. 'I miss her terribly.'

Her mother. His wife.

'But she is dead,' Desma said, choking back a sob. 'She is dead.'

'I can't do this anymore.' He drew a shuddering breath. 'She is everything to me. My life, my purpose, my love.'

'What about me? What am I to you?'

'You don't need me, Desma,' he said gently, his breathing coming too fast. 'Not anymore. You need to be free. I will not have you trap your life here because of me. And I do not want to live here without my Timothea.'

'But, Father, don't you understand what you've done?' She was almost shouting. 'You won't be allowed to cross the river. No Charun will carry you. You won't be allowed to enter the Vale!'

Her father knew all of this. Everyone did. To take your own life without purpose was an affront to all the Holy Twelve. The souls of those who chose this ending were never allowed to enter the realm of Aita, to sit in judgement of the Three-Who-Speak-Doom, to be reborn if given the honour. Her father would stand on the stony shores for one hundred and twenty years – ten years for each of the Twelve – being able to see and hear the Vale and its inhabitants. But he would be invisible to those who reside there. And once the years of his sentence pass, he would fade into mist and be scattered along the undead rivers.

His body began to shake. He was losing too much blood. He must have missed his heart otherwise he would have died long before she had time to climb the stairs.

'I am sorry, I am not strong enough,' he said. 'She was more than my other half. She was the greatest part of me. I cannot be ... without her.'

'But how can I be without both of you?' Her hands were wet and red. There was so much blood. 'Why is it okay for you to leave me as well?'

'Because you are stronger than us,' he said with a sudden fierceness. 'Your whole life I wanted nothing but a humble path for you, to bind your fate and power. I didn't realise how I wanted to stifle you. For that, I am so sorry.' He grimaced in pain. 'I need to go, daughter mine. I know I will not be with your mother, but perhaps I can watch her from the shores of Beneath and see her be happy and peaceful. I am but a potter, remembrance was never in the stars for me. But it is for you.'

'No,' she said, shaking her head violently. 'I cannot let you.'

'I love you, Desma,' he whispered, his eyes starting to glaze. His breathing became low and far between. 'I love you.'

'I love you, too, Father," she said, her voice cracking. She took his face in her hands, leaving bloody prints on his cheeks as she gently pressed her lips against his brow. 'And that is why I have to do this.'

Her hand darted to the floor and grabbed the knife. In less than a moment, with her thought barely taking form, her soul moving faster, she plunged the blade into his heart, finishing what her father had started.

She watched his eyes flare, shock and horror lancing across his face, air grappling to form words, but it was too late. Where her father had missed, she had not. Deep, dark heart blood pumped out with the last of his strength.

She leaned down and pressed another kiss to his forehead. 'Go and be with her. Tell mother I love her, as much as I love you.'

The last light faded from his eyes and she knew his soul had gone. It would travel the greyness of the living until it reached the rivers of blood far Beneath. The Charuns would have to carry him across now. They had to.

She stayed with his body for several hours. The second time she held watch over a parent. The sun had disappeared behind the other buildings and the room was suffused with the warm scarlet and deep blues of twilight.

She heard Korinna knock on the shop door, heard her enter cautiously, calling for them both, her loud footsteps as she walked up the stairs, and her gasp at the sight of Desma sitting hunched over her father, hand still wrapped around the knife sticking out of his chest, blood covering them both, Palamaon's face twisted in horror.

'Ethausva and Tinia preserve us all,' she swore, hand clutching her chest. 'What did you do?'

Desma sat up with a groan, uncurling her hand from the knife, everything numb and in pain. She looked at Korinna with eyes as bleak as the frosty sea. Her voice was hoarse when she spoke. 'They are together again.'

'Father-Killer,' Korinna said, her voice filled with revulsion.

Desma nodded. 'Father-Killer,' she agreed.

Cela waited with the rest of the assemblage in the megaron, the great throne hall of King Sophocles. The room was filled with hushed whispers, disdain and revulsion clear in the voices of the nobles, statesmen, and merchants.

The same feelings that roiled in her own heart, giving battle to her love for Desma.

It was three days since her father's death. Three days since his murder.

She had been heading to the shop to check on Desma and her father when she had heard a commotion from several streets away. She had gathered her dress in her hands and sprinted, arriving in time to see a flash of hair red as wine between the burly shoulders of city guards.

'Desma,' she had shouted, to no avail.

Faces turned towards her, eyes shadowed with fear and sorrow.

'What has happened?' she asked the nearest person, but they shook their heads and moved away, kissing their fingers and circling their heart, a call for the goddess.

Cela pushed her way to the shop to find Korinna standing in the doorway, face white as lamb fleece. 'Aunt, tell me what is happening!'

Korinna turned to her, eyes filling with tears though she held them in check. 'Cela, sweet child, I am so sorry ...' In broken sobs she spoke dark words, words that felt like a blight in the air, hideous and foul.

'It cannot be,' Cela said, pushing Korinna aside, ignoring her shouts, and running up the stairs. His door had been left open and she slowed, afraid to take the final steps.

A blanket had been draped over his body but it had soaked with blood. More pooled around the bed, red sandal-marks marring the floor from footsteps.

A small knife laid on the table beside the bed, dripping scarlet.

It was too much.

She ran from the building, taking side streets to avoid the crowd that followed the group of warriors as they marched up the cliff to the palace, a small, defeated figure huddled in their midst.

Cela eventually made it to the palace, a few minutes ahead of Desma. Built on the side of a protruding cliff face that kept the palace out of sight from most of Apasa, when one rounded the rock on the main road it often caught the viewer by surprise. Like the rest of the city, the palace was mostly carved directly from the sea-cliff, inseparable from Apasa herself. Rows of terrace gardens swept upwards until a wall of columns seemed to grow out of the rock. Though much of the palace was open to the air and ocean, the white marble and creamy brown stone made the palace feel warm and rich. Its roof was tiled in beige clay and rose quartz that sparkled at noon and blazed at sunset. Clevers from Trilos had engineered pumps that sourced water from the sea so it fell in twin rivers on either side of the palace, setting off rainbows at different times of the day and filling the air with invigorating salt.

It was a place Cela had visited often as a child with her mother, but it had been years since she stepped foot inside. Cela, Desma, Timothea, and her mother had all been invited to a feast which was planned for after the temple celebrations and for the king to announce the new square he would build in their honour.

Instead, she had watched Desma be escorted inside as a criminal. Cela hid behind a marble chariot bearing Laran, keeping out of sight. This was her sister, a woman she followed into wine and battle without hesitation. And now her hands were red with their father's blood. Her lips had remained silent as Desma passed, unable to bring herself to call her attention. Desma had disappeared through a set of doors and Cela was left alone, bereft suddenly of father and sister.

Cela was brought back from her reverie by the creak of the doors to the megaron opening. Two guards walked in, spears glinting brightly in the shafts of afternoon light that shone through the sungaps in the ceiling.

Desma was still wearing the same yellow peplos from when she had been arrested, though now it was stiff and brown. Her hands and face were still stained with old blood. She had torn a strip from the bottom of her dress and tied her hair back, trying to keep it from her face.

She walked in silence through the hall, her face blank and unnoticing of those around her. Cela could see the fear on the faces of the servants. The disgust from nobles. The anger from the warriors. One woman spat as Desma passed her.

Desma did not react.

Cela was to Desma's left, several rows in between them. Part of her wanted to be seen, to show Desma she was not alone, to give her the love and support that came as naturally as breathing.

But how was she to do that? Desma had killed their father. Cela knew it was to save his soul, to let him be with Timothea again in the Vales. But how could she have taken up the knife? Where did she find the will to follow through her act of salvation and patricide?

She watched Desma stumble when she caught sight of Melitta watching. The older priestess' face was cold as she stood with a dozen other women from the temple, all who had helped raise and teach her. None offered a smile or supportive look; they had already passed sentence.

Desma was stopped a dozen paces from the throne, one of the guards forcing her shoulders down into a bow.

Cela looked to the king.

Sophocles, Hero-King of Apasa, was a man past fifty. He sat in a chair of solid marble, carved with images of the Lovers, its back curved and arched. He was still a strong man, taking care to keep his skill with sword and spear keen as well as often visiting the Library of Kelus to study and debate. His face bore the slightest marks of age, thin lines radiating from his eyes and patterning his brow. His eyes were like the deep earth, as brown as the stones of the city in the shade.

He was admired by his people and his peers across the waves for being a fair and good-natured man, brave and thoughtful, always thinking before taking action. He had brought Apasa into a peaceful time of prosperity and was always the first to offer help when needed. But his trust was conditional. When broken, it was as likely to be regained as putting a shattered vase back together without cracks.

'Desma,' he said, his voice like rumbling rocks falling down a cliff. 'I have heard your story as you told it to my advisor. I have heard from your neighbour, Korinna. I have heard from people who have known you since you were in swaddling.' He leaned forward. 'But I am no closer to understanding your thoughts behind this action. Your father made a terrible choice, but what you did was worse. Do you understand, truly understand, what it is you have done?'

She nodded.

His eyes were intense. 'Do you? You stand here, in my court, before Apasa, covered in the dried blood of your father. Your mother is not even a month Beneath and now you send her husband to an early grave. You might claim you understand, but I doubt I ever will. But, to pass true and just judgement, I must strive. Do you wish to say anything?'

Cela wondered what she would say. Desma had three days alone in a cell to think about it. What speech would she give, what moving words to evoke passion and feeling, to share what Desma had seen and done with her hands? How would she bare her soul before her king and beg Apasa to understand?

Desma shook her head. 'No, my King.'

Cela's gasp was echoed around her, as condemning as the final stroke of a sword.

Sophocles leaned back in his chair, running a hand through his hair. 'Desma, if you do not speak, I must pass judgement on what I know. The law allows you a voice – use it! For the friendship I had with your mother, I will ask you one more time. Do you have anything to say?'

Cela's heart was like a rock in her chest, each beat pounding her sternum until it ached. Her stomach was crushing in its hunger and nausea as she looked upon her friend, her sister.

Desma had killed their father.

She had stabbed a knife into his heart and ended his life.

The law was clear.

Desma squared her shoulders, gathering the shreds of whatever strength she had left, and met the king's eyes. 'No.'

Cela saw when the merciful king, the man who looked down at his departed friend's daughter standing helpless before him, disappear. The king who took his place was the one trying to keep his city together, trying to heal the wounds of losing temple, priestess, goddess. He had to act.

'Then I will pass sentence,' he intoned. 'Desma, daughter of High Priestess Timothea and potter Palamaon, you have committed the crime of patricide.

You have slain your own father in his home and bed. Your hand alone wielded the knife, and his blood stains your skin. I hereby banish you from Apasa. Never again can you set foot in Turan's city while you are polluted.'

Desma's face was slate, clear of any emotion, an empty vessel. Cela had never seen her so devoid of fight, of strength and fire. She was like an unlit hearth.

The king continued. 'You are free to seek purification from king, priest, or oracle. As King of Apasa, I announce to all the world that I will never offer to purify this sin from you. As there is no oracle or high priestess to be made the request, there is no salvation for you here. All you own will be taken. If they do not belong to another, then they are ceded to the crown. You will be given one set of clothes, food for three days, and a coin each of gold and silver and copper.

'Your feet are now on a path of repentance and pilgrimage. As by the divine rule set by Tinia, you are not to request help in your journey but may accept it if offered. You must tell anyone you meet of your crimes so they know with whom they speak. If none offer to cleanse you, then your only hope is a life of service and prayer to be judged by the gods when you leave this life as to whether the Vale will be open to you. You are to leave the city before the next rain or you will be put to death by drowning. Such is the judgement of your king!'

He took the proffered clay cup from one of his attendants and cast it before him. The cup shattered on the marble floor, wine rich and purple splashing Desma's feet.

Hospitality had been revoked.

Citizenship had been revoked.

Family had been revoked.

'You are released under guard to make whatever arrangements you require. Remember, you cannot be in the city by the next rain. Begone.'

Desma did not take her eyes from the shards of the cup. The guards grabbed her arms and began to pull her back. She did not fight, allowing them to drag her from the court.

She had been cast from her home. Where would she go? Who would take her in? Where would she be safe?

Cela saw the choice she now had before her: stand with her city, help them to rebuild … or follow her friend. She stared at the spreading pool of red liquid, her mind flashing back to the shop. Wine as dark as the sea. As dark as Desma's hair. As dark as her father's blood.

CHAPTER SEVENTEEN

Four guards were ordered to escort Desma through the city. She was handed a bag with one set of travelling clothes and sandals, food, and her three coins as the law allowed.

She knew that word of her judgement by the king was already running through the city. The guards were there to protect her as much as to watch her. People she knew and people she had never spoken to cast curses at her, calling her father-killer and filthblood and outcast.

Her city, her home, turned against her with all their hatred and fear and useless rage at the misfortunes of Apasa. She now embodied them all. Several times during her journey she had to duck a piece of fruit or rock that was thrown.

The sky had darkened with the gathering of clouds. It was as if the gods themselves were hastening her departure. At the speed they were swelling, she doubted she had more than an hour or two to leave.

One man even tried to push his way past the guards, ignoring them in his bid to get to her. They shoved him to the ground with their shields and kept marching, tightening their circle around her. Their duty was to get her out of the city and they would fulfil their loyalty to their king. From the expressions on their faces, Desma knew they would prefer to leave her to the mercy of the citizens.

Desma could not remember the last time someone was banished from Apasa, and certainly no one in her lifetime. She knew the consequences that would come from what she did. But experiencing it was nothing compared to what she imagined.

But she had to do it.

She had to save her father. For her mother and for him.

For the love they had for each other.

It was worth the sacrifice.

They eventually made it relatively unscathed to her home. They entered the dim shop and Desma paused at the stairs, but she could not bring herself to climb them. She called Cela's name, but there was no response. She wasn't there.

She turned to her father's worktable, his wheel forever still. There was a parcel wrapped in orange cloth sitting on the wheel. She picked it up and carefully unwrapped it. It was a brooch. One of her mother's. A dove in flight, carved from a giant pearl, and entwined with sea glass myrtle. Her mother had a hundred brooches of similar designs. She wondered who would have left it here. Arete maybe? Or Cela – but then, where was she?

'Am I allowed to take this?' she asked, her voice shaking slightly. By law, all she owned was forfeit, but this was clearly a gift and she was allowed to accept help, in whatever fashion, if offered and not asked. She hoped they would see this as such.

The guards glanced at each other, frowns evident on their faces.

'It was my mother's,' she said quietly, her eyes darting to each of their faces. 'Please.'

Finally one of the guards, the oldest, nodded with a grunt.

Grateful, Desma went to slip it into her pocket but instead pinned it to her chest. She needed her mother close.

'Am I allowed to get changed?'

The same guard replied. 'No. You own nothing here. You were given one set of clothes. If you wish to change into those, you may.'

'Can I bathe?'

'You own nothing in this building. You cannot use the public baths, as you are banished from the city and not entitled to its amenities. You cannot ask a citizen to use their bath.'

'Can I use the sea?' she asked, flinging an arm westward. 'Am I allowed to use what is owned by Nethuns and none other?'

The guard hesitated. He withdrew to discuss it with his companions. Desma was furious at them and the king, and even at her father for putting her in this position. For gods' sake, she just wanted to take one damn bath.

The older guard stepped toward her. "Not within the harbour of Apasa," he said with a finality that ended any debate.

'Damn you all,' she swore. 'May your hearts be filled with cowardice in battle and Laran turn his head away in shame at your actions!'

His eyes darkened. 'If that is all you wanted to do, then I suggest we start heading for the cliffs. The clouds are heavy and your life is at stake.' His hand brushed his sword, his meaning clear. The second the first drop fell, they would drag her to the sea.

Desma opened the shop door and looked about, hoping that she would see a familiar head of golden wheat, hear her friend's voice. But what was she expecting? Her father was as much Cela's. What sister would stand by her side after what she had done?

The weight of the sky felt like it was settling on her shoulders. 'Let's go.'

They left the shop, a crowd having gathered in the street, their eyes flashing and words stinging. Father-killer, filthblood, outcast.

As they walked through the city, she kept looking around her, searching for Cela – or Khufu, or Arete, or Delphinus. Anyone.

Faster than she could believe, they were at the base of the main path up the cliffs. She looked back one last time, hoping she would see a familiar face. Nothing.

'We will wait here,' the older guard said. 'If we see you on the path when we feel the first drop of rain, your life is forfeit and we will hunt you down. Go.'

There was nothing else for her to do.

Desma began the climb.

She entered the dark, sulphurous workroom, choking on the stench and soot in the air.

Following the sound of a heavy hammer falling endlessly, metal ringing on metal, and the fierce crackle of fires that never grew cold, she folded her wings as tightly as she could to her body, but she knew a number of baths would be required to clean the oil and smoke from the feathers. Creation was a messy and dirty business. But a necessary one.

She ducked beneath an array of armour that hung from the ceiling, some made for men and others for giants, brushing past a row of spears that screamed silently for blood. The sound, unheard by mortals, made her cringe. Though as she passed by a doorway, she couldn't resist glancing through. Gold and silver and orichalcum, rubies and sapphires and amethyst – all wrought into items of such beauty they were decreed to never leave the domain of the divine, for the mortals would tear themselves apart for such treasure.

There was a reason she had chosen to marry the Forge God.

She eventually found him where he spent all his time, in his workroom. The forge in one corner heated the space to unbearable levels, a variety of tools older than most mountains hung neatly in their places, tables groaned with a thousand projects in various stages of completion.

Sethlans was in the far corner, hunched over a glowing rock that shimmered with the colours of sunset. He was slowly tapping away with a chisel, his face alight with fiery yellows and oranges. She took a moment to study him.

He was akin to a large boulder, skin constantly black from soot and red from flames, arms bulging with strength to bend metal and smash stone. His chest was wide and hairy, muscles rippling from ten thousand years of toil, but his back had a permanent hunch from bending over his craft without pause. His legs were trunks of massive trees which ended in feet that were turned backwards, causing him to walk with a limp and a cane, an imperfection that she did her best to not acknowledge.

It was said that during the war with the Beings, Tinia ordered Sethlans to build him fearsome weapons. The Forge God refused, claiming he was meant to create not destroy, and tried to forsake his craft altogether. Tinia descended from his throne and wrestled the mighty god to the ground, sat on his back, and twisted Sethlans' feet around, sending bolts of his power flowing into the shattered bones to heal disfigured. No magic can undo that of a god, not even another deity. Tinia then sat his brother at his worktable and told him to build and if he refused again it would be his head next.

She did not know if that was the truth, as he refused to ever speak about his impairment. She let it be, as it was useless to her either way.

She stood silently, waiting. Time was irrelevant in the halls of the divine. Eventually, he grew aware of her presence. Slowly, he drew away from his glowing stone, eyes as deep and dark as the earth blinked slowly as they refocused on her. As always, a hunger flickered awake in his face as he took her in and she did not blame him.

Her dress was the colour of deep lavender, a gold belt woven with viridian stones clasped her slender hips, with sandals softer than lamb wool peeking from beneath her hem. Orichalcum bracelets wove themselves from wrist to her bare upper arm, reminiscent of rose stems. Rings, gifted by her husband, flashed on every finger, each one a startling colour that could not be found in the mortal world.

Her face was a masterpiece, her dark, copper skin smooth from a cream made from the milk of Uni's blessed cattle, lips painted a pale peach, her eyes lined in gold-flecked kohl, gentle pools of sea foam that beckoned with promises whispered on a disappearing breeze. Her hair, the colour of ambrosial wine, of crushed berries, of the deep sea alight with a drowning sun, was loose and fell in waves down her back and over her shoulders, a cloak of shimmering scarlet.

'Wife,' he whispered harshly, his throat dry from the heat of the room, his brow beaded with black sweat. His face was as blunt as his mind was clever. Nose too broad, eyes lined deeply from squinting, mouth wide with teeth that were cracked. His beard was as thick and wiry as a boar's coat, several patches always smouldering with embers.

'Husband,' she said with a smile, her voice the stuff of dreams, violent passion wrapped in silk.

'Why are you here?' he asked. He knew she hated coming here, to what mortalkind called The Workshop, in Quirinale. She much preferred her city of light and birds and beauty in Aventinus, it was true. But she had a favour to ask. And one did not ask a favour after sending a summons.

'I wish to ask a boon of you.'

Sethlans leaned back on his chair, interest replacing mild suspicion. 'It has been an age since you've needed something from me, Wife.'

'I am independent,' she said with a shrug that caused her dress to slip down one shoulder.

The fires in the forge flared in response.

'We both know where this meeting will end,' Sethlans said, not bothering to hide the reaction she was causing in his body. 'Ask your favour.'

She went to open her mouth but he held up a hand.

'And, yet ... it must be important for you to come here. Something you want from me. Desperately. So, I will grant your favour – on one condition.'

Concern began to creep in her chest. Her husband was different to the rest of the gods. Despite their marriage, she always felt she understood him the least.

'The condition?' Her dress slipped from her other shoulder, falling completely to the floor, her body exposed. Arousal exploded in the room, their bodies reacting to the power of her magic, her essence.

'You know what I want,' he grunted, his voice hoarse now from want.

She froze. She knew what he was asking. What she had withheld from him for thousands of years. What she feared it could become.

But in the next thought she shrugged away all worries. That was what separated god from mortal. Almost nothing gave them fear, for what could threaten a god?

'Agreed.'

The evening vanished in a devouring feast of body and pleasure.

CHAPTER EIGHTEEN

Desma didn't know where to go.

Apasa was no longer her home. By the law and in her heart.

She was unclean. Foul. Tainted.

She was poison. Darkness. Corruption.

She was feared. Hated. Loathed.

She looked down at the city below her, shining dimly by the darkening sea. A city in mourning, a city without a purpose now that its goddess had abandoned them. A city rocked and shattered by travesty after scandal.

The sky above was just as dark as the sea. Clouds oppressively, morbidly, pressed down on the earth, as though expressing its own distaste at recent events.

She tripped and fell on the stony path. Her knees gashed open and the skin on her palms tore. Biting back her cries, she dragged herself upright and kept climbing.

She had to be out of the city before the rainfall, and the clouds looked about to split asunder any moment.

Not that she knew where she was going. Or to who. There was no one left. Not anymore. Because of her.

Patricide. Few crimes were as heinous in the eyes of man and god. The promise-breaking of host and guest. Incest. Blasphemy. Father-killer.

But she had to. She had to save him.

Sacrifice was revered by the gods. A warrior fighting a lost battle to give his comrades time to retreat to safety. A hero perishing with the monster to save the city instead of fleeing. A mother trading her life for those of her children to satisfy the hunger of the winter-starved bear.

But to take one's life in despair and grief, knowing that it would cause nothing but pain and anguish in others, achieving nothing but losing so much. A future blacked out before it could come alight. A thread severed by mortal hand rather than Inevitable Nurtia, Goddess of Fate. It was the needlessness of the act, the wastefulness, the casting of the gods' gift of life back into their faces. That was why those who took their lives were sealed from the Underworld. No entry to the Vales. No punishment in the Plains.

They were locked out and forgotten. Drifting in fog and dark waters, held together by their own memories until they too forgot who they were and faded into a fate worse than death – being forgotten by mortal and deity and earth.

Desma knew that her act had saved his soul, allowing him to be judged by the Three-Who-Speak-Doom, hoping that the good in his life would grant him a place in the Crocus Vales. To be with his wife again.

But the last thing her father saw was his own daughter plunging a knife between his ribs and into his heart. Blood so red it was black, glistening like rubies buried deep in the earth, flowed in waves over her hand, her lap, her legs. Her dress greedily lapped at every drop, staining from yellow to crimson. Wet and hot. So hot. Burning. Blazing. The heat was her father's life, cooling fast as death fell softly about him.

A sob broke from her throat as she finally reached the top of the cliffs. Falling heavily onto the dirt, she rolled onto her back, breath jagged and sharp.

She couldn't move. She couldn't muster one thought in front of another. Her fingers grappled at the earth, trying to grip something, someone. She did not know where her next step was meant to be. She did not know what her next words were supposed to be. She was adrift.

It crashed down on her with enough strength that she felt her bones break.

But no. It wasn't her bones.

It was her soul.

Mother was dead. Father was dead. The temple burned. Their goddess abandoned them. Her city turned its back on her.

Wounds so deep she knew they would never heal. Not completely. Weeping scars and blighted soul.

Her tears were lost in the downpour that began to fall from the sky. Rain as sharp as nails and cold as frost, hammering and piercing her skin.

With a deep groan, fingers digging into the stones until she felt her nails break, she pulled herself to her knees.

The sky and sea were indistinguishable. Grey and black and deep, deep blue. The city below was lost in the sheets of water pouring from above.

She pushed herself to her feet, staring at the heavens, unblinking as the rain lashed her.

'What was I meant to do?' she whispered.

Silence.

'What was I meant to do?' she suddenly screamed. 'Tell me, you bastards. *Tell me!*'

Wind slammed into her hard enough to knock her to the ground, vision spinning and teeth rattling for a moment.

Blinking the stars from her eyes, she got back to her feet, tasting blood in her mouth.

'What?' she said to the heavens. 'You don't like to be questioned? You don't like having someone ask what you would do in an impossible situation? Well, blast you. Blast all twelve of you—'

This time the wind lifted her from her feet and threw her several feet back. The rain was now arrows, striking hard enough to bruise her, howling to draw blood.

Desma spat to clear her mouth of blood and grit, her hair plastered about her face as she snarled. The wind screamed around her, buffeting and pushing her down as she strived to get up.

Tinia was mad. To raise a hand against one's father, to strike him down, to kill him … it was the worst of the blood crimes – despite the fact that he himself slayed his own creator to gain the thrones of the divine. Hypocrite. Liar. Bloody, thrice-damned, bastard.

She got to her feet, and planted her feet firmly, hands clenched defiantly. 'Honour thy father,' she said through her teeth, her words ripped away by the wind. 'That is your commandment. Yet you would have preferred I let him take his own life and be banished from the Underworld? To be forgotten? One moment of weakness, of immeasurable grief, and ... You. Don't. Care.'

Thunder shattered the sky as lightning splintered, illuminating the world for a single moment in stark white.

Desma, alone on the sea-cliffs, her home lying below her, the sea a roiling behemoth.

Desma, alone before the gods high and low.

Desma, alone without family.

Desma alone.

'My father couldn't turn my mother into a tree, a flower, a constellation. He couldn't turn her into a new creature of earth or sea. He was powerless. He could only take what was his and his alone. And yet I am punished because I had to commit a crime that at least I have a chance to be redeemed from. Once my father was dead, he had no more chances.'

Thunder threatened to take her hearing. She could feel the ground shake and rocks go sliding off the cliffside. Lightning was striking the sea so fast one bolt hadn't ended before another was thrown.

And where was Turan in all this? Where was the goddess her family had dedicated their lives too? The Goddess of Love and Desire. A goddess who was greater. The cruellest of her family.

Her hand reached for her heart. Slowly, her fingers closed over the brooch on her chest, her mother's. The dove and myrtle entwined. With a jerk, she ripped it from her dress.

Her lips curled in contempt. Never had she felt such anger, such futile loathing. A primal scream ripped from her throat as she hurled the brooch out over the cliff. She lost sight of it immediately in the black and white flashing of the clouds and lightning, until a shaft of lightning, blush pink instead of brilliant white, shot from the clouds and struck the brooch, exploding midair that made Desma shout as her world turned a hazy red.

Then black.

She wasn't sure how long she was out but when her eyes slowly cracked open the sky above was a clear and harsh blue.

The sun was cleared above the horizon, so she must have been knocked out for at least twelve hours. Her clothes were still damp and her skin stung as she moved, breaking open still new cuts and scrapes. She sat up and froze.

Surrounding her were dozens of rose bushes, all without blooms. But each bush was filled with wickedly long thorns all pointed inwards ... towards her.

She gulped. Turan's message was as clear as the day. Desma was under the eyes of Tinia while she was on her quest for purification. But she had been warned. The goddess would not tolerate any more blasphemy from her.

With great care, she managed to get to her feet but realised she would need to make her way through the bushes. There was no path for her.

Bitch, she thought to herself, careful not to say the word aloud. It was only wise to push a goddess so far.

It took ten minutes to make her way through the bramble, each thorn sharper than glass. By the time she broke free, her dress was little more than scraps.

She couldn't start her journey this way. She quickly stripped, discarding her dress onto a rose bush, and slid on the one change of clothes the city provided her. They were damp from the night's rain, but at least they were not covered in blood both fresh and three days old. She kept her sandals, planning on cleaning them at the next river she came across, putting them in her bag. A quick search found a stout stick that came to shoulder height and would make a good walking staff.

She glanced down at the city, scoured clean by the violent rains. Ships were sailing out of the harbour, people were milling through the streets. Faint strains of music and chatter floated up the cliff. The city would recover. Her king was strong and her people brave. She turned away and scoped out her options.

She could travel south, but no major cities within the League lay that way. Eventually, she would reach the sea again and either turn east or find a ship. The east would be of no help as none of their kings or priests could cleanse her. She could find a ship and sail to Konoso, with their Bronze-King and horned priestesses. But they were a fierce and strange people. They would just as likely sacrifice her as help her.

To the west, across the sea, were the bulk of the Kingdoms. She would have to find a captain willing to take her on as a passenger and she could not ask for help. The chances were slim.

That left the north. Trilos lay that way, Apasa's closest neighbour. Mynta's home. At this moment, she might be her only friend left. And she could make it the whole way on foot, which would lessen the need to find someone who would offer her help.

She could not stop herself looking eastwards, though. To the temple. There was no reason for her to go there. There was nothing for her.

Nothing except ruins and death.

She started walking northwards.

Desma knew she was being followed.

It was the fourth day of what she estimated would take around fifteen days to walk to Trilos.

On her first night, she had camped beside a creek and spent an hour in the river scrubbing her skin and hair. And then another hour. Eventually, her arms were shaking from the effort of washing her hair but every time she ran her fingers through she still felt phantom patches of congealed blood.

As she walked, she foraged some food along the way; but it was mostly handfuls of wild herbs and a wizened apple tree that only had three pieces of fruit not already gnawed on. She ate half a loaf of bread with it, wanting to stretch the food she was given as long as possible.

Her stomach was unhappy with the measly offering, but it may be even worse in the days to come. She only had three coins to her name and could not ask for food. Yet, somehow, she had to make it to Trilos.

But she was alive. She had breath and will and strength. That gave her hope.

The next three days were the same, filling her bag with the abundance of herbs and greens she found growing alongside the road, moving aside when she passed other travellers, keeping her head down. By law, if any stopped to speak with her she would have to explain her crime. Though she knew, in her heart of hearts, that what she did was the right thing, it was still a murder. And she could not cope with having to tell it for the first time to a stranger.

At night she would find a grove or shallow spot off the road, not lighting a fire as the nights were warm and she was sheltered from the sea winds. She thought about trying to catch a rabbit, but had no ropes for snares or a knife to clean it. She did not particularly want to cook a rabbit with the fur on. Fruits and plants would have to sustain her.

By the fourth day, she was hungrier than she had ever been in her life. She made do with mint and oregano, an odd apple or fig, chewing on rosemary stalks as she walked, eating morsels of bread and dried goat. The food she was given would have barely stretched to three days and she wanted it to last at least a week, if not longer.

But an hour before noon on the fourth day, she knew someone was behind her. When she topped a rise she looked back and saw a figure. She dismissed it as another traveller and kept going. A little while on, at the top of another hill, she checked back and saw the figure was even closer and moving with haste. Thinking that perhaps they were a messenger on an errand, she decided to wait until they were closer and she would move off the road.

Not long after, she looked back again and realised they were not a messenger. Messengers were trained as youths to run for hours without stopping, carrying only a small waterskin and a bag of food they could eat on the move. And they would wear a multicoloured ribbon that would stream behind them as they ran to show they were on an errand and under the protection of Turms, Herald of the Gods.

Whoever this was had their hair swept back and under a simple cap, and kept stopping and starting as they hurried, catching their breath before moving again swiftly.

Wary, Desma moved off the road the moment she was out of sight of the person, hiding behind a shrub so she could see the stretch of road.

Ten minutes later, the runner appeared, breathing heavily. They climbed the slope of the hill and paused. She watched them shade their eyes as they peered forward. She tried to get a glimpse of their face but when she moved her staff rustled the bush.

The figure's head spun towards her and Desma swore.

She rose from her hiding place, staff in front of her, ready to fight.

'Blood and bone, you are quicker than Tinia when he sees a maiden sunning herself on a riverbank,' her pursuer laughed, pushing the cap off their head, revealing their golden wheat hair.

CHAPTER NINETEEN

'Cela,' she said, incredulous. Desma dropped her staff on the ground, tears starting to well up. 'Cela?'

'Oh my gods, Desma.' Her friend ran down the hill and threw her arms around her. It took Desma a few seconds to wrap herself around her friend in return. Her body began to shake and she let her sobs break free. Her friend smelled like cassia and wildflowers, and the familiar feel of her embrace was more than she could handle.

They both slid to the ground and Cela let her have a few moments to compose herself.

'What are you doing here?' she finally asked her friend.

'Looking for you,' Cela said. 'We figured you would head for Trilos, but we didn't think you would cover this much ground in four days. We were miles behind thinking we were ahead of you.'

'We?'

Cela blinked. 'Me and the crew.'

Desma let out a half-sob, half-laugh. 'I don't understand. Why are you following me?'

Cela cocked her head, confused. 'To ... help you.'

'No, you can't,' Desma said, shaking her head. 'I cannot ask for help.'

'But you can accept it if it is offered,' Cela reminded her. 'And I am offering. So don't be stupid and say thank you.'

Desma let out a laugh. 'Thank you. But why?'

'Because you're my sister.'

Desma's heart grew tight in her chest. 'But I killed our father.'

Cela's eyes grew sad. 'I know. And I know why. I don't know what I would have done in your stead. But I see the love behind your action. You gave him another chance to be with Timothea. For eternity. You were given an impossible choice. I know where the law stands. But you are my friend, my sister. I will help you clear your name and blood.'

'What about your mother? And the temple? You should be helping them rebuild.'

Cela waved her hands in front of Desma's face. 'Do these hands look like they were made to carve stone and dig dirt? No. And the king has an entire kingdom to draw from. No one will miss me.'

'Your mother?'

'The infection has been contained,' Cela said. 'They fear she will lose her leg, but a priest of Esplace is to arrive and has offered to lend their gift. She will be fine and will be too busy to miss me, since she was proclaimed the new high priestess.'

'Did you …?'

Her friend nodded. 'I said my goodbyes.'

There was one last, burning question Desma wanted to ask. One she feared the answer to the most.

Before she had a chance, Cela stood up and brushed the dust from her clothes.

'Come,' she said, offering her hand. 'Let's go back to the others.'

Desma took her hand gladly, the weight on her shoulders lessening slightly.

Cela shared some peaches with her as they walked back south and she refused to answer any more of Desma's questions until they met up with the rest of the crew. It was a few hours walk before they reached a shallow beach that offered a break from the cliffs. Lazing under the afternoon sun and idly chatting were her crew … her friends.

Khufu sat on a rock, whittling a small block of wood, while Arete spoke animatedly to him, drawing in the sand with a stick. Kassandra listened wistfully to Delphinus strumming away on a lyre, his eyes closed as he swayed with the music. Bion laid shirtless on the sand, napping through the heat and lulled by the waves.

Cosmas was not in sight.

Kassandra was the first to spot them. The overseer leapt to her feet with a shout, sending a spray of grit into Delphinus' face as she sped towards them. She slammed into Desma, tackling her to the ground with a laugh. Before Desma could catch her breath, Bion lifted both of them up into the air, roaring a welcome.

'Put them down, you great bear,' Cela shouted, smacking his arm.

Once she was back on her feet, Desma swept her hair back from her face, her eyes flicking to each of them. 'Do you really understand what you are all doing? You are hitching your wagon to me: a tainted woman. There is no guarantee that I will ever be cleansed. I might fail. You could be doing anything. You can go back to your homes, or to Apasa and help rebuild. Take the ship and sail around the Middle Sea, cause havoc and brawls, enjoy your lives.'

'Girl, has there ever been a time when you have set your mind to something and failed?' Bion asked in his blunt way. 'We know well what you did. I cannot say I would have done the same in your position, but I understand why you did it. Your father was a good man. And he became a sad man who made a mistake. I don't think it is just to be punished forever because of grief. You did what you did out of a desperate love. There was no hate or malice in your heart. For that reason alone, girl, I am willing to follow you. I am offering you help, without any need of persuasion or trickery, in full knowledge of your crimes. Accept it and let us be there.'

Desma laid a hand on his burly chest with a smile. 'I accept your help, Bion.'

Each of the others stepped forward and offered their assistance in turn, and for each of them she accepted until by the end she had tears once again shimmering down her face.

After the last person, Khufu, stepped back, she looked around. 'Did Cosmas stay in Apasa?'

Arete snorted. 'Would he do anything so bland? He always has to be the mysterious one.'

Desma looked at her confused.

'He's gone ahead of us to Trilos,' Cela said. 'He said that is where you would be heading and he would wait for us there.'

'He did the smart thing and went by ship. He should be there already if the winds are fair,' Khufu said with a pointed look.

'How was I meant to get on a ship if I can't ask someone?' Desma defended. 'So, I started walking.'

'Well, thank Menrva for commonsense,' Arete said, 'because we brought a ship.' She pointed to where sand met wave.

Desma's eyes swept over the ship that was not the trireme she had docked in the harbour upon their return from Urruc. It was less than a quarter of the size, needing only ten rowers, with a single mast with sails the colour of deep wine. But it was a beautiful craft of pine, fir, and cedar, stained to a deep, bronzed colour. It was obviously built by a master shipwright.

'That's not our ship,' she said slowly.

'Not exactly,' Cela admitted. 'When we heard the king's decree, we set about arranging to follow you but figured it would be best to offer our help outside of Apasa. The sentiment running through the city was unkind towards you.'

'To say the least,' Delphinus chipped in helpfully.

'But we thought dragging a trireme with over two hundred men to chase after you was a little excessive.'

'And a lot of the rowers took up Theokritos' offer to join the temple guard,' Kassandra said. 'I went with them to vouch in front of the captain.'

Cela cut in. 'So, I bought this ship. It only needs ten rowers and is as quick as a seal dodging a spear.'

'Tell her its name,' Bion said excitedly.

Desma waited expectantly.

'*The Darkling*,' Cela announced with a grand sweep of her arm.

Desma frowned. 'I don't get it.'

'She is *The Darkling* and we are her darklings,' Kassandra explained.

She was still confused.

'Because of your hair,' Cela said exasperated. 'Wine-dark, like your mother's, and like the sea. Hair famed throughout the League. It is our standard, our flag, our sigil.'

'You have not disappeared from history yet, daughter of Timothea and Palamaon,' Arete said with a still voice. 'You have not finished with the world.'

'If it makes you feel any better, I voted to be called the wine-men,' Delphinus said. 'It was not received well.'

She shifted uncomfortably. Before they had sailed together in service of the temple. Desma was in charge, Cela her second, and Khufu the captain. But they all answered to her mother and, ultimately, to Turan.

The only purpose she had left in this world was the faint hope of clearing her name and her blood. If the day she was cleansed for her crimes ever came, she had no plans for what would come after. Her friends were assembling under her and she did not know what to do. She was alone. There was no one above her to seek wisdom or guidance or orders.

Her world began to spin.

She felt someone slip a hand into hers.

'The next step is to find someone who will cleanse you,' Cela said. 'Only the gods know where this path will take us. Once we have achieved what we set out to do, then we can reassess. One plan at a time. Agreed?'

'Agreed,' she said.

'Then are we ready to head for Trilos?' Khufu asked.

Desma breathed in the salt on the wind that billowed her hair out like a flag, deep and bright and unmistakable.

'Ready,' she said.

The Darkling waited to set sail.

BOOK TWO:
UNRAVELLING

CHAPTER TWENTY

In the few days it took to sail to Trilos, Desma had planned with the others what they would do once they reached the city. They beached the ship in the section marked for travellers without goods; Khufu spoke to the beachmaster and was given an iron ring that had to be displayed on their prow while they were in the city and Bion went off to see if he could find Cosmas.

'Or wander around until he finds me,' the helmsman said.

Kassandra went to The Forge to see if she could gain an audience with the high priest, while Arete volunteered to go to the palace. Cela eventually convinced Desma that she should stay on the ship to avoid any trouble until they heard back and understood the mood of the city in the wake of events in Apasa.

It chafed her to stay on the boat. Redemption was so close and yet still fragile.

She would not be surprised if the high priest denied her request. His god was husband to their goddess. And Turan had made it abundantly clear that Apasa now meant nothing to her. They had a better hope with the king. But, as Arete pointed out, the king may not want to cause trouble with Sophocles by cleansing one he marked foul.

Towards sunset, both Arete and Kassandra returned without good news. They could not see the king or high priest that day and were told to come back in the morning.

The next three days passed the same.

Arete and Kassandra set off, while the rest of the crew took turns bringing supplies from the city back to the ship. Cela stayed onboard with Desma, trying to soothe her frayed nerves but she felt like she was going to tread a hole in the deck with her pacing. Evening on the third day had her stabbing her knife into the mast in frustration when her friends returned once more without securing an audience.

'Did you manage to talk to anyone? Tell them why you need to see them?' she asked.

Arete nodded. 'I spoke to one of his ministers yesterday and explained. He seemed ... indifferent. He said he would speak to the king. But I could not see the same man today.'

'The priest I see every day just says the same thing,' Kassandra said. 'He says, "Such requests cannot be rushed to judgement. Divine advice must be sought. Forgiveness is the province of the gods and man simply conveys the gift."'

Desma audibly gritted her teeth.

'What do you want to do?' Cela asked.

Desma looked up towards the city, backlit by the fiery glow of The Forge that never ceased. 'Perhaps it is time for me to state my own case,' she said. 'Khufu, Arete, and Kassandra, I want you to come with me.' She pulled a hooded cloak from her bag and flung it around her shoulders, tucking her hair into the hood and darkening her face in its shadows. 'To the temple.'

They walked with Khufu in front under the purpling sky, Arete by her side with the overseer taking up the rear. The hope was they could make it to the temple without Desma having to deal with anyone directly. By law, she would have to state her crime and punishment to anyone who spoke to her.

Fortunately, they made it without interruption through the city.

It was built very differently to the sea-cliff city of Apasa. Trilos was constructed in a massive square, the city portioned into even sections with straight roads. The people were similar to the Apasans with olive-brown skin, rich dark hair, and eyes that were more curved than the rest of the League.

The palace was set in the exact centre of the city, a walled keep with four towers and a central court. They skirted around the palace and headed for the temple of Sethlans to the far east of the city. The temple was built with the same straight lines that dominated the rest of the city, with one central tower set within the main gate. The entire building was covered in sheets of orichalcum, a material only the devotees of Sethlans knew how to forge. It looked like gold suspended in a liquid state and set alight within. Fire and gold, symbols of Sethlans.

Two automatons stood guard by the entrance, their helms crafted into crowns of flame, the hammer and tong burned into their chest armour. Waves of heat could be felt spilling out of the main gate as they drew near. It was said one hundred by one hundred fires burned within the temple and Desma could feel awe creep into her bones.

She had grown up in the temple at Apasa, learning to crawl and speak in the naos, playing hide and seek from priestesses – Turan's divinity had felt as natural as the ground and sky. But here was Sethlans' domain, and the fierce, wild flames of creation made her skin hot and tight, as though she had been burned by the sun

Their party entered the temple unchallenged.

'The furthest I ever got was through the left here,' Kassandra pointed down a hall. Desma moved without hesitation, Khufu having to hurry until he was again in front.

A priest, wearing gold and red robes fringed in white, stepped out of a room and held up a hand. 'What can I do for you?' he asked, his eyes narrowing on Kassandra. 'Ah, you again.'

'I need a shield that will cause blades to glance off with every stroke,' Khufu said, moving so that he blocked the priests against the wall. 'Not one that will absorb the impact, meaning the strength in my arm wanes with every blow, but one that sends the sword dancing away. How much would one of those be?' He pulled out a pouch that clinked heavily.

The priest's eyes darted to the sound of money. 'Interesting concept,' he said. 'It would be all about the angles …'

Kassandra caught Desma's hand and pulled her through another door quickly, Arete following.

They passed through three more doors and down two curving corridors before a group of Clevers, marked by an armband of gold with an orichalcum hammer, came out of a large room. Kassandra pushed Desma behind a statue.

'Wait until we leave and head down to a black door covered in flames and waves. That should be the high priest's rooms.'

The Clevers noticed the two of them and approached.

'Good evening,' Arete said. 'I've got an idea I want to discuss about a three-forked catapult.'

'You should not be here,' one of the men said. 'Who let you into this area?'

Kassandra shrugged. 'No one, if you put it that way. But technically no one stopped us either. We just wandered around until we bumped into you.'

'You need to leave,' he warned. 'One of the acolytes in the devotion rooms will take your ideas.'

'If you insist,' the overseer sighed. She turned to Arete. 'I guess they don't want to know about the prototype of Taitle's Claw you built that actually worked. Let's go.'

'Wait, hold on,' the man said. 'We'll walk with you.'

'No, no, no,' Kassandra said, shooing them away. 'We'll talk to an acolyte and make sure to let them know who sent us their way. What was your name again?'

The Clevers fell over themselves to escort them to the devotions room, peppering the stunned Arete with questions about how she built a device whose design has been long lost.

The shipwright shot a glare at Kassandra and began speaking rapidly, talking about weight distribution and leverage advantage and fulcrums. As they passed Desma, pressed up in the narrow space between the wall and statue, Kassandra gave her a wink. Once the group rounded the corner, Desma stepped out of her hiding place and kept walking.

She passed forge rooms and workshops filled with carpenters, gem cutters, sculptors, and armourers. She could have wandered for days in amazement. But she had to hurry before she bumped into someone else.

The main corridor she was on fortunately ended in the black doors Kassandra had described. It had no handles or hinges, but a single gold plate with the depression of a hand. She knocked on the wood but it made no sound. She banged harder but, besides bruising her hand, it made no difference. She looked for a rope that could be connected to a bell, like some of the rooms in Apasa's palace had, but nothing.

She moved to the gold plate. The handprint was large, far larger than even Bion's hand. With no other option, she placed her hand in the depression and pushed. It warmed and then cooled under her palm. She heard a great whirring and grinding before the door split along an invisible seam and swung open silently.

Desma walked in.

It was a large room, made up of several galleries with thin windows spaced across the walls to peer out over the city. The floor was red flagstone and the walls unblemished white marble; the ceiling featured a mural, rimmed in gold, of Sethlans sitting at a table with the world between his hands, his tools scattered around him. The office was filled with dozens of tables covered in projects at various stages of completion. Like any of his priests and acolytes and Clevers, the high priest was skilled in the art of creation.

The man himself was sitting at one such table with his back to Desma. His robes of office were cast over a stool and he was wearing a simple chiton. A strip of cloth was bound across his brow to keep his sweaty brown hair from his eyes. He was hunched over whatever he was working on, completely absorbed in his task and unaware of her presence.

She gave a polite cough.

There was an audible crack and a plume of purple smoke filled with lightning rose above the table.

'Shit and fire,' the high priests cursed, rolling away from the table on a stool that Desma could now see had little wheels attached to the bottom of the legs.

As he moved away from the smoke, the stool spun slowly and came to a stop with the high priest's surprised and annoyed eyes piercing across the room at her. He was an older man, in his late forties, his upper body well-muscled from hours at the forge, his hands scarred yet delicate. A bushy beard covered the lower half of his face and his eyes were hazel with flecks of gold. He stood slowly up, cracking his back as he stretched and shaking his legs. 'Gods, how long was I sitting there?' he groaned.

'High Priest,' Desma said respectfully, bowing with her arms outstretched, her hair falling from her hood and spilling across her shoulders.

The priests sighed. 'Timothea's daughter. Your friend is persistent. I see part of her persistence was to find out where my rooms were located.'

'She is forward-thinking,' she agreed. 'High Priest.'

'Call me Castur,' he said with a wave as he turned back to his project. 'Damn, this is ruined.'

'Sorry,' she said. 'I did try to knock.'

'The door is designed to absorb sound. And powerful enough to stop one of those elephants from the Great Lands. When you put your hand in the key it rings a bell for me to hear ...' He fell quiet. Slowly, he turned back around to face her, eyes blazing with interest. 'But it didn't ring. Why?'

Desma felt the question was not for her.

'That door only opens to the high priest, those anointed by Sethlans himself, a descendant of the god ...' He stood up and walked over, his bronze-studded sandals ringing against the floor. When he got near he grabbed her arm, squeezing with considerable strength.

'Ow, release me!' She struggled in his grasp until he let go.

'You are not a daughter of Sethlans,' he stated.

'Good to know,' she said, rubbing her arm.

'Fascinating,' he said again. 'What is it you want, Timothea's daughter?'

'My name is Desma,' she said. 'And I have come to ask for the act of purification. As decreed by the laws of Tinia, I must share my story so you know with whom you speak.'

'I know what you did, daughter of priestess and potter,' Castur said, folding his bulging arms. 'You slaughtered your own father to help him escape the gods' punishment. Sophocles will not cleanse you and a high priestess was chosen only after you left, and I doubt she would have helped you. The closest city to offer you a chance was Trilos. So, now you stand in The Forge before me to ask if I will perform the rites of purification.'

Desma allowed the smallest flutter of hope. 'Will you?'

Castur was silent for several long moments, small eternities it felt to her. 'No. I will not.'

Anger, hot and fast, flashed through her before she clamped down on it.

'I see what you feel, Timothea's daughter,' he said, not unkindly. 'But I cannot help you. My god is husband to your goddess. Turan has withdrawn her hand from Apasa, clear for all the world to see. The Empire is her home. Her displeasure is plain in Apasa and in you. I will not come between my god's wife and her outcasts. Your journey will have to continue.'

Desma reached for a nearby stool and sat down, not caring that she wasn't invited to take a seat. 'The king is my next option.'

Castur rolled on his stool to be next to her. 'I do not speak for the king and I try to have as little to do with his court as possible. However, my advice to you would be not to have too much hope with him.'

'You think he will say no?' she asked.

'Perhaps, if it was his decision alone, he would choose to help you,' Castur said carefully. 'But the king has not inherited the strength of will of his father. The Council grows stronger each passing year, and some voices are heard more than others.'

'Should I search elsewhere?' Why waste her time in Trilos if she had little chance?

'I am not Aplu,' Castur smiled, naming the God of Foresight. 'I cannot see the future. But I do not think this quest will be an easy or quick one. I have only now met you, but I can see that you have much to do in this world, should you choose to walk that way. Our lives are threads woven into a great tapestry, but some people are themselves weavers who can change both the weave of their own fates and the threads of those around them – in both remarkable and ofttimes disastrous ways.

'At every step of your life you have a choice. What you choose will always be up to you, but that does not mean there is a right or wrong, better or worse path.'

A faint chime began to ring out in the room, growing louder with each passing second.

'Someone is at the door,' the high priest said, standing up and offering his hand.

Desma took it and got to her feet. 'Thank you for at least hearing my words,' she said.

'I am sorry it took so many days,' he said. 'I suppose I did not wish to have to look you in the eye when I denied your request. Your mother and I were friends. I miss her.'

Desma blinked away a tear and nodded.

Castur placed a heavy hand on the crown of her head. 'May the fires of his Forge light your path, daughter of Timothea.'

'Thank you,' she said with a bow.

Castur waved his hand and the black door opened to allow two priests to enter. They both started when they saw her.

'Ah, good timing. Can one of you please escort Desma back to the city?'

One of the priests nodded and beckoned her to follow.

When they passed the door, she turned and waved farewell before Castur was lost from view, and she wondered why his face was so sad.

The priest walked in silence and she was glad to not have to talk. When they arrived at the gates, Arete and Kassandra were waiting, the former sketching on paper and the latter pacing nervously.

'There you are,' Kassandra said, relief clear in her voice. 'Any luck?'

Desma shook her head. 'Where's Khufu?'

Arete jerked her head towards the beach. 'Went to see if anyone has found Cosmas yet.'

'Let's go,' Desma said. 'I'm tired.'

And she was. The hope that had been quietly burning inside her while they sailed grew a little dimmer. Perhaps Castur was right. This would not be as easy as she wished. 'We'll go to the palace in the morning.'

CHAPTER TWENTY-ONE

A half hour later, they arrived back at the beach to find a group of thirty men with weapons and torches surrounding the ship.

Her crew were facing them, swords in hand, with Khufu and Cela arguing with the beachmaster.

Desma and the others pushed their way through. 'What is happening?'

'This piece of *gribushu*,' Khufu said, swearing in his native language, 'is telling us that our berth has been revoked. He arrived with these *men* to retrieve the iron ring and to ensure we set sail.'

The beachmaster, an average sized man darkened from spending everyday under the sun, waved a scroll towards them. 'I have received orders to have your ship leave the beaches of Trilos tonight. My men are here to keep the peace. We will give you one hour.'

Desma stepped towards him and attempted to take the scroll. 'Who ordered it?'

The beachmaster moved away from her and two of his men blocked her from getting closer.

Desma grew furious. 'How do we know this is legal if you will not let us see the paperwork?'

His men rattled their swords. 'That is the paperwork,' the beachmaster said with a mean grin. 'Please direct your complaints to them.'

Desma gave him another glare and moved back to her crew.

'We could take them,' Delphinus said, 'but it will be bloody.'

She shook her head. 'No, it will just bring the city guards. I don't know who is behind this but it might play into their hands if we attack.'

'Are we just to leave?' Kassandra asked. 'We haven't spoken to the king yet.'

'Maybe it is the king's orders,' Delphinus suggested.

'I don't think so,' Desma said, thinking back to what Castur said.

'What do you think we should do?' Cela asked.

An idea struck her. 'Cela, did Mynta not say to us that we are welcome to Trilos at any time to see her?'

Cela nodded slowly. 'She did. But why ... oh!'

'Exactly.' Desma turned back to the beachmaster. 'We will happily return the iron ring to you,' she said loudly for all to hear. 'And, in return, we would like you to fetch us a silver ring.'

The beachmaster laughed. 'Why would I give you a silver ring?'

'As we have an open invitation from Amynta, daughter of Emissary Linos, we are entitled to a silver ring as guests of a city official,' Desma explained with painstaking slowness. 'Or do you wish to force us to offer insult to Emissary Linos for not visiting our dear, *dear*, friend, his daughter? Will you convey word yourself to offer our apologies?'

The beachmaster looked uncomfortable. He opened the scroll and beckoned one of his men closer with a torch. He read the words again, peering closer to the bottom of the scroll where the person who ordered it no doubt had their name. Eventually, he pushed the man away, winding the scroll back up, and cleared his throat.

'As guests to Emissary Linos, Councilor to the King, you are welcome in Trilos. We will give you a silver ring and, as is customary, you have one day to provide proof of friendship or invitation, otherwise the ring will be rescinded.'

'Understood,' Desma said with a smile. 'I bid you a goodnight, beachmaster.' She turned away.

'One moment,' he called after her.

She looked at him, wondering what was next.

'I know who you are,' he said slyly. 'And I know what judgement hangs over you.'

Dread filled her stomach, blooming upwards into her chest and throat. She had forgotten. She had spoken to the beachmaster and his men.

'The law is clear,' he continued. 'You must tell anyone who speaks with you what you have done so they know with whom they are dealing. You have failed to do so.'

She was frozen.

He gestured around him. 'We are listening.'

Her crew tightened with white-hot tension around her. She stepped forward, so she was between the two groups, a placating hand held toward her friends.

'I am Desma, daughter of the High Priestess of Turan from Apasa and her husband, Palamaon the potter. After the death of my mother during the destruction of the temple at the hands of Empyrean warriors, my father succumbed to his grief.' She paused to take a deep, shaking breath.

The beachmaster tapped his foot impatiently.

'I found him after he had stuck a knife into his chest,' she continued. 'He was still alive. I knew that if he died by his own hands he would be barred from entering the Vale.' The sight of him bleeding on his bed returned vividly. 'I could not let that happen to him. I picked up his knife and I stabbed him in the heart.'

The men hissed.

She could feel again the hot blood pouring over her hands, the horror in his eyes, the frail gasps of his last breaths. 'I killed him so that he could gain entry to the Vale and be with his wife, my mother, until time ends.'

'Father-Killer,' one of the men spat.

'Hero-King Sophocles decreed my blood is filth,' she continued, each word heavier than the last. 'I am on a path of redemption to cleanse my blood and my life.'

The beachmaster bared his teeth when he grinned. 'As I understand the law, you failed to provide your story before we spoke, and I am granted the right to ask for a gesture of contrition. Is that not so?'

Desma's teeth felt like they would shatter with how hard she was grinding them. 'True.'

'What should I ask for, boys?' he asked.

The men began hollering out suggestions, each cruder than the last until Bion had to hold Delphinus back from unleashing himself on those closest to them.

'Get him on the ship,' Cela snarled at Bion.

The beachmaster held up a hand, quietening the group. 'Get on your stomach and beg for my forgiveness.'

The bastard.

She didn't move.

He leaned forward, an edge entering his voice. 'Get on your stomach like a worm and beg that I forgive your transgression. Or should I seek a priest of Tinia to report your blasphemy?'

Death. His. Long and slow and bloody. She imagined it in intricate detail..

But he was in the right. She broke the law, and it was his right to demand an act as long as it would not inhibit her ultimate quest for purification.

She began to kneel.

'At my feet, if you please.'

Forcing herself to walk over to him, she kept her eyes on the ground, unable to look into his leering face as she lowered herself into the sand, her face hovering just above the ground. 'I ask your forgiveness.'

'And I am most graciously willing to accept it, on one last condition.' He laughed. 'Eat the sand.'

Desma's chest was leaden; where before there was fiery anger, there was nothing but a cold emptiness. Swallowing her disgust, she took a bite of the beach.

Sand and grit crunched in her mouth as she chewed, the clump becoming heavy and thick as it soaked up her saliva. She tried to force it down but as soon as it touched her throat she began to cough. She pushed herself up, hacking and gagging as she spat. When she was finally able to take a clear breath, she looked up at the beachmaster, on her hands and knees, eyes red and teary.

The man gave her one final grin. 'Apology accepted,' he said with a noble air. 'Have a pleasant evening.' Laughing, he left with the other men.

Desma stayed on ground until Cela and Arete ran over, pulling her to her feet. Khufu and Kassandra were aggressively dispersing the crowd that had gathered from the other ships to watch the display. They all knew who she was now. And had seen what she had to do.

Shame. Disgust. Filth.

Mynta knew the moment the ship was secured on the golden beach who had arrived in Trilos.

For whom else would travel on a ship with sails the colour of dark wine?

She had waited for three days but no friend had brightened her door. Would they come to visit her? It had been a year since they had last seen each other and so much had changed for the three of them.

She had wept when news of the attack on Apasa reached her city. She had begged her father to let her sail south, to make sure Desma and Cela were alive, but he had refused. She had sent a dozen messengers, handing out gold drachmae without care, until she finally had a reply from Cela.

She could not imagine the pain they were going through, and to learn High Priestess Timothea was killed ... she had again pleaded with her father to let her go, but he was resolute.

And then word came later of a new father-killer, cursed by Tinia and banished by Hero-King Sophocles. A daughter who slew her own father as he drowned in his grief. Mynta's father had told her over breakfast, matter-of-factly, as she reached for another bread roll. Her hand had frozen, face gone slack, as her mind grappled with his words. He had simply finished his last mouthful before leaving the table, leaving her alone to deal with the news her best friend was a murderer.

It was her nursemaid who told her the rest of the details later that night. Mynta had cried again, both in relief that Desma was not a cold-blooded killer but also at the terrible ordeal of her friend. To lose both parents in a span of weeks – and one at her own hands. She did not know the strength Desma would have had to draw from to save Palamaon's soul and risk her own. But Desma was the kind of woman who would not hesitate to step into darkness to save those she loved.

The sun had long set and the evening meal was approaching when she heard her father's secretary announce the arrival of a messenger. Mynta crept from her room and through the central garden, keeping a screen of branches and columns between her and her father who waited outside his office.

The messenger gave a low bow and produced his medallion bearing the emblem of the Council. 'Councilman Linos, the Council has been called by King Hilarion. The matter before you: a petition from Desma of Apasa, daughter of the former High Priestess, to speak with the King to request to be cleansed from her blood crime. The Council is voluntary so long as a quorum of thirteen is achieved. Prime Nicander has chosen dawn tomorrow.' With that, the messenger bowed again and left, no doubt heading to the next Councilman's home to repeat the message.

Her father dismissed his secretary and retreated into his office.

Mynta stood in the shadows of the garden, her mind racing. Of course her friends would have been visiting the palace to speak with the king. The temple, too, most likely. The king must be considering the request if he was putting it to the Council. Although she knew from listening to her father that the king was not as strong as his father before him. Many decisions that came before the throne were either delegated to the Council or sent to them for recommendations before the king would make his judgement. She had seen Hilarion many times over the years, even danced occasionally, but he had never been a talkative man.

The Council would vote tomorrow as to whether Desma could make her request to the king. Her father had to support Desma's request. But ... why would he?

She was knocking on the doorway before she even realised where her feet had carried her.

Her father looked up from the scroll he was rolling and raised an eyebrow. 'Daughter.'

Linos was copper-skinned, with black hair and a beard that she remembered she used to love grabbing with both hands as a child, giggling as it was soft and ticklish. His eyes were brown with a heavy brow, slightly taller than the stockier men of Trilos, but showing none of the usual signs of excess in a rounded belly and heavy limbs. His voice was full of gravel and his words rumbled even after he stopped speaking.

'Father,' she said demurely. What was she doing? Her heart was beating raggedly, skipping beats as though it was trying to both freeze and run. She and her father rarely spoke, exchanging pleasantries during meals, lanced with verbal spears to her heart when he expressed his disappointment in her. She would never be the prize mare he wanted her to be, sold to the highest bidder so his star could continue ascending off her lying on a marital bed and bearing children.

She had chosen herself and he would never forgive her.

But this wasn't for her. This was for Desma.

'I heard the council summons,' she said, stepping into the room that had never felt safe.

'You have nothing better to do than lurk in shadows, eavesdropping on state matters? I thought you would have been in the dining room, as it is close to supper.'

She had no armour against him. His words raked over her soul, but she kept on. 'Will you go to the meeting?'

He shrugged. 'It is unusual for only a single matter to be discussed. And foolish for Nicander to call it at dawn. Many Councilmen will not be bothered to go for such a foreign concern. Who cares for the fate of a Father-Killer?'

She is my friend, she wanted to cry but she bit her tongue. He was baiting her, needling her where he knew it would hurt. 'I saw Galen in the Copper Markets today,' she said quietly. Galen was a young member of the Council and a constant thorn in her father's side.

His head flicked up sharply. 'And why would you think that would be of interest to me? You lost the chance to wed him after ...' He waved at her body.

Shame burned her face. 'He is back from his trip to the eastern towns. No doubt he will attend the meeting.'

He grunted. 'Why would Galen care for an Apasan girl?'

'He doesn't. But he cares about power, and any chance to impose his will on the Council and king. He will attend, if only to make sure his opinion should be heard.'

'Let him, then,' her father said. 'I am growing tired of this conversation.'

'I think some people may find it strange that the Emissary to Apasa would not be present to speak on Apasan matters. In fact, you have not been to Apasa for quite some time. You even chose not to attend the celebration in the first place.'

'And thank Sethlans I did not, for we would have been in the city during the attack.'

'How fortunate, indeed, that you managed to avoid such a terrible conflict. One that nobody could have seen coming.'

His eyes glittered angrily as he met her gaze. 'Your words are dangerously slippery, Amynta,' he growled. 'I will not bother to warn you never to speak them aloud again, as you know full well how destructive such implications can be among the court.'

She bowed her head. 'It might win much favour with Apasa if Desma was to be cleansed.'

He laughed. 'Ha, they are the ones who banished her!'

'Instead of executing her,' she snapped back before biting her tongue. 'She is not a lowly citizen who killed out of greed or anger. She is daughter of the last High Priestess, looter of Urruc. Her name, whether for good or ill, is inscribed in history and tales. All I ask is that you not dismiss her so quickly. Good night, Father.'

She left quickly, hurrying to her room before she lost her nerve or her father called her back. Never before had she stepped into his political realm – it had filled her with a thrill, despite the churning in her stomach.

All she could do now was pray he would heed her words on the morrow.

CHAPTER TWENTY-TWO

The crew were quiet for the rest of the night. Dinner was served but Desma had no appetite. She sat at the stern of the ship, watching the dark waves pattering against the beach, the thin sliver of moon limning the nearby clouds. The stars moved as though trapped in honey, slow and unmindful of what was happening below. How she wished she could be up there. No longer having to care. No longer having to feel. Was that peace? Apathy?

She knew who was approaching without having to turn around.

'I'm okay, Cela,' she said.

'Liar,' her friend said, sitting beside her and sharing her blanket by draping it across her shoulders. 'The wind feels colder here than at home.'

Home. Apasa was Cela's home. She had her mother and the temple.

Desma had nothing.

'What are you thinking?' Cela asked.

'What someone would have to do to piss the gods off enough to be turned into a star,' she joked.

Cela gazed up into the sky. 'I think they usually do that to people they like. Maybe you should aim for a cow or a rock.'

Desma shoved her laughing. 'A cow? How dare you?'

'A nice one with a creamy coat and shiny horns and the most beautiful eyes,' she said. 'You could be brushed every day and fed sweet grass and give forth rich milk from your bountiful teats.'

'Every girl's dream.'

Cela sighed. 'Do you think Mynta has changed at all?'

'Maybe. It's been a year since we've seen her.' She remembered how hollow their friend had looked. 'I hope she's not married.'

'Or, if she is, let us hope he is kind,' Cela said, her eyes worried.

They settled into a quietness that was comfortable. Desma could not count the number of times they had sat together on their trireme, sailing across the Middle Sea, watching the sky wheel overhead and the sea part way.

But in the three days it took to reach Trilos, they never had a moment together. Arete, or Kassandra, or Delphinus, or someone else was always with them. She decided to seize the chance to ask the question that was gnawing a hole inside her.

'Have you forgiven me?' she asked into the stillness, the only immediate answer was the creak of ropes and the flutter of canvas.

Cela did not look at her, but gazed westwards. Her hair was silver and black in the night, her skin almost luminous. She was always the brighter of the two, happier and freer, willing to laugh when given the slightest chance.

Desma was the darker. Seeing the shadows for what they were, having the bronze in her spine to make the choices she would never allow Cela to make. Cela looked towards the sun and Desma would watch her back against the darkness.

Desma did not push for an answer. She let the faint movement of the ship half in the water ease some of the weariness from her bones. The minutes stretched to a point she thought Cela would not answer when she finally spoke.

'Not yet.'

It was not the answer she yearned to hear, but far better than what she feared. There was hope. She wondered at how her life was now filled only with these faint glimpses of hope, where before there was surety supported by a hundred-more gilded columns.

'I understand.'

'I don't know if you do,' Cela said into the night. 'Just as I would not understand if I were you. He was my father, just as much as yours. He said so all my life. He was a gift given to me out of love. And both of you took it away.'

Desma had not thought of it that way. If her father had succeeded, if she had not found him, he would have still died and robbed them both of his life.

'I do not know what I would have done if I was the one who found him – I hope I will never be in such circumstances. There are days when I know I would never have had the will to pick up that knife … but there are nights when I know just as strongly that I would do anything for him.' She sniffed and wiped her nose on the blanket. 'I don't know when I can forgive you. And I don't know if I ever will. You are my sister. I love you with such fierceness sometimes I think my heart will break itself apart. But I am not ready. My heart, my head, my *soul* cannot yet figure out what I am feeling.'

She turned to Desma, her eyes dim in the darkness. 'I do love you, Desma. Love is there even when I feel hate, imagining you in that room with … and the blood.' Her voice cracked and Desma felt it reflected inside her. She would never understand the pain she put her friend through – the shock and betrayal. She tried to imagine what it would have been like if their fates were reversed but she could not bring herself to place Cela in the room, have the blood on her hands. For her friend, Desma would pick up that knife a hundred times, clutching the tatters of her own heart in her chest, if it would spare Cela.

'But it is strange to have two opposing forces inside me,' Cela continued, 'I feel as though I am caught in a riptide and not sure yet whether I will make it back to shore or be cast out into the unending horizon.'

Desma leaned forward and pressed her lips to Cela's brow. 'I'm sorry,' she said softly. 'I had to ask. And I am grateful you could find the words to talk to me. I will always be your sister and friend.' Cela laid her head on Desma's shoulder, moving closer until the blanket cocooned them both, their heads peeking out to watch the ocean. Desma lowered her head to rest atop Cela's. 'We will see where the winds of fate take us.'

Briny sea air and the smoke from nearby fires fluttered across them in the quiet breeze, a scent that felt like home almost as much as roses and apples. Desma could feel Cela take a breath, deep and slow and calming.

'Maybe I will find a rich prince to marry and build me a palace on an island. You can live there with me and we'll sail the straits and search for sea nymphs, sending out wishes on the breeze.'

Desma smiled at the dream. 'Sounds wonderful.'

'Or we could get caught in a storm and drown the next time we set sail.'

'Aren't you a delight?'

'Always.'

Mynta was not allowed in the Council chamber but she had to hear for herself what happened.

She accompanied her father before dawn to the palace to visit her mother, who had been staying in their chambers there. She had grown up in the palace, with her father being a powerful noble, and his position had only grown stronger. She knew the places where no one looked.

Once in the palace, Mynta had slipped away and crept into an unseen corner of the chamber before the Councilmen arrived. She sat on the floor behind the base of a statue of one of Aplu's lovers, a large tapestry conveniently placed against the wall that her cloak blended into.

The councillors were all men, though no law forbade women from joining. Only a majority vote from the presiding councillors or a command from the king could permit a new member and, somehow, a woman had never made it.

They ranged in age from late twenties to well into their sixties. There were nobles from old families, some claiming royal or divine heritage. Others were wealthy merchants, or controlled important roads or fleets of ships. Some, like her father, were ambassadors to the other Kingdoms and beyond. The numbers varied given the year, but there were currently forty-two councillors and thirty-seven had arrived for the meeting. A large number for a dawn meeting that was only called late the night before.

The Council Prime, an old man called Nicander, opened the meeting with the customary request for the gods to guide their wisdom. He was one of the few men in the room with a beard, as they had fallen out of favour, but his reached his chest and was white like down. His eyes were slightly glazed in blindness but his mind was as sharp as a winter wind.

'We have gathered at the behest of the King, Hilarion, son of Hesperos, to discuss the petition of Desma, daughter of the slain priestess of Turan.

Hilarion has asked us to discuss the merits of her request and our obligations. I open the floor to my brothers.'

The first to step forward was Galen, a man in the zenith of his youth, strong jawed with a powerful voice. He often dominated the council meetings through either unassailable rhetoric or intimidation – whichever gave him the greater chance of winning. His father, a powerful man who controlled the three great roads into Trilos in the king's name, had died unexpectedly in his fortieth year. Galen was invited into the Council more out of respect for his newly gained influence than any sense of comradeship.

Mynta never liked when he was invited to her father's parties and was grateful when he married the daughter of another councillor, for he received fewer invitations while her parents hunted after other prospects for a husband.

'I feel that I speak for every man in this room,' Galen began, 'when I express my disgust that this agendum was brought to our attention, let alone our glorious king! She is filthblood, unclean and shadowed by the gods' displeasures. We invite angering Tinia and our patron god, Sethlans, by allowing her in the city and giving her a voice. We should decline her request and send her on her way. There are kings and priests aplenty across the Icarii Sea – let her search for some fool to resolve her blood crime elsewhere.'

There were murmurs of assent flickering across the room.

Nicander gestured towards another councillor. Etule, Master of the Copper Markets, rose from his seat, a great necklace of copper with fine carvings filled with tin across his chest. 'Perhaps we should not be too hasty to speed to a decision,' he said in a voice rich as syrup. 'Despite the severity of her crime and that fact she did not deny it – indeed she confessed without a fight – Sophocles was well within his right to claim her life. Instead, he sentenced her to a fate many of us would deem worse. But there is the possibility for redemption. Why would he choose such a judgement, is what we should be asking ourselves.' He sat down. A few men around him nodded and one even clapped his shoulder.

Galen spoke again, as it was his right to respond. 'We should not forget that she is the daughter to Turan's high priestess, a woman of fiery will, famed beauty, and wise grace. They were friends and, if rumours are to be believed, even lovers at some of their festivals. The king no doubt cared for her daughter and chose this judgement as one last gift to a farewelled friend. We should not read into this as some clue into this woman's character, but a consequence of Sophocles' friendship to her mother. She stabbed her own father in the heart. Remember that.'

'Xanthos, speak,' Nicander said.

Mynta could not see the man who spoke next from her vantagepoint. 'As well as the reason why she did it,' he said, 'one must consider the murky greyness of saving the soul of a beloved with the foulness of patricide. A crime to right a crime. A darker side to an already dark coin.'

'Emissary Linos,' Nicander called out.

Mynta shifted slightly so she could see her father, standing with his supporters directly opposite to Galen. He was dressed in a long, green chiton with a large beige himation that reached his feet. A gold chain clasped in his hair allowed a ruby to dangle on his forehead. As he spoke, he gestured with arms and hands glittering with jewellery.

'It is interesting timing that this Council gathers to discuss this issue,' he said, his eyes sweeping across the assemblage. 'I only received word an hour before this meeting that Desma and her crew have been granted a silver ring by the beachmaster.'

Whispers sprung up like a breeze.

Her father continued. 'This was after a confrontation with the beachmaster last night when he attempted to revoke her iron ring and force her out of the city.'

More whispers.

'And why was she granted a silver ring?' Galen called out over the other voices. 'She would have no official charge, so it must be as a guest. Of who?'

Linos met his eyes across the room. 'Mine, through my daughter Amynta.'

Galen's eyes sparked. 'That *is* interesting.'

'What I found intriguing was that when my men arrived at the beachmaster's office to request the scroll containing the orders for her to leave, mysteriously, said scroll was allegedly destroyed in the scuffle with Desma and her crew. Even more curiously, the beachmaster's memory suddenly failed him when asked to recall the name of the person who sent the scroll.'

Galen shrugged. 'The risks of bureaucracy.'

'Indeed.'

'I wonder why you would choose to extend the hand of friendship to one who has been condemned as she has, Linos?' Galen asked, tilting his head to the side. 'To allow your family to consort with someone with such a venomous nature ...'

Mynta had to stop from flinging herself at the bastard.

Her father stroked his beard. 'I do not understand. Do you wish me to apologise for not having the power of foresight which belongs only to Aplu and his chosen? How am I to foresee what a friend of my daughter does in another kingdom? Do you wish me to beg your forgiveness for not being divine, Galen?'

Laughter bounced around the room. Even old Nicander allowed himself a small grin. 'Serapion, you may speak.'

A thin man stepped from the group standing near her father. 'I say we allow her audience with the king. Her mother was priestess to Turan, wife of Sethlans, our patron god. While many speculate that the misfortune that has befallen Apasa of late is an indication of Turan abandoning them – this is a fact we know for certain through our priests. But as far as the world is aware, we only know what Sophocles has proclaimed – that it was a terrible attack on their city and they are rebuilding in their goddess' name. As such, we must show an open mind to the daughter of Timothea. Allow her to make her case, and let the king render judgement under the guiding hand of Sethlans and Tinia.'

He stepped back and Mynta sent a silent prayer of blessings for the man.

Nicander spoke. 'I call the Council to vote. All those who accept Desma's petition, raise your cup.'

Arms raised high and Nicander counted aloud.

'Fourteen for rejection. Twenty-three for acceptance. The petition is granted. Linos, as she is granted a silver ring in your name, I charge you with informing Desma and arranging with the king's First Advisor for when the meeting shall take place. Council has ended. Praise to Sethlans and the Holy Twelve.' Nicander lowered his cup and drank the rest of his wine before slowly getting to his feet.

Mynta waited until the chamber was emptied before she moved from her hiding place, running to get back to their rooms before her father arrived.

She would wait for her father to mention the meeting's outcome before suggesting they invite Desma and Cela to lunch at their house in the city.

Desma's chances looked hopeful with her father's open support.

She couldn't wait to tell them.

CHAPTER TWENTY-THREE

Desma and her crew waited outside the doors to Emissary Linos' house, standing under the warm morning sun in the main courtyard.

She and Cela decided to forgo their travelling clothes for this occasion. Desma was wearing a damask peplos with a dark yellow belt, her red hair swept out of her face and held back with a thin band of gold patterned with sage leaves. Cela was wearing a light grey dress that left one shoulder bare, a red belt girdled at her hips, with red ribbons tangled in her hair. She also had a necklace of garnets and a large bracelet of gold that covered her forearm. Desma knew she should never have doubted that Cela would not have packed for every occasion – including dressing for royalty.

Desma had been awake eating a late breakfast with Arete when there was loud knocking on the hull of the ship and someone shouting. It was a messenger from Mynta's house requesting their presence. While the crew readied themselves, Arete had gone with the messenger to see the beachmaster to provide the required proof of invitation.

They then left their rowers on *The Darkling* with coin enough for food, wine, and entertainment. They had all come from the two hundred who used to row on the trireme, and Desma and Cela trusted them to care for the ship.

Bion had still not been able to find Cosmas. Desma was not sure if she should be worried. It was not unusual for him to disappear for great lengths of time, but it was strange he had not reached out at least once since their arrival. Her reverie was broken by the doors of Linos' house opening and a servant ushering them inside.

Mynta's family lived in a beautiful house in the city when they were not staying at the palace. Made from bricks of warm, golden stone, it was surrounded by a high wall that provided shelter for a large garden and small artificial creek set in the middle of the house. All the rooms opened to a covered walkway held up with slender pillars that allowed one to step directly into the garden. A private oasis.

Past the gate in the wall and the entry courtyard, the first room was the welcoming hall with couches and pillows for guests to repose, with a splendid view of the rest of the dwelling. Linos and his wife were seated there on simple chairs, smiling benignly at them, and off to the side was a mirror-opposite to the Mynta they had seen a year ago.

Before, her beauty was tainted by gauntness, pale beneath sun-kissed skin, hair glimmering with expensive oils yet still lank and flat, and eyes made large by dark rings. A rose tightly closed was still beautiful, but nothing compared to when its petals bloomed. That was Mynta now – a woman in full bloom.

Copper skin and flowing, ink-dark hair, eyes bright and flashing, lips straining to keep the smile from bursting through. She wore a long dress the colour of crocus petals, with amethysts sewn with pearls through her hair. Radiant was the only way Desma could describe her. She almost forgot to make the traditional greeting to her friend's father, reminded only by Cela's sly elbow.

Once the pleasantries were done and the welcome wine poured, Desma and her party joined the family in reclining on the pillows. Servants brought beaten gold platters of bread and grapes, figs and the choicest pieces of beef. Small bowls of olive oil were passed around to dip each morsel into before transferring to their mouths while two young girls in the shadows of a column sang softly in the background, their melodies soothing and the words low enough to be indiscernible. A cool breeze made its way over the stone wall, gathering scents from the garden to disperse throughout the house.

It reminded Desma of the many times they had visited Mynta in Trilos, accompanying Timothea on divine visits to The Forge. And she was shocked to see Mynta help herself liberally to the food in front of her, her plate never half emptied before she filled it again – all without a sharp word or slap to the wrist from her mother. Though the lady of the house's lips were thinned and her eyes filled with disapproval, she said nothing. Linos did not look at his daughter once. Desma could not wait to have a moment alone with Mynta and Cela.

'We have heard of the recent events in Apasa,' Linos said with his gravelly voice. 'It has been a difficult time for the city ... and yourself.'

'Your sorrows are ours,' Mynta's mother slid in smoothly. 'The loss of one's family in such situations cannot be imagined.'

Desma bowed her head slightly from her position lying on her side on cushions of rich silks. 'Thank you for your kindness.' She wondered at their real thoughts beneath the honey words and warm gestures. She doubted they would have been allowed in the door, let alone by their direct invitation, if it would cause Linos any harm politically. But did he hope to gain anything by their visit? Would he intercede on their behalf to the king and council? She took a deep breath. The law is the law. She had stretched propriety by waiting until after the meal but it was also Tinia's custom for hosts to feed their guests before sharing news. 'Before we proceed any further, I must speak the truth. As decreed by the laws of Tinia, I must share my story so you know with whom you speak and dine with ...'

It was the second time she had to tell her story, her crime, and her sentence. The words were foul and heavy, and she finished in a rush like she could not spew the words out fast enough.

She did not realise she was panting, sweat beading her brow as her eyes flicked from Linos, to his wife, to Mynta and back. Linos knew what she had done but now was the moment when he could turn his back on her and nothing under the gods could change his mind.

Linos' brown eyes did not waver from her face and he stroked his beard one-handed, drops of olive oil rubbing from his fingers. The tension was broken by his words. 'I offer what help I can.'

Desma took a moment to sip her wine, blinking back tears that threatened to form. Though she counted Mynta as her closest friend behind Cela, her parents had never warmed entirely to the two girls from Apasa. Mynta's mother was kind enough and always took care of them when they came to Trilos; Linos was ever distant, though cordial. Much as he was to his own daughter. But Desma always felt he tolerated them because of who her mother was, rather than their friendship with Mynta. Now that Timothea had passed

...

Relief was an understatement.

'Thank you, Councilman Linos,' Desma said formally. Cela echoed her words.

'I understand you have already spoken to the High Priest?' he asked.

She nodded.

'No oracles reside within Trilos, so your hopes rest with King Hilarion.' His eyes glinted under his heavy brow. 'The fact he did not turn you away immediately shows that he is open to the idea of purification. However, because he passed the decision of whether to speak to you to the Council reveals that he is waiting to see what the public opinion of the Council and the city would be.'

'He is waiting to see where the scales will tip without realising that as king he *is* the scale,' Khufu suddenly spoke from where he crouched on his feet on the other side of Cela.

Linos turned to him. 'I do not know much of the land you hail from, Captain,' he said flatly, 'but in Trilos the Council and the King act in balance. Our history contains enough examples of the dangers when ruled by a single man. The King is checked by the Council, and the Council cannot act without the King. Thus, only that which truly benefits our kingdom is proclaimed.'

Khufu gave a grunt in response that brought a sneer to Linos' face.

Cela placed herself between the two men with her words. 'Has the Council met yet to discuss Desma's request?'

Linos turned to her, but his eyes kept flicking back to Khufu. 'We met this morning, though no decision has been reached yet—' He cut off as Mynta suddenly began coughing.

Her mother chided her for eating grapes too quickly, but Linos simply dismissed her. 'I understand your eagerness for a decision, but to Trilos this question must come after more pressing matters of state.'

'I understand.' As much as she wanted to demand an audience with the king right now, to march to the palace directly and beg on her knees for cleansing, she knew that her plight meant nothing to anyone else beyond her in the great scheme of the cosmos.

'But you and your friends are welcome to remain in the house until a decision is made,' Mynta's mother said, nodding to Cela and the others.

After expressing their thanks for the hospitality, Linos rose from the cushions, claiming that he must see about some business and that they no doubt were eager to spend time with his daughter. Without further word to his wife or Mynta, he swept out of the house, calling out to some men who were waiting with clutched papers in the courtyard.

Mynta's mother told them to ask anything of the servants they desired before excusing herself from the hall and leaving into an adjacent room. Desma asked the rest of the crew to return to the ship and continue seeking word of Cosmas. He should have made contact already and she was growing concerned something foul may have occurred.

Soon Desma, Cela, and Mynta were alone.

Mynta wasted no time in hurling herself at the two of them, the group falling over onto the pillows and rugs on the floor in a laughing heap, dresses askew and hair twisting.

'Oh, how I have missed you!' Mynta cried, joy flashing across her face. 'A whole year you've abandoned me with scarcely a letter from either of you.'

'We have missed you terribly, too.' Cela laughed as she propped herself up on a cushion, her wheat-gold hair pooling around her shoulders, looking for all the world like a nymph.

The dark-haired woman squeezed her hand before reaching over to stroke Desma's cheek. 'I know you have heard this a hundred times,' she said softly. 'But I am so sorry. For everything you have gone through. For everything you've had to do.'

Desma did not even try to keep the tears from her face. 'Thank you. But let us keep to happier things. Tell us – what happened to the skin-and-bones girl from a year ago?'

Cela pinched Mynta's side. 'And here I was thinking the secret to happiness was sex and all the time it was food!'

Mynta swatted her hand away, laughing.

The morning brightened into true day while the three of them chatted of more pleasant times. Desma could almost – almost – forget why she was in Trilos for a few hours.

Cela sat with Mynta as the household began to quieten for the night.

Mynta had wanted to take them out into the city during the day but Desma had begged off, afraid of the chance that she would have to tell someone her crime – or forget and again suffer the consequences.

Cela had to convince Kassandra and Delphinus from hunting down the beachmaster. As much as she also hated the vile worm, he was right before the eyes of the gods. To harm him was to invite divine vengeance. That did not stop her from daydreaming about his office on fire with him locked inside.

So, instead they lounged around the house, talking and eating, swapping stories of the past year, skirting the events of the last few weeks.

Eventually Desma excused herself early to bathe and go to bed, though Cela noted the jug of wine she took with her.

'It is so good to see you both,' Mynta said softly, rolling a grape across her plate idly. 'I was worried.'

'What about?' Cela asked, lying back on her couch, arms stretched over her head to drape over the side. The warm night was lulling her to sleep.

'How you two would be faring together.'

'We are friends, family – we will always be by each other's side.'

'Love does not negate the troubles that come up on the road,' Mynta said. 'Sometimes love can make things worse.'

Cela rolled onto her side. 'How so?'

Mynta shrugged. 'A stranger insults you and, while their words can hurt, they are sticks thrown at you. But have a family member speak the same words and suddenly the sticks become spears, the wounds they inflict so much greater. Why? Because you love them.'

'Desma did what she had to. She did it out of love. Even if ...' Cela took a deep breath.

'Even if it was an evil act,' Mynta finished.

Cela could only gape at her.

'Only the innocent and fools think that love is only good. Love can also be cruel and dark and painful. It is the *intent*, not the action, that is the love.' Mynta rose from her couch and sat beside Cela, lying a hand on her hip. 'To a child, a parent smacking their backside for running in front of a horse is cruel. But to the parent it is an act of love, teaching them of danger and showing the fear they have of losing their child. To my mother and father, what I have done, ignoring their wishes and being who I was born to be, is selfish and stupid. But it is because of the love I found for myself, with the help of my nursemaid, that changes the intent of my decisions.'

Cela brushed a hand across her eyes. 'Stop it, Mynta. I do not wish to speak about it anymore. I just ... don't.'

'But I think you need to hear it, Cela.' Mynta took her hand, wet with her tears. 'You might never forgive Desma. You might always feel a part of what you are feeling now and it is alright for you to share what is in your heart. You don't always have to be the sun to her shade. You are allowed to stumble in the dark. She will catch you. *I* will catch you.'

Why was Mynta saying these things? When did her friend grow so wise? This was not the same person they visited a year ago – a woman beaten down by her mother and father, starved in body and in her spirit.

Cela couldn't take it anymore. To constantly be asked about her feelings, the guilt and hatred that flared inside her at times, the sadness that her father was gone, the horror when she dreamt of Desma's hands red with his blood. She loved Desma, *loved her*. Oh why did the gods have to make difficult what should only be beautiful?

She rolled off the other side of the couch, getting to her feet with her face turned away from Mynta. 'I am tired,' she said, cursing her trembling voice. 'I am going to bed. Sleep well, Mynta.' She reached out a hand behind her. She felt her friend take it and press a soft kiss into her palm.

'Peaceful dreams, Cela.'

CHAPTER TWENTY-FOUR

Seven days they waited in the house of Linos.

Seven days plus the three since they landed on the beaches of Trilos.

Still no word from the Council.

Every day at breakfast Desma hurried from her room she shared with Cela to catch the emissary before he departed for the day. She always received the same response.

'Not yet,' he would say with barely a glance at her. Always something more pressing had his attention. 'The Council has many matters to deal with. And almost all more important than the fate of one girl.' He would try to soften his words with a smile but it never reached his eyes.

It was on the tenth day, when she was left standing alone in the garden watching his receding back as he headed for the palace, that Mynta finally told them that the Council had in fact already decided that she be granted an audience with the king.

'I am sorry I said nothing sooner,' she said in a rush. 'I have no idea what my father is planning – I thought there must be a reason he did not tell you the truth. But I heard just last night a messenger came from Nicander – he is the Prime of the Council – asking for news on the audience. My father has yet to even speak to the King's First Advisor.'

'And you said he argued for the audience to be granted,' Cela said, more to herself than as an actual question. 'Could this Galen be a threat?'

Mynta shook her head. 'I think he was the one who sent the order to revoke your iron ring. Perhaps he hoped that you would leave before the matter was brought to the Council and not have to risk losing the vote.'

Desma twitched the skirts of her pale-yellow dress and moved to sit on a bench under the shade of a lemon tree in the private garden. Her patience was nothing but dust she kept sweeping into her hands and hoping it would hold, despite the wind that tore it from her grasp. Yet she was in no position to push her host and only friend on the Council. How could she demand he do any more than he was?

She was the criminal. She was filth in the eyes of every citizen in the Kingdoms. She knew that this was her punishment, as Tinia intended. The journey to salvation was paved in shame and pain. Memory of chewing grit and sand on her belly in front of the beachmaster caused embarrassment to claw her insides.

She shoved the feeling away roughly. Now was not the time. She kept those feelings firmly locked up until she was sure Cela was asleep at night. That was when she let them free to wrack and wreck her until she felt like a wrung-out rag.

'There is nothing we can do,' she said resignedly. 'Linos was charged with arranging my meeting with the king. We just have to wait.'

She had not noticed Mynta absentmindedly walking away until Cela called after her. She looked up to see her friend tapping her chin thoughtfully. 'What is it?'

Mynta turned with the face of someone who was slowly piecing a puzzle together. 'Maybe ...' she said quietly, eyes drifting yet sharp.

Desma and Cela exchanged glances. Most of their troubles when the three of them were together sprang from one of their minds. Mynta usually went along with whatever one of them suggested. Yet, the few times she proposed an adventure usually ended up with them being kept under the watchful eyes of the city guards until Timothea or Leontia collected them with a face like a thunderhead. Silence stretched while they waited.

'For Uni's sake, tell us!' Cela finally snapped.

Mynta turned to them. 'My nursemaid says, "When the feather fails, try the hammer." Come with me.'

They followed her into her rooms. She clapped her hands and maids rushed in, followed by Mynta's nursemaid, an older woman with severe eyes, grey-gold hair tied in a loose tail, and a mouth that seemed ready to twitch into either a smile or a scowl.

'We are going to the palace,' Mynta told the assembled women. 'We need to be readied appropriately.' The women began moving briskly, some running to the closets, others to jewellery chests, while others dashed to the kitchen to order hot water for baths. Desma found herself being poked and prodded by two maids towards a second room that had a shallow pool lined with delicate green tiles that was no deeper than her ankle, all the while they stripped her of her dress.

Other maids rushed in with jugs of warm water that they unceremoniously dumped over her head. She spluttered and tried to push her hair out of her face, sneezing water from her nose. Soft cloths were rubbed over her skin vigorously before another dumping of water. The cool breeze coming in from the sea and through the garden pebbled her skin and she shivered slightly.

She was towelled dry gently and her hair brushed from brow to tip in long, unbroken strokes. The maids chattered about the deep colour of her hair, each claiming to know the best tinctures to make the colours more vibrant, her hair more voluptuous, its length wavier.

Mynta's nursemaid appeared holding three small, clay bottles. 'Clove and fennel, cinnamon and rose, apple and jasmine,' she said pointing at each bottle in turn.

She thought for a moment before pointing at the middle one. The nursemaid gave a knowing smile before passing the cinnamon and rose oil to another maid who began liberally massaging it into her scalp and coating every strand of hair.

'Not so much,' the nursemaid snapped. 'Only enough to entice the nose, not clobber a bull senseless!'

The maid gave a squeak and grabbed a towel, roughly wiping away as much excess oil as she could. She seemed not to notice she was almost pulling Desma's hair out.

Once she was dry and anointed, the maids produced a peplos the colour of persimmon that was snug around her waist and almost did not need the burnt ochre belt embellished with running horses. Sandals studded with silver were slipped onto her feet and, once she was dressed, Mynta's nursemaid appeared once more and pointed to a small olivewood chest.

The maids withdrew the contents from the chest and Desma almost gasped. Jewels and rings and necklaces that would not look out of place on a queen were presented before her. She knew Linos was a powerful and wealthy man, yet this was just one of several chests scattered in Mynta's rooms.

One of the maids, a sweet girl who was not yet of marriageable age, gave a small smile. 'Lady Amynta received many gifts from sons of lords and princes of the city,' she explained. 'However, it has been nearly a year since any courting gift has arrived.'

A year since she refused to continue starving herself, Desma thought bitterly.

She selected a few items and sat patiently in front of the buffed bronze mirror while she was bedecked.

A necklace of rubies strung in delicate gold wires fell in tiers down her neck and chest. Two rings, each with flashing garnets encircled by white quartz, went on both hands. Silver earrings fashioned like leaping dolphins were attached to her ears. A silver net was artfully entangled in her hair until it shimmered and sparkled in the morning sun that flowed through the arabesque window.

Lastly, paints were delicately applied to her face. The maid added fine white powder to a bowl followed by other powders of different yellow and brown and orange shades. Soon she had a mixture that matched Desma's skin and she gently brushed it across her face with a goat-hair brush. Charcoal and olive oil were mixed together and painted under her eyes and next came a rich cream of beeswax the colour of cedar that was applied to her lips, which the maid blew gently upon until it dried.

As the maid stepped away, Mynta's nursemaid returned and gave her a once-over with her critical eye before nodding approvingly. 'That will do,' she said simply. 'Come.'

Desma hurried to catch the old woman's arm. 'Pardon, mistress, but could I ask your name? I'm afraid I do not know it.'

The nursemaid studied her with unreadable eyes. 'Anesidora,' she said quietly. 'Though few use it.'

'Thank you,' Desma said, for some reason feeling as though the older woman had given her a gift.

Her friends met her in the central garden. Cela was almost incandescent, covered in jewellery studded with topaz, her hair catching every ray of sunlight, and a golden dress that only made her shine brighter. She smelled of apple and jasmine.

Mynta was clothed in a green that was almost black, her raven hair scattered with rubies, with a necklace holding a single, large emerald. She swept from her room like a queen, the dress cut to highlight every curve of her body, her ankles flashing from beneath the hem, and her belt carved with images of Horta's blessings: sheaves of wheat, figs, loaves of bread, grapevines. She was scented with clove and fennel.

'What is the plan, Mynta?' Desma asked. 'We cannot just barge in to see the king.' That plan may have worked with High Priest Castur, but she did not for a moment think it would work with Hilarion. She doubted they would make it pass the palace doors, let alone to the royal chambers.

'We do not need to see the king,' her friend said as she rifled through a small box proffered by Anesidora. 'We need to see Phokas.' She withdrew a thin veil of palest purple with a single wavy line of amethysts sewn across it. Mynta attached it to Desma's hair with clips so that the veil covered the lower half of her face from nose to chin. 'Perfect,' she said before throwing a long white shawl over Desma so her hair was completely covered.

'Who is Phokas?' Cela asked, studying the veil.

'The King's First Advisor,' Mynta said with a clever smile. 'Now, this is very important for you to remember, Desma, and no doubt the hardest instruction you have received to this day. Don't speak.'

Desma opened her mouth to do just that and found Mynta's finger pressed firmly on her lips, all but pushing the veil into her mouth. 'Shh,' she said with a twinkle in her eye.

They did not have far to walk through the city. The palace was in the centre of Trilos and Linos kept his house within easy walking distance to ensure he was never far from the corridors of power.

Almost plain in comparison to the palace in Apasa, Hilarion's home was a walled fort with four square towers in each corner, the open gates depicting the forge of Sethlans. The buildings within the inner walls were a sprawling affair. Bright towers of warm, yellow stone capped in bronze and gold, banners and great-shields topped each spire, proudly displaying the red hammer and gold flames. Small grottos provided relief from the stone, with flashing fountains and the fresh scent of citrus.

When they reached the gates, Mynta waved for them to stop a dozen paces from the guards and she glided forward to speak with the men quietly. Desma strained to catch the words exchanged, but the rattle of carts and the constant banging of the thousand forges throughout the city provided a backdrop of noise that would foil the most tenacious eavesdropper. After what seemed an age, Mynta gestured for them to join her and they swept past the guards, who watched her with open interest.

She held her breath in fear that one would speak to her.

But no one did.

On the way to the city, Mynta had explained the significance of the veil. Trilos had a sect of women who served as Handmaidens of the Smiths. Mynta explained that the Handmaidens were not well-known beyond the temple and palace as they only had one function. The priests and workers at The Forge often had trouble sleeping due to the constant noise and the proximity to the divine fires of inspiration that often had them dragging their feet from their beds at all hours to create their inventions. The handmaidens would stand in the bedrooms of the men of the temples and sing while they slept. What Mynta had tried and failed to hide from them was that they sang while wearing nothing else besides the veil!

Desma had almost torn it off then, but was eventually convinced to keep it on. It was known that the women never spoke in front of anyone who was not a handmaiden and they were not an uncommon sight within the palace, as the royal family often requested their assistance in sleeping. Desma had blushed furiously while Cela laughed at Mynta's suggestion that the men of the royal family may also need other assistance to fall asleep.

Desma swallowed the idea and the embarrassment she felt. As she was fast learning since arriving in Trilos, anything she had to endure was part of her punishment.

And no matter how much she scrubbed her teeth with a twig and washed it out with wine, she still found the odd grain of sand in her mouth.

They entered the palace proper and, as plain as it was on the outside, it was filled with marvels on the inside. Giant gears turned pumps that sent water running along small aqueducts that disappeared into the palace walls. Lights that did not flicker and changed colour from white to yellow to orange glowed from sconces shaped like an open hand. They walked past an upside down glass pyramid, as large as a wagon, balancing on its point on a small obsidian sphere the size of Desma's fist.

Several times they walked passed an automaton the size of a tall man. They looked like fearsome warriors from ancient times, standing silent and immobile, but capable of utter destruction. How anyone in the palace could pass one without a shudder, Desma did not know.

They followed Mynta silently as they made their way through the palace. She wanted to ask where they were going, how long it would take, but she did not dare speak. The veil kept anyone from talking to her, thus saving her the shame of telling her story.

Eventually, they arrived at a wooden door with a group of clerks waiting patiently outside, some making notes on chalk tablets, others rereading scrolls, but all stopped when they approached.

'Good morning,' Mynta said cheerfully with a bow of her head. 'I believe this is the office of First Advisor Phokas? Thank you.' She went to push passed the men to reach the door but the clerks moved as one to block her way as efficiently as any warrior with spear and shield.

'I am sorry,' said the oldest clerk, a man with greying hair and a slight hunch, his hands gnarled but still spry. 'First Advisor Phokas is currently engaged and I do not recall any meeting scheduled this morning with ... yourself,' he finished with a sniff.

Mynta's face was the image of mild surprise, which very quickly turned to shock as her eyes slid past the clerk's shoulder to look down the hall. 'My King,' she said, dropping low, her dress splaying around her.

The clerks all spun around and, without hesitating a moment, Mynta popped back to her feet and threw the door open, sweeping into the room without waiting for Desma or Cela.

'No ... wait ... come back,' the old clerk spluttered but made no move to give chase. Desma slid passed him and Cela shut the door in his outraged face with a little too much satisfaction. She shrugged at Desma's raised eyebrow.

Desma turned to see the man they had come to find.

The first advisor to King Hilarion was not a young man but strength still radiated from his broad shoulders and straight back. His hair fell in waves that flicked back from eyes that tilted slightly, warmly dark and intelligent. His mouth twitched in a bemused smile, but no sign of alarm registered. He was dressed in well-made robes of red and cream, the ends pinned to his chest by a golden ship with green sails.

The man seated across the table from him had a strong face and deep eyes, his black hair was worn slightly longer, whose muscles rippled beneath his chiton, his overcloak a rich garment of scarlet brocaded with gold silk ribbon. His expression clearly conveyed his annoyance at the interruption.

Mynta staggered for a moment at the sight of the younger man before promptly dropping to her knees in a deep bow, one hand on the tiled floor and the other on her heart. 'First Advisor Phokas. Councilman Galen. Apologies for the intrusion.' She waved for them to join her.

As Desma knelt, her mind was racing. Galen. He was the man who argued for her petition to be rejected. It was most likely his name was on the order sent to the beachmaster.

Her hands gripped her dress tightly. With her head bowed almost into her lap she surreptitiously snatched the veil from her face and balled it up in her hand.

When she rose to her feet, she hoped the two men had been too preoccupied by Mynta to notice she was no longer wearing a veil or what design it had been.

'I know your face,' Phokas said in a cultured voice. 'You are Linos' daughter.' It was a statement.

Galen's eyes became like daggers.

Mynta kept her gaze steadily on the advisor and nodded.

'I was unaware I had a meeting with you today,' Phokas said with little emotion. 'And I doubt I would have arranged such a conflict of scheduling to have you intrude on my discussion with Councilman Galen.'

'Our apologies, once again, First Advisor,' Mynta said, her hands clasped modestly in front of her, the image of innocence. 'We meant no disrespect to your noble office. But once we heard, we were driven by honour to attend you as soon as possible.'

His brows knitted in confusion. 'Heard what?'

Mynta gestured vaguely, encompassing nothing yet indicating everything. 'Why, that the petition of my good friend, Desma of Apasa, has not yet been brought to you to arrange an audience with King Hilarion, as per the consensus of the Council.'

Both men's eyes flew to Desma, taking in her deep red hair as she pushed back the shawl. They would have met her mother when she visited Trilos, and there were none other in all the Kingdoms who had her hair.

'You ...' Galen started to rise from his chair.

Desma stepped forward, spreading her arms wide in the posture of a supplicant. 'I am Desma, daughter of the High Priestess of Turan, Timothea, and her husband, Palamaon the potter, from Apasa.' She kept her voice unwavering and her eyes firm. She would have to get used to speaking these words. She would not break every time, would not allow tears or a crack in her voice. But shame, deep and sharp, sliced into her soul with each sentence.

'I killed my father after he tried to take his own life, despairing at the death of his wife at the hands of Empyrean traitors who tore down the Grand Temple. I killed him to save his soul from the punishment of a death-crime.' The horror on her father's face when the knife slid into his heart was as stark and clear as if she was still stuck in that moment. 'Hero-King Sophocles decreed my blood tainted. I am on a path of redemption to cleanse my blood, sheltered under the judging hand of Tinia until my journey is complete. I have come to ask King Hilarion whether he will acquiesce to conducting the cleansing rites.'

She stayed standing, arms stretched, palms held upwards, looking over the heads of the two men, waiting.

It was Phokas who spoke first. 'I am reaching my fifty-sixth year in the world of the living,' he said slowly, as though each word was weighted. 'And never have I heard the announcement speech of one cursed by the gods for a blood crime. I had hoped I never would.'

'Father-Killer,' Galen growled. 'How dare you presume you can make filthy the halls of Trilos with your presence. None summoned you. If you truly wish to make up for your unforgivable act, then leave our city. Find an island with some goats and die, unburied and without honours, away from fair people.'

Desma was barely aware of Mynta grabbing hold of Cela's arm as she tried to reach forward and slap the councilman. She was caught in the hatred that roiled in Galen's eyes. It was like a punch to the gut. He saw her as dirty, a diseased scab in his city, her plague threatening to infect his way of life. She found herself rubbing her hand on her arm, as though scrubbing at her skin. She forced herself to stop.

'Have a care for your words, Councilman,' Phokas said with a hint of reprimand. 'You had your time at the gathering and lost. Do not gain shame by being sullen.'

Though his words were delivered in a mild manner, Galen flinched as though Cela's slap had reached its mark.

'How can I be of assistance?' The first advisor's eyes went from Mynta to Desma and back. 'I am sure that now you are here it will take nothing short of armed guards to remove you.' He raised a hand as Galen went to speak. 'We are talking about whether you or the king is responsible for repairs to the Strait Road. It is an argument we have had a hundred times before and will no doubt argue about in the future. It can wait.' Galen settled back with a glower.

Mynta smoothed her dress before speaking. 'Word has reached my friends and I that, due to extenuating circumstances, a meeting with King Hilarion has yet to be arranged through your noble self with Desma for her to present her petition for purification. We at once set forth to the palace to speak with you. We understand this meeting is of some importance with the king as he has sought the guidance of his Council.' She gave the barest nod to Galen. 'The king shows wisdom to ensure that his steps are in line with the city and kingdom. We much desire to prostrate ourselves in front of King Hilarion and beg his forgiveness, but would never dream of intruding on his royal duties outside of proper process. Which, of course, is through yourself, First Advisor.'

Cela clutched at Desma's hand and she gripped it back just as tightly. She knew she was holding her breath but did not dare exhale. Mynta had explained her plan on the way but it still seemed farfetched. Barging in on arguably the second most powerful man in the city and coating their demand to see the king in honey, completely bypassing her own father and the Council. Madness.

Phokas clasped his forearms on the table as he listened, his eyes taking everything in but revealing nothing. Once Mynta's speech was over he shrugged and pulled a wax tablet over. 'The king is available in two days time one hour after noon. I trust all parties can attend?' He looked at Desma expectantly.

She let out her breath quickly. 'Yes, of course. Thank you.'

'Wonderful,' he said as he inscribed onto the tablet. 'Galen, I entrust you to alert all members of the Council. All are invited to attend but their presence is not compulsory.' Galen grunted. 'And Amynta,' Phokas glanced up at her. 'Please let your father know that the meeting he requested for next month has been cancelled as the matter he wished to discuss has been decided upon now.'

Mynta's mouth gaped open and Desma nudged her. Her mouth slammed shut and she bobbed another curtsy. 'Thank you, First Advisor. I will pass along your message. May Sethlans' fires warm and inspire you.'

'And to you three,' Phokas bowed his head. 'Now that your business is concluded, please allow me to continue my originally scheduled meeting with the councilman.'

The three of them bowed again and once more to Galen who continued to glare at them all, especially at Desma, and they hurried out the door.

'I cannot believe that worked,' Cela squealed, once they were far enough away from the glowering clerks who muttered darkly at them.

'Only two more days,' Desma breathed, relief plain in her voice.

Mynta caught her arm and stopped her in a section of hallway empty of other people. 'We are making progress,' she said. 'But this is far from over. The Council may have met officially but now the real game begins. I bet every gem I own that over the next two days the king will meet with all the influential councillors. He will want to gauge their position on your petition. It is rare for the king to go against the majority of the Council, and he will not risk anything greatly over you. We must pray that enough councillors either support your plight, or do not care enough one way or another. Because if they don't care then they are more likely to support the purification if only to settle the matter.' She sighed heavily. 'Come, let us stop by the Ethausva's temple and light some incense. We will need her grace tonight.'

'Why?' Cela asked as they started moving again.

'Because my father will kill us once he finds out what we did,' Mynta said bluntly, her face cold.

CHAPTER TWENTY-FIVE

It was not long before the evening meal when they heard the gates to the main courtyard slam open and Mynta's father's voice cut through the hubbub of the household with a growl. 'Where is my daughter?'

The sun was low in the sky but still bright enough to light the yellow stone of the buildings with a warm glow. The welcoming hall was clad in purpling shadows. Several braziers and torches were scattered about to push back the gloom but not enough to heat the still balmy air.

The three of them had been sitting in their chairs since returning from the palace. Mynta had been very clear in her instructions to her two friends. She rarely went against her father and to have his own daughter subvert his designs amounted to a political blackeye.

Her mother had returned earlier in the day. Mynta had explained what they had done and urged her to let them deal with the repercussions. After a few worried words and biting her lips, her mother had smoothed Mynta's hair and kissed her gently on the lips.

'Menrva be with you,' she had whispered before leaving them to their dangerous game, summoning her maids to prepare a bath.

She had taken her mother's seat instead of her own. Desma sat on a stool by her left hand and one pace forward, the position of a supplicant under her wardship. Cela stood to Desma's left but two steps back so she was behind Mynta. Her father's chair had been left where it was, next to where Mynta sat, but all other seats were removed except for a stool that sat directly in front of Mynta five paces away.

Her father could either take his usual seat next to her, thereby forcing both of them to turn to face each other, a stare of equals. Or he could take the stool in front of her.

She knew he would do neither.

Her nursemaid had watched as she readied the hall and taken her seat, her wrinkled face unreadable. She simply waited until Mynta was settled, her dress adjusted just so, before shuffling forward to hold out a diadem of gold set with emeralds. It was three waves high, set with a larger gem at each crest, with strings hanging down and ending in smaller emeralds. Mynta hesitated before nodding. She stayed still as her nursemaid placed it in her hair and held up a small mirror. The diadem sparkled among her ink-dark hair, the small strings hanging down her brow with the emeralds resting just above her eyes. She looked ...

'Beautiful,' Desma said quietly, her hair, the colour of rich wine, coiled about her head, a powerful lady in grey with rubies and silver. Always, the daughter of the high priestess had looked a queen-in-training. Confident and strong, sure in every step she took, command in her voice and care in her eyes. She was who Mynta tried to emulate, the image she sought to project.

The Desma that had come to Trilos was changed. Before, it was clear she knew where every step would fall, but now it seemed that though she still held the belief in her choices, fear flashed in her eyes while the foot was still falling. Her decisions were made with the same abrupt clarity, but shadowed by doubt afterwards. Afraid to speak to anyone beyond the household. Worried to leave its walls where she might be forced to interact with a stranger. Mynta could not imagine what it would be like to go about her day, never knowing if she would have to share her story, tell people how she had killed her own father.

Celadine was always the bright yellow flower to Desma's dark rose. Free and joyful, she never appeared to allow the world to touch her when she did not want it to. But Mynta knew better. Cela saw and experienced the world, the same as anyone else. But she chose how it affected her. And she always chose the light.

But the death of Desma's father – his murder – was an infection that she had not cleaned out properly. He had in all but blood been Cela's father as well and he had been taken away from her twice – first at his own hands, then by her sister. She could not imagine what such a betrayal by two loved ones would feel like and she doubted that Cela knew at this time. She was still fleeing from the wound and one day it would overtake her. Mynta just hoped she was strong enough to survive it.

But first she had to survive her own father.

Linos was like one of the fabled lions of old, snarling at anyone who came close, eyes aglow in the twilight dim. He soon saw her from across the courtyard and stalked towards them; if he had a tail it would have been lashing. He was wearing a short chiton cast around his shoulders. Though he was only a little taller than most men in Trilos, he towered above the three of them seated. She noticed that his beard had been dusted with gold. What the mind noticed at the oddest times.

'You foolish girl,' he snarled, his deep voice even more like gravel than usual, the rumble hardly ending before he spoke again. 'You stupid, meddlesome, *fat* girl. Do you know what you have cost me? Do you realise what you have made me lose because you could not sit at home and *stay silent.*'

His tirade halted as he realised where she was sitting. He had automatically been heading for his chair. He noticed the stool in front of her and kicked it with such force it broke apart when it hit one of the columns.

He took the final steps towards her, grabbed her shoulder, and hurled her from the seat.

Mynta could not help letting out a gasp as she hit the tiled floor but she flung out a hand towards Desma and Cela.

Her friends stopped in their tracks, both having gone for their belts where Mynta had wisely made them put their knives away. No blood would be drawn. Not in her home.

She slowly, carefully, picked herself up, dusting her dress. She rose to her full height, a foot shorter than her father, eyes not flinching from his face. With measured steps, she walked back to her mother's chair and sat back down.

Her father's eyes bulged. He reached for her again.

'Do not lay your hands on me, Emissary Linos,' Mynta said in a level voice, leaching all emotion away.

His hand froze. 'What?'

'I am under the protection and hospitality of Councilman Linos,' she said, back straight and hands clasped in her lap. Pure, demure defiance.

'What?' he strangled out, his hand flexing but no longer moving forward.

'If you harm me any further, I will be forced to call upon the Law of Council Kin.' She was surprised at how steady her voice remained. 'By law, I will become a guest of the king and remain in his palace while a tribunal is formed by no less than seven councillors to investigate the claim of harm against myself.'

'I am your father,' he snarled, looking as though he could chew through stone. 'I rule this household and all who live in it.' His eyes darted towards Desma and Cela but Mynta clapped her hands, once, to bring his attention back to her.

Mynta eyed him coolly. 'That is correct. Yet, by the rules of Trilos, a councillor's authority is only superseded by the prime, and his only by the king, or whomever the king places over them. *As your daughter,*' she said bitingly, 'I am automatically granted protections by the Law of Council Kin. None may lay their hands on me for it will be interpreted as an act of extortion against the councillor and thereby treason against the order of the city.'

Linos reared up to his full height, staring down at her, his breath coming hard and heavy. His face was dark and frightening, and Mynta felt her resolve quail. But, peering up at him, she caught a flash of green from one of the beads on her diadem hanging against her brown and drew strength from it.

'As a councilman,' he said, calm forced into each word. 'I can do what I deem right for the city. You interfered with Council affairs.' He suddenly dropped down to grip each arm of the chair, his face inches from hers. Mynta felt shame at the small gasp that slipped out. 'If I must bring you down to earth with my own hands, then I am within my right.'

Mynta moved her face forward, forcing him back or risk getting headbutted. 'But you did not enter as councillor to citizen,' she said. 'You entered and asked *"where is my daughter?"* and I have witnesses.' She gestured to Desma and Cela and then off to the side. Her father jerked his eyes and gave a surprised grunt. The maids of the household were lined up on the east side of the main garden, their faces impassive. 'All will agree to be called upon to testify to the tribunal.'

'And risk dismissal?' he asked them as much as her.

Her nursemaid, Uni grant her every blessing, stepped forward. 'For justice and the truth, we risk dismissal.'

Her father moved away and crossed his arms, studying her. 'You want something. Otherwise, you would not have entrapped me. You know that I will not risk you calling upon the law. I will be disgraced. The shame alone will drive me from the city and the Council will strip me of my position for violating their rules. Despite the fact that it will ensure the destruction of our family, I ... believe that you would go through with it.' He jerked his head at her friends. 'All for a filthy Father-Killer and a whore.'

In a moment, Mynta was out of the chair, had crossed the intervening space, and slapped her father. The crack of flesh against flesh shattered the gloom. The maids gasped. Even Desma and Cela could not keep quiet their shock. This was not part of the plan – but she would not let him speak of her friends like that.

She calmly returned to her seat. 'What I require,' she said as though nothing had happened, 'is for you to spend the next two days gathering all the support you can among the councillors to promote the purification of Desma. I have never asked anything of you. I have been silent at every harsh word, every ignored greeting, all of the coldness that a daughter should never experience from her father. But this ... this I will fight for because it is from these two women that I learned what to be loved meant.' He flinched. 'I don't care what you have to do. I don't even care if you have to *whore yourself* to get those men to agree – you will ensure that the king performs the cleansing rites. Afterwards, I do not care if we never speak again. You can send me to the other side of the League or to a temple of Horta. Do you understand what I am asking of you?' Demanding of him.

Silence deafened her, nothing but the crackle of flames and the splashing of the creek breaking the tension that spread like a cavern between her and her father.

He was a veteran politician. There were probably a dozen ways he could wiggle out of agreeing. A hundred ways this plan could fail. But she had hedged all her bets that the shock of her standing up to him would be enough. To challenge him in his own house. To use his position as a weapon against him. To twist him in knots so tight he could not breath. All done by his daughter he saw as nothing more than a bejewelled cup he was waiting to sell to the highest bidder.

'I understand,' he said quietly. Without further words, he spun on his heel and walked out into the night and into the city.

It was only after he turned out the gate and was out of sight that she became aware of how hard her heart was beating in her chest. Her skin felt on fire and when she touched her brow she was amazed to find it dry from perspiration.

Desma and Cela flung themselves on her, both praising her bravery. She looked up to see her mother standing at the door of her rooms. Her face was tight but she gave the smallest nod before disappearing inside. But it was not her Mynta was looking for.

Her nursemaid was still standing by the column where she had spoken, a smile splitting her face, pride clear in her eyes.

And deep within her, she felt as though something had opened. Something dangerous and bright, something she had never been brave enough to look at before. But perhaps now she would be.

CHAPTER TWENTY-SIX

The morning of the audience dawned without a blemish in the sky, bright blue and wavering in heat, the fisherman proclaiming it would be a good day at sea and good fortunes were coming.

Mynta had risen early to prepare everything for her friends, ensuring what they wore would be suitable for a royal audience but still humble enough for a supplicant. For Desma, she chose a plain pink peplos, plain yellow belt and sandals, and simple jewellery. Cela was wearing a similar outfit in green, and Mynta chose a warm brown dress.

The house had changed drastically since Mynta confronted her father. After Linos departed, men later arrived to collect her mother and most of the servants, claiming that they were going to stay in their apartments in the city indefinitely. She had been left with Anesidora and her other maids, a cook, two male servants, messenger boys, and twelve guards out of a complement of sixty.

She had asked her mother to stay and she had looked as though she would give in, disobey her husband, but with a wrench she shook her hands from Mynta and turned to leave. But, in a flash, she had spun around and grabbed Mynta's head in a fierce grip, pressing a kiss to her brow.

'I have to go,' she had whispered. 'Be what I can never be.' She then swept from the house, a column of servants bearing chests and baskets following.

Now, they left the house escorted by the crew and four of Mynta's remaining household guards. The streets were busy and many people stopped to watch their odd procession. Mynta kept Desma in the centre, almost unseen behind the shoulders of the others. Desma kept a smile on her face, but Mynta could see the tightness in her muscles.

Her father had not returned to the house again but during the two days he occasionally sent messages back with his secretary to update them on his progress. As hard as he was working to convince the councillors to support the petition, Galen was putting as much effort against her. The Council seemed split evenly in half, with a small percentage avoiding both Linos and Galen, appearing to want to wait until the assembly before casting their support one way or the other.

Mynta could not predict what way the day would go.

They passed swiftly through the city to the palace, crossing its corridors quickly until they came to the great hall. The megaron of the palace was a wonderment. Automatons towered above them all, helms brushing the ceiling fifty feet above them. Metal vines and gemstone flowers wrapped around every column and moved though no breeze flowed. On one side of the hall was a fountain with a waterfall of liquid silver that felt cold when approached.

King Hilarion sat on his throne that looked like solid flame frozen into stone. A hammer twice the height of the throne towered behind him and danced with actual flames that shimmered from red to green to white.

The king himself was a younger man – no more than a handful of years older than Mynta. He was robed in red and deep green, a circlet of orichalcum settled on his windswept brow; more orichalcum covered his fingers and chest, the pride of his kingdom on display. His eyes were warm and kind, but already threads of care spread from their edges and gave creases to his mouth. His skin was the pale flesh of a shelled walnut, the colour of someone who used to spend much of their days outdoors but had not seen the sun for some time.

He was surrounded on either side by members of the Council. Out of the current forty-two members, only seventeen were in attendance. On the king's left she saw her father with five other men, though he refused to meet her eyes. On the king's right was Galen with the rest of the councillors, his grin smug and triumphant. Her heart sank.

First advisor Phokas waited patiently by the king's right hand. When they were within ten steps, he bid them halt.

'King Hilarion of Trilos has considered your petition, Desma, daughter of Timothea,' he proclaimed in a strong voice, clear of any emotion. 'Word of your deeds reached the city long before your arrival. Sophocles of Apasa had also sent a letter to both King Hilarion and High Priest Castur.' Mynta felt Desma stiffen beside her. 'The Hero-King in no way attempted to persuade King Hilarion in his decision, but simply wished to convey a true account of events, clean of rumours or exaggerations that may have occurred on the tongues of travellers and sailors. The king has proclaimed he knows all he needs to be able to make his decision.'

Mynta froze. This was not the way. Desma had the right to speak, to plead her case, to answer any questions. Myta went to open her mouth but the first advisor thudded his copper-butted rod onto the stone floor, silencing her.

'King Hilarion, in his wisdom and in service to our god, Sethlans of the Forge and Flame, declares that you will not find purification by his hand. Our ties to Apasa and our god's wife, Serene Turan, are too tight to allow any dissension – we cannot pardon what they have sentenced. The hospitality of Trilos is extended to you for the grace of four nights. By the following dawn, you are to be out of the city either on foot or by your ship. Thus is the judgement of King Hilarion, blessed of Sethlans.' He struck the floor again with his rod and the king rose without another look, stepping away to go through a door off to the side, Galen and his followers walking after him.

Mynta spun towards her father but he had already disappeared through another door. They were alone. This couldn't be happening. How could the king and his advisor ignore the rights of petitioners? How could her father have failed so miserably?

Mynta turned to her friend, who was left standing before an empty throne, her mouth open, her eyes darkened. Cela and Arete had to practically carry Desma out of the megaron with the king's men urging them with stern faces. Mynta followed behind, too shocked to offer any words of comfort to her friend.

Desma could not sleep.

Her head ached and her eyes burned with each blink from tiredness. But it did not matter how exhausted she was, for sleep either eluded her or was driven away by her own thoughts.

It had been three days since the king had rejected her petition to be purified by his hand. Rage had burned brightly the first day – so hot and wild she honestly thought her skin should be red and raw. In her mind, a whirlwind of destruction surrounded her with chairs smashing and tables flying, trees toppling and stone walls shattering. But nothing happened beyond her hands clenching so tightly that her nails drew blood from her palms.

The second day brought despondency. She could not rise from her bed. No matter what Cela and Mynta did to try to convince her. Food was mud, wine was vinegar, honey was as tasteless as water. Anesidora even threw a bucket of water over her on the bed. But she simply dragged herself up and plopped into a nearby chair, not bothering to change her clothes, its dripping the only company long after the nursemaid left with a sigh.

She felt stupid. She was an idiot. She wanted to shake and slap herself. She wanted to reach inside her chest, rip out this gripping pressure that was strangling her and hurl it into the fire. But she couldn't. She just couldn't.

Despondency sank into despair.

Desma wondered briefly if these feelings were anything like what her father had felt on … that day. There were a hundred stories of men and women with broken hearts, of falling into dark pits, of seeing no way forward. But there was a way. There had to be. It was finding the strength to walk it. And she felt as weak as a lamb.

Her petition had been rejected.

Trilos had abandoned her.

She knew there were other cities, other kings and priests and oracles. Dozens of chances at salvation. People she would have to beg for help. Strangers with whom she would have to share her story, her crime. People who would spit on her, call her father-killer, cast her out from under their roofs, deny wine and bread. And under the law of Tinia, they were within their right. She was filth until she was cleansed.

She knew that she only had two nights left before she had to leave. There was much to prepare. But she could not bear the thought of moving or talking. The shame of having to tell her crew that she still needed their help. The embarrassment of failure. Darkness, bottomless and cold, spread from her chest until she was huddled on her bed, shivering despite the heat.

She thought about her mother – proud and powerful, strength beyond breaking, calm above every storm. How she wanted to be like her, to be with her. She needed her words and comfort. She craved her embrace. She wanted to smell her rose oil and apple smoke. She would know how to stand up again. *She* never would have fallen. High priestesses could not falter for they bore the weight of her people's faith, were the speaker to the divine on behalf of mortals. Strength beyond imagining.

And her father. As solid as the earth. As dependable as the clay he worked with, always sure of what it would be under his hands. Kind and quiet, a warm boulder that would always offer her shelter. But even he had stumbled and lost his way.

Was she like her mother or her father? One never fell and the other fell too deep. Where did her strength come from? The one that had kept her brave when she steered her ship through a storm. The one that kept her hand steady upon her sword when screaming savages ran towards her. The one that led her into the terrors of Urruc to claim its treasures despite everything the cursed land could throw at her. Who was she?

She did not know what time it was when she woke, but the room was dark. She rolled over and saw the half-moon, bright and high in the sky, limned in silver light as it sailed above. It took her a moment to realise she was not alone.

She looked over, expecting it to be Cela or Mynta, or even Anesidora.

The figure that rose up was tall and thin, pale hair shining in the moonlight. With a gasp she flung herself out of the bed, hands searching for her knife but only finding clothes strewn on the floor. She opened her mouth to shout when the figure gave an amused chuckle.

'I remember when you would sleep with a dagger under your pillow and would throw first, ask questions later,' a distinctly quiet voice said.

She paused in her search, panting on her hands and knees. 'Cosmas?'

The quartermaster stepped into the beam of moonlight to reveal his face, his muted blue eyes almost silver. 'Desma.'

'Where in the freezing Beneath have you been?' she cursed, getting to her feet and clasping his forearm in a tight grip. 'Bion has nearly gone bald looking for you.'

His eyes twinkled in amusement. 'I know. He all but strolled the streets hollering my name like a bannerman.'

She gestured at a pitcher of wine on the table but he waved it away. 'And you couldn't swing by the ship to at least report to Khufu? You know he will strap your feet once he gets his hands on you.' They both knew that to be a lie. Though Khufu was the captain, Desma had always allowed Cosmas leeway as long as it did not threaten the safety of the crew. As per their agreement.

'I'm reporting to you now,' he said with a shrug. 'I had to be in too many places at once to spare a moment. You know I would come to you if it was necessary.'

It was true. Though she rarely knew his methods she was aware of the results he produced. And sometimes she was glad to be ignorant of his methods.

'What do you know?' she asked, settling on her bed.

He leaned against the wall, arms folded loosely in front of him, seeming at ease. As much as a leopard was ever at ease, at least. She noted that, from where he stood, he could see both windows and the door.

'Though it means little now, Amynta's father worked hard to win support for you,' he said, keeping his voice low. 'He was actually making headway – which is why Galen probably did what he did.' He explained how, the night before the audience, many of the sons of the councillors had sailed into the harbour, as they did on occasion, with wine and musicians and women. Children of the powerful often become friends, growing up together and always ready to cut each other down when their turn at power came around. But the ship never returned to the city at dawn. By early morning, the councillors were aware their sons were missing. A promise was whispered around the palace of their safe return if the daughter of Apasa was refused.

'That bastard,' she swore again. Resorting to blackmail to win the support he needed. There was no surprise the councillors did as he wanted. They probably knocked themselves over in their rush to speak with the king before the appointed hour. They did not care what happened to her – there was no benefit or profit to them if she was cleansed.

She could hardly blame them; but what she wanted to know was why Galen was working so hard against her. What did he hope to gain? She had never heard of him before now and she doubted her mother ever had anything to do with him. What plans did he have in place?

'There are more bastards in the world than olives,' Cosmas said.

She poured herself some wine and took a gulp. There was also some cheese and grapes on a plate beside the pitcher. She helped herself. 'That explains two of the days in Trilos. You got here before we did. What else did you do?'

He picked at a thread on his shirt. 'I tried to get a sense of the city's feelings towards what happened at Apasa with the temple, on the Empyreans, and on you. It was split down the middle. Most were either indifferent or sympathised. The other half cursed your name and said you were lucky Sophocles only pronounced you polluted instead of the more visceral punishments available. I figured you would find that out yourself easily enough so moved on.'

'Moved on to what?' She reached for some bread. It was slightly dry but she swallowed it down with more wine.

'It looked like a coin toss on what the king would decide. So I went searching in case the coin fell unfavourably and found your next best chance.'

Desma felt the cup quiver in her hand. 'Where?'

He leaned forward with a grin. 'Koriithos.'

'Koriithos?' she said slowly. On a map, Koriithos was almost exactly due west of Apasa but to reach it by ship you had to sail south, around Athanai. It was situated on the small bridge of land that connected the southern peninsula to the mainland. It was not truly connected, as there was a canal over seven miles long that allowed ships to sail from the Gulf of Koriithos to the Icarii Sea, instead of sailing all the way round the peninsula. It was a proud city with a severe people, ancient home of the Father of the Deeps, Nethuns, before he abandoned them for Viminalis in the Empire.

'Why there?' she asked.

'Because only recently the king has made it known beyond their lands that the city has been terrorised by a horrible monster for the last ten years.'

Her mouth dropped. 'What? How could that news be hidden from the League?'

Cosmas shrugged. 'Apparently, the monster only attacks those born within the city. Travellers and merchants and visiting nobles are left alone. Hundreds of men have been sent to hunt it down and only some ever return, babbling of burning blood and frozen skin and tearing flesh.' Even he gave a little shudder. 'The mildest of stories are not pleasant. Koriithosans are a private people and tight-lipped. None wanted to announce they are being hounded by a creature from a godling's nightmares, nor that they cannot vanquish it themselves. And it is not consistent. It might attack five times in a row and then disappear for a six-month, only to reappear for another attack and vanish again. Several weeks ago marked ten years since the first attack and the king has sent word for a hero.'

'Why would this be of interest to me?' She knew there must be a reason.

'Because the king has promised to grant a single request, if it lay within his power to give, to anyone who vanquishes the monster.'

Her hand paused as she reached for more bread. 'But that means...' Purification was only possible by a select few. Oracles were few and far between. Two of the Holy Twelve had already rejected her, as well as Sophocles and Hilarion. Konoso was far to the south, the Dramakians were unpredictable at best, and listened to the moon and wind more than their own thoughts. Athanai had no king – only archons who, much to their anger, were not granted the king's right of cleansing. Thevai was roughly the same distance to sail as Koriithos. But Koriithos was offering a clear chance.

Word would spread throughout the League, lighting a fire in the hearts of youths and glory-chasers. Veterans of battles would no doubt try their hand, thinking their experience would tip the scales in their favour. Some would even doubt there was a monster – probably only a large bear or wild boar. Monsters were not uncommon in the League; offspring of gods, cursed creatures, ancient things that emerged occasionally. And all it would take was one lucky sword blow, a well-aimed arrow, a firm spear thrust, to snatch her chance away.

A path was suddenly clear in front of her, well-paved but leading into a forest. Whether she would emerge from the other side remained to be seen.

'We're sailing for Koriithos,' she said, decisiveness ringing in her voice. Her hand hit the tray beside her and she was stunned to see that she had eaten every morsel and drank the entire pitcher of wine. 'If you will wake Cela and Mynta, I will head to the ship to speak with Khufu.' She went to rise but found Cosmas standing very close to her, all but forcing her to remain seated unless she wanted to slide up his body.

'While I am grateful to once more see some fire in you, Desma,' he said carefully, 'as well the return of your appetite, it is best if you sleep. Dawn is in a few hours and we still have plenty of time to depart Trilos.'

She tried to wriggle around him on the bed but he pushed her shoulder, gently but with indomitable pressure, until she was lying on her back.

'I am not a child,' she growled as he lifted the blanket over her.

'Of course not,' he said, with too much care to keep his voice neutral. 'Sleep, Desma.'

She was tired. The food and wine were contentedly heavy in her stomach and her eyes were burning with tiredness. Perhaps an hour or so of sleep would be good. But no more. She knew where to place her feet again. All she had to do was figure out how to kill a monster ...

Dim greyness took her.

CHAPTER TWENTY-SEVEN

The Darkling cut through the waters off the beach of Trilos as though as eager to leave the city as Desma felt. Sixteen days since they arrived in the city. Sixteen days of effort that had culminated in ash – though not for all of them.

Mynta's father had not returned home. He had sent a messenger saying that they would be remaining in the palace apartments for the foreseeable future. He had arranged an allowance for Mynta to run the household and for anything else she may need. Her friend had become mistress of a major house. Instead of worrying, she was excited. Desma almost imagined cogs, like in one of automatons, churring away in her friend's mind. So much had changed in the past year between visits that she wondered who she would find if she returned to Trilos.

When she returned to Trilos again.

They had said farewell on the docks at morning high tide, the three of them unable to let go of each other.

When they eventually disentangled themselves, tears clear on all their faces, Desma and Cela boarded the ship, the rowers already at their stations and the crew waiting by the railing. The sails unfurled, the colour of deep wine, the wind catching at them straight away, as harbour men pushed the bow of the ship back into the waves. As the ship slipped away from the shore, Desma had thrown the silver ring onto the sand at the beachmaster's feet, making an astonishingly rude gesture at him. Cela let loose a peal of laughter at his outraged face and spluttering, mimicking the gesture as well.

Trilos, with its proud walls and ever-present billow of smoke that rose from The Forge, fell behind quickly, the wind favouring them as it blew from the east. If the wind remained steady they would reach Koriithos in four days.

Desma took the chance to stand at the helm, letting the salt-scrubbed wind ripple through her hair, the clean scent of the sea both sharp and soothing. As much as she wanted to let all her troubles go, scattering them to the eight corners of the world, she knew it was impossible; so she shoved them down into the darkest hold in the ship, hoping to leave them there until they reached the city.

Arete joined her after an hour, seeming content to also enjoy the peace of the open water.

'I haven't taken the chance yet to thank you,' Desma said, continuing to gaze forward. The sea was a deep blue that turned black at times and crystal green at others.

She saw the shipwright's puzzlement out the corner of her eye. 'Thanks for what?' the smaller woman asked carefully.

Desma patted the wood of the rail beside her. 'Do you think I would not recognise your work? This is your ship. Built by your hands and your hands alone.'

Arete glanced back at Cela, who was teasing Bion as he tried to eat a long pepper in peace, a blush turning him bright red while Delphinus roared with laughter.

'She said nothing,' Desma said. 'She only told me that she bought the ship. I hope for a fair price?'

Arete snorted. 'She could have bought five triremes for what I asked. I thought that would dissuade her thoroughly. She only frowned and left, returning an hour later with Bion carrying two chests filled with gold drachmae. What could I do? She honoured the price I set and I was not going to go against my word, may Turms strike me dumb,' she said, calling upon the God of Merchants and Trade.

'I promise to look after her as best I can,' Desma promised, her hand still on the railing.

The smaller woman shrugged. 'We cannot see what will happen. All we can pray is that we reach safe harbours if anything does befall us while at sea.' She looked up at the taunt sails above, a ghost of a smile alighting on her lips.

'But I am proud of *The Darkling*. Proud that she is under your command and that I can still be with her. '

Desma reached down and took Arete's hand, squeezing it tight. 'I am proud to be sailing her with you.'

Arete leaned against Desma and they stood together, watching the horizon stretch far ahead, the wind tugging at their hands and clothes.

Spurts of water burst from the waves on the port side of the ship, crystallising in the air before shattering when they hit the surface.

They both gasped but then another eruption happened on the starboard side.

More spurts of water shot into the sky all around the ship; some turning a brilliant blue and some vibrant green. Desma began to hear sounds like rocks clattering down a cliff. She leaned over the rail and stared below the surface. A face, distinct from the water but still part of it, coalesced below and gave a shy smile. Its eyes were like teardrops, the iris bright white, with hair that floated like spilled ink, and lips like coral. A little hand, webbed and covered in pearls, gave a small wave before it vanished.

'Sea sprites,' Desma cried out in delight. 'They're sea sprites,' she called again to the crew. Bion and Khufu took their hands from their weapons while Kassandra lowered a bow.

Sea sprites were the cast-off children of the ocean nymphs. Creatures barely able to hold corporeal form, they floated in large, adopted families that rarely came into sight of people. But they had on occasion helped guide a ship through fog, their light leading the way.

'Do we have any ...' Desma began to ask, turning from the water.

'Already ahead of you,' Cela said, coming up beside her with a small amphora. She broke the seal with her knife and began to pour. Golden mead flowed into the water. Within moments, the sea turned into a roiling explosion of lights. Sea sprites loved honey above all else, and had been known to almost blind crews in trying to impress them with their lights in the hope of an offering.

Once fed, the sprites followed them for the rest of the day, shooting geysers of blue and green and white over and over again. They ended up feeding them another three amphoras of mead, until Bion began to grumble and stalked into the hold to stand guard over the rest.

As sunset was starting to bleed into twilight, the sprites began to slowly disperse. Delphinus brought out his lyre and strummed lightly on its strings.

It was peaceful and Desma savoured every moment. In a few days, they would be in Koriithos with all the challenges and hardship it would bring. But until then she would be surrounded with friends and the worries of the future could stay in the future. For now.

She waited until the final girl had gathered her discarded robes of ceremony and carried them from her chambers to be washed. She never wore the same clothes two days in a row. In fact, she rarely kept any garment for longer than a year, summoning seamstresses during midwinter to measure her for the new year to come.

She gazed at herself in a mirror of purest glass, so clear and clean that it seemed as though two women stood in the room. The Empire was known for its glass works – fabled throughout the Middle Sea and even beyond. Her body was on the fuller side of slim, age keeping a tight grasp on every ounce of weight, where before youth would shed it almost as fast as the food was consumed. Her hair was long, hanging to the middle of her back when loose. Once a luxurious cascade of earthy gold, it was streaked with more grey than anything else now. Of average height for an Empyrean woman, she held herself as though she towered above the greatest man. Senators bowed when she walked by, lesser lords falling to their knees, and commoners all but grovelling in the dirt. She demanded no less.

Touching her face with her fingers, she almost marvelled at the changes that seemed to have occurred when she was not looking. Her eyes were the same cutting green as from her youth, but the creases that multiplied daily were prominent. She pushed at her cheeks that slightly sagged, almost being able to gather the loose skin between her fingers. She viciously ripped out a hair she found on her chin, somehow growing to an inch long despite her morning ritual hunt for new growth.

She was clad in only an undergarment of cotton, cut well enough to cling to her body, highlighting what once was proud and tight but now was low and heavy. She shuddered and turned away from the sight.

When had she grown old? She could no longer pretend she was mature. She was older than most grandmothers she knew. A hag serving the Goddess of Beauty. What irony!

Another girl, no older than twelve, entered after a timid knock, her eyes kept low to the ground. She dropped to her knees, bent over with both hands clasped over her heart until bidden to rise.

The girl moved to a chest and drew out soft robes of pleasant green with gold thread. She helped her dress, deftly working her grey-with-a-touch-of-brown hair into a hive with pins of quartz, sliding sandals on her feet, and dabbing oil of rose and apple on her wrists and neck.

'Thank you, child,' she said dismissively, pleased that her voice had lost none of its musical quality. 'Please send Bishop Camillus in to see me.'

She moved over to a table and let her fingers run over the objects. A small knife with a hooded serpent handle; a bowl with geometric black and red markings; a beaded bracelet with a clasp that looked as though the moon and sun had collided into a new celestial object; a jug so thin she thought it would shatter with a touch, but had instead practically bounced when she accidentally dropped it. A dozen more items laid on soft silk pillows or stands carved from ivory. Treasures from Urruc, plundered from the temple in Apasa. Salvaged from the outcasts and brought to the true home of her goddess.

In thanks, her Goddess had allowed her to keep one small chest. Though she had seen other items of such beauty she thought she would weep, what laid before her now was worth almost as much as the city of Aventinus itself.

She moved over to her balcony and looked out on the city. Built on the far east of the Great Island that was south of the mainland Empire, it was a city of lacework bridges and slender spires, red and pink quartz domes, golden statues, streets paved with white and grey marble and lined with walls of silver and sea glass. The sea shimmered around the arrowhead of land that the city was built on, the harbour split in two as they fell on either side into protected coves.

Here bloomed all the plants that pleased her goddess: apple trees and rosemary bushes, myrtle trees and sweet roses, riots of spring flowers and sea jasmine. Incense burned at every church and shrine, and in many households, until it was almost too heady to walk through the city without a spinning head; but always the crisp sea wind blew the air clear and left the very stones scented.

It was known as the City of Birds and it lived true to its name. The sky was filled with sparrows that flitted and chirped from the first hint of dawn. Doves from brilliant white to the faintest blush festooned churches and arabesque windows. The sparkling ponds and rivulets of the city were dotted with swans, geese, and ducks of a dozen varieties, all blessed and sheltered under Turan's hand.

In the few places where the land suddenly dropped away into the ocean, creating cliffs sheer and shallow, stood statues of her goddess carved by Sethlans himself. Some were nude, others with nothing but a loose robe fluttering away from her body, and others in full regalia.

The praetor of Aventinus was holding a public audience in the Heraclaen Square in front of his palace, a collection of towers and spires encased in sheets of bronze with red tops and domes. He was the third praetor in ten years, but finally this one seemed to grasp the understanding that she ruled this city in the name of her goddess, not for the Empire.

The knock at the door heralded her guest.

Camillus was born in a peasant hovel and spent his childhood growing the grain that fed Aventinus. A priest of Golden Turan had paused in his village for the night on his way back to the city and was a guest of Camillus' family. The priest had spoken of the Goddess of Love and in the morning Camillus had left with him, the fires of a zealot burning in his eyes. In thirty years, he was now a Bishop of the Church, proud and learned, with a neat-trimmed beard that was the style of the day, brown hair, and a smile that set most people on edge. But she knew him to the core of his being, having been the one to raise him through the ranks. A scorpion on a leash, but she never forgot the sting at the end of his tail.

He bowed deeply, his cerulean stole held to his robes with a pin shaped like a spray of orange roses. 'Holy Mother Valeriana, may the blessings of Turan the Golden rain on your heart,' he intoned.

'And on you, my son,' she said back, kissing her fingertips and touching them briefly to the top of his head. 'How are you enjoying your new home?'

'Very much, Holy Mother,' Camillus said after standing. As a reward for his deeds in Apasa, she had gifted him a beautiful sea palace with servants and riches.

'And how are you healing?' she asked.

She watched as he stiffened slightly, eyes going hard. As punishment for his failure in Apasa, she had him strapped in the Hall of Mortification in front of all the bishops in residence.

'Slowly,' he said in a flat voice. 'As is the will of Turan.'

He would come for her title one day. She had no doubt and expected nothing less. It was that drive and ambition that had drawn her notice. But he would not be high priest any time soon. Not if all her plans come to fruition.

'You have a chance at redemption,' she said. 'Come, sit with me and pour us some wine.'

They moved to a set of chairs padded with silk, a small table between them with a silver pitcher and cups studded with amethyst. Camillus poured the rich wine from Tuscanai and handed her cup before filling his own.

'I will do anything in service of Turan,' he said quietly, but she saw his fist clenching the stem of the wine cup. He was shamed in front of his kin, but his failure could not go unpunished.

'You failed to retrieve the Belt of our Goddess from Apasa,' she said, taking a sip. Excellent vintage. 'Despite Timothea's attempts to hide the news from reaching us, she had told Turan. That, above anything else in that temple, She wanted. And it was the one thing you did not bring back.'

Camillus bowed his head. There was nothing for him to say. He had told her everything when his ships had returned and she had personally watched every man on the ship stripped in front of her and every crate searched before she finally agreed he did not have it. She later had the three quinqueremes pulled into the dry dock and torn apart to ensure it was not secreted in a smuggler's hold.

The Church had walked in fear of encountering her for several weeks after. She had not held back her temper.

'Golden Turan has come to me in my meditations and blessed you with another chance,' Valeriana explained. 'The Belt must have been removed from the temple for safekeeping. Timothea would never have given it to Sophocles to guard. The Belt is divinity itself and could only be trusted to an initiate of the temple, or an extraordinary member.'

Camillus looked up puzzled before understanding dawned. 'The daughter.'

She nodded. 'Desma. She either has it or knows its location. And after the death of her mother and murdering her own father,' she shuddered at the words – even to her, patricide was sickening, 'she may very well have decided to hide it forever. You are to find her and find the Belt. At any cost. You are granted dispensation by the Church and by Turan's hand. All crimes committed from now until the return of the Belt, so long as they are in service to this order, are pardoned and annulled within the Empire. *Bring back the Belt.* Do you understand me?'

Camillus placed his wine cup on the table and knelt on both knees, palms placed over his heart, eyes lowered. 'By my love and passion, I vow to bring the Belt of Turan back to Aventinus and lay it into your hands, Holy Mother, or I will die in the attempt and my soul wander the stony shores, never to feel the touch of a Charun's hands.'

She again kissed her fingers and placed them lightly on his crown of hair. 'Go, my son, and may all the gods guide you.'

The young bishop left the room quickly, barely nodding again as he walked out the door.

She took another sip of wine and noticed that he had never touched his own. Clever man. He would one day be high priest. But only when she gave up the post willingly. Either in death, or to move on to greater heights. And she very much wanted the latter.

CHAPTER TWENTY-EIGHT

Koriithos was a city of bright white stone, red tiled roofs, and sweeping green stairs. Water fell from a thousand spouts and fountains, some fresh and others seawater. It was a sprawling city more than twice the size of Apasa. Pine trees, some towering more than a hundred feet in height, spotted the city. The land surrounding was rolling hills of grass and rock outcroppings, interrupted by golden patches of wheat or groves of olives and grapes.

The north of the city was bordered by the spear-straight blue line of the canal that cut across the seven-mile-wide isthmus. Koriithos held the land connecting the peninsula to the mainland and had grown rich on the taxes and tolls paid by merchants. Wars had been waged between the city and most of the League at one point in time. Phoroniaa had started no less than four wars in the past five centuries, while Athanai had launched three. But the city had never fallen. Some said it was because of the God of the Deeps, Nethuns, who grew angry when his favourite people were threatened. But though Koriithos tried to keep it secret, it was widely known that Nethuns had not visited the city in over two hundred years, preferring to spend his days floating among the canals of Viminalis.

As *The Darkling* sailed into the famous harbour, the crew all stood on deck to gape wide-eyed. None of them had been to Koriithos before, and even Cosmas could not resist coming out of the hold to stare, though his mouth was kept firmly closed.

The harbour was over two miles wide with sheer white cliffs rising towards the eastern side where the Temple of Nethuns and royal palace proudly strutted into the sky. Scattered throughout the water were rocks and several small islands, only large enough to hold a single building. The smaller rocks held statues of Nethuns carved from green marble and obsidian. The God of the Deeps sat on thrones of shells, or atop cresting waves, or towered over slain beasts, hand held out either in benediction or in warning – depending on the mood of the petitioner. The islands held open-air temples with only a half dozen columns on each side holding up the roof.

A single island held a temple to Turan, identified by the rose quartz columns and rose bushes festooning the rocks despite the salt. She was a goddess of the sea, after all, and the Koriithosans were wise enough not to offend her entirely by disputing her rule over the waves. Sailors knew above all others how fickle sea gods could be.

They docked their ship and Arete went to speak with the Master of Quays to record their ship and pay the fees.

'Let the men stay in the nearby inns,' Desma said to Khufu, the towering Opuni man eyeing the dockworkers warily. 'Keep three men on the ship at all times and rotate them. Kassandra, I'll leave it to you to find us an inn closer to the palace. Nothing too extravagant,' she warned as the overseer beamed excitedly and vaulted down the ramp.

It was a little over an hour later when she returned, four large men following her, all of them looking a little dazed as they watched the diminutive overseer. She directed them to start gathering their chests and crates.

'I found a serviceable inn,' she said casually. 'Close to the palace and we can all stay there. Ah ... we will need the bigger one,' she said to Bion who had gone below to grab the smaller coin chest.

Desma groaned.

'You will love it,' Kassandra promised with a sweet smile.

They made an interesting group walking through the city, clearly not from the kingdom. Koriithosans were a somber people, their clothes drifting towards dark greens, browns, and greys. What was strange to Desma was that it seemed only the men wore jewellery; the women kept their hair in tight bundles or tails, with only ribbons to keep them in place. Occasionally a woman wore a ring with a dark stone, or a bronze bracelet.

In comparison, Desma, Cela, and Kassandra all wore bright coloured peplos, most of their hair left flowing freely, draped in what they thought was an austere amount of gold and jewels. Arete wore a chiton of dull grey but enough silver to sink a rowboat.

Most inns in the League were sparsely furnished, as they focused their efforts on serving good food and drink. Many of the people who stayed at inns were short term visitors, merchants and sailors, wanderers and farmers come to market. People who needed longer term residence stayed with friends or paid to rent rooms in private homes.

This inn, due to its proximity to the palace, catered for a richer clientele. Bronze statues of Nethuns and Horta, friends and lovers, stood in welcome beside the door. Nethuns turned to waves below his waist, his beard sweeping low and a crown of starfish on his brow, eyes wide like a deep-sea fish, and his four-prong fishing spear by his side. Horta was clothed in a dress that became sheaves of wheat, her hair coiled loosely around her head with a coronet of pomegranate seeds.

Inside, the common room was spacious, filled with men in dark robes with glints of a gold bracelet or bejewelled ring. Women sat in small groups, adorned only with ribbons, and whispered as though careful not to create a disturbance.

The owner was a large man, pale as mountain snow with only his face and hands tinted a light copper from being touched by the sun. His hair was thinning and he had a slightly unkempt beard. But his eyes were warm and he welcomed them, though he seemed to pay most attention to Bion. 'Your woman let me know that your stay is indefinite at this point in time,' he said to the helmsman, ushering him to a large trestle table. 'I would appreciate that the fee for the accommodation be paid in instalments of three days, first payable now. And if every meal can be paid before the last leaves the table. Not that I don't think you are a trustworthy fellow, but one can never be too careful with … these times.' His hesitation was clear he had meant to say something else.

Bion shrugged his broad shoulders and gestured towards Cela. 'She's in charge. Best to work out the details with her.' Desma thought it best if Cela led until they could speak to the king to avoid having to tell her story.

The owner peered around Bion at Cela who stood with a scowl on her face. 'Oh,' he said carefully before understanding seemed to dawn. 'I understand. Of course, you might be here a good while and it is always best to have a woman to run the house, as it were.' He snapped his fingers at Cela. 'Eight gold drachmae for three days. Konosoan weight, mind you.'

Cela looked about ready to bite the man's head off when Kassandra leaned over and whispered in her ear. She nodded and took a deep breath to calm herself. 'Six drachmae and in Apasan weight. Only fools carry Konosoan gold in their purse to fling about for bread and figs.'

The owner looked ready to swallow his own tongue rather than haggle with her. Desma let them be and Arete asked a serving girl to show the rest of them to their rooms.

The inn was a sprawling affair all on one floor. Their group had five rooms. Four for each of the men and one room for the women to share. Desma looked at the two small beds on either side, with a pallet on the floor between them; a small table and washstand were pushed up next to the door and a hollow in the wall served as their storage.

'To the Beneath with this,' she swore and reordered the rooms. Delphinus and Bion would share what was the women's room. Cela and Desma would share a room and bed, Kassandra and Arete another. Khufu and Cosmas got their own rooms.

'There is still plenty of light,' Arete said. 'We might as well get started.' She nodded to Kassandra and the two of them headed outside.

Desma sighed and laid back on her feather-stuffed bed, arms folded under her head. They would do the same as when they arrived in Trilos. Arete would head to the palace and request an audience with the king to petition for purification. They figured it would be best to ask for cleansing first before volunteering to go hunting monsters. Gods only knew what the king would say. Kassandra headed to the Temple of Nethuns to ask the same of the high priest.

Desma held little hope. Especially after Trilos. It seems Tinia did not mean for this to be an easy punishment. Not that it should be. She had killed her father. Regardless that she knew it was the right thing to do, to save his soul and to reunite him with her mother, it was still murder. And the gods had judged her.

She wondered how big the monster's teeth were ...

Dinner was roast lamb with sweet onions in vine leaves, brined olives, seafood soup, and crusty rolls with chunks of dried figs. Wine and mead were served liberally to wash it all down.

Musicians played in the corner, strumming at lyres and beating softly on drums, candles casting warm glows in the darkening corners, though the sun had not yet sunk below the water. Desma's group was quiet.

She thought that her petition would be rejected eventually, but both the temple and palace had declined her request in a way that brooked no argument. They suggested she seek one of the more liberal cities, such as Delphon or Thevai.

'At least they did not waste our time, like the fools in Trilos,' Khufu said around a mouthful of lamb. 'As stark as these people appear, they are forthright.'

'Did anyone find out how we go about offering to kill the monster?' Cela asked.

Bion raised his hand as he took a deep drink of mead. They waited until he put his now empty cup down and gave a small belch. 'We need to approach the Second Astronomer. He will "read our stars for voids and flashes" and, if he is happy, then he will allow us to approach the king.'

'What does he mean, "read our stars"?' Cela asked. 'What do the stars have to do with us? Everyone knows they are strings of light set by the gods to honour heroes and lost godlings.'

'Koriithosans believe stars to be sentient beings of power and light that affect our lives through their movements,' Cosmas said from his seat in the corner, back to the wall, a shredded loaf in front of him. 'Astronomers are revered in this kingdom and the king does not act until he consults his First Astronomer. A man named Kalchas. The Second Astronomer is his student, although he would be known as a master anywhere outside the palace. He is called Hyllos.'

Bion grunted. 'You seem to know a lot about a place you've never visited before.'

Cosmas gave a slight shrug. 'I've been here for nearly a whole day.'

The helmsman laughed and thudded Cosmas on the back, nearly sending the slight man tumbling off his seat.

'So how does one meet the Second Astronomer?' Desma asked. She did not enjoy the idea of waiting in line with other monster hunters, any of them able to strike up a conversation with her, and she could not send Cela or Arete to speak on her behalf. She had to make the offer in order to claim the prize.

'He spends the hour before dawn watching the last glimmer of the stars, by the statue of Nethuns' Admonition on the harbour wall,' Cosmas said.

They all turned to him.

'What?' he said, popping a small sliver of bread into his mouth. 'I said I've been here for a day.'

CHAPTER TWENTY-NINE

Desma slept in fits and starts during the night, waking in a breathless rush in fear the time had gone past. She need not have worried. When the sky had turned from purplish-black to purplish-grey, the door to the room opened and Cosmas peered in. 'Let's go,' he whispered.

She rose from her bed, already dressed in a peplos of soft brown, and drew on a himation of cream. She strapped a small knife to her belt, and decided against any jewellery to avoid drawing attention. When she slipped out of the room, Cela still mumbling in her sleep gently, Cosmas was waiting patiently, clothed in a long chiton of deep green, soft boots instead of sandals on his feet. 'Do you really need two daggers?' she asked as they padded through the inn.

'Should I mention the other four?' he asked with a small grin.

Desma decided to ignore him.

It took about fifteen minutes to reach the statue. The Father of the Deeps was carved from green-veined marble, his strong legs almost invisible in the stone waves that seemed to swirl in the eye. The god's bare chest was wide, crisscrossed with scars from ruling the oceans. His beard fell to his waist, tangled in nets and studded with pearls. His face was as stern as rock, with wide eyes, shark teeth, and an eagle nose. His hair fell to his shoulders, twice as broad as Bion's, and a crown of scales and sea froth on his brow.

He stood with arms crossed, one hand clutching his fishing spear, and the other with a single finger raised. He glared down at the sea as though it was a disobedient child, his frown frightening and harsh – Nethuns' Admonition. A fitting name for the statue.

Sitting on the small step at the base of the statue's plinth was a robed figure, several charts spread out in front of him, his face staring wide-eyed up at the sky. Desma followed his gaze and saw a handful of stars that had not yet become lost in the predawn gloom. They shone fiercely, as though aware they were about to disappear.

One in particular shone a deep blue, and another off to the west was a garnet gleaming. Time passed and the three of them watched as the stars continued to swim through the sky as it lightened into grey, slowly becoming stained by fingers of colour. Finally, the last star vanished and, after a moment, the man shook himself as though out of a slumber and gathered up his charts. He dusted off his robe and turned around, only to gasp at the sight of them and nearly drop his papers.

'You startled me,' he said accusatorily, straightening himself. He was tall and the colour of milk not yet separated from the cream. Freckles spattered his nose and his brown eyes were wary and intelligent. His head was shorn around the sides but the hair on his crown was long and curly. He was not large, nor was he overly slight, with hands more used to wielding a stylus and ink over chisel or plough. His voice was rich and commanding, clearly used to telling people what would be and what would not.

'Apologies, Second Astronomer Hyllos,' Desma said with a polite nod. 'We did not wish to disturb your celestial studies and yet we have urgent business. Thus, our seeing you at this early hour.'

'Indeed,' he said intrigued. 'Thesan has scarcely flung open the doors of her palace to farewell the night and already I have advocates. For what cause, is the question.'

Desma knelt smoothly onto her knees, her hair spreading over her shoulders as the cream fabric of her cloak slipped off. She kept her eyes firmly on his face as it creased in further puzzlement.

'That hair ...' he said.

'I am Desma, daughter of High Priestess Timothea and the potter Palamaon,' she said with a clear voice, though her chest quivered. 'I killed my father to save his soul, to ensure it would be carried by the Charuns across the river so he could spend the afterlife with my mother, his wife. I did it out of love for them both. But it was still a blood crime.'

The astronomer watched her with intelligent eyes as she told her story. When she had completed the account, she continued, 'I have come to Koriithos to offer my services to the kingdom to slay the monster that terrorises its citizens. I understand you are the man to speak to in order to arrange a meeting with the king.' She was careful to phrase it as a statement and not a request for assistance, which was forbidden under the law of Tinia.

Hyllos looked at a loss for a moment, before he smoothed his features and glanced at Cosmas. 'And you are?' he asked.

'Hungry for my breakfast,' the quartermaster replied dryly. 'Your expedition in reading her stars would be appreciated.'

Hyllos turned back to Desma, who remained kneeling in front of him, her hands hidden in the folds of her dress as they were clamped tightly together. 'Please stand,' he said. 'Second Astronomers do not receive such obeisance.'

Desma rose and waited patiently. She expected this man to be filled with ideas of his own importance, inflated like a pig's bladder children kicked around in the streets. But Hyllos appeared ... uncertain of himself.

'Perhaps it was best you came at this time,' he said thoughtfully. 'Maybe some of these star movements will make sense now. Come.' He moved to a nearby stone bench and she joined him. Cosmas leaned against the plinth and watched silently.

'Interesting bodyguard,' the astronomer noted, eyeing Cosmas warily.

'He is actually my ship's quartermaster.'

'I think I would prefer starvation rather than risk what he would put in my food.'

Desma let out a laugh. 'Too much cinnamon is what you can expect.' She could feel Cosmas eyes boring holes into her back.

They fell into a silence while Hyllos studied her, his eyes moving slowly from her hair, to her eyes, to her hands, to her feet, and everywhere in between. She began to feel like a specimen about to be dissected. 'How do we begin?'

'We already have,' he said cryptically. 'Do you know what stars are?'

'I was taught they were creations of the gods to remember their children who died and great heroes of the world,' she said. 'But I have since learned that Koriithosans believe differently.'

'They are spheres, further away than any mind could fathom,' he explained, 'some larger than our entire world by over a thousand times, tens of thousands. Imagine.'

Desma could not. Such size was impossible. She didn't even know how far the lands stretched more than a thousand miles north of Dramaki, or the same length east of Apasa. Was there even an end to the Middle Sea out west? She suddenly felt very small.

'We believe that they have a consciousness, imbued by the magic of the cosmos, by a fragment of everything that had been, will be, and is.' Hyllos waved his hands as he explained, caught up in the excitement of his work, his charts spilling onto the bench. 'Their movements are messages, warnings, promises. Only through long study can one learn to read what they are trying to say. It is by doing this that astronomers can read the aura of someone's life and their story, both told and untold. But it can be fickle and unclear, a jumble of cords and twisted wires and broken paths. Weak minds have broken trying to see the patterns.'

'Sounds like a dangerous occupation,' she said. What would he see when he read her stars? Did she have a void? Could he see if she would slay the monster and be cleansed? 'What do you see with me?'

He plucked a chart from the pile and rolled it open. It was filled with circles that intertangled with coloured orbs and waving lines. It was gibberish. 'What I saw this morning,' he said slowly, picking his words carefully, 'as I have been seeing for the last week, is a star that is sometimes bright, catching the first rays of dawn, red as new birth blood, and becoming pink. But sometimes that same star would become almost lightless, only seen because it is a deeper dark than the gloom around it. If a star could be said to be at war with the skies, that is how I would phrase it. A constant battle of light and dark, colours and bleakness, voids and brilliance. It follows no set pattern, yet will not deviate even when all the knowledge gathered says it should move before celestial bodies far larger than it. It rises and falls and is never where I expect it to be. I could not understand what it meant until I saw you before me. Your hair ...' He reached out and took a stand in his finger, examining it against his pale skin.

'It is the same as the last colour of the star each night before dawn arrives. It can only mean you.'

She swallowed, feeling uneasy. 'What does that mean for me?'

Hyllos let go of her hair and looked at the chart in his hand. 'I don't know,' he said. 'Greatness and disaster. Breaking and binding. More breaking, I think. But breaking what? Love and pain are intertwined deeply but they do not mean what you think they would mean. You are anathema and antithesis. But for who and for what, I still cannot say.' Frustration crept into his voice. 'It is a conundrum I would very much be happy to have solved already.'

She looked out over the harbour at the grey water that was slowly turning blue, the warm breeze promising a cloudless, hot day. She thought back to her mother and father. They had both said to stay home, find a husband, and be forgotten. She did not regret doing what she did to save her father, but sometimes she wondered what it would be like to find peace in obscurity. She did not understand half of what Hyllos said, but if love and pain were involved then so was Turan. And she did not want to fall under the goddess' eyes ever again.

'I suppose I can head to Phoroniaa next, and then maybe to Pallan if they say no,' she said to herself.

'What do you mean?' Hyllos asked confused. 'You are leaving already?'

'It is clear you will not grant me admittance to see the king. He and the high priest have already declined my request to be cleansed, so I need to move on.'

'Are you an oracle yourself, Desma?' the astronomer asked. 'Able to predict my decision and words? Nevertheless, you would make a poor one and would be cast out by Aplu.'

She blinked. 'Does that mean ...?'

He nodded. 'I will grant your request. Aside from all that I do not understand, I see something that ties you to this city. Though it, too, has strains of darkness, it is predominately bright. You are not finished with Koriithos.'

Relief flowed like warm honey through her chest. She flung her arms around his shoulders, not caring when he stiffened and did not return the embrace. 'Thank you,' she whispered.

It seemed she was going to need to sharpen her monster fighting skills –
and find out how many teeth were involved.

Another city, another king.

Those were Arete's dry words as they were escorted to the main chamber
of the palace. And Desma could not disagree. Since leaving Apasa, she had met
councilmen, kings, advisors, high priests, and now astronomers. She wondered
what her mother would think if she could witness what was happening.

The palace was a marvel of white marble and green sea glass. Small pools
of seawater lined the halls and filled corners of every room, available for anyone
to soak their feet and feel connected to the sea. Salt and pine filled the air,
cleansing and invigorating. It was at odds with the people who occupied the
halls. Men and women in muted greens, reds, and browns, only men wearing
any jewellery, hair kept simple on the women, and most pale – as though they
did not often stand in the sun. Those they passed were quiet as they watched
behind even quieter eyes, studying the newest batch of hunters come to claim
the prize of the kingdom.

Desma had asked Cosmas, Arete, and Cela to accompany her. They had
all wanted to come, arguing that the king seeing the whole crew together
would better convince him of their chances at succeeding. She simply said that
whether she came with three or three hundred, there was little chance he would
deny her. The city was desperate.

They had heard the stories in the two days they waited until the king could
see them.

Citizens of Koriithos were killed when they left the city by land. It did
not matter if they were heading east or west, the monster found them. And
if their party contained people from other kingdoms in the League, they were
left unharmed. Occasionally, a bruise or a cut would occur during the attack
but the survivors all said the monster took great pains to avoid them, knowing
who was Koriithosan and who was not.

Desma soon discovered that it was not only natural-born citizens who were killed. There was a man from the Great Lands south of the Middle Sea who had lived in the city for forty years and became a citizen only three months before he was killed. While his family, who had come to visit, were left unscathed.

'How can a monster tell such things?' Bion had asked. No one knew the answer.

Reports of the creature varied greatly. Some said it was as large as a bear, others a lion, and some twice or three times as big as that. It had green skin. No, red skin. No, mottled yellow skin, like leather, with black feathers. No, it had red fur and orange eyes, with a tail like flame.

It had five hands, and three hands, and two fingers on each hand, and also eight fingers. It had wings and a tail, or it was only comprised of tails. It spat saliva that burned, shot ice from his nostrils. It sang as it killed. It roared like a lion. It squealed like a pig.

It attacked during the day, at night, at dawn and twilight. It ate its victims, or tore them apart, or burned them.

The only consistency was what the monster left behind. A bough of solid gold, with leaves like from an oak tree. The king had ordered every bough be brought to the city but the moment it passed through the gate it turned to liquid, splashing onto the stone road, and washing away into the sea like rain.

None of them had ever heard anything like it and Desma was beginning to seriously rethink this idea. But as the doors to the chamber opened, she knew it was too late to back out now. The guards stayed at the door and the four of them continued alone.

The king sat on a throne carved like a wave hitting a rock, fountaining high above his head in green-streaked marble. The queen sat on a smaller throne shaped like a shell, her hands busy with needle and thread in her lap. Nobles and advisors stood to the side, some interested to see the newest hunters, others bored at yet another group eager to win the prize – and undoubtedly fail.

Desma saw Hyllos off to the king's left, standing a few steps behind a heavily robed, older man with deep lines in his face, a small hunch, and peppery hair. Kalchas, the first astronomer. He watched her with sharp, assessing eyes.

To the queen's right was a young man wearing dark green clothes and a necklace of colourful sea glass, a coronet of silver waves with a pale blue moonstone in the centre resting on his brow. The prince. He was a handsome youth, not much older than twenty, with windswept black hair, skin that could almost be called coppery, strong shoulders and well-muscled calves. But his eyes gave Desma pause. They glittered with a furious light.

She swallowed and kept going, trying her best to ignore the angry youth and focus on the king.

Gylippus was an old man. He had ruled Koriithos for over forty years, having ascended to the throne as a mere youth when his father had died suddenly out at sea. Despite his advanced age, his hair was still full and black, with only two small streaks of grey. But his skin reminded her of the old seadogs who fished the harbour every day, wrinkled and lined. His clothes were black, and she could see under his hem that he was barefoot. His crown was a band of solid sapphire, with Nethuns' four-prong spear above his brow. If his people were severe, they looked jolly next to their king.

Their party reached a line of blue tile that broke up the white marble and halted, bowing deeply.

The king waved for them to speak.

Desma took a deep breath. 'King Gylippus, I am Desma.'

'The Father-Killer,' he grunted. 'We all know. You are not here to ask for my hand to cleanse you. That has already been denied. I will not sully Koriithos with the dirty affairs of Apasa.'

She bit her lip and schooled her features into a calm mask. She had been warned by Hyllos that the king often unbalanced people with his abrupt manner. Some said he took pleasure in it, though few had ever seen him smile.

'I will send an announcement through the palace and city detailing your story and your presence here,' he continued. 'That should satisfy Tinia's requirement.'

She forced bile back down her throat. *The entire city?* 'I thank you, King Gylippus.'

He gave a dismissive wave. 'I have already decided that you may lend what help you can for the city,' he said. 'My First Astronomer has informed me that, if you succeed, you will ask me to cleanse you. Which many here may see as a contradiction to my previous decision. But they are forgetting an important detail.'

He leaned forward. 'You are a woman. In all the history of Koriithos, there has never been a warrior-queen, or battle-priestess, or *heroine*'—his voice was laced with amusement—'and there never will be. But you are welcome to try, along with your other women. There is at least one man among you.' He gestured apathetically at Cosmas. 'Perhaps that will help, though I doubt it.'

He laughed, his advisors and many in the room joining him.

'Thank you, King Gylippus.' The words were bitter on Desma's tongue, but it was all she could force out.

The king continued, still chuckling. 'I promised to grant any wish within my power to grant. As king, I am able to offer the rite of purification. I vow, here in front of the might of Koriithos, that if you succeed in ridding the kingdom of the monster, I will cleanse you. May Nethuns strike me down!' He clapped his hands sharply. 'Now, begone. I have other matters to attend to. Good luck, my man,' he said to Cosmas. 'I hope you can keep these girls in line.'

The quartermaster gave the king a cold smile. 'I go where my commander says,' he said with a sweeping bow to Desma.

Some of the men in the chamber gave stifled gasps and the king gave a grunt before turning away from them.

Desma led them out of the chamber, looking back as they reached the door. The queen had not looked up once from her needlework. The king was talking to Kalchas. Hyllos gave her a wry smile. And the man in the coronet ... he was still staring at her – and his eyes all but blazed with fury.

She was glad when the doors boomed shut behind her.

CHAPTER THIRTY

'The king does not think all that well of women,' Cosmas said quietly, using a thin blade to poke holes in a strip of leather. 'It will be a pleasure to prove him wrong.'

'I do not like Koriithos,' Arete said, her solemn grey eyes staring daggers at the men around the common room. 'It appears that in this city women are to be seen and not heard. Men hold all positions of power besides the queen, who is nothing but a living doll for the king to sit beside him as a paragon of womanly virtue.'

'Keep your voice low,' Desma warned, her eyes searching for anyone who may have overheard the shipwright's heated words. Some of the men glanced their way, but not in response to Arete. They were clearly mostly displeased with so many women in such bright clothes, obviously not deferring to the men in their group.

'Who cares what these goats think?' she spat but at a lower volume.

'Perhaps this would be a good place for me to find a wife?' Bion joked, stroking his beard that he was slowly growing. 'I could finally have some peace and quiet.'

Four piercing stares were his only response from the women.

'When do we head out?' Khufu asked. It had grown cold as night fell and the captain was wearing a scarf large enough for Desma to use as a blanket.

'Dawn tomorrow,' she said. 'We've learned all we can in the city. We know there are at least two other groups of hunters out there. The rest have given up but more could come any day. We'll start north and travel along the canal until we hit the bridge, then turn west and south around the city. So let's get some sleep because there are going to be some hard days ahead of us.'

Bion swapped a look with Delphinus. 'Well,' the giant man said hesitantly. 'I thought I might stay up for a bit and finish my mead. And Delphinus promised the owner he would play a song or two. Better stay here and keep him out of trouble.' The piper nodded vigorously in agreement.

'And we better watch them to make sure they *actually* stay out of trouble,' Kassandra said, nudging Arete.

Desma sighed. 'Fine, but we are leaving at dawn even if I have to have Khufu dunk your heads in the harbour.' The captain grunted a laugh.

After many promises of only finishing the drink in their cups and coming to bed soon, Cela followed Desma to their room and they readied for bed.

Desma laid awake for a long while, staring at the clay-plastered ceiling and studying the swirling dips and handprints left by the builder. She wondered if she would ever have a house with a similar ceiling, maybe at the base of a small hill so it was sheltered from the wind. There might be a small lake or slow stream nearby, enough soil for a few fruit trees, a herd of goats, a little garden for herbs and vegetables. Maybe she would find a nearby beehive for honey. She would have to learn how to make wine. Or she could travel to the local village every so often for a jug or three.

She was only twenty years old. So much life left to live. But she had found the greatest trove of treasure from Urruc and delivered it from the cursed land. That alone was worth a few songs, at least. Maybe that was all the gods had planned for her. It was never wise to tempt blind Nurtia, Goddess of Chance; no one ever knew what path she would end up pointing towards. Maybe goats and honeybees would be enough for her.

She remembered her promise to her mother as she held her on the temple floor, to forget the Empire and the pain they had caused her and fade from the world. To grow old and wizened under the sun, with maybe an occasional visit from a friend. She would stay near Apasa. Drop in to see Cela, or she could come to her. She could learn the lyre ...

'What is swirling around that head of yours?' Cela asked softly.

Desma started, thinking her friend had been asleep. Not that she knew how long had passed. The sky was just as dark outside the small window set high in the wall as when they climbed into the bed. 'Life. What it could be.'

'You never told me what the Second Astronomer said when you met him,' Cela said. 'Cosmas played mute when I asked him.'

'You shouldn't pry,' Desma said, still staring at the ceiling. 'Ow,' she gasped when Cela's finger poked her ribs. Hard.

'You do not get to start hiding secrets from me just because you're on a tragic adventure like a character out of a playwright's story,' Cela scolded.

'Let's hope we get a happier ending,' Desma said wistfully. Most playwrights tended towards tragedies. She shifted away from Cela's finger when it poked her again. 'Okay, stop doing that! He didn't really know what he was saying, let alone me understanding it. He just said I was somehow tied to Koriithos and I need to stay around longer to see what unfurls. He didn't say why, or even if I would succeed in killing the monster. You know as well as I that even Aplu's oracles are as clear as mud. Now, if you're not going to sleep then put that mind of yours to figuring out how we are going to find and fight this beast instead of bothering me awake.'

Cela rolled away mumbling something particularly unsavoury under her breath.

'Goodnight to you, too,' Desma said, pulling the wool blanket tight around her.

Desma woke standing by the statue of Nethuns' Admonition. The sky was stained black and blush with billowing grey clouds that moved far swifter than even a storm's winds. Below was the harbour of Koriithos but all the ships were capsized in the water, their hulls bleached white like bone. Every small island and rock in the harbour were festooned with brambles and thorns, red leaching into the water around them, turning the sea to blood.

She stepped back, bumping into the statue's plinth, and felt a sharp pain. Turning, she saw that it was covered in roses, all as green as sea glass, with thorns longer than her fingers. As Desma raised her eyes to trace the height of Nethuns' figure, the marble began to writhe and melt and reform until a young man with the wings of a black swan smiled down at her, his grin vicious and his eyes wild.

Desma jumped away and cried out as her ankle twisted on the pavement that was now water, gasping at it flooded her mouth with the taste of sand. She spat and scrabbled with her hands but gained no purchase.

Eventually she found a rope, gnarled and slimy, covered in bumps that oozed, but she clung on. Bit by bit, she dragged herself up the raging river of salt and sand until her head broke free and she gasped air filled with applewood incense. Nearby was a broken marble column, jutting out of the sea. She swam to it, hauling herself up until she was only half left in the water. The column was white and grey marble, gilded with gold and silver. She traced a carving of myrtle and Desma knew it was a column from the temple in Apasa, before it was burned to the ground.

A shout caught her attention. She pushed her wet hair from her face and saw a ship approaching, it sails bronze and blue. Its prow was a blush swan, hissing, enraged as it lunged towards her, only held in place by its rear forming the rest of the ship. Around its neck was a crown of roses.

Desma started shaking, but there was nowhere to go. She was no longer in Koriithos' harbour and the column was the only firm land in sight. On the deck of the ship, men bearing wicked crooks gathered, faces obscured by the setting sun. Still the swan hissed and shrieked, the sound devouring everything else. Spittle and sharp teeth flew from its mouth, falling into the waves to form doves that burst into the air, blood pouring from their wings. They swarmed around her and Desma cried out, but it was drowned out by the swan. Waves of red, dark as wine, and winds of bronze, sharp as ice, consumed her.

She screamed.

Dawn rose weak and chilled. A light rain had fallen during the night and everything glistened with moisture. The sea was subdued, more grey than blue, with pale clouds obscuring most of the sky. Desma had her cloak wrapped tightly around her as they left the city, three donkeys bearing their supplies led by Bion at the rear of the group.

She had woken well before dawn, the vestiges of her nightmare haunting her long after she awoke. It still felt as though the swan's screams were echoing in her head but she knew it was her imagination. Once the sky had begun to lighten, Desma had found a grim joy in throwing a bucket of water over most of her crew. Though she did have to duck a knife thrown by Kassandra before the overseer realised she was not being attacked. Desma had waved away her red-faced apologies. They were about to hunt a monster; she would prefer if her crew had sharper reactions rather than dull.

The first unpleasant surprise for the day met them at the Canal Gate. Two men bearing spears and shields blazoned with the fishing spear and sail of Koriithos rose from where they crouched just inside the gate. One was tall, pale-skinned and broad shouldered, with long hair tied into three braids. He had a golden beard and green eyes, and a scar that ran from behind his left ear and down his neck to his shoulder. The other man was small, only a little taller than Cela, with almost the same colour hair as her, and his skin was dark for a Koriithosan, the colour of weak honey. He was slim with a squarish jaw, slanted nose, and wide brown eyes.

Both were wearing hard travelling sandals, brown chitons, and muted green cloaks. Besides the spear and shield, they each carried a short blade and a large bundle by their feet. They waited until they drew closer, and then the taller one addressed Bion, who was standing to Desma's right.

'We have been ordered to accompany you ... what?' The question was directed to his companion, who had elbowed him. He barely came up to the taller man's shoulder. Now that they were closer, Desma could see that the older man was at least ten years senior to the smaller man – closer to forty, she would guess. The younger man thrust his chin towards Desma and eyed her significantly. He gave her a small grin.

The older man grunted and turned to Desma, a faint sneer on his lips. 'As I was saying, we have been ordered to go with you. To make sure there is no trickery or ... exaggerations.'

Desma ground her teeth. They were to make sure it was actually her who did the killing so she could claim the wish. If the monster was killed. Others must have tried some subterfuge previously to win the prize.

'As long as you don't get in our way,' Desma said chillingly. 'I won't have you sabotage our efforts. By accident, of course.'

The older man nodded and shouldered his bundle, stepping aside to let them pass.

The younger man did the same, saying, 'I'm Actor and he is Peteos, by the way,' as they passed.

Cela grabbed the younger man by the arm and pulled him along with her. 'You just stick by me, Actor,' she said warmly. 'I'll need a strong arm to keep me from tripping on any roots.'

Desma snorted loudly and her friend cast her a stone-faced look.

The group of now ten set off down the road that ran parallel to the canal that split the isthmus and technically made the peninsula an island. It was only a half mile from the gate but hidden by rolling stony hills. It took a little over twenty minutes to get there, the road well paved with many houses and shops right up until the bridge that spanned the distance. It was a dour looking bridge, built with dull grey stone, wide enough for four people walking abreast, and almost completely flat with no arching. The Icarii Sea end of the canal was the deepest part. The sides were sheer cliffs varying between a half mile to a full mile along most of the canal's length until it reached the Gulf of Koriithos, where the land was sea level.

The canal had been a gift from Nethuns when the city was founded, as thanks for their prayers asking him to be their patron god. He had stridden from the sea to the sand, climbed the cliffs by the harbour, and struck the stone with his fishing spear. The earth had quivered and quaked, splitting apart with a thundering crack as the break in the earth raced seven miles to the Gulf. From the canal and the control of the isthmus, the city had grown rich from trade and taxes.

The plan was to search the isthmus as it made most sense the monster would be near the city. However, the isthmus was twelve miles at its longest point and over ten miles at its widest. The Kingdom of Koriithos extended beyond the land bridge for about thirty miles towards Athanai and twenty to Phoroniaa westwards. Like most of the League, the area was mountainous with sporadic woods, a thousand valleys and dales, a few rivers and a hundred coves. They agreed to concentrate their search in the immediate vicinity of the city, though some attacks had occurred over two days travel away.

The next hurdle was how they were going to conduct the search.

Desma had wanted everyone to work in pairs, within calling distance to the next pair and make their way north-west from the canal in a wide loop around the city.

Arete argued that they could cover twice the ground if they searched alone, as it should be safe as only the guardsmen were native-born. That earned a sour look from the Koriithosans.

Khufu was of the opinion that they should separate into three groups, one stationed west of the city, one north, and the last east.

Bion decided to complicate matters by suggesting the monster could be sea-bound and dwell under the waves until it was ready to hunt. 'Makes sense,' he said when Desma rounded on him angrily. 'This is Nethuns' ancestral home and he has sired most of the monsters from stories. Maybe this is one of his children.' It was a dark thought.

It was Cosmas who eventually settled the debate. He pointed out that they could spend days and weeks searching everywhere they thought the monster *might* be, but perhaps they should first check where it *had* been.

Delphinus was quick to add his support to Cosmas. The piper had little wish to be traipsing through the wet countryside, as he had already slipped twice on the slick paved road.

Fortunately, the guardsmen knew the location of each attack and had been to several as part of the patrols. Peteos did not look pleased at returning to the sites but he started leading them to the closest one that was only a few miles off the road. Cela continued to chat with Actor but the smaller man became quieter the closer they got to the spot.

As they made their way through the few pine trees that seem to spring up from behind each rise and hill, tension began to build. Desma noted Delphinus loosening his twin swords and Bion carried his bronze axe in his hand, hefting it occasionally as he kept his other hand firmly on the donkeys' leads. Khufu didn't finger his weapons but his eyes never rested. Cosmas seemed to ghost from tree to rock, disappearing and reappearing.

'Here,' Peteos said, waving his hand towards a copse of cypress and fir trees. He made no move to venture closer.

Desma left him and approached cautiously, despite telling herself there was nothing to worry about here. Peteos had explained that it had been a group of youths who were picnicking in the countryside, four men and three women. All slain.

From the signs left behind, it was clear it was not a quick killing. Despite the attack being four months ago, the trees still bore the scars of deep claw marks, some trunks missing large pieces altogether. One tree had been smashed from its trunk altogether. The ground bore deep prints that had been marred by time and weather but were distinct enough to count that the beast had six toes. How many feet and hands were still in question. And there was a ... smell. Desma's nose wrinkled when she tried to take a deeper sniff. It was rancid, like oil gone bad, but underlaid with a minty scent that she could not quite place. A quick look revealed no patches of mint or spearmint in the undergrowth.

There was nothing else to see. Khufu followed the tracks east but they disappeared as soon as they reached a rocky hill. They checked the surrounding area but failed to pick up the track.

CHAPTER THIRTY-ONE

The rest of their day and the following three days followed a similar pattern. Peteos knew where most of the attacks had taken place as he had been a patrolman for over twenty years. But there had been at least a hundred attacks in the last ten years. Some locations held no clues as any signs had faded away. Sometimes there was a cracked tree that grew crookedly that could have been from being hit by a large beast. One had shattered rocks that could have been made by a hammer. Another was in a natural overhang where the walls were clay. Six claw marks rent the wall of the shelter, an inch wide and continuing for two feet. More than one of the group shivered.

In the last year there had been twelve attacks. The most recent was only days before they had arrived and was on the other side of the city. By the time they had worked their way south and reached the site, the area had been washed clean by the rain. It was on the hard-packed dirt of the road heading towards Phoroniaa and little sign of anything happening remained, only a snapped branch from a poplar.

Their fourth night was spent a little away from the last attack site, in a natural gap in the trees large enough for them to set up camp. The persistent clouds had finally dissipated and the stars were crisp and clear. Desma and her crew had set about clearing the ground and gathering what dry wood they could find. Bion shambled off into the trees to dig a latrine pit, while Kassandra and Arete went to fill everyone's waterskins from a nearby creek.

Cosmas began to slice up some potatoes and green beans, throwing baby wild onions and garlic stalks into the cookpot Khufu had just heaved over the flames. Desma blessed the day he had tried to poison them all. The talk they had when she discovered him trying to kill them was something she kept safeguarded between them. Not even Cela knew the circumstances that had led to her offering him a place on the crew. But they had eaten well ever since thanks to his never-ending supply of herbs and spices. Even the cinnamon.

Peteos rarely did more than lay out his bedroll. He was near enough to their fire to get some warmth but not so close as to be included. He ate the food in his bag, filled his own water, and spent the rest of the time glowering at Actor.

The younger guardsmen had taken to Cela and Kassandra. He walked with them during the day, and shared stories at night. On the third night, Kassandra had slapped him when he had pinched her bottom. The shock on his face had set the camp roaring. Bion had clapped him on the shoulder roughly as Cela followed the overseer to the other side of the fire in a huff. 'But she pinched mine,' he had said to the giant man.

Bion chuckled. 'You welcomed the pinch, no? She did not. That's the difference.' And left the younger man in puzzlement.

Desma had caught Bion's sleeve as he walked passed. 'You know if he did that to Arete, she would stab, not slap him.' She laughed quietly and Bion threw back his head and bellowed loudly, wiping his eyes as he cast a glance at Arete, who grew very still as she surveyed the two of them.

After dinner and the one cup of wine Desma allowed, for she kept a close watch on the wineskins strapped to the side of one of the donkeys, Delphinus would pull out his lyre or pipes and play merrily. But, on this night, he had only just started strumming an Apasan folk song when the sharp warble of a rosewing sparrow cut through the camp.

For a second they were all frozen, save the Koriithosans, who looked side to side at everyone, before they all leapt to their feet. Khufu was on watch and that was the call they had for *men approaching, be wary.*

They stood in a circle around the fire, Peteos finally deciding this was a situation where he would join them, hands on weapons. Arete limberly climbed a nearby tree and sat perched among the branches with an arrow half-drawn.

It was a few minutes more before they heard the crunch of feet. Soon enough, they spied figures approaching from the dark and they resolved into twenty men, who seemed surprised to find them waiting armed.

To a man, they were scruffy and dirty, faces unshaven or beards unkempt, their clothes patched and their eyes narrowed in suspicion. Three of the men had the bronze skin and tilted eyes of the eastern kingdoms. Most seemed to be from Pallan or Phoroniaa, going by their smaller stature and black hair. Two men were clearly from Tethalia, with their white hair and almost golden eyes. There was even a Konosoan, though he was not as large as Bion. Some of the men drew their swords but a man with light eyes stepped forward, hands held out towards them all, an ingratiating smile on his face. He wore a bright red sash around his chest and one side of his head was shaven.

'Evening, friends,' he said in a smooth voice that marked him from Athanai. That kingdom had schools for children where it was law they must attend until their twelfth birthday. They learned writing, rhetoric, and arithmetic. Those most promising were snapped up by officials, generals, or scribes, and the rest were allowed to pursue their own lives. Mostly building ships for their navy or harvesting their olive groves. 'I am Stolos, from the town of Marce, from the Crownless Kingdom.' That was what Athanains called their land, because they had cast down their last king centuries ago and appointed the three archons, who ruled for three-year terms. They wore the name as a badge of honour. 'We are in service to the Koriithosan king to hunt the monster terrorising the city. Are you travellers?' His eyes dashed from one of their crew to another, trying to determine the leader.

Here we go again, Desma thought bitterly. She went to speak when Cela stepped forward.

'We are also in service to the king,' she said flatly. 'Are you passing through or looking for a camp?'

Stolos eyed her slowly up and down, eyes moving to Bion and Peteos. 'If you have no objections,' he said carefully, eyes flicking back to Cela, 'we would be happy to camp nearby. It has been a week or so since we had any company beyond ourselves.'

Desma tried to catch her notice but Cela was staring steadfastly at the strangers. 'Under Tinia's eyes, if you bear no harm or ill will, and are not followed by misfortune, we can share camp.'

'Under Tinia's eyes,' Stolos repeated, holding out a mud-stained hand.

Cela took it without hesitation and shook it once.

The man started, though, when Arete suddenly dropped from the tree, shouldering her bow. He swore when Khufu materialised from next to him, stepping into the light where the fire glinted on his wing-bladed axe. 'How many are you?' he said shakily.

'Enough,' Khufu said harshly, thrusting his axe into his belt and crossing his arms, making an imposing sight, half shrouded in darkness.

Stolos scurried off through the trees to where his men were setting about clearing brush and collecting wood. There were only a dozen paces separating the two camps, with a few trees in between.

'I think watches of three tonight would be wise,' the captain grumbled quietly to Desma. 'Two watching their camp and a third in case anyone tries to come from the other side.'

She nodded and he walked away to arrange it. She caught Cela's cloak as she walked past and pulled her aside. 'Thank you,' she whispered. 'But come morning I will probably have to tell them.'

Cela cast a disgusted look at the newcomers. 'They are fortune hunters and would no doubt try to slit our throats if they could. I would be surprised if they were still here when dawn rose.'

Desma made sure she had the last watch of the night and sure enough, just as the sky began to lighten to a murky grey, Stolos rose from his bedroll and went about kicking men awake, quietly cursing anyone who moved too slowly. Within ten minutes they were leaving camp. Desma stepped away from the tree she had been leaning against, framed neatly between two trunks, and caught Stolos' eye. The man paused before cutting a mocking bow and following his men.

Desma very much doubted that was the last they would see of them.

The next two days brought no sign of the monster that was haunting the area.

On the sixth day of their search, Desma finally agreed they should split up but they still searched in groups of three, with Desma's group numbering four. They had not seen Stolos' band but no one trusted him as far as they could spit.

Desma was with Actor, Cela, and Delphinus, and the weather had warmed enough for her to bundle her cloak away. They were currently west of the city, about five miles away, and if they stood on a tall hill they could almost see the gleam from the palace and temple. The wind brought warm salty breezes and the scent of pine from the trees that grew all along the sandy coast. Sweat trickled down her back and her legs were wet from where she had washed the mud from her dress after she had fallen when the strap on her sandal had broken.

She was just wondering whether they should have headed for another city to see if their king or priest were more amenable to helping her, or perhaps visit Delphon to see the Young Oracle, when she broke through the trees and found a road. They must have been heading more south than she thought. It was smaller than the main road that led to Phoroniaa, probably leading to a village or town not far past the isthmus.

A rumble warned her of someone approaching and she waved the others who had followed back into the shrubbery. She waited by the side of the road – hot, sweaty, leaves in her hair, probably looking like a dryad who forgot how to be a tree.

A cart rounded the corner, pulled by two dusty-grey cattle, filled with amphora packed with hay. An old man was on the driving seat, switch in hand that he prodded the cattle with though they hardly needed direction on the flat road.

A youth walked alongside, barely into manhood, and wearing only a chiton that he had let slip from his shoulder so his torso was bare in the heat of the day. He was slightly bronzed, with unruly brown hair, and was carrying a small girl on his shoulders. Another boy, no more than ten, ran about his feet, chattering away.

The old man saw her first and poked the youth with his stick. The young man turned and gave her a hard eye. He lifted the child from his shoulders and set her on the seat, scooping up the other boy to add alongside. He drew a large knife from his belt and kept to the side of the road she was on, between her and the cart.

As they drew near, she lifted a hand and waved. 'I mean no harm,' she called out as friendly as she could. 'I've just turned myself around and am trying to get my bearings. Where does this road lead?'

The old man grunted as he pulled on the reins to bring the cart to a stop. 'Maybe your friends hiding behind can help you find your way.'

The youth stiffened, raising his knife higher.

Desma sighed and waved for the others to join her. The old man had sharper eyes than she thought, despite his squinting. The other three joined her, trying to look as least threatening as possible – though Delphinus grinned like a madman.

'We mean you no harm,' she said again.

'Then why are you prowling the trees instead of walking the road like goodfolk?' the youth demanded, his knife giving a slight shake. She doubted he had ever used it for anything other than farm work.

Actor stepped forward before Cela could grab him and brandished his spear. 'I am a warrior in King Gylippus' army. We are in service to the king and go where we will, citizen.'

The youth glared further. 'Come, grandfather. If they truly mean us no harm then they will let us continue in peace.' He smacked one of the cows on the rump and they started forward again.

Desma shot a scowl at Actor and moved to keep aligned with the cart, still remaining off the road. 'Forgive me, my companion can be brusque at times.' A spluttered response was swiftly silenced by Cela. 'May we walk with you? I have a few questions that perhaps you may be able to answer. And if you are headed towards a village, I would not mind stopping for some wine and bread.'

The youth opened his mouth but the old man cut him off. 'You are searching for the monster.' It was not a question. 'None of you are from Koriithos except the soldier,' he said, gesturing to Actor, who had regained his composure and tried to appear looming despite his small stature. 'You have a fortune-hunter's swagger, but there is something else about you.'

Fortune-hunter's swagger! She swallowed her tongue.

'Come,' the grandfather said. 'We are heading home, but we will pass through Irna on the way. You may accompany us that far. Sheathe your blade, Timo, before you stab yourself with it. Can't you see any of these four could kill you with barely a blink.'

The youth jumped at his grandfather's words, sheathing the blade quickly, but never taking his eyes off them.

Desma moved to join the old man, walking beside him. The youth, Timo, moved back to the rear so he could watch them all at once. Cela gave him a kind smile but it changed nothing on his face. 'I am Desma, from Apasa,' she said slowly. 'You have travelled from the city?'

The old man nodded. He wore a broadbrim woven hat that kept most of the sun off but let the breeze through. His white hair was scraggly with bald patches and his skin heavily lined from a lifetime of working outside. But his eyes had lost none of their sparkle.

'I have. I saw the proclamations, and your hair is not something one sees every day. I hear that in the far, far north there are people with hair like bright fire, but yours must be a gift from Turan herself.'

Desma's face tightened.

He touched his fingers to his lips. 'Apologies. That was ill spoken.'

'You have no fault,' she said. Turan had betrayed her mother, or one could look at it as though her mother had betrayed Turan, had disobeyed a divine order. But death and destruction did not fit the crime. No matter what any king or priest said.

She heard Cela telling jokes to Timo who, despite his best attempts, could not keep the smile from his face at Cela's unstaunched cheerfulness. The two children had hopped down from the cart and were running circles around Delphinus, who was juggling four rocks as he danced around them.

'I am Thales,' the man said. 'Is it easier?'

Desma jerked back to look at him. 'What?'

'Is it easier to ask if we have heard the proclamation than to have to tell your story yourself?' His words were said in a kind voice but they still felt like hammer blows.

She was taken aback from the question. 'I suppose it is. Having to say, over and again, the words …' she trailed off. Having to say she killed her father. Stabbed him. An unbidden tear fell down her cheek and Thales' gnarled finger was there in an instant, catching it before it fell.

'Again, I find myself begging for your pardon,' he said gently. He lifted his hand and placed the tear onto the top of her head. He chuckled at her confused face. 'It is custom in Koriithos to never let tears fall unless at a funeral or wedding. Tears are to be caught, to not share any sadness with the earth or water. There is enough pain without us adding to it.'

'Strange custom,' she said, rubbing her eyes nevertheless.

'Tears have power, dear girl,' Thales said. 'More than most think.'

They rode in silence for a while, listening to the shrieks of the children and Delphinus stomping after them, one eye closed and booming in a loud voice, declaring himself Prog, King of Cyclops. Even Timo laughed freely when the piper went sprawling after tripping on a large rock. Actor had warmed to the youth and began to show him some simple moves with the knife, how to stab properly, block and parry. He even promised to show him how to throw it once they stopped at Irna.

'Has your village suffered any attacks from the monster?' Desma asked.

Thales shook his head, a frown appearing on his face. 'No, thanks be to Horta.' The Goddess of Harvests was honoured by all farmers and shepherds, regardless of what kingdom they lived in. 'It is not country folk it is after.'

'What do you mean?'

'Not that those in Koriithos would have noticed, but the monster only attacks those who *live* in the city itself and are citizens. No one in any farm or village on the isthmus has been killed by it. I swear by the sickle and hoe.'

'What kind of monster is this?' Desma mused. 'Most are offspring of Nethuns, though some are cursed men and women. Maybe something left over from the destruction of Urruc? Stories say that terrible creatures were birthed during the war between gods and Beings.'

Thales shrugged. 'I am just a farmer. I know little beyond the seasons and when to harvest. You cannot know the sunshine of tomorrow, only work in the rain today.'

'I think the very wise would find they know little when speaking to a farmer.' Desma laughed.

'Peace, children, please,' Delphinus cried out in mock-despair. 'I will tell you a story. But of what, I wonder? Shall I speak of Laran and his battle with the Boar of Melcindes? Or maybe of Anthusa, founder of Artas, who defeated her sister, Aketa of the Green Flame? Maybe the story of the mighty Queen Koritto, who seduced Esia, Goddess of Peace, and brought stability to Pallan with her willowy legs and broad ... actually, not that story. How about—'

'Tells us of Cisra and Vikare,' the boy shouted. 'And how Cisra destroyed the palace, shooting fire from her eyes and spewing evil fog from her mouth.'

'And how she had giant scorpions,' the girl squealed. 'But don't make it too scary!' She shook a warning finger under Delphinus' nose, even though she only came up to his knee.

'Why, I only learned that story myself recently,' he said, scooping them both up in his arms. 'But do we have time to tell it?'

'Aye,' Thales nodded. 'We have a good mile or two left.'

Tale of Vikare and Cisra

Two hundred years ago, during the reign of King Soranus and Queen Iphys, Koriithos gave shelter to Vikare and the barbarian woman, Cisra.

Vikare was, as he believed, the rightful king of Thevai, but he had been spirited away from his city as a babe by servants to his mother. She was blood-queen, while his father was wed-king. But the king had fears that the child was in fact the product of his brother, who he later had beheaded, and it was said that the king tried to have the boy killed.

When he discovered the babe had vanished, he flew in a rage and killed all the faithful servants to the queen. He then locked her up and ensured he held the only key. A year later, she gave birth to a baby as blue as the sky, a daughter who the king took away. It was only then he released the queen, banishing her from Thevai with only an old hag for company, declaring himself regent. But we will return to Thevai later.

Vikare was taken to a mountain where he was raised by wizened old men, children of Selvans and Tiur, who could turn into dancing lights or flowers as they chose. Selvades or Tiurades, they call themselves. They taught him all the pastoral arts, herblore, piping, carpentry, and languishing in fields of wildflowers like a godling waiting for his lover.

But one night, when he was well into manhood and content with his life as a woodsman, Turnu, son of Turan and Summanus, came to him. The god is said to have feathered wings of flashing red, midnight hair long and braided into a single tail, eyes like molten rubies flecked with gold, and a smile both bewitching and frightening. He came like a star from the heavens and claimed him as his son.

He told Vikare how he had come to his mother in a storm of passion one night and left her with child. It was then the god told him his story and how he was the lost king of Thevai, the true king.

He returned to Thevai, after many trials and journeys, to find his sister, who was born close to death but had blossomed into a sumptuous woman of fire and wit, was now queen. The king had died, unexpectedly, one year before. Some said Phaidra – for that was the sister's name – had killed him to gain the throne. She refused to believe Vikare's story and cast him out of the city. Vikare vowed he would return with an army and in response Phaidra picked up a bow herself and shot him in the leg, forever giving him a slight limp.

Vikare travelled to Koriithos, intending to ask King Soranus for assistance, for he knew relations between the two kingdoms were uneasy. Koriithos had been attacked by an Empyrean navy and requested assistance, which Phaidra had refused. They had barely defeated the invaders but it had left their warriors depleted.

The king sympathised with Vikare and promised that if he could bring him back a treasure that would grant his kingdom unending wealth, he would be able to help fund an army for him. Vikare was eager for any chance and agreed. King Soranus charged him with finding and retrieving the fabled Golden Bough, an oak branch of solid gold that, when planted in a pot of silver, would continually grow gold leaves that could be harvested.

Vikare left Koriithos that night with a crew of the drunkest and most unruly men he could convince on the docks to follow him. The king had gifted him a vessel, an ill-maintained ship with torn sails, but the godling was undeterred. There were stories in abundance that the Golden Bough was in the possession of one of the barbarian chiefs of the Cold Sea. After months of searching, they happened across a river that flowed for miles inland, through dank and tangled forests, until it came upon a large town. The buildings were as strange as its populace. Black tiled roofs with patches of thatch, on buildings made from grey stone and ironwood that were wider at the top than at the base. The people wore their hair wild and unbound, black as coal and thick as vines. Their skin was brown with eyes black, earthen, and grey. A proud and volatile people; they were not afraid to fight in the streets and just as quickly help someone unload a cart.

Vikare had come across Arydor, their savage chieftain Evas, and his exotic daughter Cisra.

Evas indeed had possession of the Golden Bough; it had made his petty kingdom strong among his neighbours and led to him having many wives. He found Vikare's demands for the Bough amusing and set him tasks to complete, impossible tasks that only a god could accomplish. But, to the chief's surprise, Vikare succeeded no matter the trial. Eventually, the chief tried to have Vikare and his crew killed but they were warned by an unexpected ally: Cisra.

She had been helping Vikare with strange and wild magic for she was known throughout the Cold Sea as a powerful sorceress – and she was in love with Vikare. It was said that she fell so quickly in love, the fall swift and resounding, that even Turan was astonished. When Cisra heard of her father's plan to kill Vikare, she crept to where the Bough was hidden – in a cave protected by her brothers – stole the Bough, and fled to the ship with Vikare.

A harrowing chase down the river and across the Cold Sea followed, the chief commanding a hundred ships, until Cisra cast a terrible spell that made it appear as though she set their own ship alight rather than risk being caught and returned home. It is said the screams Chief Evas gave as he watched his only daughter burn into the water can still be heard on the waves of the Cold Sea.

Triumphant, they sailed back to Koriithos and presented the Golden Bough to King Soranus, who made Vikare a lord of the city and a close advisor. But it would take years for the kingdom to build back its strength from the Empyrean attack to restore him to the Thevan throne.

As time passed, Vikare began to spend more and more time with the kings' daughter, young Dirce, who was as beautiful as a winter bloom kissed by dawn's golden light. Despite having two children with Cisra – for they had married not four days after returning to Koriithos – Vikare all but abandoned her in his pursuit of Dirce.

Cisra grew angry and jealous. And when the king announced that her husband and the princess were to marry, that Vikare's marriage to her was annulled, that anger grew into balefire. Disguising her rage with sweetness, she claimed she was happy her husband had found true love and that she would leave the city with her children. But Vikare refused, claiming the children as his own, untainted by savage Arydorian blood. She begged him, on her knees with breast bare and tearing her hair, she begged him to release her sons. But with voice like ice and eyes like granite, he denied her mother's right.

This was his mistake.

He knew that she was a powerful sorceress but he thought that by keeping his sons, she would never dare harm him. What he did not know, for she did not reveal it until then, was that she was also a godling twice over. Her father's mother was Vanth, the fearsome Goddess of the Beneath who keeps the dead in check. And her mother's mother was Tiur, the Moon Itself. Cisra was the wild and savage daughter of Demoness and Moon – vengeance was her blood.

CHAPTER THIRTY-TWO

'No more,' both children cried, huddling into Cela's and Actor's arms.

'Let's leave it here for now, Delphinus,' Desma said. 'The poor parents will never get them to sleep tonight after this.'

The girl raised her head up, eyes red, and looked straight at Desma. 'Mother and Father are dead.'

Desma froze. 'I am so sorry, little one.'

The boy mumbled something into Actor's shoulder. 'What was that? Head up, like a good soldier.'

The boy looked him in the eye. 'The monster killed them both and ate them.'

'Holy sh—' the piper began to say with wide eyes.

'Why don't you tell them about the drunk ox and the blind musician?' Desma suggested, cutting him off. That was the cheeriest story she knew and always had her giggling as a child.

Delphinus nodded and pulled out his pipe, speaking softly until the children started to peek up at him with small smiles. Timo had fallen back and had a sullen expression.

Thales had gone stone-faced and prodded the cattle to speed up although they did not move any faster.

Desma laid a hand on his. 'Your son or daughter?'

'Son, although she was just as much my daughter,' he said gruffly. 'The five of them all lived in the city. They were coming to visit me when the two younger ones wanted to rush ahead so Timo went with them. They were only just out of sight when they heard screams. Timo hid the younglings in a tree and ran back. He found their heads and nothing else. It was about two miles back from where you found us. That's why he was so on edge. They came to my farm and lived with me ever since.'

'I'm sorry,' she said, not knowing what else to say.

They continued on for a while, the only sounds the plodding of the cows, the creak of the cart, the clatter of clay amphora bumping, and the soft voice of Delphinus.

'Do you know the rest of the story?' Desma eventually asked.

Thales nodded. 'It's a favourite of Koriithos.'

'Tell me the rest.'

He cleared his throat. 'I'm not much of a storyteller, not like your friend there, but I can say it plain.'

There were few who could compare to Delphinus. The King of Delphon had once offered a dozen chests of gold and gems to have him as his royal poet. Desma had told him he was free to go as he wished but was silently thankful he refused the offer. Which led to his attempted kidnapping by the king, which now made a good story around the campfire.

She leaned back against the seat, propped her feet up on the cow's rump in front of her, and waited.

Thales cleared his throat again and poked the cattle. 'Let's see ... he left off right when Cisra really got mad. Not wise to anger any woman, let alone a sorceress, and a godling on top of that! If you know a wolf is a wolf, don't kick it thinking it will act like a puppy.

'Anyhow, Cisra ended up gathering her maids – she brought a crowd of her people along when she fled. And together they made these beautiful slippers which they presented to the princess to wear on her wedding day. But they were so lovely the princess put them on the night before the wedding and burst into a green flame that consumed her and her entire room, killing all her friends.

'The king and Vikare tried to save them but the fire did not touch them. It only burned the women. Well, you can imagine the king's despair and anger. He sent the whole palace to hunt down Cisra but Vikare found her first. She was in the courtyard of their home on a chariot being pulled by winged scorpions. Imagine that!

'She had her children with them as well as the Golden Bough. Vikare asked her why and she laughed at him and it was said the city rang with her madness. She said that while her love for him was as deep as Aita's House, her hatred reached forever into the heavens. She took flight and while in the air she slit her own children's throat and let their blood fall upon the city.

'Where each drop fell, flames grew until Koriithos was ablaze. And when she flew over the palace, she hurled their bodies from the sky. When they struck the ground, the earth shook and hurled itself upwards, splintering the palace and feeding the flames of the burning city. Only by Nethuns' grace was it saved, though not without great damage, and the princess was dead.

'In his grief, King Soranus ordered Vikare to be beheaded and his body sunk into the harbour. Cisra vanished into the east, never to be seen again.'

Desma was aghast. *That* was Koriithos' favourite tale? A barbarian witch killing her own children and ravaging a city out of spite? Vikare was a pig, but to slay one's own flesh and blood ... like Desma had. No, she was nothing like Cisra. As contradictory as it sounded, what she did was filled with love. Cisra's actions were nothing but selfishness and hatred.

'Let it pass from your mind,' Thales said. 'It is not a pleasant story and the children should know not to ask for something that would upset them. I let it be because I assumed your friend would sugar-coat the worst parts.'

Desma chuckled. 'For him, that was sugar-coated. I've heard him describe scenes so viscerally that others have vomited.'

He wrinkled his nose. 'Sounds pleasant. Remind me not to request the story of the ugliest man and the pig he mistook for his wife.'

Desma threw back her head and laughed loudly.

Thales and his family farewelled them once they reached the town. A collection of houses, one shrine to Horta, and a small agora did not quite make a town, but that was what the locals called Irna.

Actor went with Delphinus to ask around if anyone knew of strange tracks in the hills, or odd noises, missing flocks, or weird smells. Desma and Cela bought some cool wine and hard cheese, sitting on a low wall under a linden tree, kicking their sandals off while they relaxed. It would take several hours to get back to where they agreed to meet the others for camp but they had time.

The sun was only a little passed noon and summer was just ending, meaning the days were still long.

The men returned shortly with no news or clues. They finished their lunch and headed off into the mountains again, receiving odd looks from the townsfolk. As the sun nestled into the horizon they found their campsite where Khufu, Peteos, and Cosmas were already waiting. The others tramped in about an hour later, all covered in mud and twigs. They refused to answer any questions and Bion even cracked his knuckles threateningly when Delphinus would not stop guessing.

They set two watchers as usual, to keep an eye out for the monster as well as Stolos' band. None of them felt comfortable knowing they were out there. Cosmas even remarked that he felt eyes on their group during the day but no matter what trick he pulled he never found anyone.

Desma agreed to take second watch and settled into her blanket, propped up against a small log near the embers, trying to will herself to sleep with little success. When Arete gently tapped her shoulder some hours later, she only opened her eyes with a sigh and dragged herself to her feet.

She walked over to a young poplar and hung her cloak over a low branch. The night was cool but refreshing, and now she was on her feet she felt tired. The area they chose for camp was next to a low hill with a spattering of trees that meant they did not have to go far for firewood. A small stream was nearby for water and Arete had managed to shoot four rabbits just on the other side of the hill. There must be a warren. She would ask whoever had dawn watch to try and catch a few more for next night's supper.

The night air was filled with the sounds of small animals, the occasional owl as it caught its prey, the lowing of distant cattle as something spooked them. The sky was clear and the stars looked almost within reach. There was Arekles with his silver arm. Trastor the Ancient Lion. Neresta who mixed honey with her tears and grew the first lavender. Bellamia who saw truth but could only speak lies.

A hundred stories danced above her head, each as comical and tragic as she felt her life was sometimes. Yet in every tale, the heroine never gave up.

Theodora, First Spear of Konoso, did not surrender when her men were pushed into the sea by the Pallan. She did not turn and walk away, giving up her weapons for a shepherd crook.

Pero, daughter of Turms' High Priest, kept going even when her city cut her hair and strapped her feet, stripping her of name and title because she took herbs to farewell a child in her womb. She did not run into the wilds of Thethalia, but lived on the street and helped women who needed it.

Even Orthia, Maiden of the Sun, did not stay home and weep when her husband's ship was sunk by pirates. She walked from the far north of the mainland to Athanai, bought a trireme, and became the bane of sea bandits, hunting them all until she cut down the pirate captain who killed her husband.

It was of these women she thought, whose strength she wished could flood her veins. Mynta was another. She had never seen such fire in her friend in the years she had known her. To stand up to her father in his own house, to twist him with her words and set him on the path she wanted, to be so unabashedly *herself*, was such a beautiful sight to witness.

She glanced over at Cela, her wheat-gold hair spilling out and turned silver by the moon. Desma wondered what she would have been doing if she had stayed in Apasa. Her mother was high priestess now. Leontia was a kind, fair woman. Softer than Desma's mother, what sometimes could be construed as weakness by some or merciful by others. She would be what the temple and city needed. A healing presence. Cela would have been her right hand woman, as Desma had been Timothea's. Cela could have held the crew together, continued their work, maybe even gone back to Urruc, though none of them ever wished to return to that godsforsaken land. Did she sometimes resent Desma? Her family had taken everything from Cela. Her high priestess had caused the destruction of the temple. Her adopted father had given up. Her sister had taken his life.

Desma sometimes tried to swap their stories, to imagine what she would have done in her friend's position, but she knew she would never know the truth. Only fools pretended to know who they were. The wise understood that people were mysteries even to themselves.

Her mind drifted back to Urruc, the constant foul wind that blew, smelling of a midden heap. Sand that scratched and burned like shards of glass heated by a sun that wanted to burn the ground, even though nothing grew in that cracked and parched earth. The buildings, once glorious and without equal, were empty and silent. Echoes of a past lost.

Sometimes the wind sounded like screams and shrieks as it swept through broken palaces and homes, rising and falling for hours at a time. At night, clouds swept from the sea, blocking the moon and stars, smothering the land with a darkness so thick it hurt to breathe. And when rain fell, twice in the three months they were there, it stank of rot and decay, tasting like a swamp when they tried to drink it. They had to keep sending the ship to a nearby island for fresh water.

But it was the day they had discovered the tomb. When they had broken through the sealed up wall ...

A scream, sudden and piercing, swept through the camp. Desma jerked out of her reverie, standing stock still as she tried to determine from what direction it had come from. The others roused themselves in a rush, weapons drawn as they readied for an attack that did not come.

'What in Soranus' flaming beard was that?' Bion shouted, his great axe gleaming in the starlight.

Desma held her breath, waiting.

A second scream, carried by the wind, came from the west.

'This way,' she shouted, taking off up the hill and past the few trees. She realised that it might not be the monster. It could be brigands raiding a merchant train. Or a raid on a village. Nevertheless, she pushed herself harder, feet pounding the rocky terrain as her chest heaved for more air, hair flaring out behind her like a banner. Monster or no monster, it did not matter.

That second scream had been from a child.

CHAPTER THIRTY-THREE

Desma heard the others giving chase behind her. She did not know where she was heading but the screams could not have been too far away.

She hoped there would not be any more screams. Or did she? Screams at least meant whoever they were would still be alive. And she needed more guidance.

To her relief – and fear – there were more screams and she veered slightly south. She did not know how far she had to run but she refused to slow down. Branches whipped her face, stones threatened to turn her ankles, hidden creeks splashed her with water. All were secondary to finding the source of the noise. Of the terror.

Bright lights began to appear ahead and she lessened her pace. Drawing her sword, she approached with care. The hills had given way again to woodlands, the trees tall and old, having survived the axe and plough of farmers. She slipped between the trunks, taking care where she placed her feet to avoid any twigs snapping, though whoever was ahead was making enough noise for an army. Off to the side she spotted a large rock, towering ten feet in the air and covered in moss. She carefully pulled herself up the slanted surface and, once she was at the top, she inched her eyes over the rim and found she had a perfect view of below.

A glade several dozen feet wide was encircled with giant bonfires, except for a small gap. In the middle of the flames was a large wooden cage filled with men, women, and children, at least twenty of them. Their clothes were dirty and some had bruises. She even spotted two men wearing linen shirts with bronze greaves – warriors from the city, no doubt. Were all these people from the city?

Horror, deep and sharp, flooded her veins.

They were bait for the monster.

Another search revealed more men on the outside of the fire circle. Some hid behind or up trees, others crouched behind rocks or bushes. Except for one who stood openly in view, red sash gleaming in the light and only one side of his head shaved. Stolos.

Desma gritted her teeth. The bastard. He was trying to lure the monster with citizens. The people in the cage all huddled around each other, men on the outside, then the women, the children in the centre.

Occasionally, one of Stolos' men in the trees would sling a rock, hard, into the cage, causing someone to cry out.

'My blood isn't curdling.' Stolos laughed in his cultured voice. 'Scream louder, or the next thing we shoot at you will be a little pointier.'

The prisoners were sobbing and one of the men gripped the bars and hurled insults at Stolos, face red and spittle flying. The band leader grinned viciously and motioned to one of his men. An arrow flickered from the darkness and struck the prisoner in the stomach. He doubled over, screaming as blood gushed onto his hands. The others in the cage took up the shouts, cramming as far as away from the injured man as possible.

Stolos laughed.

A terrible bellow, like a bear roaring and a horse screaming, thundered through the glade. A moment's hush followed, everyone falling silent in surprise, before the prisoners took up their cries once more. Stolos walked into the darkness, calling orders.

Desma went to climb down and saw her crew, with Peteos and Actor, waiting below. 'About twenty prisoners in the cage,' she said as she dropped to the forest floor. 'Children included. One man badly hurt. I think there are probably more than forty men in Stolos' band now, all around.'

A crackle of leaves spun her around with sword raised.

Cosmas floated into sight, as grey as a wolf and almost as silent. 'I would put the number at fifty, give or take,' he whispered. 'Minus three,' he added with teeth bared.

Another roar shook the trees.

'Whatever is coming, is coming fast,' Desma said hurriedly. 'We are going to get those people out.'

'Why?' Peteos burst in. 'A murderous creature is coming and we are outnumbered. There is nothing we can do for them. Leave them.'

Before Desma could speak, Actor rounded on his older companion. 'Be silent,' the small warrior hissed, fist raised. 'I don't care if you are the lowest, slimiest coward to ever crawl this land. There are children down there. You will draw your sword and go where Desma commands, or *I will cut you down myself!*'

Peteos, eyes wide in shock, swallowed and nodded, moving back to the fringe.

Actor caught Desma's eye and nodded as well.

Desma turned to Arete, waiting expectedly.

'Right,' the shipwright said, solemn eyes bright in the flickering shadows. 'Here's the plan.'

As everyone took up their position, Desma remembered the last time they had bled their blades together. The beach near Apasa where they had tracked the Empyrean men left behind to find the Belt of Turan. They had left none alive.

Desma waited with Bion, Actor, and Arete near the rock. Bion hefted a large log, a felled young tree covered in branches, like it was a sack of wheat. Kassandra and Cela had gone north; Khufu and Delphinus south. Cosmas had turned into a ghost. Peteos stood alone further east, keeping their retreat clear, to attack any hunters if they tried to follow, and ensure all the prisoners were sent back to their camp.

The roars continued, unabated and growing louder in the few minutes it took for them to be ready. If the creature was so loud yet so far, she dreaded to think how large it was. They killed two more of Stolos' men as they circled near the rock. Bion snapped one's neck and Arete had skewered the other in the eye with a knife. Both had been tossed in a depression with leaves kicked over them. They deserved little else.

The people in the cage were still throwing themselves at the bars, ripping their nails as they tore at the straps holding the bars in place. Stolos had ordered two more arrows into the group; one hitting a bearded man and the other a mature woman with brown hair. They were wounding shots, to maximise pain, and they writhed on the ground with the first victim. Desma's hands flexed as she imagined them around Stolos' throat.

They had to wait for the monster. Desma did not care about killing it herself, gods damn what she had at stake. She just needed it to be close enough to distract most of the hunters.

Bits of loose stone on the large rock they hid behind started to rattle. She knelt down and pressed her hand to the ground and felt slight vibrations. Whatever was coming was *big*.

'Get ready,' she said unnecessarily. Her group all had grim, determined faces.

There was crashing from the south, the direction where there was a gap in the bonfires.

'Fires,' Stolos called from somewhere in the night. Twin fire arrows flew down and hit the ground outside the opening. Two lines of fire raced away into the forest, a path of burning oil to lead the monster straight into the circle. And to the cage.

'Tinia shit in my beard,' Bion cursed as the monster came into view, illuminated by the lanes of fire.

Desma wholeheartedly echoed his sentiment.

The creature looked as though it had been spat out of every child's most terrifying nightmare.

It was so large it could have cradled Bion like a babe in its arms. Right before it ate him. Towering above them all, its skin was a green so dark it was almost black, with grey striations radiating from its neck and across the length of its body. Its hands were as large as shields, with tufts of coarse hair, six claws ending in talons like spearheads. It had a stumpy tail like a lizard in the process of growing a new one, swinging like a club. Its body was hardened leather with scales at its joints. Oozing gashes and gnarled pustules covered its back and stomach, smelling of rancid oil and mint.

With a neck long like a horse but far more flexible, its head swinging about as it sniffed the air, its face was hideously human but distorted. Pale grey, like the striations, with a bulbous nose bright with red veins. Its ears were wide, like a bat's, shooting horizontally from the sides of its bald head. And its eyes were like plates, round and black with slashes of green. Its mouth was a gash with a mixture of teeth, some needlelike, others flat like a cow, and others like a shark. Its tongue was black and long, flopping between its teeth. It didn't seem to notice when it bit down and brought forth murky white blood from its own tongue, smearing it over its lips like the froth of the deranged.

Desma heard Peteos vomit behind them and she clamped down on her own stomach.

The beast roared again and began to hurl towards the prisoners, between the twin lines of fire.

'Khufu, now!' she screamed, though there was little need. Three heavy spears, taken from the slain men, slammed into the monster, two hitting its side and the other the top of its back leg.

It let out a squeal of pain and outrage. Before it could recover, three more spears hit it, pushing it through one of the fire lines, its skin crackling as it passed through the flame. At the same time, men began to curse as arrows and rocks rained down on them, forcing them into the light of the bonfires.

The monster, moving with a slight limp, had ripped the spears from its flesh, releasing waves of white blood and the smell of rot and mint. Its head swung around and towered above the hunters. It gaped open its mouth and screamed down at them. The men scattered but one foolishly drew his sword and stabbed at it.

Whatever prohibition that had kept the monster from killing foreigners and country-dwelling Koriithosans did not appear to stop it from attacking those who harmed it. With a swipe of one claw, it tore the man's sword arm off and, in a blink, snapped its mouth over him, chewing messily, blood and gore dripping down its chin.

It raised its head and caught sight of the other men in the trees and bellowed as it lunged after them.

'Quick,' Desma said, moving away from the rock. 'We need ...'

Actor's shout made her duck, a knife causing sparks as it struck the rock where her head had been a second before. She whirled around to see Stolos with ten of his band around him, eyes furious and teeth bared.

'Bion, save them,' she said, moving between the two groups.

'Desma,' he started to growl.

'Do you want them to die like those men?' she snapped, screams of the dying spilling through the woods.

The Konosoan glanced at the prisoners, still beating at the wooden bars, and with his own roar ran towards them with his log, gripping one end. He swung the small tree back and forth, smashing a hole through the bonfire. Actor followed him.

Arete stepped beside her, sword and dagger drawn, face set.

'Go help them,' Desma ordered as Stolos began to approach.

The shipwright snorted and swung her blades in lazy circles. 'Even for you, one against eleven is pushing the odds. And, lately, the Corded Goddess has not been in your favour.'

Desma gritted her teeth but said nothing. It was ridiculous to think she could hold all of them off. Her own blade, crafted from iron and copper in the traditional double-edge leaf shape, was made by the finest smiths in Apasa. It had gone to Cela when King Sophocles had stripped her of her belongings and her friend had made sure to bring it along. Though it was not as great as swords forged in Pallan, and nothing compared to one made in The Forge in Trilos, it was still a fine blade.

With a nod, both women lunged forward, catching Stolos and his men off guard. Arete's sword tore through the first man's neck but Stolos recovered quicker. He ducked Desma's swing and stabbed. Desma twisted to the side, foot flying as she kicked him in the shoulder. He stumbled away, face outraged, but two of his men rushed forward and it was all Desma could do to avoid their spears. One jabbed at her feet and she sprung up, brandishing her sword wildly to force him back, landing to only spin again to thwack the other spear away with the flat of her blade. Two more joined and she was now facing four spears.

Arete was faring no better, surrounded by swords, never seeming to pause as she danced and evaded.

Desma could not let her four surround her. In a mad move, she threw herself to the ground, rolling until she slammed into someone's shins, toppling him over. She lashed out with her sword and heard a curse as it struck another. She scrambled back to her feet. One man was down, clutching his side where she had cut him. The man she had tripped was climbing back up.

She had never been a great swordsman. Her teachers had been strict and hard, pushing her as far as she could go, but she would never be Hamphiare, who slayed a thousand men on a battlefield by herself. But she could fight dirty. Honour was for a warrior. She was a fighter.

She batted away a spear, stepping close, and slammed her knee into his groin. As he crumpled she banged her hilt into his temple, causing his eyes to roll upwards and glaze. She grabbed another spear as that man stabbed, wrenching him closer to punch him in the throat with a hand wrapped around her hilt, crushing his ability to breathe.

One man left. He stumbled as he jabbed with his spear, still hurt from being knocked to the ground. Almost lazily, she parried, stepped forward, and thrust her sword into his chest.

Instinctively, she ducked. Another knife hit the already dead man in the forehead.

She spun and prowled towards Stolos. He was backing away, two men guarding him as he drew another knife. Gods, how many did he have?

'Fight me, coward,' she shouted.

His two men paled. Backlit by tall flames, dark hair flowing in the breeze, sword dripping blood, and her face ferocious, Desma was not surprised when they turned to flee.

Stolos screamed after them but they kept running. He kept his eyes on Desma, knife still raised.

Arete suddenly cried out. Desma glanced over and ducked the knife Stolos threw. He turned to run towards the trees. Desma moved towards the shipwright. She had felled two of the men but had taken injuries. Cuts on both arms sent streams of blood down to her hands but she kept the other two at a distance. She was slowing, however.

Desma fell on them like lightning, her sword slashing across the back of one neck and embedding halfway into another. She wrenched it free, letting the body topple as she wiped the blade clean. 'You all right?' she asked.

Arete nodded, eyes tight with pain.

'Coming through,' Bion called, running towards them. He had one child on his shoulders, arms wrapped around his head with eyes squeezed shut. He carried three more in his arms. Actor had two children himself and the rest followed them.

'The injured?' Desma asked.

The large man shook his head, anger tinging the movement.

Desma's lips tightened. Bastard Stolos. She pointed towards camp. 'Keep going. Find Peteos and get them to safety.'

Bion nodded and started moving again, the men and women following after him like ducklings in a stream, most of them too dazed but to go where he led.

'Go with them,' Desma said to Arete. She opened her mouth to argue but Desma cut her off. 'How are you going to be of any help against *that* if you can't even lift your arms? Go!'

Arete gave a final frown and followed after the others.

Desma turned and went in the opposite direction.

She could hear men yelling, the occasional clash of weapons, and, above all, the sounds of the monster.

As she rounded the bonfire circle, her foot slipped and she barely caught herself on a tree trunk. She looked down and gagged. Half a man was on the ground, everything from his navel down was missing and her foot had stepped on what looked like his spleen.

'Menrva and Artimi preserve us,' she whispered, stepping around the mess and continuing.

She soon came upon a scene that would have made bards fall over themselves to write a tale about. Trees felled, earth ripped in great chunks, fires flung like water, the dead and dying scattered in pieces. The monster, half-lit and half-shadowed, gambolled about the darkness, killing men. She saw her crew scattered throughout the woods. Khufu fought three hunters at once.

Cela was firing arrow after arrow at the beast. Delphinus, sword and spear in hand, screamed words to an old battle song, a whirlwind of death and madness as he flew across the glade. Men ran from him in fear, and the piper cut them down from behind.

And, towering above it all, the beast still roared.

CHAPTER THIRTY-FOUR

The beast crushed one of the hunters with its claw, fist slamming into the earth hard enough to make the ground tremble. And Delphinus turned towards the monster.

'No, stop,' Desma shouted after the piper but he did not hear. She set off at a run but he was far closer. With a wild scream, he threw himself up at the monster's shoulder, sword and spear stabbing into its flesh as he pulled himself up onto its back. The beast let out a terrible squeal that was half-horse, half-lion, spinning around as it tried to reach around itself to grab the piper.

But Delphinus scampered about, dodging its claws, laughing as he stabbed and slashed. White blood, thick and unctuous, splattered him but he did not care, barely pausing to wipe it from his face so he could see.

'Get down before you get killed, you idiot,' Desma yelled, cutting down a wiry fellow who leapt out at her. 'Khufu!'

Her captain turned and saw her pointing. His eyes widened as he killed the last man in front of him. He dashed forward, roaring in the same voice he used on the trireme to be heard over the fiercest storm. 'Piper, attend!'

The words cut through the battle-fog and Delphinus blinked repeatedly, barely registering where he was until the beast finally managed to backhand him from its back. The piper went flying and crashed into Khufu, sending them both to the ground.

Still gushing blood like a fountain from its back, the monster went to pounce on the two men when arrows began to sting its face, Cela barely releasing one arrow before she was drawing the next.

'Stop.' Desma threw herself between, hand thrust up as though by will alone she could stop the beast. Her palm grazed the monster's skin.

A resounding *boom* echoed through the glade. A shockwave of air seemed to move slowly outwards, buffeting rather than pushing, and everything felt charged with tiny bolts of lightning. Where her hand connected with the monster a light welled, rose and black, brilliant in its illumination, and the creature screamed.

It threw itself away from her, crashing into the large rock and breaking through it. It scrambled to its feet and began to run, away from them and into the woods, careless of the trees it smashed it.

Desma looked down at Khufu and Delphinus. 'Can you move?'

Khufu nodded as he got to his knees, taking deep breaths and checking himself over. 'We can still fight.'

'Then finish these men,' she said flatly. Most of Stolos' gang had fled but Cela and Kassandra still fought. Cosmas was no doubt in the woods waiting for the stragglers to try and run. 'I'm going hunting.' And she took off into the night, leaving Khufu's shocked expression behind.

The beast was faster than any horse Desma had seen but in its pain it did nothing to hide its trail. She followed the torn vegetation, cracked branches, and crushed rocks with ease. Her breath was ragged in her own ears and her side burned, but she pushed ahead.

She did not know what she was going to do when she caught up to it but it had to end. Though the men in Stolos' band deserved what happened to them, she thought about all the innocents it had killed. Men and women and children. And it would have done the same to the people in the cage if they had not stopped it from reaching them.

And that *force* when she touched it. She had no clue what it was or why it sent the creature running. Had it come from her? Impossible. She was no witch or godling or priestess gifted with divine magic. Why would her touch have hurt it? If it even was her touch – everything happened so fast. Was it something Delphinus had done?

Soon, she lost sight of the monster and after a few minutes even the sound of it crashing through the forest faded. Occasionally she heard it roar but, eventually, silence. She did not stop.

She did not know how far she had gone or even if they had travelled in a straight line. She only concentrated on putting one foot in front of another, glancing up occasionally to make sure she still saw signs of its passage.

Eventually, she reached a sheer rock wall covered in moss and lichen, roughly forty feet in length. It looked like it was one side of a gully but the other had fallen away in a landslide. The soft forest floor had turned to large slabs of stone and crushed rock. But the path led directly there. She slowed down, taking a moment to rest her burning legs and take deep, shuddering breaths.

Her sword still in hand, Desma stalked around the gully wall, listening for any sound but the woods were silent. There was no opening or cave in the wall itself so she walked around and up the cliff. It reached twenty feet at its peak but there was still no sign of the monster. She went back down and walked along the wall's length, hand on the stone in case there was a gap she was missing in the darkness. Only a little light from the stars and crescent moon was filtering through the branches.

She was about halfway along the wall when something slithered under her palm. She jerked her hand back, thinking it was a snake but nothing moved. She poked the spot with the tip of her sword but there was nothing but stone. Not even a vine. Frowning, she placed her hand back and again felt a strange slithering motion. She pushed harder and a light welled underneath her palm, rose and black. There was a faint concussion of air and suddenly the stone wall was no longer there.

Desma stumbled back in amazement. A section of wall, about ten feet wide, was gone and she was staring into the gaping maw of a cave. *Was* it her? She pushed the question away. She needed to focus on the task in front of her. Though the question burned in the back of her mind.

She hesitated before gripping her sword tight and heading inside. She had briefly considered returning to the others and coming back as a group when they were rested but dismissed the idea. They were here because she needed them. She was the one tainted and the one who needed to be cleansed.

They had all offered their help but that did not mean they had to die.

No one else she loved was going to die because of her!

If Nurtia, Goddess of Fate, and the Diviners, her three daughters, decided this was where she would meet her end, then so be it. Tinia's protection only went so far for one of the damned.

She walked with one hand on the smooth tunnel wall and the other holding her sword in front of her. As soon as she entered the cave the little light from the sky vanished. Breathing as shallowly as she could, she stepped carefully and was thankful the floor was just as smooth, no leaves, or sticks ... or bones.

As she walked, she started to feel the same slithering sensation as before but now it was around her. Her skin, hair, inside her clothes. Like a thousand dry worms were wriggling over her. She shuddered.

A light appeared ahead and she heard the sounds of something snuffling. The beast, she assumed. As she got closer, the warm golden light growing brighter, she heard a new sound.

Someone was speaking.

Desma was still too far away to discern what the voice was saying but the tone was calming. She heard a whine and whimper, something banged loudly followed by gently shushing.

She crouched down low, edging forward slowly until she was able to peer around the edge of an opening.

The tunnel led to a large chamber, far taller than the height of the gully wall, though she had not felt the passage sloping downwards. It was circular in shape with a domed ceiling. Giant rushes covered the floor and the scent of rancid oil and vibrant mint filled the air. Smaller tunnels led off, presumably to other chambers, but this one was large enough to hold the monster. As well as a second monster.

Desma froze, too afraid to move.

The second monster was just as big but covered in dark red scales, with tufts of white fur sprouting randomly. It had no tail but two stubby wings that it flapped anxiously as it hovered over its kin. Its face was just as hideously deformed but its eyes were long, horizontal slits the colour of yellow pus.

The first monster was lying on its side, kicking its feet and groaning, head thrashing in pain as it let out the occasional hiss.

'Be calm, Ector,' the voice from earlier said. 'I need to make sure none of those nasty arrows or spearheads are stuck before I can heal you. Alexon, help soothe your brother.'

Desma stifled a gasp.

There was a woman between the two monsters.

She was clothed in a homespun dress of good brown wool, her mane of black hair held back by a strip of the same cloth, and a belt of white leather wrapped her waist. She was of stocky build but with slender arms, with skin the colour of walnut wood, and she was at least a foot taller than Desma. Her face was strong and strange. It was the face of a mature woman, wise with the experience life brought but it was still lit beneath with youthful vigour. It held an almost agelessness, and Desma could only place her somewhere between twenty and fifty years old.

She was currently elbow deep inside the wounded monster, her arms drenched with thick, white blood. She continued to speak placating words, humming snatches of songs, and whispering encouragement to the creature. It obeyed every command, rolling when asked, lifting an arm where directed.

Once the woman was satisfied, she patted the creature's head and moved to a long trestle table. Pots and cups and bowls covered its surface, along with bundles of plants, nuts, and gems.

She moved across the table with surety, never hesitating as she selected one item after another. Some were grounded in a mortar, others roughly chopped, and some tossed whole into a large bowl. Eventually, she lifted a silver jug and poured glistening water into the bowl. She picked up a cracked wooden spoon and started to stir slowly. Four times east and then four times west. Repeat.

She began to speak.

'Dark Artimi, adopted goddess of my people,' she said, her voice old and young. 'I call upon your wildness and your new dominion. You who picked up the mantle of the Old One, who gathered my sisters when we were lost. I ask you now to bless this desire, to bring your will to bear and to alter what is not yet set.'

She spat into the bowl.

'Take a gem of blue and shatter it nigh. Accept parsley young and bracken sea. Let herbs of night and dawn, twins and enemies, meld and mix and turn to light. Bind and seal, fill and soothe. By Tiur and Thesan, take my rage and steal my fire. By Artimi and Horta, steal my pain and gift my love. Turn mundane into power. Let my will wrought the world. Let me change what is my right!'

Whatever mixture was in the bowl began to bubble and hiss though no flame came near it.

'Witch,' Desma breathed silently.

The woman grabbed the bowl and moved back to the wounded monster – Ector, she had called him. 'Hold him, for this will be painful,' she said to the other creature. Alexon.

The red beast arranged itself carefully on top of its brother and the woman began to smear the sage-colour mixture across Ector's wounds. The creature squealed and writhed but his brother held him firm, grunting as it struggled.

The woman slapped the healing tincture on like a bricklayer with mortar, moving swiftly and without mercy until every stab and scrape was coated thickly. When it was done, she put the bowl down and grabbed a packet from the table. 'Eat, my dear,' she whispered gently, holding it to Ector's mouth, unafraid of his many teeth.

He carefully wrapped his tongue around the packet and swallowed. She stayed, kneeling beside his head, stroking his brow with her arms still covered in blood, speaking kindly. She looked at the monster with such tenderness. Who was she?

Soon the monster closed its eyes and its breathing deepened, sleep claiming him.

The woman rose to her feet with a groan and moved to a bucket to wash herself. 'He will be fine, Alexon,' she said to the other monster who followed her with a worried look. 'He will need sleep and lots of meat. You will need to do much hunting in the days to come. But you are strong and brave. You will care for both of us well.' The red beast grunted happily.

The woman frowned as she scrubbed her arms. 'It is strange how hurt he was,' she said more to herself than to the monster. 'Perhaps he grew careless.'

Desma decided that was enough. She was uncertain how she would fare against one monster, let alone two. And a witch.

She began to edge slowly backwards.

A strong breeze blew down the tunnel, ruffling her hair as it swept into the chamber.

The red monster sniffed loudly and its head whipped around on its long neck, eyes narrowing even further when it spied her. The woman stood with mouth agape.

'Oh shit,' Desma cursed, scrambling to her feet.

The monster roared in anger and charged towards her, knocking the trestle table over in its rush.

Desma tripped and fell heavily. The creature would be on her in seconds and she would die. Torn apart by tooth and claw and eaten. She screamed.

The woman shouted words in a harsh and cold language and the monster froze.

Desma stared into the jaws of the creature, its teeth covered in spittle, its eyes roving wildly, but it did not budge. It had not been a command but a spell.

The woman walked around the beast and looked down at Desma, her face more intrigued than angry. 'Get up,' she said.

Desma clumsily got to her feet and noticed she was still gripping her sword. Realising that this woman could kill her by beast or by word easily enough, she sheathed it.

'Wise,' the witch said. 'Come.' She turned and walked back to the upended table.

Desma followed, carefully avoiding the monster's limbs. It was stopped mid-lunge, as though turned into a statue.

'Help me with this,' the woman said, gripping one end of the table

'What?'

The witch flashed her an impatient look. 'Grab the other end of the table and turn. Was I wrong to call you wise? Jump!'

Desma jumped. She hurried to the other end and together they righted the table. It was solid oak and heavy, scarred from much use.

'Help me pick these up. I cannot be bothered gathering these all over again. And you'—she shot a scolding look at the red monster's rear—'need to be more careful. Move.' She snapped her fingers and the beast completed its lunge right into the ground. It heaved itself up and turned around, rubbing its nose, and stared balefully at Desma.

'Leave us, Alexon,' the witch commanded. 'Ensure the entrance is hidden. And do not try to eat her again.'

Alexon did not look pleased but stomped up the tunnel towards the entrance, indignation clear in its movement.

'May I ask a question?' Desma said, kneeling to carefully start picking up scattered gemstones.

'Yes,' the woman said as she righted her large bowl.

'What the freezing rivers is happening? And who are you?'

The woman looked up and met Desma's gaze and she suddenly felt very, very frightened.

'You tried to kill my son,' the witch said in a cold voice. 'And I am Cisra.'

CHAPTER THIRTY-FIVE

Cisra.

The name rang like a bell in her head.

The only Cisra she knew was from the story. The Arydorian who almost destroyed Koriithos and killed her own children. The sorceress.

Desma dropped the items she had picked up and stepped away, hand on her hilt though she did not draw her sword. What use would it have been anyway?

Cisra straightened as well, face imperious but calm.

The silence stretched.

'Are you going to kill me?' Desma finally asked, heart pounding but she refused to let fear show on her face.

'At this present moment, I am,' the witch replied, as though discussing whether she would head to market that day.

'Is there anything I can do to avert my death?'

'Why were you trying to kill my son?'

Desma hesitated. Cisra must know what he had been doing. He had killed dozens of people. And she assumed his brother was no less innocent. Did she also go out on the hunt, and kill?

She saw no choice. Honesty was all that was left for her.

'Though it was not the reason that set my feet on this path,' she said carefully, 'knowing now what I have witnessed, I would do my best to stop both your children. They have attacked and killed so many innocent citizens of Koriithos. Children included. Such heinousness cannot be allowed to exist.' She took a deep breath. 'But my true motivation is far more selfish. I am tainted.'

'Yes,' Cisra breathed, eyes half-lidded as though she was looking at something else. 'I can see bonds about you, gold and crackling. A law of Tinia?'

Desma nodded. Did she need to go into full detail? Surely this woman did not deserve her story.

Cisra must have read her thoughts in her face. 'I have never been denounced by the gods. I am twice over daughter to goddesses and I have the right!'

Bitterness coated Desma's tongue but she spoke the words that carved open the wounds afresh. 'I am Desma, daughter of the High Priestess of Turan from Apasa and her husband, Palamaon the potter.' Words like rust and bile. But she spoke them, almost spitting them out by the end, but at last her story was over and the witch watched her with unreadable eyes.

'A Father-Killer,' she mused, moving to place the objects she picked up onto the table. 'It was far more common in olden days, hence why Tinia made that law. But still, life is better than death.'

'It does not always feel so,' Desma said, for some reason moving to continue helping. Maybe it was better to keep her hands busy.

'Such whining,' Cisra scoffed. 'Are you telling me that since you were punished you have felt no joy? No happiness or laughter or wonder? Experienced nothing new?'

Desma had to concede. She loved seeing Mynta again, to see her friend blossom into an intelligent and gorgeous woman. She thought of the starlit nights on the sea, sitting with Cela or Arete and listening to the waves, chatting with Khufu or joking with Bion. The wonder of Koriithos. Meeting Thales and his grandchildren. Such simple, good things. No, she would never have traded her punishment for death.

'I guess I only thought about the pain of what happened,' she admitted. 'And the fear every time I talked to someone new.' Memories of lying at the feet of Trilos' beachmaster and eating sand flickered into her mind before she forcibly shoved them away.

'It would not be punishment if you were not punished,' Cisra said simply, picking up the last bundle of herbs. 'There, all righted now.'

Desma realised they were standing across the worn table from each other. Cisra met her eyes and held it. Fear, like a dark cold washing down her body, returned.

'Would you care for some warmed wine?' the sorceress asked. Without waiting for an answer, she moved off to the side and went through one of the small openings in the chamber.

Desma glanced back to the exit tunnel. But Alexon was waiting at the other end and she doubted Cisra would let her go so easily. She was still planning to kill her. But the least she could do was offer her some wine. She followed the witch.

The doorway led to a more comfortably decorated chamber. It was lit with torches that did not flicker, warm light flooding the circular room. It held fleece covered chairs, a small and large table, several rugs on the floor, and a fireplace that burned with white flame and gave no smoke. The walls held murals of wild woodlands and sharp mountains, wolves howling at the moon, and sand dunes softened by reed-lined rivers. The room smelled even more strongly of mint but without the spoiled grease. But the crisp mint was softened by something else. 'Marjoram?'

'Close,' Cisra said, taking a seat on a simple wooden chair with a fleece of black wool. Her voice was mildly surprised. Desma had not realised she had spoken aloud. 'It is called calamint. It smells like mint and marjoram. Please, sit.'

Desma chose a seat opposite Cisra, facing the doorway. She accepted the cup of warmed wine. It smelled heavenly of spices. She took a sip and it was wonderful. 'I smelled it when we inspected some of the ... sites. And it is very strong in your ... home.'

Cisra sipped her own wine, eyes studying Desma over the cup's rim. 'I suppose there is no harm in telling you. Each witch has a scent to their magic, a sacred herb so we may know each other without words. It is one of the last gifts from the Old One before Artimi adopted our covens. My magic smells of calamint. My sister smelled of sorrel. My brother smells like old thyme. My aunt ... indescribable.'

If this truly was Cisra from two hundred years ago, legend said she killed her own sons. Did she use her magic to resurrect them and transform them into monsters? Is that why they smelled of calamint, because they were made of her spells?

'Tell me how you came to be in my home,' Cisra said, taking another sip.

Desma opened her mouth but paused. For just a moment, the witch's eyes had turned ravenous, nearly hidden by the movement of her cup. Why? It clicked in her mind. No one had found her home for ten years of searching for the monster. She had been shocked to see Desma, which she would not have been if others had stumbled onto the tunnel. She did not know how Desma found them and she was desperate to know.

She leaned back in her chair. 'Tell me why you are allowing your sons to kill Koriithosans.'

Cisra's face turned to thunder and the air felt cold. Desma's throat went dry but she kept her face clear. The room darkened and the shadows around Cisra's chair began to writhe. Still Desma did not move beyond taking another sip. Was it wise to drink a witch's wine? Too late now. Cracks began to appear on the floor, webbing towards her chair. Desma flicked her eyes towards the murals, letting them rove slowly over the images, as though content with enjoying the artistry.

The room brightened and warmed, the cracks vanished, and the shadows became still. She glanced back at the witch, who struggled to hide her puzzlement.

'Finished with your tantrum?' she asked mildly.

Too far. Whips of air suddenly bound her arms to the chair, her cup spilling across the floor. Her head was wrenched back and the smell of calamint was overpowering. Cisra stood slowly from her seat, towering higher and higher until she dwarfed the chamber. 'Tantrum?' Her voice set the room rumbling. 'I am Cisra, Uncrowned Queen of Arydor. I am monstress and arcane godling. I could keep you here for a hundred years and you would know pain to break the strongest heart every day without end. I could carve off pieces of your flesh and feed them to my sons while you watch. I could delve into your mind and poison all the beloved memories you possess. Do not trifle with me!'

Desma met her eyes that had become voids as black as the cavern between stars. Darkness to be lost in forever. Falling upward, higher and lower, until …

'If you want to go through all that effort,' she found herself saying, bravado fortifying her voice. 'But how long until I spoke? How would you know my words are true? When will the others come?' Doubt at what she was doing tried to crash through the panic she kept it tightly held down. 'You live in a cave. A very nice cave, but a cave nonetheless. You are hiding and don't want to be found. What will happen when I am tracked and all of Koriithos comes through that tunnel?'

The world shifted.

Cisra was suddenly sitting in her chair, her own size, drinking her wine. Desma's arms were free and her cup sat by her feet right way up and filled with dark wine. She blinked at the disorientation.

'You show remarkable insight for one so young,' said Cisra. 'Perhaps we can talk for a while.'

'And are you still planning on killing me?'

'Oh, yes.'

'We better make it a fascinating discussion, then.'

Cela nearly tore her hair out. 'What do you mean you *lost* the trail?'

Cosmas gave her a flat stare, towering over her with his slim height. 'I mean, it was here and now it is gone. It ends on the stony ground and we cannot find it again.'

They were standing in front of a large gully wall. Arete and Khufu were with them as well. The rest had gone back to camp.

It had been a ferocious battle. Arete's plan had worked and the prisoners had been saved. Most of the brigands had been killed but Cosmas said Stolos had managed to flee with at least a handful of men. Kassandra had bandaged up the cuts on the shipwright's arms but she had still insisted on coming with them. Remarkably, there were few injuries among the crew. Bion probably had it worst with burns from clearing the fire but they would heal.

Cela had seen Desma give chase to the monster and she cursed her childhood friend vigorously. Who runs *after* a monster – and alone? Fool!

As soon as they had the prisoners clear, were certain there would be no counter-attack from Stolos, and everyone's wounds checked, she had set off after them. The trail had been easy to follow. The monster was too injured to care about erasing its tracks. But now they were at a dead end.

Everyone had taken a turn walking around and up the gully wall looking for an entrance but there was nothing. The only oddity was at one point she was hit by a heavy cloud of mint but could not see the plant. It was as dark as Nethuns' armpit. A few clouds had gathered which blocked out some of the precious little light filtering through. They had not brought any torches in case they came across the monster. Stealth was preferred.

'Circle outwards and let's see if we can pick up the trail,' Cela said, heading north. The others picked a different direction.

She was furious at Desma. It would have taken moments to call out to her and Cela would have followed. She would follow Desma anywhere, even into the Beneath if she had reason. But she left her behind. There was a time when that would have been unthinkable. They had walked hand-in-hand into every danger and prank and adventure together. She had *abandoned* her home for Desma, leaving her mother lying on her sick bed with a leg black and green. She had received her mother's blessing to go after Desma and knew a priest of Esplace was on his way to heal her, but the decision still weighed heavily on her. Apasa was her home and it was injured. But Desma was her sister and she was in a way just as hurt.

There were times, when the night was deep and the silence shrouding, that she questioned the wisdom in her choice. It was easy, in the bright light of the day, standing with Desma as they figured out their next steps, argued to see priests and kings, travelled the sea from city to city, to feel proud to be by her friend. But in those quiet, lonely hours when Thesan was far from announcing the dawn, she wondered how far the binds of friendship and sisterhood stretched.

But she and Desma had been friends since they were barely out of swaddling. She sometimes did not know who she was when her darker, fiery friend was not by her side. Fire and light, wine and honey, that was who they were.

But they could not return to those days. Her mother would never take them both back into the temple. Desma, even if – no, *when* – she was purified, would not be welcomed in the city. She had the whole world. But Celadine, daughter of High Priestess Leontia of the Grand Temple of Turan, knew her duty. But why did it feel like a knife in her chest?

She angrily kicked a rock and sent it scattering into the darkness. There were no tracks to be found. What had Desma got herself into now?

CHAPTER THIRTY-SIX

Desma watched Cisra tap her chin thoughtfully as she stared at her.

She was gambling with everything and with nothing. Balancing on a knife's tip and knowing the only way down was sliding on the blade's edge.

'Do you know my story?' asked Cisra. 'Tell it to me.'

Desma swallowed. 'Vikare believed he was the rightful king of Thevai after Turnu revealed his true lineage. He returned to the kingdom to claim the throne and was cast out by the queen, his sister, Phaidra.'

'Noxious woman but strong,' Cisra said begrudgingly. She waved for her to continue.

Desma tried her best to remember how Delphinus recited the tale but she was no poet. She gave it blunt and simple. She did fumble when she got to the part where Cisra killed the princess, flew away on a chariot borne by winged scorpions, killed her sons, and cast their bodies onto the city. The witch's face was murderous.

'I hope that bastard is freezing in the Blasted Depths of the underworld,' she spat. She had discarded her winecup and her nails were renting furrows in the chair arm.

'Is any of it true?' Desma asked.

'Oh, parts of it are true. That is how you make a lie believable and live this long. You use truth to bind the falsehoods together.' She visibly took control of herself, taking a settling breath. 'I never loved Vikare,' she proclaimed. 'I remember seeing him for the first time. A proud, limping buffoon who thought to demand my father's treasures to claim a throne hundreds of leagues away. What cares do we have for his childish concerns? He came to my house two times, begging me to betray my father, my king, my people. Twice I denied him, turning him away with threats to stay his advances. But when he came the third time I was attacked.'

'He attacked you?' Desma was incredulous. 'That makes no sense.'

Cisra waved her hand. 'No, not by him. Magic, more powerful than anything I have ever witnessed. This was not a simple god's magic. This was one of the Twelve. *Turan.*' The name was filled with hatred. 'Love, visceral and binding and utterly false, filled me. I *adored* Vikare. I would have done anything he asked of me. I do not know what bargain he struck with the Love Goddess but what she did to me was not love. It was rape. I was forced to love that man and betray everything that was mine. Everything I did was because of that spell I could not break. For years, living in that frigid and stoic kingdom, I worked at the knot of god-magic inside of me though I knew it was no use as nothing can undo what a god has wrought. But I had to try ... despite the pain.' She trailed off, staring into the distance, sadness seeping into her features. Desma was spellbound. 'When he told me of his intent to marry Dirce, I was so happy. Finally, a way out. I forgot – we are but the playthings of gods. I discovered later that Uni was angry at Turan for some cruel joke. When she saw Turan's fingers in the love between Dirce and Vikare, she cast her own cruel spell and filled me with wifely spite, for she ruled social order and, in her eyes, divorce tears at its very fabric. I killed Dirce how they said, but I had no anger for the sweet girl in my heart, none that was my own.' She lowered her head and heaved a sigh.

Desma almost wanted to reach out and comfort the woman. To be used by two goddesses; to have no control over her own body. 'And your children? Did you kill them?'

Cisra's head jerked up, anger twisting her face. 'No,' she snarled. 'I *love* my children with my own love and none of Turan's foul magicks. Vikare got drunk one night, the last he ever spent in my bed, and told me that while I could leave – for he knew that I was too powerful for him to kill – he could not allow children with his blood to roam free to later lay claim to Koriithos. Only his children with Dirce could rule and he needed to safeguard their future.'

She stared into the fire. 'I tried to flee with Ector and Alexon. I summoned 'winged scorpions' – they are called *scriporiia*, by the way – but Vikare was already looking for me as Dirce had tried on the slippers that killed her. As we took flight, he fired two arrows and pierced both of my sons' hearts. He had always been a terrible shot but the dark fates aligned and he struck true. But my children are mortal through and through as they inherited none of my divine heritage. Their blood was only blood. It was I who wrought destruction on the city.' Her voice grew fierce and harsh. 'I summoned fire from clouds and ice from the sea. I scattered the earth like ripples on a pond. I wanted to destroy what had been my prison for so long, break those people who cast me aside. But I had to hurry. My sons were hurt and time was of the essence.

'As we flew, I used my craft to hold them to this world. We landed on a little spit of land almost at the edge of the League. There I cast spells I have never before voiced. Magic that I should never touch. I used it all. But still that harridan's magic held inside me and it twisted my weavings. My craft was vulnerable to Turan because I cast it out of love, her domain, and she slithered into my magic. True, it saved my sons and kept them living, but it created ... what they are today.'

Desma could barely get the words out of her mouth. 'Why did you come back here? Why are you killing people?'

Cisra focused on her. She had regained some of her composure and she looked regal, as stately and powerful as any queen. 'I spent close to two hundred years travelling the world with my sons trying to undo the magic. It is known that nothing can undo the magic of a god. But I thought since the core of the spell was mine, perhaps I had a chance. I was wrong – as difficult as that is for me to say. Only my aunt and brother surpass my skills with the craft and even they had no help to give me.' She shrugged. 'Ten years ago ... I gave up. Something called me back here and I let my sons run free. They choose to seek vengeance on the city who turned its back on us, harming those who wronged me so long ago.

'I tried to stop them. But when I denied them the chance to sate their bestial nature, they began to lose their humanity. Another cruel quirk of Turan's magic. The only remedy I could find was if King Soranus forgave us for the death of his daughter. He refused. When he died, I tried with his nephew who succeeded him. He refused. I tried with his son when he gained the crown. He refused. I grew tired.'

'But they killed innocent people,' Desma exclaimed. 'Young men and women, grandparents, children. They ate them!'

'THEY ARE MONSTERS,' Cisra thundered, rising to her feet. 'I did not make them so. Turan, Goddess of Love, turned them into these things. And I *love* them. I will always love them. Not all of us can turn a blade onto our family,' she spat.

Desma stiffened. She got to her feet as well, though she was a head shorter than the sorceress. 'I hate Turan as much as you,' she said, her very body quivering with anger. 'She abandoned my temple, sent Empyreans to slaughter my people and steal our treasures. She killed my mother because she loved her goddess so much she disobeyed for a chance to entice her home. My father, for love of his wife, could no longer stand to live in this world without her. Everything that has happened to me is because of Turan and *I loathe her.*'

Desma could not keep her hands, now clenched into fists, from shaking. It was true, though she had not dared voice it aloud. She hated the goddess. Every vein and thread of her existence wished pain on Turan and the futility of her emotions made it an agony. Both her and Cisra had been puppets of the goddess' desires, collateral damage so she could get what she wanted. The Goddess of Love loved no one but herself and the devotion she received from others. How Desma wished she could raise up a hand and strike her down. But she was mortal. She might as well stop a storm by blowing.

'Maybe we are not too dissimilar,' Cisra said, quietly. 'Dry your tears, child.' Desma had not realised she had been crying. 'Sit, please. You have heard my story and my sorry excuses. I have heard most of yours. I know that you hunt my children for the king's prize and now I know it is so you can claim his gift to request cleansing. But I still have one question: how did you find my home? I have laid spells that would challenge a lesser god. I sense no magic in you. Please, explain it to me?'

Desma took a shuddering breath and thought. How had she found it? She had smelled calamint, searched for an opening with no luck. She walked along the wall, touching it when it ...

She explained it to Cisra as best she could, including the strange light and explosion of air. She hesitated but also told her about when she had laid a hand on Ector's skin and her son's reaction.

Cisra's face was stone as she listened.

'It cannot be,' she whispered once Desma had finished. 'It is almost as though ...' She trailed off. 'Follow me.' She rose to her feet and left the room swiftly. Desma scrambled to follow.

They walked back to the main chamber and over to another doorway that had a strange, opaque covering. Cisra gestured towards it. 'Lay your hand upon its surface. Please,' she added at Desma's hesitation.

Warily, Desma did as asked and placed her hand on the surface. It felt like mud, giving way slightly and then resisting. She pushed harder, and it grew firmer. She gave it a shove, wanting to be able to enter what was beyond, and the sensation of slithering returned. Although, now that she was ready for it, it was not quite the right description. It was not like holding a snake. It was more like something was *unravelling*. The strange rose and black light shone from her hand and the opaqueness vanished. Desma stepped through into a small room filled with artefacts that made her uneasy.

She turned and found Cisra staring, wide-eyed and open-mouthed. 'Did I do something wrong?' she asked, although she did not know what she was meant to be doing at all.

'It can't be,' Cisra repeated. She suddenly dropped to her knees, hands held out in supplication. 'Desma, I beg your help. I know that we have no reason to trust each other but I can only hope that after hearing the true story of my life you can summon a shred of mercy. I beg on my knees, as a mother, for your help.' She leaned forward, pressing her forehead to the ground, arms straight ahead with palms up.

Uneasy, Desma did not know what to say. What had she done? 'Cisra, please, get up. I don't understand.'

Cisra did not move. 'Promise me you will help my children.'

Desma looked over at Ector who snored and snuffled in his sleep, his blood drying grey on his dark green scales. This was a boy, killed by his selfish father, and turned into a terrible beast because of Turan. For any one of those reasons she would have said yes. 'Tell me what to do.'

Cisra was on her feet in a moment, grabbing Desma's hand and dragging her over to Ector. 'Place your hands on him,' she instructed. 'But before you do, think about what he was before. Imagine the child, the young boy with black hair and olive skin and dark eyes, boisterous and loud, constantly having scraped knees and bumped elbows. Imagine a web around him and cut it away.'

Without pausing to consider what she was doing, Desma stepped forward and placed both hands on Ector's neck. She pictured the child Cisra described and felt the slithering, the unravelling, begin. It was greater this time. Like the ropes used to tie the mightiest ships to a pier, thicker than a man's waist. It moved sluggishly, not wanting to unknot but she pushed harder. How she pushed harder she could not say but she did it anyway. Deep rose and glittering black shone from her hands. She felt it encompassing her and, from the look on Cisra's face when she glanced up, she knew she made an awesome sight. But in that moment's lag in concentration, she felt the ropes begin to slide back into place. She shoved again. Inch by inch, she gritted her teeth and heaved. A concussion of air blew out from her in a circle and she fell forward as Ector's body was no longer there.

She collapsed to the ground in a heap, exhaustion flooding her body. When she finally managed to raise her head, she saw Cisra kneeling beside a body considerably larger than a child's, but definitely human. Alexon had returned from the entrance tunnel and was howling as he scrabbled around the two figures, careful not to crush either of them.

Desma pushed herself to her feet and walked over. 'Did it work?' The body was unnaturally still.

Cisra looked up, her face sparkling with tears, but she smiled. 'My son is back,' she sobbed. The figure in her arm was a man of about thirty, solidly built, wavy dark hair, and handsome features. And naked. But she saw his hairy chest rise and fall and knew he was alive.

'He is not a boy,' Desma pointed out uselessly.

Cisra shook her head. 'He grew, even as a monster. But he is my son and he is back and he is alive. Thank you, Desma. Bless you.'

Alexon huffed and whined beside her.

Cisra looked from him to Desma and opened her mouth.

Before she could speak, Desma walked over and slammed both hands onto Alexon's red scaled chest. Now that she knew what she was looking for it happened a lot faster. Light exploded, air concussed, and the ship-rope knot unravelled. In the space of a few breaths the monster was gone and in its place was a naked man a little younger than Ector, with the same dark hair but covered in freckles. Alexon looked down, hands clapping over his body in disbelief and he let out a wild laugh. 'I could kiss you,' he crowed, grabbing Desma in a hug and swinging her around. Desma could not help but join in, giggling as she swatted at his shoulders.

'Alexon, put her down' Cisra scolded, but joy softened the words.

He let her down gently and knelt beside his mother and brother, embracing them both.

Desma felt dizzy and leaned against the nearby table, her bones like water, and she was ravenous. Her skin felt feverishly hot. Were there side effects to whatever she just did?

'What *did* I do?' she asked, more to herself than to the room.

Cisra answered anyway. 'You undid Turan's magic.' Her eyes grew grim. 'No being in creation can do that.'

Desma felt faint.

CHAPTER THIRTY-SEVEN

Once they had moved Ector to Cisra's bed – there was only the one – and left Alexon to watch over him with a plate of food and wine, they both returned to the sorceress' sitting chamber.

Cisra also gave Desma a plate of bread, cheese, figs, and smoked beef. Desma ate it hungrily and asked for more. She also drank a whole pitcher of wine and water each. Once her stomach was no longer panging for food and she felt she could walk a reasonable distance again without toppling, she put down her plate and wiped her chin on her sleeve.

Cisra had watched her silently as she ate, only moving to bring more food and drink. Now, she spoke. 'You are something not seen in this world before, Desma, daughter of priestess and potter.'

Desma cursed inwardly. 'I don't want to be whatever I am. I just wanted to finish this journey Tinia has given me and find a nice quiet farm somewhere. Maybe near the sea so I can keep a boat for fishing. Some lemon trees, a few fat sheep, a little herb garden ...' she realised she was rambling.

'Nothing says you cannot do that,' Cisra said. She smiled. 'But somehow I doubt you would let yourself fall into such anonymity.'

She was suddenly reminded of Arete's words: *You have not finished with the world.* She squashed down the ominous feeling gathering in her gut.

'I know nothing of magic beyond stories and priestesses,' Desma said. 'Can you explain what I did?'

Cisra sighed. 'I dearly wish I could, Desma. But it has never been done before. The magic of a god is absolute. No exceptions. No loopholes. Tinia himself, King of the Gods, cannot undo the spell of the smallest deity. Oh, he can order and coerce and beguile, true. But he himself cannot unweave what another god has woven. Witches can undo other witches' spells, fae creatures of earth and sea and sky can undo each others' magic. But never a god's spell. I have not ... Desma!' Cisra leapt to her feet as Desma suddenly doubled over, pain like shattered iron tearing at her insides. 'What's wrong?'

Desma forced her mouth open to speak but instead vomited blood. The sorceress stepped back in surprise but then rushed forward, kneeling in the spreading red puddle, pushing Desma's hair back and feeling her face, neck, brow. Desma let out a groan as she felt something building inside her. She tried to speak but the air in her throat was thick and copper burned her throat and nose. The building sensation kept growing and she began to tremble. Within moments her body was wracked with seizures. And whatever had been building suddenly popped.

Desma screamed.

Pain like rivers of molten metal poured into every vein. Bones cracked, brittle by frost that bit deeply. Needles in her eyes. Hot coals in her ears. Every tendon stretched until it snapped. Overwhelming pain. Utter agony.

And then all at once it was over.

She blinked as her vision cleared, the blurriness and colour flashes disappearing. She took a ragged breath. Then another. Then another. She realised she was lying on her back in Cisra's lap, the witch's eyes wide and face pale.

'What ...' she croaked. She licked her lips and tried again. 'What happened?'

'Here, Mother,' Alexon said from the doorway, handing a small cup of water. He looked shaken as well.

'Drink, Desma,' Cisra said gently, letting drops of water fall between her lips. She drank slowly, and it gradually soothed her throat. Cisra traded the cup for a damp cloth and softly wiped her face. Desma saw the cloth come away red.

'What happened?' she asked again. She went to sit up but felt no strength in her limbs.

'There was a *warping*,' Cisra said. 'It is the best way I can describe it. I think there were repercussions to unravelling the curse.'

Worry flared up inside Desma, though she was almost too tired to acknowledge it. 'Am I dying?'

'No, your heartbeat is strong, and your breathing has come back. You kept flickering between fever and chills until I swear my own arm should have burn marks on it. But just as quickly as it came, it was over.'

'I'll live,' she said quietly.

'Most people would be joyous at the news,' Cisra tried to joke. 'Alexon, help me get her back to the chair.'

Between them, they carefully manoeuvred her back into her seat. When she tried to put any weight on her feet she immediately sank.

'Will you be all right for the moment?' Cisra asked. 'Alexon can keep you company.'

Desma nodded and Cisra left the room, not without leaving firm instructions to summon her the moment anything changed.

Cisra's younger son took the seat across from Desma and gave a reassuring smile. She gave a small grin in reply. Her eyes fell on the large pool of blood that was congealing on the floor. Her smile faded.

About ten minutes later, Cisra returned bearing a steaming bowl that smelled pungent and peppery. The scent of calamint followed her. 'Here,' she said kneeling down beside her. 'Drink this. All at once. You'll want to throw it back up, but that will pass. Here we go.' It was blistering in its spiciness and musky. Desma gagged but Cisra gave her no choice but to keep swallowing as she tipped the bowl into her mouth. When it was empty, Desma made a horrid face but felt better. The nausea passed and she flexed her arms.

'That is wonderful,' she said, marvelling at how strong she felt. She stood up. Her legs held her but her head swam a little. She sat back down slowly. 'What an eventful night,' she said ruefully.

Cisra laughed as, with a wave of her hand, all signs of mess vanished. 'You set out to save lives and kill a monster. Instead, you met a mother, gave her back her sons, and discovered a power that should not exist.'

A power. She had magic. What did it mean and where did it come from? She never learned magic and her mother certainly never displayed any abilities. There were stories that her grandmother's mother, Desma's greatmother, was blessed with powers but the tales were always unclear. She had also been a high priestess for Turan. Cisra said she could unravel magic, undo what the gods have decreed, but with a horrible backlash. Though her body had no mark, the memory of the pain sent her shivering. This was something she needed to keep hidden, for now. Until she learned more about it.

'Do you think that perhaps now we can reopen the discussion on killing me?' Desma asked with a weak smile.

Cisra let out another laugh. 'I believe we can.'

It was nearing dawn and there was still no sign of Desma.

They had searched for miles in every direction from where the tracks had ended at the gully wall without success. They had stumbled across a few members of Stolos' band and dealt with them swiftly and without hesitation. There had been *children* in that cage.

Cela had eventually gathered the others and they were currently resting on a grassy knoll a little distance from the wall. Bion had put together a small fire, saying he doubted the monster would come back after the hurts it received. Cela allowed it, if only so she could warm her toes. The predawn cool was biting.

'We'll need to check on the others,' she said eventually, her displeasure clear. 'Get the people back to the city. And then start searching the forest.' This time for Desma. Gods blast her impulsiveness!

Arete was looking around, sometimes twisting to look behind her, with a deep frown marring her face.

'What is it?' Cela asked the shipwright.

Arete shook her head. 'I keep smelling mint. I wouldn't have noticed it, but it is getting stronger the longer we sit here.'

'So?'

'I can't see any.'

They all turned to survey the area, Cosmas standing to walk around, prodding clumps of plants with his foot, searching. Now that she had mentioned it, the air was strong with mint as it was earlier by the gully wall. And it seemed to be growing stronger.

'Perhaps we should be going ...' Bion suggested.

They all stood, throwing dirt onto the small fire, Arete turning in slow circles, trying to see everything at once.

'Let's go,' Cela ordered.

The four of them passed her, heading back to their camp. Cela gave one last look around. As she turned she let out a gasp. The others spun around, drawing weapons only to slowly lower them, surprise clear on all their faces.

There was Desma, leader of their ragtag darkling crew. The tunic and skirt she had changed into when they made camp was torn and covered in blood, both red and white. Her face was tired and drawn, haggard almost, and her hair was a wild nest of dark rubies. But she walked with a resolute step, a smile spreading across her face when she saw them. She had no weapons but carried a large sack in both hands.

Cela hit her like a hurricane.

Desma dropped her bundle and clasped her back just as tight. 'I'm all right,' she said.

'Well, I'm not,' Cela snapped, pulling back and shaking a fist at her friend. 'Where have you been? No sign of you. No sign of the monster. If you *ever* go running off again by yourself, I am going to have Bion tie you to the mast *upside down*. Am I clear?' She ignored Bion's flabbergasted expression at being part of her plans.

'I promise to take someone with me the next time I kill a monster,' Desma vowed solemnly, a sparkle in her eye.

'Very good,' Cela nodded. 'Now ... wait, what?' She looked down at the large bag at their feet and noticed the wet patch at the bottom. 'Is that ... its head?'

Desma knelt and untied the top, pushing it open to display the gruesome contents.

Cela exclaimed in disgust. It was the size of a large rock, disturbingly human, yet not. Its face was pale grey, like a fish's belly, with a red-streaked nose, too many different teeth, a black tongue – at least a foot long – and wide, black and green eyes. Its neck was severed right under the chin, hacked like it had taken effort to chop through its skin. How did Desma do it?

'How?' Bion asked, echoing Cela's unspoken question.

Desma sat down tiredly on a fallen log. 'To be honest, the details are a blur. I think it believed it had escaped me and stopped to rest. But I was faster than it thought. I jumped onto its back. It went running – at times I thought we were flying, how far it leapt about – and I kept stabbing and stabbing until it stopped. I think it had already lost too much blood. I just finished it off. And then'—her lip curled—'I cut its head off.'

'I would not want to have done this alone,' Arete said quietly. 'But you did it. You fulfilled the king's request. He will cleanse you. It is over.'

Cela realised she was right. It was over.

Cela helped tie the bag back up and Bion offered to carry it. She pulled Desma to her feet and offered an arm for support. They walked the distance back to their camp, arm in arm, with Desma sometimes putting her head on Cela's shoulder. Her eyes kept fading off to the distance and Cela wondered what her friend was thinking about. Though she had never questioned Desma before, she began to wonder if there was something else to her story. Did it happen as simply as she said? She did not see any wounds on her body, so perhaps it was just exhaustion. Maybe when she had time to rest she would recall more details. She would be telling this story for the rest of her life.

'Thank you for looking for me,' Desma said quietly.

'What else did you think we would do? Sit down for some wine and honey cakes?'

'Sometimes I wonder just how far this bond of loyalty will stretch,' Desma said. 'Arete is cut on both arms. The burns on Bion's hands. Cosmas ... well, he is too slippery to be hit.'

The quartermaster glanced back from his position at the front as though he heard her, yet he was too far and she was speaking too quietly.

'It is over now,' Cela tried to say reassuringly. 'We will meet up with the others and return to the city so the king can cleanse you. And it will all be over.'

She could see what Desma was thinking. It was over for Cela. She could go home. To Apasa.

Desma was abandoned by her kingdom. They had never spoken of what exactly was planned afterwards. Who would the crew follow – Cela or Desma? Did Desma even want the crew? She mentioned a fishing boat or a house in the mountains. She talked about travelling the League, visiting Opuni and Anama, maybe venturing north. Never to the Empire. When this was over, would she see her friend again?

It was a chilling thought.

CHAPTER THIRTY-EIGHT

They stood in the open-air courtyard outside the throne room.

Almond trees ringed the grey and green tiled area, patches of tiny, white-pink blossoms still clinging despite the lateness of summer. Large, tiled pots filled with carefully pruned citrus trees circled a fountain of Nethuns in a swirl of water, concealing nothing as he stood naked for the world, long beard covered in sea glass, fishing spear held aloft with a large fish impaled but apparently happy.

Desma had insisted her entire crew accompany her. Cela had made sure everyone had dressed in their finest, which involved a lot of unnecessary shouting. Arete had refused the dress Cela offered. And when the determined, golden-haired woman had physically tried to stuff her into the dress, Arete had neatly flipped her overboard.

Khufu and Bion had pulled a sopping Cela back aboard to riotous laughter from all onboard. Her glare had been murderous and Desma had to step in, letting Arete wear a finely cut grey tunic and cloak, but the shipwright did bend when it came to jewels and wore moonstones and amethysts in her hair.

Cosmas was the plainest of the lot. Clothes of pale grey, with a single necklace hung with an uncut sapphire. He waited quietly by one of the almond trees but Desma noticed he kept a close watch on her.

Desma had agreed to let Cela dress her in red so pale it was almost pink, a red leather belt with thick black stitching, golden sandals, and a wide necklace studded with chips of garnet and obsidian with matching bracelets. The river of her hair was contained in a loose braid, tied with golden ribbon.

They had returned to the city a little after midday, leading the freed captives to one of the city's officials and explaining the situation. The bureaucrat was stunned at the sight of twenty dirty, tired, and slightly shocked people as well as their tale. When Bion let him peep into the bag, he went green and quickly summoned a small army of servants and messengers with promises to look after the citizens. Desma had also asked if the man could arrange for a message to be sent to the palace requesting an audience, and advised where they were staying. Actor and Peteos stayed with the released captives.

Just before dinner, a royal messenger arrived with summons to attend the king the next morning.

Now, they waited.

Desma strolled over to join Cosmas, enjoying the shade of the almond tree. The courtyard was already warm from the sun and the sea breeze did not reach here.

They both rested against the trunk and watched the goings of the palace, the rattle of spears, the swish of scrolls, the murmur of nobles and servants. It was peaceful busyness and she found it oddly relaxing.

'I assume there is a reason why you lied to us,' Cosmas murmured, barely moving his lips.

Desma started and quickly covered it by brushing imaginary dirt from her dress. 'I don't recall telling any falsehoods,' she replied calmly. Blast Cosmas, what did he know?

'I am not offended,' he explained. 'Curious. As to the real tale and why the lie needed to be told.'

'And what is this lie exactly?' Perhaps he was just guessing.

'That is what I do not know. I just know you lied.'

Maybe she would be able to get away with this. 'How?'

Cosmas gestured towards the sack that held the monster's head. They had placed it in another, thicker bag as the blood was leaking and no one wanted to touch the head itself. It sat on a silver platter provided by a servant between Bion's feet. 'Where did you get the bag?'

Where did she get the ...? It clicked. She had chased the monster into the forest. Killed it in a secluded area. She told them she had walked right back to the gully. And why would she have had an overly large sack going into battle? Cosmas read volumes in the brief hesitation while she tried to think of a plausible story.

'Again,' he said quietly, his muted blue eyes missing nothing, 'I do not care that you lied. Just why.' He held up a hand. 'If you cannot tell me, then please do not break any oath. I just wanted to let you know.'

Desma glanced at the others but no one was paying attention to the two of them chatting. And it appeared the king was going to make them wait. So, in hushed tones, she told him about Cisra, her sons, and what actually happened to them two hundred years ago. She skirted releasing them from their curse and instead explained that their mutual hatred of Turan was what ultimately led to the sorceress agreeing to leave Koriithos.

'And the head?' he asked, raising an eyebrow.

'A rock,' she said. 'Enchanted to look, feel, smell like Ector's head. It will not fade and will decay as though it was real.' And hopefully the king would choose to get rid of it rather than keep such a gruesome trophy. Cisra had warned that a priest of Aplu would be able to see through the subterfuge.

'So, you met Cisra of Arydor,' Cosmas breathed. 'A living legend. I would have very much liked to have had the chance to speak with her.' He shook himself out of his thoughts. 'You have revealed enough. I will let you keep your last nugget.' He pushed himself off the tree and joined the others, leaving Desma gaping after him. How did he know? Theirs was a relationship of secrets and she knew he would never press her. And Aita would sooner fling open the doors to Beneath than Cosmas let a secret slip from his lips.

Desma thought back to her farewell with Cisra.

'Where will you go?' she asked the sorceress after she had come back from checking on Ector, who was improving.

'I might take my boys to my aunt. She has not met them as their true selves and her island is peaceful. We need that in our lives right now. Stability. And somewhere they can learn to be men.' She ruffled Alexon's hair playfully.

'I don't know what god led me to your doorstep today, or what twist of fate,' Desma said, 'but I am glad to have made a new friend. If I may call you that?'

Cisra paused, eyes growing thoughtful. 'It has been many years since I had a friend. I think that I would like that very much.'

Alexon gave a large grin from where he sat on a chair turned backwards. 'Both Ector and I would be glad to have a cousin,' he said, his words tinged with shyness.

It was so odd to look at the youth before her, who sometimes was a little awkward in movement and speech, as though unused to his body, and think of the terrifying beast he had been hours before. But how could she blame him for a fate he was cruelly burdened with when he was a child? The gods have little regard for their lives. She smiled back. 'As would I, Cousin Alexon.'

'As for fulfilling your quest for the king,' said Cisra. 'I will bewitch a rock to seem like Ector's head ... as unappealing as that sounds. It will fool most except a high witch or one of Aplu's disciples. But you should be clear of them in Gylippus's court.'

Desma nodded her thanks. 'I hope that one day we meet again.'

'I would invite you to my sister's island but she has an unfortunate tendency to turn strangers into livestock,' Cisra laughed. Desma did not find the idea all that amusing. 'But I also wish the same. You cannot know where your feet or sail will take you. Look where you are now. A year ago you could not have imagined such a possibility. Some take heart in the idea, and some are fearful. But the future is the future. Walk your path and keep your eyes open and life will happen regardless of your worries and hopes.'

She picked up Desma's hands and held her gaze. 'You have a volatile gift. I do not think you will be able to sink into the world's shadows. Nor do I think you could let yourself. I am eager to see where you will go, dear Desma. And I hope it will give Turan a restless night or two.' She gave a ferocious grin.

Desma gave an equally vicious smile. 'The possibilities are endless.'

A servant in plain robes edged with green slipped out of the doors to the throne room and spoke to an official. Desma went to touch another necklace but remembered she had left it hidden safely on the ship. It was strung on simple leather and looked like a frond of calamint flowers, purple and green. It appeared smooth like glass but was rough when touched.

'Take this,' Cisra said, handing her the pendant, a wave of calamint flowing from her. 'If ever you need me, for whatever reason, be it because you have foes or because you need a friend, shatter it on stone and I will come. No matter where you are, what realm, I will know and will follow to the place it struck the stone. A token of our friendship and common adversary.'

Another secret. She did not really know why she did not tell her friends, especially Cela, but when she tried she found herself swallowing her words. Let Cisra be free. The only people who knew were her and now Cosmas. There was always time.

The servant finished speaking with the official who gestured for them to approach. Desma joined the others as Bion hefted the bag, still looking uneasy to be carrying it, as though afraid it would suddenly come alive and start biting. He had refused to keep it in his room and made Desma store it under her bed.

They were ready, assembled in their finery, to finish the quest they started what seemed a lifetime ago – but it had only been a matter of weeks. And the event that set her feet on this path was only months, not years, ago. Strange how one's mind made time seem longer the more painful the emotion.

Cela moved to stand beside her and grabbed her hand, giving it a squeeze.

Arete appeared on her other side and did the same.

The doors began to open and Desma took a deep breath.

Hand-in-hand with her friends, she entered the throne room of King Gylippus.

Nothing could go wrong now.

Camillus knew she was up in the palace. The city was abuzz with news of some abomination's death and how the city's salvation was delivered by a fearsome woman with wine-dark hair.

He spat on the ground and ignored the glares of a husband and wife who sidestepped him. These people were Abandoned, like most of the League of Kingdoms. Squabbling cities that for most of their history fought each other as much as they fought the Celestial Empire now. But one day they would be ground beneath the Empyreans' feet and be added to the Boundless Crowns.

He was wrapped in a thick brown cloak, lined with fine gold stitching, though the colour certainly left much to be desired. He was loathed to part with his robes and dress like one of these stoic, drab Koriithosans. But it would not bode well to announce his presence in the city.

He was here by order of the Holy Mother, who spoke for his Goddess Herself. His Goddess had spoken of him! His face had been in Her mind and his name on Her tongue. He felt flushed with ecstasy at the thought. He took it as a great omen. His star would rise ascendant in the Church and he would rule through beloved fear.

But he had to please Her. He had to find the Belt and that wretched orphan had it.

He would wait. He must be patient. He could not let it slip through his fingers again.

He glanced at the palace, high above from the docks where he walked. His informant would meet him in an empty warehouse later to report on what was happening and he would twist his plans to accommodate.

He would succeed.

He would not fail Her!

CHAPTER THIRTY-NINE

The chamber was almost identical to when Desma had first been there only days ago.

Nobles and officials lined the chamber, clustered thickly in rows. The king sat on his cresting wave throne, skin as weathered as the untreated hull of a ship. His clothes were dull grey, hemmed in black, and the sapphire-banded crown sat proudly on his black hair, Nethuns fishing spear centred above his brow. He leaned on the arm of his throne, head resting on a hand, appearing as nonchalant as if this was a feastday; but Desma noted how rigid he was sitting and how dangerous his eyes shone.

The queen – whose name Desma had never learned – sat on her smaller chair and again appeared busy with her needle and thread but her shoulders were tight and her hands clenched. She was as taut as a bowstring.

Both the first and second astronomers were standing by the king in what looked like a heated whispered discussion. They broke off as Desma's party entered, smoothing tan robes cinched in bronze, eyes hard and unreadable. Desma gave a small smile to Hyllos. He did not return it.

The young man she had seen last time by the queen's side was also there. He wore the same dark green chiton and himation, trimmed in silver with matching coronet. Where last time she had seen inexplicable fury in his eyes, this time she saw *hatred*. It was so strong she paused in her approach, taken aback by the power of the emotion, but Cela and Arete tugged her forward. She had to force her eyes away from him but, still, she felt his gaze boring into her.

They paused at the line of blue tile that marked the boundary to the thrones and they bowed as a group.

'The woman returns,' King Gylippus snorted. 'Triumphant, so I hear. Show me.'

Desma bit her tongue at his tone but gestured for Bion to bring forward the bag. The helmsman untied it and left it at her feet.

Once he stepped back, Desma looked the king in the eye and kicked the bag. The head, followed swiftly by a rank stench, rolled onto the gleaming tiles, stopping halfway between them, its tongue landing with an audible flop.

The queen gave a soft gasp.

Someone off to the side started to retch.

The king's eyes opened in disbelief.

The young man was quivering in anger.

Hyllos finally smiled.

Kalchas looked troubled.

Desma purposefully stepped over the blue line. 'As promised, I have rid your kingdom of the monster who plagued your countryside and slaughtered your citizens. I claim my prize: as you vowed, here, before your court, I request the rite of purification for my blood crime. Tinia *and* Nethuns as our witnesses.'

The king was at a loss for words for a moment. Clearly, he had not believed she would have brought back any evidence, let alone a head. It continued to ooze on the tiles. Cisra's magic was very convincing.

Gylippus looked over her crew. 'How do I know it was not one of these men behind you that slayed the beast,' he said. 'That man there looks like he could have ripped this head off with his bare hands.' He gestured at Bion.

Bion shook his head. 'Was not I, King.'

Gylippus glared at him. 'My point is that I have little more than the word of a Father-Killer for proof. Fortunately, I expected such subterfuge and planned accordingly. I call upon my general, War Leader Actor.'

Desma gave out a startled gasp, echoed by her crew, as they all spun around to see Actor stride into the chamber. The small man with hair the colour of young wheat, skin like new spring honey, and slim-bodied, came towards them but met none of their eyes.

He wore a cream, sleeveless tunic that came down to just below his knees under a polished bronze breastplate. Bronze greaves covered his shins and hard leather sandals were strapped to his feet. He carried a green plumed helmet under one arm with only two slits for the eyes and a vertical slit for the mouth. A plain sword was strapped to his hip.

Desma could scarcely wrap her head around it. He was not even ten years older than her and he was leader of this kingdom's armies. The same man who Kassandra slapped when he pinched her, who followed Cela like a puppy. The man who treated Desma as the leader of their group.

Actor came to a halt beside Desma and gave a sharp bow to Gylippus. 'My King.'

Desma forced her mouth to close.

Gylippus had a smug smile on his face. 'War Leader Actor, I have summoned you to court to provide your report. I swear under the waves of Nethuns' realm that I have not heard from you until this moment. Do you also swear?'

'I swear,' Actor said, eyes straight ahead.

'This woman claims to have killed the terror that has haunted our city for ten years. Tell me and all assembled here that her words are lies. Tell us who truly rid our city of this creature.'

Desma felt her heart stop. Actor had stayed with the captives. He had not followed with the others and could not even vouch that he knew for certain they had not killed it. And that was even if he did not twist the truth further. Gylippus had sworn he had not spoken to Actor until now but he could have given him orders before ordering him to accompany them.

'While I did not see the killing blow with my own eye,' Actor said in a voice loud and clear, 'I have no doubt that Desma speaks truth. She killed the monster and saved Koriithos. She has the right to the King's gift.' A ghost of a smile visited his lips.

These were obviously not the words the king was expecting to hear. His face grew darker and his eyes wide. 'If you did not see her strike the blow, then we have no way of verifying her words. I am under no obligation to grant wishes to liars.'

Actor dropped to his knees, drawing his sword. Several gasps broke out and two men stepped forward but he made no threatening movements. Instead, he flipped the sword so the hilt was offered to the king. 'I vow before man and god, before wave and stone, that Desma, daughter of Apasa, killed the monster. I trust her with my sight and breath and strength of limb. To disprove her word is to disprove mine. I offer my honour to the King for judgement.'

Desma crouched down next to him before the king could respond. 'Do not do this, Actor. Please.'

'I do what is right,' he said, loud enough for the king to hear.

She could do nothing. With his speech, Actor had tied his honour to her. If the king called her a liar and cast her out, he would also be casting out his general. And by swearing, Actor proclaimed for the court that he believed her enough to risk his standing.

The king looked ready to take the sword but Hyllos stepped forward, leaning down to whisper in his ear. 'I know,' Gylippus snapped at the astronomer, who simply bowed and moved back into place. Kalchas cast him a mean look.

The king turned back to Actor and waved him to stand up. 'I accept your word, Actor. Step aside.'

The young general bowed at the waist and moved away. He caught Desma's eyes and gave a reassuring smile, which disappeared quickly.

'Fine, let us get this over with,' the king snarled. 'Priests!'

Four priests of Nethuns, clothed in robes of green and purple, fluttered from the sides and crowded around her.

'Let the rite of purification begin,' the king called out.

Now? Desma thought as priests began stripping her clothes away, throwing them and her jewellery into the arms of Cela and Arete who looked ready to tackle them to the ground. Desma shook her head at them. She had assumed there would be time before the cleansing but the king was eager to have it done with. She let them do what they must.

Soon she was naked. Despite the warmth of the day, she felt her skin pebble under the gaze of so many people. Embarrassment heated her face and she allowed it. This was the final act. One last trial of shame.

The king approached with three servants bearing a silver pitcher each. Gylippus had a white strip of cloth tied around his head. On one cheek was a streak of ash and on the other was blood. His face was set in stone. The power of purification was sacred and allowed only to kings, priests, and oracles. This was a solemn duty and he would perform it with respect, despite his feelings towards her. She knelt before him.

'You come before me,' he began, 'befouled by acts cursed by the gods. Your blood is filth, your flesh is tainted, your soul is stained. By the grace of Tinia, King of the Gods and Doomspeaker, and by the waters of Nethuns, Lord of Oceans, I, King Gylippus of the Kingdom of Koriithos, stand before you with clean hands and pure spirit. As you requested to be purified by my hand and I said yes, so I now offer purification to you and await your response.'

Desma almost found it hard to speak the words. 'I accept your offer of purification.'

'Let it begin.' He turned to the first servant and took his pitcher. 'By blood you were tainted and by blood you are cleansed.' He poured the contents over her head. Lamb's blood, pungent and thick, coated her head and fell down her back, breasts, navel, thighs. It spread around her in a pool. He took the next pitcher. 'With oil, the foulness of your deed is forgiven.' Olive oil, peppery and green, washed over her, slicking her limbs, and forming bubbles in the blood on the tiles. He took the last pitcher. 'With water sweet and water salt, you are washed clean. The gods and man open their arms to you once again.' Water, so pure and silver, dashed upon her and swept away all traces of blood and oil. She rose to her feet, as clean as though she had stepped from a bath. A priest appeared with a robe of soft cream and placed it on her shoulders. She wrapped it around her and cinched it tight. The king offered her a cup of wine, as dark as her hair and as the wild sea. 'I offer you the return of guest-rights. May hearth and home and protection be offered to you as for any citizen.' Desma accepted the cup and drank deeply.

When she finished, Gylippus clapped his hands together loudly. 'You are purified!'

There was a moment of silence before it was broken by roars behind her. Her crew, her friends, appeared around her, hugging and kissing her cheeks, dancing in circles. Delphinus broke into song and even Cosmas took her hand to press a soft kiss upon it. Cela refused to let go of her arm and Kassandra was crying.

Desma beamed.

She had done it. They had done it. Three cities and three kings. Hundreds of miles over land and sea. Filled with pain and heartbreak and doubt. No more. She was free!

'Seize her,' the king ordered.

'What?' Dozens of soldiers appeared from among the nobles and swept down on her group.

Bion threw two of them across the room before he was brought to the ground.

Cosmas struck like the snake, felling six men before others arrived through the doors and beat him down with the butts of their spears.

Kassandra was knocked unconscious with Khufu quickly following.

Cela and Arete fought like wild cats but weaponless they could do little against men in armour.

Delphinus went mad. He punched one guard in the throat, spun to kick another, before launching himself at a third, sinking his teeth into the man's arm. A shield was slammed into the back of his head.

Desma did not move when two men grabbed her arms. She was dumbfounded. She looked at the king, who glowered at her. He waved at his first astronomer who approached, face equally unhappy. She looked at Hyllos but he avoided her eyes. Actor was a little alarmed but did nothing.

'Are you certain?' she heard Gylippus ask Kalchas.

'Yes, my King,' the first astronomer replied, his voice like paper rustling. 'She is the one.'

'Blast Aplu and all his children,' the king swore before rounding on her.

'What are you doing?' Desma demanded. 'We have done nothing to harm you or your people. We *saved* you! We will go in peace. Please!'

It was Kalchas who responded. 'I am afraid we cannot let you leave.'

'Why?'

'Because,' Gylippus growled, 'you are to marry my son.'

CHAPTER FORTY

Desma was stunned.

She did not struggle as they dragged her from the chamber. Her eyes could not leave the prince.

He had not moved but he seemed to grow harder. His face was stone carved and a snarl twisted the corner of his lips. The queen reached over to touch his arm but he paid her no mind. He only glared at Desma.

The doors slammed shut in her face as she was dragged backwards.

They took her to an opulent set of rooms, built from blocks of white stone with inlays of green-streaked marble. Thin windows looked out over the harbour, covered with sheer cloths that twisted in the slightest breeze. Well-made furniture of pine and cypress filled the rooms, made soft with rugs and blankets.

When they pushed her into the rooms and shut the door, she had gathered some of her thoughts and began to bang on the wood, shouting for the king, Hyllos, Actor, anyone. But she was half-hearted. She was still dazed.

She was to marry the prince. That angry, furious man who seemed to loathe her. She had never met him or slighted his honour. Why would he hate her so?

She found a chair and sank into it, clutching the white robe tight. She was still wet from the cleansing, had no sandals or boots, and felt naked despite the robe.

She listened to the drip of water as it fell from her legs to the floor. She could hear the murmurs of the city below, the cry of a gull, the creak of ships at the quay. But in the room, silence reigned.

Gylippus cared nothing for her. He thought women were dolls to be dressed up when needed and shoved into a corner to wait. Why did he want her? She had no land, no money, no power or prestige or influence.

Parents had offered their sons to her mother as Desma grew up but Timothea had always rebuffed them. She knew that Desma was never going to be high priestess after her and would not use her for political gain. She had married for love, so why would she deny her daughter the same if she wished?

Not that Desma had ever seriously thought of marriage. Even before the attack on the temple, she had never looked to her future and seen a husband and children. And now one was being forced on her.

It suddenly struck her.

If she married the prince – she did not even know his name! – she would one day be the Queen of Koriithos. Queen Desma.

Dread, deep and tangible, moved through her chest. *Live and be forgotten,* was what her mother had said before she died. *Remembrance was never in the stars for me. But it is for you,* were her father's last words.

One path led to safety and a long, peaceful life away from the eyes of the gods.

The other would keep her in the mind of Turan, a goddess who killed her devoted.

Why was it that the harder she strove for the first path, the further she was pushed down the second?

She shivered.

She had to find some clothes. Her eyes flicked to the door but she knew it would be guarded. She crept over and pressed her ear against the crack; there were men chatting beyond, their voices too muffled to make out words. Wherever her crew had been taken, she prayed they were alright. Surely they would not have harmed them.

Letting the robe drop to the floor, she headed over to the closet and pulled open the doors.

Dresses, muted and dull, filled the inside. Soft greys, dark greens, earthy browns. And a single, muddy red dress.

She pulled it out and slipped into it. It fit almost perfectly.

There was a knock at the door.

Desma turned towards it and waited.

Another knock.

She waited.

A third knock.

Waited.

The fourth knock sounded like a bang.

'Enter,' she called softly.

Hyllos stepped into the room and nodded at a guard who had the butt of his spear raised to hit the door again. 'Desma,' he said warmly, with a brief bow. 'I am sorry for the dramatics.'

'You mean grabbing me and my crew, telling me about my forced marriage, locking me in a pretty prison, and somehow having dresses that fit me exactly?' Desma knew she sounded petulant and hated herself but she could not help it. She could barely stop herself from folding her arms. 'Are you here to explain what is happening? And they are just going to hope that I won't break your neck.'

The astronomer smiled but it faded at her expression when he realised it was a real possibility. 'Yes, well,' he cleared his throat. 'Such steps had to be taken. Before you arrived in the city, your reputation was renowned. The child who sailed the seas with a ship full of troublemakers, a child who became a woman as fierce and bright as flame. The Daughter of Passion. The Looter of Urruc. The Despised Beloved. And still only twenty years of age.'

The Despised Beloved. Those words made her cold. 'Nearly twenty-one,' she said, moving back to her chair. 'Where are my friends?'

'They are safe and well. They have rooms in another part of the palace. Nice rooms,' he said quickly when she opened her mouth. 'They have a private courtyard, windows to look into the harbour. And only one door.'

Hyllos took a chair as well, though she did not offer one. His freckles were like drops of rich honey on cream. His eyes were warm, yet sharp, offering kindness but still being wary. She wondered how he had come to his position. As second astronomer he was in the king's inner circle, behind only the first astronomer and Actor. She still could scarcely believe that Actor was general of the kingdom but, in light of everything else that had happened, it was low on the list of surprises.

'Do you feel different?' he asked.

Different? He meant the purification. For a moment it had slipped her mind. It was over. She was cleansed by blood, oil, and water at the hands of a king. Tinia's punishment had been revoked. She was again a citizen of the League. Now that it was over, it seemed like she had left Apasa only yesterday. The begging, the fighting, the humiliation, and worry – all faded into one condensed emotion. She felt cleaner. Perhaps because she would no longer feel the stares of people looking at a father-killer. The purification wiped clean the slate. People may still whisper behind their hands, gazes may linger with morbid curiosity just a little too long, but few would mention it outright. And she could again speak with ease to any person she met.

She realised Hyllos was still waiting for her answer patiently. 'It is like when you have fallen into a muddy ditch and had to walk a day's march home. And you sink into a hot bath and watch the dirt breakaway from your skin, bit by bit. It feels like the moment you stand up out of the water, the filth falling off your body and you are yourself once again.' She levelled a look at him. 'Until someone barges into your home and kidnaps you.'

'We assumed that you would prove difficult and try to leave if we attempted to discuss it with you in a civil manner,' he explained. 'For the record, I was opposed to the idea but there was little I could do when Kalchas overruled me.'

'Why do the king and Kalchas think I need to marry the prince – what is his name?'

'Lycon.'

'He does not like me.'

The astronomer eyed her carefully. 'True. For now. Perhaps over time that could change.'

She highly doubted that. 'What happens when I refuse to be wed?'

He grew uncomfortable. 'You do not have a choice. If need be, you will be dragged to the temple and married with a gag in your mouth.'

Desma was aghast. They would force marriage on her? They would perform such sacrilege under the eyes of the Queen of the Heavens, Goddess of Marriage? 'Why?'

'There is a prophecy,' he said slowly. 'It spoke of the monster and how someone would come who could defeat it. And that person would be the monarch Koriithos would need in the days to come. What those days are … we don't know. War, famine, plague. Or perhaps a great discovery, trade, new alliances. Will this person be a warrior or healer? A skilled diplomat or cunning merchant? Hero and saviour?' He shrugged. 'The skies give a hundred hints but no answers. That is why for ten years the king kept news of the monster quiet from the rest of the world. At first, only nobles and sons of lords and princes were sent out to fight the beast. King Gylippus is not opposed to his son marrying a man. In fact, I believe he would have preferred it. But many died. Then soldiers. Then it was open to any citizen. But a few months ago, Kalchas came to the king and said that the stars foretold the person we needed would come from another land but would hold Koriithos high. We assumed that meant a far-off son or daughter of the kingdom. But we are presented with you, daughter of Apasa. You *must* be the next Queen of Koriithos.'

'Or what?' she asked angrily. How dare these people think that, after everything she had been through, they could force this upon her? She had no desire to be queen. Nor did she want to marry into a family that despised her.

Hyllos looked at her long and hard before finally sighing, throwing his hands in the air. 'I can see that you will not be an easy-going queen. I fear you will break us as much as you save us. This must come to pass, the wedding and crowning. All the astronomers in the city have looked down that path and all of us, each and every one, have seen the same thing. This is wildly unheard of. Ten of us can see the same stars and have ten different answers. Those who rise to First and Second in the city are those whose readings are almost always correct. To have a hundred see the same thing again and again … that is the will of the gods.'

'What do you see?' she breathed.

'An axe felling a wave. Crowns emerging from deep cracks in the earth. A horizon of ships with sails of flame. An arm of marble. A river turning into a serpent.' He spoke with a dark voice, his eyes moving far away, as though looking once more at the stars in the blackness.

'What do they mean?'

'The end of Koriithos.'

Desma realised her hands were clenched in the folds of her dress and forced them to open, smoothing the material as her mind was in turmoil. Was this truth he spoke? Or lies to trick her? But why would they lie to her? There was no reason for them to imprison her and marry her into the royal family. All she currently owned was what was on her back, a small bag in her room at the inn, and a chest of clothes on the ship. Not much of a dowry or groom-gift. She was allowed back in Apasa but she doubted the king would be pleased by her presence, and despite the love Leontia had for her she would be happier if Desma steered clear of the temple.

She shook her head. Was she truly considering this? Only Koriithosans looked at the stars for the future. The rest of the world relied on Aplu and his oracles. Did she want to be queen? No. Would she, if it meant something terrible would happen otherwise ...

'I need wine,' she said.

'I wholeheartedly agree,' Hyllos said, rising to walk to the door. 'Let's see if there is a servant loitering nearby.'

'Get two pitchers!'

'How many of them do you think we could kill?' Cela asked with a serious face.

Arete placed her hands on Cela's shoulders and pushed her back down on the bed. 'Not enough. There is an army and we are seven. Let's think of something else beyond a doomed rescue mission.'

The shipwright spoke truth, though Cela hated her for it. Not truly, but she was frustrated at the situation. It had taken thirty men in the end to escort them down into the lower palace that was carved into the cliff itself. The rooms were all interconnected with each other, five bedrooms, a dining room, two bathing rooms. There was one long balcony that spanned the length of their chambers and a small courtyard at the end ringed with high walls. It was warmly, if not colourfully, decorated, with good furnishings. Two trestle tables of cold food, wine, water, and juice waited untouched except for the plate of figs Bion kept eating while trying to remain unnoticed.

But it was a cage. Two full squadrons of guards filled the hallway outside the single door in or out of the rooms. Heavily armed guards. And they had no weapons.

'We could smash some chairs and tables and use their legs for clubs?' Delphinus suggested.

'Yes, and arm ourselves with these fruit knives,' Cosmas said drily, flipping one such knife that was little longer than his finger. 'They don't stand a chance.'

'Choke on a peach pit, Cosmas,' the piper growled.

'You terrify me so, mad-singer.'

'That's it, I'm going to ...'

'You are going to do nothing,' Khufu said calmly from his spot by one of the thin, arched windows. 'Or I will bend you all over my knee.'

They all looked at him askance.

Delphinus raised his hand. 'I volunteer to go first ...'

Cela let them bicker among themselves. They were all as frustrated as she was. It had finally appeared that everything was going in their favour. Desma was cleansed for the horrible thing she had done. Cela tried not to think too deeply on it, because there was always a little bubble of anger that grew in her gut. She did her best to quench it but sometimes it flared up. She had not yet forgiven her friend. She wanted to – gods, she *craved* to forgive her. But whenever she tried to bring the words to mouth or mind, they dissipated like sand in the wind. She was not ready yet.

Most nights she prayed to Munthukh. She was one of Turan's attendants, Goddess of Healing, sister to Esplace. Munthukh cared for emotional wounds and spiritual pains, helping guide people to forgiving those who had hurt them so much. Cela was still walking that path, guided by the goddess' patient hands. Munthukh knew that these wounds could not be rushed towards healing, but that the path itself was the remedy. If only it was a shorter journey.

'Maybe Cela could seduce the guard captain,' she heard Bion suggest. 'Worked that time in Artas.'

'There were only four men watching us then and, somehow, I don't think it will work this time,' Arete responded. 'We aren't locked up because we tried to rob the treasury of a thief-lord. They want Desma to marry the prince of Koriithos!'

'I've always wanted to be a queen,' Kassandra mused. 'But not if my king would be that man. Did you see how he glowered at us?' She shuddered.

Cela had been taken aback both times they saw the prince and the anger in his eyes. He must have known that there was a chance he would marry Desma. And when they came back with the monster's head he knew his fate was sealed. Why his rage, though, she could not say.

She wanted to know that almost as much as why Desma had lied to her about what really happened when she chased the creature into the woods. Did she really think she could not tell when Desma was lying to her? Cela had assumed she would tell her that night when they were alone but all Desma did was go to sleep. What had happened? And what did she and Cosmas talk about when they were waiting to see the king?

Her eyes darted over to Cosmas and she started when she saw he was watching her as he cleaned his fingernails with the fruit knife. She trusted Desma with her life, as she had done a dozen times over, but still she wished she had never allowed that man into their group. He had never once given her cause to doubt his loyalty. But there was always something too ... *much* in his eyes. She did not know how to explain it better.

She got up from the bed, grabbing an apple on her way past the table, and stepped out onto the balcony. She looked out over the sparkling harbour, ships of different sizes sailing around the small island temples and lone statues in the water, long fingers of clouds stretching across the blue sky, gull cries and salt on the wind. The murmur of people in the streets and the shouts of dockworkers and hawkers in the agoras. It was peaceful if she ignored the unseen bars holding them.

She sent a silent prayer, to no goddess in particular, that Desma was all right, letting her thoughts drift on the breeze. As much as she was angry at her friend, she would defend her with her life if needed. But, this time, whatever was happening, wherever she was, it was her battle to fight alone.

Desma had pulled a chair up to one of the thin windows and sat gazing out at the moonlit sea. Ribbons of white light danced on the harbour, interrupted by dark patches of ships sailing through or studded with lantern lights.

Her head swam and sometimes the ships in the bay doubled. She and Hyllos had ended up calling a servant twice more after he brought the first two amphoras of wine. The astronomer had eventually stumbled out of the room, falling into the guards and chuckling at nothing. One of the men had stuck his head in to check on her and she had waggled her fingers at him before she burst out laughing.

She remembered at one point in the evening thinking on the wisdom of getting drunk with one of the men responsible for her kidnapping. That thought eventually fluttered its wings and flew away. Maybe around the second pitcher. Or the third. Did she juggle at one point? She noticed several apples on the floor. She dismissed them.

Hyllos was a kind man. At one point, he even started to tell her how sorry he was that she was in this position but realised what he was saying and buttoned up. It was not good for an advisor to the king to gainsay him. But she appreciated the thoughtfulness.

Koriithos was beautiful at night. The white stone gleamed under the moon, studded with the golden starlight of torches and candles, getting darker as the city fell into slumber. The ocean was wide and endless, a blanket of rippling blues and blacks that seemed as soft as wool. She rested her head against the stone, the coolness a balm against the heat of the wine.

Though the city had its beauty, it was nothing compared to her home. The deep, warm brown of Apasa's stones, the scent of rosemary and apples, the spinning of her father's pottery wheel ...

She let the tears fall on the sill unhindered, letting the wave of grief roll over her. But it was less painful than it had been several weeks ago. It was no longer sharp and stabbing, but dull and throbbing. It was no longer the pain of grief but of love remaining beyond the end. Her parents were at peace with each other in the Vale. And she was still in the world of the living.

And about to become a queen.

The thought sobered her. How was she meant to rule? To sit on a throne next to a man who detested her. Her husband.

She shut the door in her mind firmly about what that would mean. She would be his wife, which would mean she would have certain duties to carry out ...

And what about Turan? Her warning had been clear. And now Desma no longer had the protection of Tinia's punishment. What would the goddess do when Desma stepped onto the world stage as Queen in the League? She recalled Hyllos' words of prophecy. She was meant to be what Koriithos needed but what if the astronomers were wrong? What if she was what brought about the city's catastrophe? Another Cisra, cursed by Love herself?

The little cottage by the sea now seemed an impossible dream, for queens lived in palaces.

She wished Cela was by her side, the single unwavering flame in a troubled sea. Hyllos said her crew were unharmed but until she could see them herself she could not believe his word, despite his kindness. She would ask in the morning. No, demand. If she was to be queen, then they should obey her as one.

Aplu, Tinia, Uni, she prayed silently, *I do not know what you want from me, or what you can see is in my path, but please let peace be my mark upon the world. I did not ask for this and have suffered more than many. Hear my words and let your grace fall upon my head.*

She stared out at the city and the harbour, out into the kingdom that had offered her purification but chained her with a crown.

She hoped the world was ready for what was to come.

EPILOGUE

Turan sighed deeply as her attendant brushed her silky locks, sinking deeper into the silver bathtub, its waters hot and aromatic with spices. Her fingers trailed over the side, tickling the riot of roses that swayed towards her hand, longing for her touch.

A wind sprite sang softly in the corner, her voice pleasing as she wove harmonies impossible for mortals to achieve.

The room was dim, as Artume had already claimed dominion, the purple night clothed in raiment bedecked with stars. Candles scented with precious oils glittered warmly, glinting off the clothes and jewels she had shed in her haste to bathe.

She had spent another night with her husband. As hideous as the experience was to endure, none could bring a man faster to completion than her, whether he be mortal or divine. A touch here, a moan there, an arch at the right moment, and he was spent.

And she was bound by her promise, though the favour she had wrung from him was spoiled. Sethlans had decreed to both his high priest and king in Trilos that Desma was not to be cleansed. It had provided her much entertainment to watch Timothea's daughter try so hard with the Council, not knowing all her troubles were for naught.

She was surprised at the small ripple of sadness she felt at the thought of Timothea.

Even she had not seen the madness of the high priestess' love for her. To defy her like a child, not thinking of how it would play out, arrogant enough to assume she had any control over her goddess.

But perhaps Turan has been overly hasty in ordering the temple's destruction. It was beautiful. Her temple in Aventinus was wondrous, a star descendant on the earth, but there was something to Apasa that the City of Birds could never mimic.

She looked over at the gold and leather belt she had discarded on the marble floor. Her Belt had been so close, inches from her grasp. She had sensed it in the world the moment the spawn had left Urruc's cursed waters. Followed it to Apasa and all but led the Empyreans to it until … it vanished. Disappeared so abruptly she had dropped a cup at one of Turms' feasts, spilling wine down her new dress.

She would find it again. The Belt was back in the world and this time there was no Atunis to keep it hidden.

She hissed as the brush caught on a knot in her hair. The nature spirit disappeared in a flurry of autumn leaves, the brush clattering on the floor. They had learned to be quick around her when she was displeased.

She plucked the cup hovering in the air beside her, sipping the liquid ambrosia that, to her, tasted of pomegranate and honeyed rose petals. She remembered when she had given Atunis his first sip, the widening of his eyes at the vigour that lit his veins, the passion in which he grabbed her, kissed her, pushed her against the grass …

The cup broke in her hand, flooding her bath with its gold contents, adding its heady perfume to the scents.

She had not thought of Atunis in so long, and now twice in a single evening.

She had never forgiven him. Never forgotten him.

The Belt would be found. Valeriana had been given clear instructions as well as clear penalties. And now Desma no longer had Tinia's laws to protect her, since that fool Gylippus cleansed her blood.

She would be complete once again. And the world would remember why Love was her throne.

THE DEITIES MENTIONED WITHIN

THE HOLY TWELVE

Aplu – God of Light and Prophecy and Freedom.

Artimi – Goddess of Witches and the Wild.

Ethausva – Goddess of Hearth and Home and Family.

Horta – Goddess of All that Grows.

Laran – God of War.

Menrva – Goddess of Cunning and Wisdom and Learning.

Nethuns – God of the Seas and the Deeps; Father of Monsters.

Sethlans – God of Forges and Creation.

Tinia – King of the Gods; Lord of the Sky, Storms, and Judgements.

Turan – Goddess of Love.

Turms – God of Paths and Colours and Tricksters.

Uni – Queen of the Gods; Goddess of Marriage, Social Order, and the Stars.

OTHER DEITIES

Aita – Under-God of the Beneath; Keeper of Souls.

Artume – Goddess of Night.

Athrpa, Enie, Pemphetru – The Diviners; Daughters of Fate.

Charun – One of many who carry souls across the blood rivers.

Esia – Goddess of Peace.

Esplace – God of Healing.

Fufluns – God of Wine and Laughter.

Mania – Goddess of Shades.

Munthukh – Goddess of Healing.

Nurtia – Corded Goddess of Fate and Chance.

Orcus – The Punishing God.

Phersipnai – She of Two Lands.

Selvans – God of Forests and Pastures; Father of Twilight and Madness.

Soranus – God of Fire Beneath.

Summanus – God of Dark Lightning; Lord of Night Storms.

Thesan – Goddess of the Dawn.

Tiur – Goddess of the Moon.

Vanth – Demon-Goddess of the Beneath.

THE LOVERS (ALL ARE CHILDREN OF TURAN)

Aminth – son of Aita, God of Requited Love; Avenger of Unrequited Love.

Erus – son of Laran, Cruel Love.

Heran – son of Uni, God of Weddings.

Leinth – offspring of Turms, Deity of the Between and the Liminal.

Svutaf – son of Atunis, God of Yearning.

Tusna – son of Aplu, God of Sweet Talk.

Turnu – son of Summanus, God of Uncontrollable Desire and Impetuous Love.

ACKNOWLEDGEMENTS

This has been a dream since I was eight years old and I scribbled my childish imaginings on spare sheets of paper and in half-used notebooks. To know you are holding this book in your hand is such a surreal revelation – and I thank you wholeheartedly for it.

My biggest thanks go to my husband, Andrew, for your tireless support, steadfast love, and patience. For listening to me go on and on about my story and raising my floundering spirits when I hit a wall. For letting me pursue this to the end, helping me figure out the practicalities of being an author in the real-world ... for being the potter to my priestess.

I can go no further without expressing the depth of my gratitude to my brilliant editor, Danikka Taylor. From our very first coffee chat, you made me feel so safe in sharing this precious dream with you, to know that I could trust you to help me navigate the challenges and triumphs of the editing process (even when you made me rewrite all those POVs). And then for letting me be among the first to go through the publishing process with Authors Own, to get this story out into the world – you deserve your very own temple celebration!

To all my beta-readers for your feedback and inspiring enthusiasm – Charlotte, Simone, Kirsty, Allana, Sarah, Stephanie, Faye, and Alana. Thank you for being among the first to read my story and travel alongside the crew from Apasa to Koriithos.

Thank you to all the team at Authors Own who helped me make this dream a reality – I hope I get to meet you all in person one day to give you a big hug.

A big round of thanks to all my friends and family for sharing your support and love.

A special thank you to the high school teachers and university tutors who inspired me beyond measure.

Huge thanks to the authors and editors I've met along the way who have encouraged and advised, helping me grow as a writer.

And I could not have gone this far without the unfaltering support from Kim. Your adamantine strength and unceasing encouragement picked me up when I was down and gave me the fire to keep on working, to keep on dreaming – thank you.

Lastly, I need to thank someone who has never faltered in their support of my writing. Who would let me post her first drafts of some truly terrible stories as I learned to find my voice, who would text me her thoughts and constantly correct my grammar. Thank you for being my very best friend, Riana.

ABOUT THE AUTHOR

Damien J. Coluccio is an Australian epic fantasy author from Sydney, NSW. The greats of Greek and Roman literature live rent-free in his head, fuelling the passions and pursuits of the Wine-Dark characters. Fascinated by the all-consuming power of love in mythology, Damien's debut novel features a reimagined Goddess of Love inspired by lore and legends. During his forays back to the non-writer world, Damien spends his time working at a botanic garden, eating brunch, throwing ridiculous parties for his friends, and seeking out little adventures.

Website: https://www.damienjcoluccioauthor.com/
Instagram: https://www.instagram.com/damienthelibrarian/

www.ingramcontent.com/pod-product-compliance
Lightning Source LLC
Chambersburg PA
CBHW032150190726
48290CB00005BB/1500